Not Just Another Love Story

Not Just Another Love Story

Wayne G. MacDowell

CasAnanda Publishing
New York   Florida

Not Just Another Love Story

Wayne G. MacDowell

First Edition

Front Cover Art: Anthony Rocco Guarino
Editor: Bobbi Janson

If the order form in the back of this book is missing, please request additional copies from your local bookstore, or write:

CasAnanda Publishing
Post Office Box 7207
Bayonet Point, FL 34674

Library of Congress Cataloging-in-Publication Data
MacDowell, Wayne G.
Not just another love story / Wayne G. MacDowell
p. cm.
Current PPD 9905

Library of Congress Catalog Card Number: 99-62148
ISBN: 1-889131-42-3

1. Fiction I. MacDowell, Wayne G. II. Title

10 9 8 7 6 5 4 3 2 1

Dedication

Bobbi Janson, my publisher asked if I wanted to do a dedication page. Certainly, they're fun!

Here's to heroes...I count my Dad as #1. He was an absolutely outstanding person. You would have liked him.

Next in line is Gene Autry. If you and I meet someday and shake hands, well, my hand shook Gene's and patted Champ... *I hugged them both, when I was a little boy.*

Then, there's *The Duke,* John Wayne. Have you seen his statue at the Anaheim airport?

The last...I'll keep that to myself and tell you in person.

This book is dedicated to family and dear friends throughout the U.S., England, Scotland, France and New Zealand and to the littlest daughter (my poodle!), in whose memory I launched my boat, *The Spirit of Coco.*

With gratitude I also devote this book to you, dear reader. I hope you enjoy it and that one day we do shake hands.

Oh, one last thing. A fragment of my philosophy that I hope you will share with others: *Don't permit a bad day. Maybe you'll have a bad hour or two, but don't allow anyone to ruin your day!*

Wayne

Wishing you life's best –

Wayne MacDonell

One 1

It would be a rough summer from the standpoint of hard, physical work. However, that really is exactly what he needed to keep in shape for his upcoming last year of playing football for the University of Maryland.

Kirk Daniels had inquired about summer work, and work it would be, a Forest Ranger at Elk Neck State Park and Black Hills State Forest. Well, it would certainly be a change from driving the Good Humor Ice Cream truck through the streets of Baltimore.

Kirk packed and headed his old VW convertible onto the Interstate. Loaded with gear was not the word. Kirk had all his clothes and just about every other possession he owned shoved into the trunk. In fact, there was so much packed inside the little car that he had to ride with the top down. It really looked quite humorous seeing that long footlocker sticking up in the back seat . . . almost as if another person was riding back there.

As he shifted gears, listening to the putt-putt sound of the VW engine, Kirk's mind wandered to the day he first arrived on campus almost three years earlier, driving that old straight eight Buick. That engine sound was like none other . . .but well, at least the VW was cheaper to run.

Kirk had just cleared the Harbor Tunnel in Baltimore and, at the White Marsh exit of Interstate 95, he drove onto Route 40 and headed north, toward the town of North East, Maryland. The State Park and Forest were about 10 miles east of town off Route 272. As he drove through the small town, he smiled up at the movie marquee. *Double Feature Saturday Night*. Kirk wondered aloud, "Is that the name of the movie or do they just have a double feature on Saturday evenings?"

Looking off to the right, Kirk spotted a body of water just after leaving North East. The kind of excitement you feel just before a big game started to creep over him. "Damn, this is going to be all right." Well, it truly is beautiful and quite far from the Baltimore-Washington scene, but in miles it's only about an hour drive. The State Park is located on a two mile-wide peninsula leading to Turkey Point. The Elk River lies on one side, the North East on the other and while standing at Turkey Point, you can also see the Chesapeake Bay, Bohemia and Sassafras River. The Coast Guard had used this high point above the water as a lookout post during World War II.

As Kirk entered the State Park boundary lines he spotted a road off to the right and turned onto it, noticing as he turned that he had entered the area with a sign reading *North East River Picnic Area*. "Oh well," he said aloud, "I'll get to see a part of the digs before I check in." He continued to drive through the picnic area. No one was there, after all it was pre-season. Looking round at the several hundred picnic tables and trashcans throughout this section of the 5,000-acre park, Kirk could only imagine how many trashcans *he'd* have to empty during the season. "Muscle building," he told himself and said it again trying to convince himself that this was really going to be a fun summer.

Kirk stopped the VW at the main gatehouse, but no one was there, so he drove straight on this time even though there was a road off to the left with a sign reading *Elk River Camping Area.* He was right. Just ahead on the left was the *Ranger Station and Shop.* The Station, Shop and Main Office were all housed in one building, a light green, concrete block structure. There were a couple of cars, several pick-up trucks, a stake-bed truck and an old dump truck parked near the building. A tractor with its hood and name plate off was sitting in a field on the right."Well, looks like I've got help anyway," he said as he walked toward the door with the sign reading *Office*.

It was lunchtime, and the scene as he entered the office was one that would become familiar to him. Several of the men were sitting on top of desks with sandwiches spread out on wax paper. Cans of soft drinks were everywhere. "Looks like a mini picnic," Kirk said as he stuck out his hand to the man nearest him. "I'm Kirk Daniels. Looks like I'll be working with you fellows this summer." The man was *big!* Not in height, for he was just an inch over six feet, nor in weight, for he was just a little over 200 pounds, but in structure. He had broad shoulders and was solidly built. His hand was large and rough. Kirk felt a firm sincere handshake.

"Hello! Russ Thurman here. I'm the assistant Park Superintendent. Welcome aboard. Let me introduce you to the rest of the clan. Kirk, this is Spike Odonowitz. I don't know his real name. He won't tell us. They've got it on record down at Annapolis to make out his check. It must a lulu!"

"Hi Kirk. Glad to meet you. Where are you from?" The handshake surprised Kirk. It too was firm, even though Spike was a small, thin man well past fifty.

"Camden, New Jersey. How about you?"

"Originally from Yankton, South Dakota. "Got out of the Coast Guard after 30 years and liked this part of the country. So here I am.

Russ Thurman continued the introductions.

"Kirk, shake hands with Don McLean. He's the local boy made good. Married the Superintendent's sister!"

"It's not as good as they all make out, Kirk I think my brother-in-law hates me. Thinks I'm not worthy to be in the family, but deep down, he knows I'm damn good!"

"Glad to know you Don." He surveyed the big, rough looking, good-ole boy from North East. Kirk knew as he gripped Don's hand that he was the type of man who would pull his own weight, brother-in-law or not.

He was introduced to a lonely looking man in his late forties, average height, warm blue eyes, and was very thin. He had gray hair that still had some black scattered throughout and there was a scent of liquor on his breath when he greeted Kirk.

"Hello! I'm Will Romansky. Nice to meet you son."

"I'm pleased to meet *you*, Will." He looked back at Russ. "Think I'm going to enjoy the summer here."

"I hope so. Everyone here is permanent. We put in for three summer temporaries, but they only gave us one in the budget. You look like a bull, so I guess Annapolis figured you were worth three."

Everyone had a good laugh.

Spike asked, "You eat yet Kirk?"

"No, but . . ."

He was stopped in mid-sentence. "Here, shouldn't be eating two anyway." Spike handed Kirk a sandwich wrapped in wax paper.

After lunch, Russ Thurman stood up. "All right, let's get back to work. We've got a lot to do before Memorial Day." "Come on Kirk, I'll show you to your cabin."

Kirk followed from behind, which wasn't hard, because Russ kept the truck near 20 miles per hour. They made the turn onto the road marked *Elk River Camping Area*, and after passing several areas designated for camping, they entered the section marked *Cabin Area.* Russ came to a halt in front of a cabin. Kirk could not make up his mind whether it could be considered rustic or just plain ramshackled.

"We never got around to fixing this one up, but it'll do for your needs," and before Kirk could answer…"What the hell, the roof doesn't leak and you do have a great view. Kirk, move your things in and relax a bit. I'll see you later. Oh, by the way," Russ stated, as he turned toward his truck, "You're expected over at the boss's house for dinner, 'round six o'clock. Just hustle your little . . .well, VW past the office and on down that road until you see a house on the right."

"You're sure, I mean it's OK?" uttered Kirk in a bashful manner. "I don't want to imposc," hc continued.

"Come on Kirk, just be there. We aren't very formal around here," Russ said. "Ol' Stonewall would have met you at his office, except he had to go on over to Bel Air for a meeting with Mr. Halworth, the Regional Supervisor."

"Thanks Russ. See you later." He turned back to the cabin as Russ drove away. "Home Sweet Home! Guess I better clean this place up a bit before moving in!"

Kirk took one, long look around the cabin.

"Well it looks like a crap-house now, but, through superior organization, a mop, broom and elbow grease, it'll look like a *clean* crap-house."

The cabin did look rough from the outside, however it had an almost cozy charm. Right from the start, as Kirk moved things around, he began smiling to himself. The charm was winning him over. With a combination living room, dining room, kitchen, things would be within easy reach. Also the fireplace would be a very comfortable place to sit near on some cool evenings and the woods often became cool during the night. In addition, the cabin had two extremely small bedrooms and Kirk figured one would serve that purpose, while the other could be a guest-storage room. Then he opened the backdoor. Kirk was surprised to find a nice-sized screened-in porch overlooking the Elk River. It was *sort of* screened in...there were mostly holes and some screen. But with a hammer and nails and a little luck he could rebuild the screening and other parts of the cabin itself, as the summer went on.

There were nine cabins in this particular area and although they were spread out in a sort of semi-circle along the shoreline, they were serviced by a single bathhouse. The bathhouse had facilities for washing clothes. Kirk Daniels thought aloud to himself as he returned to his cabin after taking a shower. "I think I'm going to get involved in more damn things than I bargained for in taking this job!" City life had taught him many street-wise lessons, but this was certainly a long way from the city and life out here was going to be a bit different than what he'd been used to.

As he neared the cabin, a brown shaggy dog appeared wagging his tail. Kirk bent down to pat him. "Hello fellow." He rubbed the dog's head and ears. Kirk didn't notice the beautiful young stag deer that was coming up behind him. With Kirk bent over patting the dog, he posed a perfect invitation. The deer bent his head and gently rammed Kirk, pushing him down on both knees. He dropped his towel and clothes as he fell over.

"What the . . .!"

He rolled over, started picking himself up and sat face-to-face with the first deer he'd ever seen...out of a zoo, that is.

"Well I'll be!" Kirk said, and just about the time he was trying to think of what else to say, the deer and dog bolted off together. This was only the first of many such meetings between them during that summer. Kirk would have a lot of fun with the tame deer and unsuspecting victims like weekend campers.

Kirk entered the cabin and started changing his clothes for dinner at Superintendent Miles house. He put on his best slacks and a new sports shirt and looked every bit the part he played on the University of Maryland campus, a dashing football player about to go on a date. He wasn't concerned about being overdressed because making a good impression on the boss was important to him.

The VW roared to life (well, started with a putt, putt and bang). Kirk headed back down the road into the camping area, then left on the main road. He passed the office and noticed most of the forest service trucks were missing and figured that the men had taken them home with them. However, still sitting alone to the right of the Ranger Station was the beat-up tractor. Kirk wondered if they had left it there while taking a break after cutting the grass, or if it had just quit on the spot.

He pulled into the yard of the low modern ranch house that the State of Maryland provided for the Superintendent of the Park. Kirk said half aloud to himself, "My God, what a beautiful setting for a home." Beautiful did exactly describe the setting because the house had an almost entirely uninterrupted view of the Elk River, about three miles wide. In front of the house was a long clear field and a view you'd expect to see on a calendar.

Kirk opened the door of the VW. The main thought that crossed his mind at this particular instant was what, exactly, should be his opening line. As he headed for the house, those fears were washed away quickly. A voice called from the back yard. "Hello, back here…come on. I'm feeding the dog."

That voice sounds like a female-type, Kirk thought as he raised his eyebrows and headed toward the back of the house. He still hadn't seen anyone. Then his eye caught a movement from the porch.

"Hi, I'm Kirk Daniels." He stood looking at a very pretty, tall, dark-eyed girl with long auburn hair. He was pleased with himself for getting the line out without stumbling.

"I'm Sharon Lynn, boss's daughter. So be nice to me. By the way, you can call me Sharon."

As Kirk tried to think of something of an intelligent nature to say, the brown shaggy dog came off the porch wagging its tail and stopped in front of Kirk, fully expecting Kirk to pat him again.

"Well, hello again fellow." He started to pat the dog, then caught himself and quickly turned around, expecting to fend off a deer.

Sharon laughed at the awkward move.

"I see you've met not only Duke, but perhaps you've also encountered his friend Bennie. Am I right, Mr. Daniels?"

Kirk was embarrassed at the quick move.

"Yes, that is, if Bennie is a deer!"

"He is…and I taught him the bumping trick."

"He does it well."

"Practice makes perfect. I'm happy for people like you who are willing to help out."

"Who said I was willing?" retorted Kirk. "I'm a victim!"

"Come on Mr. Daniels, let's meet Mother and Daddy."

She motioned him toward the back door and before Kirk could say anything…"We only use the front door for company."

Kirk started to reply, "OK, but don't you think I'm..." and before he could finish, Sharon interrupted.

"My, my, Mr. Daniels—an ego problem?"

"I don't have an ego problem, I was just kidding Ms. Miles," retorted Kirk in a stern manner.

"Ms. Miles! Ah, Mr. Formal, do I detect an anti-fem attitude?"

"No," said Kirk somewhat embarrassed. He had to smile.

Sharon reached for Kirk's hand. They headed for the door and he thought to himself, "She's unbelievable. I've never met anyone like her before." Sharon waited as Kirk opened the door and then she flashed a cute little girl smile to tease him.

Mrs. Miles was in the kitchen fixing the salad. She looked up and smiled.

"Mom, may I present Mr. Kirk…something…Daniels."

"Sharon!"

"Hi Kirk, it's nice to meet you. I'm certain you're going to have a pleasant summer here."

"Thank you, Mrs. Miles. It's very nice to meet *you.*"

As they were talking, a man just over Kirk's height of 6'2" came into the kitchen and extended a large right hand. Kirk likewise reached out to greet the handshake. Sharon started her introduction. "Kirk this is ...," but she was stopped mid-sentence as John Miles interrupted.

"I'm Daddy!" he said in a comical way, then continued to Kirk in his regular voice, "How about a beer before dinner?"

Before Kirk could say anything except, "It's nice to meet you Mr. Miles," he had a beer in his hand. The Superintendent closed the refrigerator door. "I'm John. Mr. Miles is my father!"

"OK," laughed Kirk. Suddenly, he began to see where Sharon got her quick wit.

"Let's go out on the side porch. It's a great view of the bay and there's usually a nice breeze coming in at this time of the day," said John. They walked through the house. Kirk looked around the dining room with its table set for dinner—then the living room as they continued to the side porch. He thought to himself, "I don't know what you call this type of furniture, but it's really nice. The house is clean, neat, a nice place to live."

Kirk's evaluation was quite correct. The house, inside and out had been very carefully decorated. Dora Miles, in addition to being the wife of Elk Neck State Parks' Superintendent, was a second grade school teacher in the local town of North East and earned almost as much as John did. Through their dual income, plus the State's allocation of funds to maintain the Superintendent's house, Dora was easily able to decorate the way she liked.

As John and Kirk settled into comfortable lounge chairs on the screened-in porch, John opened the conversation.

"Dora wanted to enclose the porch so we could use it in the winter, but I enjoy it so much like this in the summer months that she just dropped the idea."

"Yes, it is very nice," responded Kirk. "The view is almost unbelievable."

"That it is Kirk. "I passed up a promotion that would have put me in the office down in Annapolis so that we could stay here. I guess a man just has to decide what's important, and staying here is what Dora and I wanted." Then motioning toward the north, he continued, "We bought a few acres just up from the State Park and I guess when I retire, we'll build a place of our own."

He looked back at Kirk.

"How did you wind up at the University of Maryland?"

"I came down on a football scholarship." Kirk was about to continue when Sharon appeared at the door and looking toward Kirk said, "Come on, Star, it's time for dinner."

John smiled as he got up and thought to himself, "I think I'm going to see a lot of this young man after working hours." He gave Kirk a slap on the back and said aloud, "OK, let's chow down!"

As they gathered around the dinner table, John held the chair for his wife Dora and Kirk likewise held the chair for Sharon. Not to let the moment pass without a needling remark, Sharon commented to her mother, "Isn't this nice, being in the company of two such gentlemen!"

Dinner was very pleasant and throughout the meal, the conversation was kept light. Laughing and joking about different things was the way most of the meal was eaten and at the base of a great deal of the conversation was, of course, Sharon. Kirk felt right at home in the free and easy atmosphere and by the time they went out to the side porch to enjoy coffee and dessert, he had become a great contributor of the conversation.

At around 10:30 Kirk said, “Thank you very much for dinner and a very enjoyable evening. I really appreciate it.”

Mrs. Miles replied, “You’re quite welcome Kirk. We enjoyed having you and I’m sure we’ll see a lot of you before the summer’s over.”

John shook hands with Kirk.

“See you at the shop at 7:00 AM.”

Kirk nodded and Sharon said, “Come on, I’ll walk you to your car.”

As they arrived at the car door Kirk started to say, “Well, this was a very...” He was stopped in mid-sentence as Sharon kissed him lightly. “I don’t usually kiss on the first date, but this wasn’t a date, so I guess it’s OK.” Then she quickly headed for the house and called back over her shoulder, “See you sometime tomorrow. I want to talk to you about going into business. I’ve got the brains—need your brawn and first paycheck!”

Before Kirk could react to what Sharon had said, she was in the house. He shook his head and started the old VW convertible back down the road toward his cabin.

Later, he lay in bed thinking of all that had happened to him since he drove off the University campus earlier that morning. Kirk smiled as he thought of the good fortune that came his way since his football coach had suggested that working at the State Park would be a good way to stay in shape over the summer. His last thoughts were of the smiling dark-eyed girl with the dark auburn hair and as he drifted off the sleep, his thoughts were, “I don’t believe in love at first sight, but that girl does grow on you pretty quickly!”

Two 2

A few minutes before six, Kirk awoke and reached out to shut off the alarm. As he did, he knocked the clock off the small night table. It didn't break. Picking up the clock and sort of wiping it off, he sat on the edge of the bed. He placed it back on the table and noticed as he did, the glass had a small crack on the lower side which gave it the look of a half-smile. "Oh brother, I've got to wake up to that look every morning!" said Kirk and he half-smiled back at the clock.

Kirk dressed and almost by habit opened the refrigerator door to find, to his surprise, that it contained milk, eggs, bacon, butter and a note from Sharon.

"Dear Sir, Mother and I wanted you to have a hot breakfast on your first day here. In addition to what you see here, there is coffee, bread and jelly, (Mother's homemade black cherry jelly) in the cabinet. Sincerely, Sharon Miles."

Kirk laughed aloud at the note, but was grateful for the thoughtfulness of Sharon and Mrs. Miles. He folded the note carefully and placed it in a drawer with his clothes for safekeeping. He fully intended to have the note framed! Kirk smiled as he cooked the bacon and eggs. Shaking his head he wondered almost aloud, "Is this the other side of our young Ms. Sharon Lynn Miles, a gentle, shy girl?"

Just as Kirk finished eating, the sound of a truck engine stopped at his cabin. Kirk looked out the window just as Russ Thurman climbed out of his green pick up truck. Kirk noticed the State Seal and *Asst. Park Supervisor* printed on the door. He headed for his door and had it opened before Russ reached it.

"Hi Russ, want a cup of coffee?"

"I brought some. Didn't know you had time to pick up stuff," replied Russ.

"I didn't. Mrs. Miles and Sharon put some things in before I got here."

"Well, that entire family is Great People!" said Russ. "By the way, I will have a cup of coffee. These containers are cold anyway because some of the early bird campers stopped me on the way in."

As Kirk poured the coffee for Russ he said, "You know, the Miles are nice people. I mean, I spent the evening with them last night and you might have thought I knew them all my life, they make you feel right at home from the first hello."

"I know...and then there's Sharon, right Kirk?"

"Com'on, you know what I mean Russ."

"Yeah, of course, I know," replied Russ.

They got up from the table and headed for the door. "You drive on over to the shop with me, then tonight you can bring one of the trucks back here with you." Kirk nodded his head and climbed into Russ's pick-up truck.

As they drove on over toward the shop, Russ teased. "Sharon said she saw a few University of Maryland games last year, but didn't remember you doing much scoring."

"I didn't do any, Russ. I play middle linebacker and I'm going to have to explain to that young lady that keeping the other team from scoring is also important. I made the All-Atlantic Coast Conference #1 team on defense and was Honorable Mention All-American, so I can't be all that bad."

Russ laughed as the truck came to a rest in a parking space in front of the shop.

"Com'on, let's go to work keeping you in shape!"

Inside the shop the smell of fresh brewed coffee as well as conversation from the rest of the crew, added to an already beautifully bright morning. "Hi Kirk," came the greeting from the men. As Kirk greeted them back he felt an instant sense of belonging. Spike gave him a container of coffee.

"Cream and sugar is on the table."

"Thanks Spike."

As Kirk headed over toward the table he heard John Miles. "Don, you take Kirk with you over to C-Station and continue to work on cutting those new camp sites."

"What truck do you want Kirk to use, John?" asked Don.

"The dump," he replied.

Don motioned to Kirk. When they got outside Kirk walked toward the dark green Chevy dump truck.

"Don, I never drove a truck. I mean, not one this size."

"So it's your big day, Kirk ole boy, your big day!"

"How do I operate the dump," Kirk asked.

"One thing at a time. Let's work on starting, 5-speed gear shift and 2 speed axle first, OK?"

"OK, I'll show you how to operate the dump later, when we take a break." Don motioned to Kirk to get in behind the wheel and then climbed in the other side to run through the gears. He set the 2 axle speed.

"Follow the diagram on the dashboard and try to get her out of the yard smoothly. You don't have to double clutch, so relax and think of it as a big VW with 5 speeds. Start out in 2nd without a load—won't hurt it."

Kirk didn't say anything. He was trying to remember what Don had just told him. He started the engine at just about the time Don reached the door of his pick-up. Don looked back and gave a pilot's high sign, thumbs up! They left the yard and he followed Don McLean over to C-Station. Kirk's face broke into a nervous smile with the excitement of a pilot's first solo that gave him the confidence the rest of the day would go well.

Kirk parked the dump truck next to the pick-up. He helped Don get out the tools they needed to start clearing out new campsites. They walked toward some brush and Don pointed to the stakes already in place, showing the boundary marks of each site. Then taking separate campsites, they started the clearing process. Don walked over several times to show Kirk how to use some of the tools and to help move the heavy brush. He also pointed out a patch of poison ivy and told Kirk to stay away from it, saying that he had a spray in the truck that would kill it. They kept at the campsites, clearing until close to 11:30, then Don came over again and motioned to Kirk.

"Bring the tools with you. We'll head over to the shop for some lunch."

They arrived at the shop just about the same time the others did and there was one extra person there. Sharon had a picnic basket. And as Kirk brought the dump to a halt, she walked over with that broad smile that had captured Kirk the evening before. "My, my, the working man has triumphed over the demons of the campsites and now the Knight of the Dump-Truck must be fed."

"Sharon…" Kirk started to say but was cut off.

"Now, Sir Kirk, if I may call you ..." and before Sharon could finish Kirk interrupted.

"Yes, you may call me Sir!"

"One, for your side," Sharon teased, "But for that, you get the egg salad sandwich and I'll eat the ham and cheese."

But she handed Kirk the ham and cheese anyway and they walked over to an area just to the right of the shop where the picnic tables were being repaired. They picked out one of the completed tables, sat down across from each other and started to have their lunch.

"By the way, you and I are sneaking off this afternoon," Sharon said without raising her head.

"What?! What do you mean," replied Kirk in a slightly raised voice. "And what's this about going into business with you and using my first paycheck and brawn?"

"One thing at a time Mr. Daniels," Sharon answered. "One thing at a time." Then Sharon continued, "I've got to go back to school and pick up some things and I told Daddy you said you'd help me load the stuff and bring it back."

Kirk looked amazed and just a little peeved, but before he could say anything, Sharon said, "Don't be angry. I volunteered to help you shop for food and things and Daddy was going to give you time off to get squared away on that, so I thought we'd take care of everything in one afternoon, and..."

Kirk interrupted, "OK, OK, we'll leave the dump truck at my cabin and take the VW."

"I don't trust it, not that it won't make it," Sharon corrected herself, "But Mom's letting us use her station wagon."

"How much do you have to bring home?" Kirk wanted to know, then…"Oh just close your mouth and eat!" Sharon took another bite of her sandwich and her dark eyes smiled at Kirk.

After Kirk washed up and put on a clean shirt, he and Sharon started out in the station wagon. "With you as pilot and me as the navigator..." Just then she was interrupted by Kirk.

"Navigator or back-seat driver?" and he winked.

Kirk knew the way to Towson State College near Baltimore, just off Interstate 695. At exit 27 Kirk left the Interstate and drove onto Route 146. A right at Towson College Drive put them on campus. As he made the last turn, he looked over to Sharon and said, "Now you can navigate me, dear!"

Sharon smiled and directed Kirk toward the dormitory where she lived during the school year. "I might not spend too much time here next year," Sharon said as she got out of the car. Kirk looked at her. "With practice teaching, I'll be out on my own part of the time."

"You ever thought of teaching in College Park?" Kirk asked with a smile on his face.

Sharon took his hand, squeezed it, and off they headed in the direction of the dormitory, hand-in-hand.

After packing the station wagon to where it could hold little else, they drove back to North East, did some shopping for Kirk then got back in the car for the ten-mile drive back to the State Park. They arrived at the Miles house just in time for a late dinner. Kirk gently turned a little to his right and with a light kiss woke Sharon, who had taken a little nap on his shoulder.

She smiled but didn't return his kiss.

"Can't kiss you just yet. Remember I don't kiss on the first date. Come to think of it, I'm a pretty cheap date !!!"

"This was our first date?" a questioned look on his face.

"Well, if you don't want a good-night kiss Saturday, after the dance, then count that as our first date." Sharon responded.

"Wow, what dance?" Kirk replied.

"The one at the VFW. It's either that or the twin-bill at the movie, or maybe you don't want to take me out at all.

"Well, I like that!" And with that little speech, Sharon started off toward the house.

"Now just a minute Sharon. Look, I was going to ask you out for Saturday, even Friday, but let me do the asking!"

"Yes, sir!" she replied.

"And one more thing while I'm at it," Kirk continued in a mock stern voice, "This thing about kissing or not kissing on the first date!"

"Yes," and in saying that Sharon ran back, put her arms around Kirk and kissed him! "Thanks for today, come on, let's eat!" They walked into the house where the Miles were waiting with dinner.

During the next few days Kirk kept quite busy learning to use the tools and other equipment that would soon seem quite easy to handle. However for now, each new tool or technique was a chore for the young man from Camden who had never spent so much as a day out in the country, let alone be called upon to become an expert in many mechanical skills.

It was also a time for thinking during the evenings, because Sharon and her parents had driven out to western Maryland to be with John's mother and father. Sharon's grandfather had fallen from a ladder and had been hospitalized. The Miles left early in the morning before Kirk was up and in the rush to get started, Sharon didn't have time to write a note of explanation. Don McLean would tell the story of what had happened at the office. Dora had called her brother-in-law, because Don's wife, Jill, would drive out to western Maryland with the Miles, to be with her and John's parents.

On the fourth evening, just after Kirk finished eating and was drying his dinner dishes, a truck stopped outside the cabin. Looking out the window by the kitchen sink, he saw Spike Odonowicz getting out of his pick-up truck. Spike waved and walked toward the door. Kirk already had it open by the time Spike got there.

"Hi Spike, still have some hot coffee if you'd like a cup."

"Thanks Kirk, I could go for some." Kirk reached into the cupboard, took out a mug and filled it with coffee.

"Powdered cream and sugar are over there on the end of the table Spike, but if I remember you drink it black."

"Right son. Seems you catch on to everything around you and remember things pretty good too."

"I only wish I did remember everything—or even some things. I keep putting the dump down too quickly and when it bangs, it jars every bone in my body. Even Will jumped a foot today after I dumped gravel off at the guardhouse," Kirk continued.

"Well, don't let it bother you. You've been here less than a week and believe me you fit right in," Spike retorted and then continued, smiling at Kirk after sipping his coffee. "You've learned fast and you're hard-working. We're all pleased that John picked you." Kirk smiled, and nodded his head, but before he could say anything, Spike put his cup of coffee in the sink and said, "Kirk, unless you're doing anything special this evening, com'on down to Turkey Point with me. Got an old friend I'm going to visit and thought you'd like to meet him."

"Sure. I was just going to turn on my Transcontinental Radio, listen to WSM and read awhile."

Spike headed for the door and Kirk followed him outside. They climbed into the pick-up. Spike drove out of the park grounds, but instead of driving on toward North East, he made a hard left on to a dirt road. It wasn't a bad road, although in parts there were ruts to contend with and Spike avoided each one, as only a person who knew a road could. They drove in silence until Kirk asked, "What did you mean about John Miles picking me? I thought I was assigned here by some kind of pool or something."

"That may be so in a lot of cases, but it seems you were hand-picked, something cooked up by your coach and John," came Spike's reply.

Kirk smiled. "You know, Coach Wyneski? We all call him 'Pappy'. He said I wasn't working hard enough during the summers, so I guess he took the bull by the horns. And I thought I got the job through the campus employment service." Kirk smiled and shook his head.

Just then, the road narrowed to a one-lane dirt track with grass growing in the middle. Kirk looked at Spike with a puzzled look that asked the question about where they were going.

Spike caught his glance and smiled. "The old friend is Bill Kemper; he owns the farm land out here at Turkey Point. It's a beauty of a spot and old Bill's willed it to the State, to become part of Elk Neck State Park. He let the Coast Guard use it during the war years as a look out point and that's how I met Bill. I was stationed here for a while." Kirk nodded, and Spike continued, "Bill must be close to eighty, but he still works and farms each day. Has about twenty head of Black Angus too. Good beef cattle."

About this time, the pick-up approached the farm and with the mercury-vapor light extending from a pole high above the area, it was easy for Kirk to see the four buildings that made up the main part of the yard. There was a house two stories high. It wasn't a large structure, but rather a compact farm house that would not be difficult to heat in the winter months. There was a large barn, well kept, but like the house, unpainted. Over to the right of the barn were the corncrib and a shed. Parked beside the shed was a tractor. As Spike and Kirk got out of the pick-up truck, Spike noticed Kirk looking around. His eyes had stopped on the old tractor. "It's a '41 John Deere, Kirk. One fine ole work horse. Still does its share," explained Spike. "That exhaust stack blows perfect smoke rings when she idles. I mean perfect!" Spike laughed, motioning Kirk to follow him toward the house.

The old man who answered the door smiled widely as he greeted Spike Odonowicz. "How're you doin' young fellow?" He shook Spike's hand.

"I'm fifty-eight years old and he still calls me young fellow," said Spike looking at Kirk, then turning to Bill Kemper. "Bill, shake hands with Kirk Daniels. He's working with us this summer, up from the University."

"Glad to know you son,"

"I'm pleased to meet you Mr. Kemper. Spike's told me quite a lot about you, about the Coast Guard being here during the Second World War," encouraged Kirk.

"Yes, those were bad years, but with all the young men around the place, they were also good years, if you know what I mean." Bill continued as he motioned Spike and Kirk to sit down. "You want some coffee Spike, and how about you son?"

Kirk started to reply, but before he could say anything Spike spoke up. "Bill, I'll have coffee with you. Kirk will just have a beer." Kirk had a questioned look on his face. Spike smiled. "The coffee is sort of Coffee-Royale or should I say… Whiskey with a little coffee in it!"

"Right!" Kirk replied quickly. "Beer will be just fine Mr. Kemper!" And all three men had a good laugh!

It was a great evening and as Kirk was getting ready for bed, he reflected aloud, "Who would have thought that this past week could have made this many changes in my life. What a warm, wonderful place this is—and then there is Miss Miles!"

Just before Kirk was climbing into bed he heard a scratch at the door. He walked over to investigate and upon opening the door, the brown shaggy dog walked in. "Hi Duke," said Kirk, half expecting an answer. His answer was a wagging tail and a dog at his feet wanting to be petted. "You hungry? I know Don's been feeding you. Well, you look hungry. How about some bacon and eggs? That's all I have now." Kirk got out the frying pan and while the bacon was cooking, he walked outside to bring in a few more logs for the fireplace. Kirk checked the bacon, saw that it was almost done and decided to speed up the operation by cooking the eggs on top of the bacon. "This is the way I make them for myself. They're not bad," Kirk said aloud, looking at Duke. It seemed ole Duke wouldn't mind at all for his nose was up, sniffing the aroma of bacon cooking. Kirk cut up the bacon and eggs, letting the egg yolks become hard. He sat by the fireplace shaking his head a little and smiling at the dog at his feet enjoying a late dinner, or more probably, a late snack. Kirk cleaned the frying pan and dish, then checking his fire, added two logs. He replaced the fire screen and looked for the dog as he reached to put out the lamp over the kitchen table. As his eye searched the semi-darkness of the room, he spotted Duke by the foot of the bed. Kirk leaned down, patted the dog on the head, rubbed his ears and climbed into bed. In no time at all, Duke heard Kirk snoring away!

It was raining the next morning as Kirk awoke. He opened his eyes and turned off the alarm clock. He felt a cold nose nudging his cheek. "Well, good morning ole man," Kirk said to Duke. He reached out to pat the dog. Kirk washed, shaved and ate breakfast, making a little extra for his guest. Then after dressing, he put Duke out on the porch, figuring that with the holes still in the screen, the dog could come and go as he pleased, especially with it raining. Kirk closed the door to the screened porch and then walked across the floor and out the front door. As he reached the dump truck and was about to open the door, running to greet him once again was the brown shaggy dog. Kirk opened the door, and in a split second, Duke was up in the seat and wagging his tail. "Move over Duke, move over," commanded Kirk. "Do you have authorization to ride in a State vehicle?" His answer was a dog with a wagging tail, panting in his face, and licking the hand that gripped the steering wheel. Kirk started the engine, backed up slightly and then started off toward the shop, with a very official looking dog perched on the seat, looking straight ahead!

Kirk arrived at the shop a short time later. Both he and Duke climbed out of the dump truck and walked toward the office in the shop.

"Mornin' Kirk, who's that you got with you?" called Don McLean from over in the corner by the coffeepot.

"My overnight guest," Kirk replied.

"I had wondered where he went," replied Don. "Stopped by the house this morning, saw he ate—called him, but no Duke. Figured he was out running with the deer."

"Well he came over, had a late snack and when I saw him laying in my bed, I decided my guest was staying for the night so I hit the sack," responded Kirk.

Russ Thurman, the Assistant Park Superintendent, came into the office from the door in the shop. "Morning! With the rain coming down this hard, we'll get busy and finish repairing the picnic tables," he said. Don and Kirk nodded approval for being able to stay inside for the day and out of the weather. Russ went over and poured himself a cup of coffee and raised the pot, saying, "Fill-up, anyone?"

Spike Odonowicz and Will Romansky were coming in the door as Russ was speaking. Spike called out, "As you lower that pot Russ, fill two!"

"Coming right up. I want to thank you again Spike for taking me with you last night," Kirk told Spike, as Spike was raising his cup of coffee to taste the first of the morning brew.

"Man, does that taste good!"

"Oh, you're quite welcome. It was a nice evening wasn't it?" By now, of course, the rest of the men were tuned in to the conversation between Spike and Kirk and wondering where they had been. Spike saw this and said, "We went over to see Bill Kemper."

"One fine gentleman," said Will.

"Yes, he certainly is," responded Don.

"Let's hit the deck and get those picnic tables repaired," said Russ, then he continued. "We should stay right on this project through tomorrow, finish it up and start painting the shop."

With that, the men broke from having coffee and while Russ, Spike and Will went into the shop to start working on the three tables already on the shop floor, Don motioned to Kirk to come outside with him and bring in another picnic table to work on. As they walked quickly through the rain, which was now only light rain, Don said to Kirk, "Grab the other end of this thing and we'll get it inside." They carried the heavy oak table toward the overhead door of the shop. Will Romansky reached over to the switch box and hit the "up" button, opening the door. The door was about half way up and just as the men carrying the picnic table cleared the door, Will pushed the "stop" button. Once inside, the work of replacing the boards, bolts and painting the tables went on like an assembly line. Well maybe not like the auto assembly line in Detroit. Let's just say that each man did his share and the work was completed quickly with an air of fun. Conversations with a lot of light-hearted talk and a degree of kidding made the workday seem to go by quickly. It seemed that hardly any time at all had passed before Russ made the statement, "Four o'clock! Quitting time." The men cleaned up the tools and paint brushes before heading home. The echo of, "Good-bye, see you in the morning" was heard as the men filed out through the office door into the still falling light rain.

Kirk had just finished dressing, after taking a shower from the centrally located bath house. He was brushing his hair when the sound of a horn blowing made him stop and look out the bath house door to see who was making all the noise.

"Come on, shake a leg!"

Sharon called out from the station wagon.

"Shake a leg?" questioned Kirk as his smile broke into a wide grin at seeing Sharon was back.

"How does hurry up sound?" Sharon called back.

Kirk didn't answer, just smiled, shook his head a little and went back in to finish up. He made a mad dash from the bathhouse to his cabin.

By this time Sharon had parked the station wagon and was waiting in the doorway for Kirk.

"If that's how you run, no wonder Maryland had a lousy season," Sharon mocked as Kirk bounded into the cabin.

"Hey, we were 7-4 and anyway, you weren't carrying a ball, so I didn't see a need to charge in here full tilt."

As Kirk was placing the things he was carrying on the table, Sharon came over behind him and gave him a bear hug. With her head resting on his back, she said, "Miss me?"

"What, were you away?" Kirk joked, as he turned around to return the hug, then continued, "Seriously, how's your grandfather?"

"He'll be just fine. Can you believe he didn't break anything? Of course Granddad was shaken and he's sore from the twelve-foot fall, but otherwise looks as if he'll be just fine."

"That's great!" said Kirk. And then almost as if both thought waves meshed into one, their eyes focused on the other's face and they kissed, long and meaningful. "It's so good to see you...hold you, Sharon," said Kirk.

"I know what you mean," responded Sharon. They held each other and kissed again, then Sharon said, "Come on, you're expected for dinner."

Kirk and Sharon ran into the light rain and as they did, Kirk started to run toward his old VW. "No," called Sharon. "Come with me!"

As Kirk got into the passenger's side of the Miles station wagon, Sharon started the car and as she turned the key she said, "See this way, I'll have to drive you back, Mr. Daniels, then I get to spend a little more time with you."

"Ah, a madness to your method," responded Kirk.

"Isn't that the other way around," questioned Sharon as she broke into a wide grin over Kirk's quickness to retort.

"Must be learning from your Dad," he smiled and motioned with his fingers as if to chalk up two!

"Huh," said Sharon loudly. "I see, Mr. Daniels!"

"Well, well," exclaimed Kirk. "I see I've hit a tender spot. Our little Ms. Miles' ego." Sharon looked over and wrinkled her nose at Kirk and both of them had to laugh.

Sharon was just pulling the station wagon into the yard and as she put the gearshift into the park position she said half aloud, "It's a good thing I've fallen in love with you or just maybe I'd drop you, Mr. Daniels." Then before Kirk could respond she quickly said, "I'm sorry. I didn't mean that!"

"Which part didn't you mean?" questioned Kirk.

"The part about dropping you. Oh Kirk, I shouldn't have," cried Sharon.

"Well now, let me get this straight," started Kirk. Then after adjusting himself in the corner of the front seat as Sharon looked straight ahead over the steering wheel, he continued.

"Are you telling me that after knowing me for this short amount of time you think you've fallen in love with me?"

Sharon still looked straight ahead, then turning toward Kirk she responded, "Yes, but you..."

Kirk held up a halt sign. Then he continued talking,

"You see, I don't, or rather didn't believe in love at first sight. I know we're both 21 and that you've probably dated as much as I have, so this shouldn't be any teenage crush thing we're speaking of. So let me say this about the subject matter at hand. Sharon, I fell in love with you the first night we met. I didn't want to rush you along, felt I might scare you away."

Sharon wiped away the tears from her eyes and both she and Kirk reached over and kissed.

"Hey, you two coming in or do you want curb-service?" called John Miles from the front porch. Sharon just waved as they got out of the car, running through the rain to the house.

As Kirk was taking off his coat and handing it to John Miles who was standing by the hall closet, Kirk said, "Sharon said that your father is going to be all right."

John smiled and answered, "Yes, tough stock, but I think my mother will make certain he stays off ladders for a while."

John motioned Kirk toward the living room and said as Kirk sat down on a comfortable over-stuffed chair, "Too cold to sit on the side porch this evening. How about a beer or scotch before dinner?"

"Beer would be just fine, John. I haven't graduated to scotch yet." Dora came in from the kitchen and greeted Kirk.

"Hello Kirk. How are you?"

"Just fine Mrs. Miles. It's very nice of you and John to have me over for dinner, especially since you just got home from a long drive."

"Oh, we were expecting you."

Dora smiled, looking toward John.

"Yes, Sharon made sure we left on time to get home and even made me push the speed limit a bit to be sure you hadn't started dinner at the cabin," said John as he smiled back at Dora. Kirk didn't say anything, but he did look a little embarrassed as he lifted the can of beer and took a long drink.

"I'll get back to the kitchen and help Sharon with the salad. Dinner is about five minutes away," said Dora, and she left the room for the kitchen.

The dinner, like almost all meals served at the Miles' was kept light and lively with conversation. Kirk felt quite at home by now in the Miles household and participated quite freely in the conversation that seemed to go on non-stop throughout the meal. It was during dessert that the subject was brought up which Kirk had kept very much to himself.

"Kirk, you've never spoken about home, your parents or relatives," questioned Dora.

Kirk smiled slightly as one does when he ponders exactly what to say in answer to a question and how to say it. It was only a few seconds yet it seemed as if a long silence was broken when he started to speak. "Well, I don't talk much about my parents because they died when I was very young. They were killed in an auto crash," said Kirk and then continued as everyone looked on, quite stunned at what they had heard. "As for relatives, I think I have an uncle who lives in Colorado or California, being small at the time I don't remember. Anyway he never showed up and I was raised in the Camden Orphanage."

"Oh my, I'm so sorry Kirk," exclaimed Dora.

Kirk said, "I didn't mean to shock you. I thought Coach Wyneski had told John."

"Pappy didn't say anything about your folks."

"Well," said Kirk, as Sharon, not saying anything, but in reaching for his hand and forcing a smile, moved closer to Kirk. "There isn't much to talk about," Kirk continued. "It happened so long ago and when I was in the

11th grade, my high school football coach took me in and helped me get a scholarship, so things are okay. I've just learned through the years to make the best of the situation at hand and work to improve it from there." Before anyone could react Kirk smiled and in a loud cheerful voice said, "Can I have another piece of pie and some more coffee?"

That broke the tension. Sharon got up and reached for the coffeepot. Everyone seemed to settle down again and Kirk started to tell John about fixing the picnic tables at the shop. "One thing I can't understand is how those heavy oak tables can be broken by campers and picnickers. That wood is so hard!"

Three 3

Early the next morning, Sharon drove over to Kirk's cabin. Kirk was just starting breakfast as he spotted Sharon getting out of the station wagon. He walked over to the door, opened it and held it as Sharon walked up the steps and planted a good-morning kiss on him.

"Eat yet?" he asked.

"No and I'm starved," came Sharon's reply. "Have any special plans for your day off?"

"No, nothing special, just figured I'd go down to the Elk River and throw stones, maybe some rocks, or better yet..." He was interrupted by Sharon.

"Well, I'm glad your mind is thinking in a constructive manner, because we've got two very heavy things to talk about, at least to me they're important," said Sharon as she tried to bring the conversation to a serious note.

"OK," said Kirk as he poured a cup of coffee for Sharon and himself, "Seems by your expression that you've got something on your mind."

"Right," said Sharon as she took the cup of coffee from Kirk. She circled the room before sitting in a chair, half looking out at the river, but really staring at nothing. Then finally, Sharon spoke again, "I've got two subjects to talk about with you, one fun and...well, one that bothers me and at the same time worries me." Sharon took a deep breath and started to speak again when Kirk turned off the cooking range and picking up another chair, walked over to Sharon and sat before her.

"Which subject do you want to discuss first," interrupted Kirk, as he leaned forward and planted a kiss on Sharon's forehead.

"OK, let's discuss premarital sex first!" Sharon blurted out, her eyes fixed on Kirk's.

"OK, nothing like skirting an issue and sneaking up on it." Kirk broke into a wide grin, "By the way, is this the serious subject or the fun subject?"

"Kirk, this is serious!" Sharon half-shouted, but she also had to break into a smile as she realized how she was saying things and how they sounded.

"Look," said Kirk as he spotted Sharon's expression of trying what to say next,"I've tried not to put too much pressure on you."

"I know, I know," Sharon interrupted. "It's me, I've never felt this way with anyone. I always said that my wedding night would be the first time and I'd like to keep, well, you see, I..." Looking into Kirk's eyes, Sharon's began to tear.

"OK, then it's settled," said Kirk in a matter-of-fact tone to calm Sharon down.

"What's settled?" asked Sharon in a searching, but hopefully reassuring voice.

"We don't go all the way until our wedding night," said Kirk, again in the matter-of-fact tone, then Kirk reached for Sharon's hand and they both stood and embraced.

"Oh God, do I love you," Sharon said, as she quietly held onto the young man that her girlhood dreams told her she'd someday meet. Then Sharon leaned away from Kirk and said in an excited tone, "Did you just officially propose to me?"

Kirk smiling, reached down and kissed Sharon again, then said, "Yes, I guess this could hold up in court as an official proposal, especially if I asked you to be present on my Wedding Night!"

"Well, I accept!" She started toward the cooking stove. "And, as a gesture of good will - I shall cook your eggs. How do you like them?"

"Over easy." Kirk finished setting the table. "By the way, what's the other subject for discussion or shouldn't I ask?"

"It's our business venture," Sharon said, then continued as she noticed the puzzled look on Kirk's face. "Don't you remember, the first night we met, I told you my brains and your brawn and pay check!"

"Really! And what business are we going into?"

"Commercial crabbing," said Sharon in a matter-of-fact tone. "Kirk, close your mouth and, well, eat your eggs. Three pieces of bacon OK or do you want all six?"

"Three is fine, you take half." Then in a puzzled tone he continued, "Now that we've finished the bacon and egg math problem, I don't know the first thing about crabbing."

"Of course you don't, that's why I gave you the responsibility of securing capital and labor," said Sharon, half-laughing.

"I supply the capital and labor!" repeated Kirk throwing his hands in the air.

"OK, OK, boy do you drive a hard bargain," said Sharon still smiling, "I'll tell you what, you can be President of the company, how's that?"

"President of what company?" questioned Kirk. "Look Sharon..." but he was cut off by Sharon.

"Yes, you're right, what company? How about *Elk Neck Crabbers Co-op*, see, that way if we get enough orders, then we can hire other people, say on a piece meal basis, so much per dozen. Very good Kirk, you're thinking like a President already!"

"Sharon, I've never even been crabbing," explained Kirk. "I don't know how to crab. Also, I do have a job, remember, working for your Dad."

"Look," said Sharon, as she reached in her pocketbook for a pen and small note pad. "You work seven to four. By four-thirty we have Dad's boat out in the bay laying the taut lines and if all works well, by six-thirty or quarter-to-seven at the latest we should be finished. I'll have Mr. Campbell pick up the catch right at the T-dock, and that's it, except for cleaning the boat and maybe rebaiting the lines with salt-eel."

"What's a taut line and what's salt-eel?" questioned Kirk, now somewhat interested as he sensed Sharon seemed to know what she was talking about.

"OK, good question. Here, I'll draw it for you." Then Sharon took the pen and pad, placing them and herself so that Kirk could follow along, then she continued. "Taut line first. You take a float, tie a rope to it and about 10-12 feet later you tie a sinker, for example a concrete block. Then about a hundred yards away is the same set up. OK, now in between and starting at about three feet below the surface is a line running to each stationary float set-up. Now, you buy salted-eel; don't look like that, plain ole eel works much better than chicken necks and backs. OK, well, you tie the bait on at say three-feet intervals, oh, you also cut the eel in about three or four parts, so he goes further..."

"Sharon!" exclaimed Kirk as he wrinkled his nose in disgust.

"I know, I know! But *you* have to cut the bait, after all I'm a girl... and anyway, Daddy always did it."

"This is a fine time to become a dainty little lady," said Kirk as he slowly shook his head. "The President of the firm should not have to cut bait!"

"Pour me another cup of coffee and let me finish," Sharon continued. "Where was I? Oh yes, well we make up three of these taut lines and we'll lay them in a large triangle, that way we close in on all the crabs in that area. Then we simply go back to the starting point, ease the first long-line onto the spool on the boat, and with the outboard motor set at a craw, we net them. It's easy!"

"And we can make money doing this?" questioned Kirk.

"Look Star, ever buy a dozen cooked crabs in Baltimore? What'd they cost? And where do you think they came from?"

“This almost makes sense Sharon,” said Kirk. “And I also have a day off...”

But before he could continue, Sharon broke in, “Don’t get too carried away, Mr. President, on your day off and what happens to also be my day off, we can play half a day. After all, we brains of the business owe ourselves some R. & R.”

On a serious note, Kirk then asked, “Where do we get all the taut line stuff?”

“No problem, Daddy already has a complete set-up, after-all last year you weren’t around and anyway with his job as Superintendent now, he doesn’t have the extra time to help me.”

“Have I just been set-up myself?” questioned Kirk.

“Oh, not really. Think of it as an opportunity, the investment in bait is small and the labor is right at hand, come to think of it, you’ve got a pretty good deal.” replied Sharon.

“Yeah, cutting up eels!” exclaimed Kirk.

Sharon, not paying attention to Kirk’s last remark said, “I’ve got to go into Elkton for some shopping. Want to come?”

“Thanks, but no. I’ve got some tools from the shop and I’d like to do some more work on the cabin.”

“Oh, well, can you make it over for dinner tonight? Daddy’s cooking steaks on his kamado.”

“Certainly I can make it. Thank you. What’s a kamado?”

“It’s a Japanese cooking pot with a large lid and sort of chimney top with a damper down below. I don’t really know how to describe it, but it cooks meals that are unbelievable. We cooked our Christmas turkey in the thing. Daddy’s been so busy lately that we haven’t used it, but you’ll see it.”

“One more thing before you leave for Elkton,” questioned Kirk. “What did you mean by your day off. Do you also work in the Park?”

“Four years,” said Sharon in a proud voice. “Up at the gatehouse they call me the reservations lady. Are you the reservations lady I spoke with on the phone? I tell them to pay up front. No pay, no play in the Park!” And both Kirk and Sharon laughed.

Sharon started toward the door. Kirk said, “Want to take in the *Elkton Drive-In Movie* after dinner?”

“Sure, but how about if I pick you up for dinner?” asked Sharon.

“Why, I can come over in the VW?”

“I know, but the VW has bucket seats and a stick-shift. I’d rather be closer to you at thc drive-in.”

“Right. You pick me up because the VW’s been acting up lately.”

Sharon smiled, kissed Kirk as she walked out the door and toward the station wagon, calling back, "Glad you catch on fast, Star."

Kirk smiled and waved as Sharon drove out of the cabin area. He closed the door, shaking his head in amazement as he thought of what transpired in the past hour. The question of sex before marrying Sharon, getting engaged, I guess, and going into the crabbing business! "I just don't believe the last hour," Kirk said to himself. "That's some lady!" Then Kirk picked up some tools, opened the door to the porch and started repairing the screening.

Later, after showering, Kirk started walking back to his cabin and just as he crossed the road in front of the cabin, a horn from a car tooted. Kirk turned to his right and saw Sharon's smiling face behind the wheel of her mother's station wagon. Kirk walked over to open the car door. "Are you early or am I late?"

"I'm a bit early," explained Sharon. "I bought something for you."

"What's in the package? Let me open it."

"Not so fast," said Sharon in a mock stern voice. "I want to be sure you don't just love me for my wealth."

"I want your wealth, of course," exclaimed Kirk. "Spotted your wealth the first time I saw you, even in front of your mother and father, I looked at you and said to myself, man, there's wealth! Now, can I see what you bought me?"

"You're too damned fresh, Mr. Daniels," Sharon retorted, then as her grin broke into a full smile she handed Kirk the package.

Kirk took the present and sat at the table to open it while Sharon sat down across from him. Kirk looked up smiling as he opened it and said, "You know, growing up as I did, well, there were never many presents, so you'll have to forgive me if I get excited."

"Ah, the little boy in you, I like that," said Sharon as Kirk opened the box and held up the beautiful tan sweater.

Kirk didn't say anything at first, still looking at the sweater, then looking up at Sharon he said a quiet, "Thanks, it's really fantastic. I'll wear it tonight."

"You're welcome Star."

Kirk reached over the table with a thank you kiss. "I thought you'd look great in it." Then to break the quiet which started to set in as Kirk put the sweater on Sharon continued, "Com'on, we'll be late for dinner."

"OK, just about ready. I'm looking forward to those kamado steaks!"

After driving over from Kirk's cabin, Sharon and Kirk got out of the station wagon and walked hand-in-hand toward the back porch. "Thought we'd use the back door since all the smoke was coming from back here," said Sharon as they approached John cooking on the Japanese cooking pot.

"Just putting the steaks on," answered John.

"I thought as much," said Sharon. "Either that or the back of the house was on fire. How come all the smoke?"

"Hickory chips," explained John. "Makes the steaks taste even better."

"That's some good looking beef you've got there," Kirk joined in.

"Yep! Got them from Bud's Butcher Shop. By the way, Sharon's I know is medium rare, Kirk how about yours?"

"That's fine with me," answered Kirk.

Just then Dora came outside to see how things were progressing. "How soon will the meat be ready John?" she questioned.

"I figure seven minutes on each side," answered John.

"You care for a cold beer, Kirk?" asked Dora.

But John answered, "Make that three Dora!"

"Three?" questioned Dora. "Sharon is watching her waistline."

"Kirk, the chef and one for the steaks," came John's reply.

"All this makes me thirsty," said Sharon. "I'm going to make Mom and me a gin and tonic." Sharon walked over to the door but before going in, she bent down and patted their dog, Duke. Duke wagged his tail, acknowledging Sharon, but all the time keeping a watchful eye on John as he reopened the Kamado lid and turned the steaks. It certainly seemed to Duke that one of those steaks was being cooked for him. That wasn't too far off, because Sharon always saved some for what was the most spoiled member of the family. Duke could also count on Kirk for a handout!

Shortly thereafter, with everyone seated at the table eating and enjoying light conversation, Sharon took a long drink from her glass of iced tea and just as the conversation lagged for what seemed a second, she spoke. "Kirk and I had a long conversation about premarital sex today."

With that announcement Kirk, who had just raised his glass of iced tea to drink grabbed it with both hands and lowered it to the table. His face, which had an astonished look on it, also reddened a bit.

John choked on a piece of meat, but then started chewing faster, as least his gums were moving rapidly. His right hand also dropped to the table with the fork clanging as it hit the table. John's face was almost as disbelieving as to what he thought he had just heard.

Dora, who was almost as shocked, smiled at Kirk and John's reaction and said in a cool, calm voice, "Well Sharon, tell us about the conversation. I'm sure your Dad is interested. You seem to have his undivided attention!"

At this point John and Kirk seemed to have regained most of their composure. John started to mumble something which only sounded like jumbled words that certainly didn't make sense. Sharon, who now had to smile, in fact a wide grin covered her face as she realized the bomb she had laid, continued, "Well, what is upsetting everyone? Kirk and I simply agreed to wait for our wedding night."

By now, all ears were intently listening to Sharon and the first one to relax was Kirk. John reached for his iced tea, still not knowing what to say and looking to Dora to take charge. Dora caught John's eye and knew as only those who have been close in marriage, that it was her turn to speak on the current subject.

"Well, it seems that you've both thought about this and we're proud of the way you're handling it. I know that it's a hard decision to come up with in the times that we live in. It was hard for your Dad and me."

John, who was getting embarrassed as Dora started speaking of their relationship, chimed in, "Yes, you're showing good sense!" and John took another long drink of iced tea.

Sharon looked at Kirk, who had been keeping his mouth full of food, so that he didn't have to speak and slowly shook her head at him. "Well Star, what do you have to say for yourself?"

"Sharon, you're doing just fine, just fine!" was Kirk's reply.

"Just fine, I see, well unless you plan on breaking our short-lived engagement, you'd better speak to my parents," said Sharon with a mock stern look toward Kirk.

"But we only talked about this a couple of hours ago and I haven't bought a ring yet," was Kirk's answer. Then in looking at Sharon's awaiting face, he shook his head slowly and said, "OK." At this, Sharon placed her chin in her hands and rested her elbows on the table while awaiting the big message from Kirk.

"Well," started Kirk, "It seems that Sharon and I have fallen in love and while we haven't discussed a date yet, we'd like your permission to get married."

"All right Star!" exclaimed Sharon. "Very well spoken."

"Sharon!" scolded Dora.

"Your Mother's right, Sharon," Kirk joined in, "And besides that, you're pushy."

"Well I like that!" stated Sharon, again in mock anger.

"Their first fight." exclaimed John. "And we were there."

With that, Sharon got up and started to clear the dinner table when Dora said, "Don't worry about the dishes. I'll take care of them. You two had better leave for the movie or you'll be late."

"Well, com'on Star," called Sharon as she tossed Kirk his jacket. "I don't often get a reprieve from the dishes." Then, giving a big kiss to her Dad, she continued, "Anyway, Daddy will help. Right dear ole Dad?"

"Oh sure!" returned John as he smacked Sharon on the rear end.

John and Dora walked to the front door as Kirk and Sharon got into the station wagon and started down the lane. A toot of the horn and a wave from her parents brought about a very good feeling in Kirk as he looked into the rearview mirror and saw John and Dora arm-in-arm. Then, looking over at the prize he was engaged to, Kirk simply took a long look and smiled at Sharon as he placed his arm around her. Sharon smiled back with love in her eyes and moved closer to him as they left the park area on the way to the *Elkton Drive-In Movie*.

The drive, which took them back through North East on Route 272 was in quiet contentment as each with their own thoughts would look at the other. It wasn't until they turned right onto Route #40 that the silence was broken.

"Watch that truck," cautioned Sharon as they pulled into the main stream of traffic.

"Yeah, he's really moving. I thought he was staying out in the passing lane."

It was about a ten-minute drive from where they turned onto Route 40 to the *Elkton Drive-In Movie*. They turned off the highway behind a short line of cars. Kirk maneuvered the car over toward the ticket booth on the right.

"This line looks shorter," said Kirk.

"Yes, by one car," returned Sharon in a kidding manner.

As their turn came at the tollbooth, the attendant, a young man about the same age held his hand out in a "stop" fashion. "Tonight is car-load night," said the attendant. "Do you want to pay for the lady as a person or a car-load?"

Kirk had to smile to himself as he thought how ridiculous that sounded, but he thought he'd have some fun with the question.

"Let me have it broken down both ways," he kidded.

"The difference is twenty-five cents, that is, if she's the only one in the car. He winked at Sharon. Is she a cheap date or are you serious about her?" continued the attendant.

"That's a good question," returned Kirk. "Could be both, see I'm saving for an engagement ring."

"For her?" questioned the attendant.

Kirk slowly nodded, "Yes!"

"What the hell's going on here?" yelled the attendant, as the cars now behind Kirk started to toot their horns.

Kirk, a bit startled at the sudden outburst started to speak, but was interrupted as the attendant walked toward the car behind waving his hands in the air, shouting, "Hold up that horn blowing I've got a serious crisis here!"

The cars stopped tooting their horns and of course, a puzzled look on their faces took the place of anxiety.

Kirk turned to Sharon, as the attendant got back beside his opened window, "I don't believe this, Sharon."

"I don't either!" shouted the attendant in mock anger. "Sharon, how could you do this to me?" Then turning to Kirk, as the cars behind started to get into the other line, "Who the hell are you?" he said.

"OK Claude," interrupted Sharon. "Now fork over the free passes for tonight and a few more for good measure."

"Claude!" exclaimed Kirk.

"Hey, don't put me down, pal. I took this lady of yours to the high school prom," returned Claude. "Anyway, I only get Claude when someone gets angry, otherwise it's C.J."

"I understand, C.J.," said Kirk in mock sympathy.

"No you don't, whatever your name is."

"Kirk Daniels," offered Sharon.

"I still could be in love with her you know," returned C.J.

"I'll tell you what," said Kirk as he carefully chose his next words. "You said the difference between the couple rate and the car-load rate is twenty-five cents. OK, you give me the free passes as Sharon asked and I'll double the quarter and buy your rights to Sharon for a full fifty cents."

"I keep the half-a-buck and you get Sharon. I sell her affection to you, right?" returned C.J. as he smiled at finally seeing someone put one over on Sharon.

"Right!" said Kirk.

"Now wait a minute," said Sharon.

"Not now Sharon," interrupted Kirk. "C.J. and I are about to strike a deal."

"You've got a deal, Shake!" exclaimed C.J. "Here are your passes and I thank you for the four bits."

"C.J., I'm going to kill you," called Sharon.

C.J. motioned Kirk to drive ahead. "Now, now, lady, move on, sir. Come often."

"Hope he doesn't get into trouble," said Kirk as he drove into the movie parking lot looking for a space.

"Who's going to fire him, his father?" returned Sharon as she started to move toward the door on her side of the car. "Anyway," she continued, "Him, I'm going to kill. You, just half-kill, and don't come over to this side of the car, Kirk Daniels. I'm past being angry, I'm MAD!"

"You are not," retorted Kirk.

"What do you mean I'm not!" exclaimed Sharon. "I am! You embarrassed me. You SOLD ME."

"No, I BOUGHT you. Good deal too, fifty cents for you and a handful of free passes," exclaimed Kirk. "And if you don't come over here right now Ms. Miles, no popcorn!"

Sharon's smile broke into a full grin and as she moved toward Kirk, she said, "you drive a hard bargain."

"I know," said Kirk as they kissed, "especially where you're concerned."

Four 4

Early the next morning a light rain fell. Kirk was cleaning up breakfast dishes and having a second cup of coffee. He turned toward the door as he heard a quick "knock, knock" and then the door opened.

"Coffee smells good," called Sharon. "Don't bother, I'll help myself."

"Well, good morning," said Kirk. "And what brings you out on a morning like this?"

"I need to borrow the VW. Mom's got the station wagon and I've got to go to New-Ark, near Elkton, to pick up some material that just came in," said Sharon.

"New-Ark?" returned Kirk. "Is that like Newark?"

"Same spelling, but in Delaware, it's New-Ark and in New Jersey it's Newark. What can I tell you!" explained Sharon.

"OK, I'll buy that," returned Kirk.

"Seems like you buy a lot of things," kidded Sharon.

"One for your side!" said a smiling Kirk. "Here's the magic key for the VW."

"Magic key? Anyone could start that old thing with a rusty nail," said Sharon as she took the set of keys, kissed Kirk and made a dash through the lightly falling rain to the old VW convertible. Kirk watched, standing at the cabin's doorway with a cup of coffee in hand. Sharon waved and drove the VW out of the cabin area and into the light fog, which, along with the rain, gave him an uneasy feeling. Driving a car throughout the winding roads toward the town of North East would be a sports car driver's dream, however the weather conditions on this day would tax the best of drivers.

Kirk went back into the cabin, laid the cup in the sink and reached for his jacket. He drove the dump truck over to the office area. As he walked into the office, Will Romansky greeted him with a cup of coffee. "Just powdered cream, right Kirk? Uh, Kirk... powdered cream?" he called again.

"Oh, yes, sorry, Will," returned Kirk as he took the cup of coffee.

"Seems that you're a million miles away," said Russ Thurman, as he looked up from the desk where he was working on catching up with the paperwork and various State reports.

"Yes, I guess I am," said Kirk. "Sharon took the VW over to Delaware and I just hope the weather clears a bit."

"She'll be fine," said Russ. "She may drive a bit fast, but she's a good driver."

"I know, but..." said Kirk as he took another sip of coffee.

"Well, let's put you to work and maybe that will help keep your mind off Sharon," said Russ. "Got a job that will keep you busy all day."

"You mean more picnic table repairs?!" said Kirk kiddingly.

"Good guess, and with the weather like it is outside, we'll certainly keep you inside," said Russ with a devil look in his eyes and a wink to Will.

"Oh hell," said Will. "With Spike in Bel Air picking up supplies, guess I'm elected to help him."

"Glad you volunteered, Will," said Don McLean sheepishly, as he stood in a corner trying not to be noticed.

"What are you guys talking about?" inquired Kirk, using a tone of *I don't really want to know.*

"Well, it's a job designed to help strengthen the arms and shoulders," said Russ jokingly.

"And I don't need all those muscles," complained Will, as he headed for the shop.

"Before you ask any more questions Kirk ole boy," said Don, "I want to go on record as saying I'd have helped you. However, since Will already..." but Don was stopped in mid-sentence as Russ interrupted.

"Don, you're right, three can get the underground water reservoir cleaned faster than two. Anyway, I've got to complete these reports for John."

"What?! Remember I'm the boss's brother-in-law." kidded Don.

"And he'll be proud that you're not playing on the fact!" responded Russ.

"Me and my big mouth," said Don as he motioned to Kirk, with a come-on wave and they both headed for the shop.

As Don and Kirk entered the shop area, Will Romansky motioned to them to gather up the balance of the scrubbing brushes and detergent needed to clean the walls of the underground reservoir. Will already had his arms filled with boots and ponchos.

Not much was said during the trip to "B" section. Don was sitting up front with Will and Kirk was in the back seat of the crew cab pick-up truck with the tools, brushes and other things needed for the day's work. Kirk normally would have asked questions about what was to be done. And he probably would have asked why he had to climb down into an underground water reservoir with boots on his feet while wearing a poncho, and why he had to stand in a foot of water while cleaning the roof, walls and finally, floor of this 50'x50' dungeon-like looking hole. However, his mind was still on the weather that Sharon was driving through.

Don and Will noticed Kirk's silence and Don took that moment to reflect and kid Kirk out of his self-imposed silence.

"Yes, I remember the last time we did this, Will," Don started.

"You mean the time ole Spike almost got sucked down the drain when we emptied the reservoir too quickly?" answered Will.

"That sure was something. If we hadn't thrown that rope to him, he'd still be somewhere in the State Park pipe system," returned Don, as he motioned to Will with his head and winked his eye.

Kirk, who was half-listening, tuned in on the part about Spike almost being sucked down the drain and started to speak, but they were almost at the work site. And Will, looking into the rearview mirror tried to look extra serious as he half-turned away from driving and spoke to Kirk. "Now, don't you worry son, we'll take care of you, but just keep your feet away from the drain pipe."

And before Kirk could answer, Will joined in on the kidding. "We'll just tie the rope to the truck bumper and then around Kirk's waist."

"OK you guys," Kirk replied. "Sucked down the drain, come on!"

Will's smile broke into a wide grin and Don, looking at him, turned toward the window and broke into laughter. They all joined in the laughter and Kirk, getting the tools together as he climbed out of the truck, softly said to himself, "Sucked down the drain," and smiled again.

The three men walked over to the small spring house and Don took his key ring from his belt, found the right key and unlocked the door. Kirk started to open it but was stopped as Will put his hand on Kirk in restraint. "Wait a minute Kirk, let's go slow," said Will.

"Yes, about a five and one-half foot black snake lives here and we don't want him falling on you," continued Don matter-of-factly. "He might hurt himself in the fall."

"Right. Wouldn't want him to hurt himself," Kirk muttered as he stepped back very quickly.

Then Kirk caught himself and feeling the awkwardness of the possible joke he started back toward the door just as Don picked up the snake from the door ledge and lowered it to the ground. The snake, which seemed at least the size described to Kirk, started off toward the woods. Don said, "Have to move in on you for a few hours, fella."

Kirk didn't say anything as he watched the snake move away, but his heart was pounding a little rapidly at the sight of the largest snake he'd ever seen, outside of the Philadelphia Zoo. Will opened the door, flipped on the light and started to put on his boots. He threw a pair over to Kirk and Don, who did likewise. As they started to climb down the steel ladder into the underground reservoir, Don sensed that Kirk was still a bit skeptical about having seen the snake and spoke up.

"Don't be concerned about the snakes here in the State Park. Most, like that one, are non-poisonous. Flat head, diamond shaped, copper color, look out! But most, if you see any, are black and sort of round-headed. They're OK."

Kirk simply shook his head as he stepped off the last rung of the ladder and into the foot of water on the reservoir floor. He took a long look around the low-ceilinged room and as Will showed him what to do, he settled into completing the task at hand.

Meanwhile, Sharon had driven to Newark and was driving back in what had developed into a hard wind-driven rainstorm. As she made the left turn from Route 40 on to Route 272, she reached over to adjust the radio dial because the station she was listening to had developed static. Not noticing that the traffic light had turned yellow, she continued on through the turn. Just at that moment, a tractor trailer heading north from Baltimore, on seeing that the light was changing, shifted gears and continued on through the intersection. With the heavy rain, he didn't see the little VW convertible that Sharon was driving.

At the last moment, Sharon looked up and saw the huge blue truck bearing down on her. She quickly down shifted to first gear, but it was too late. The truck was now driving at 45 mph. It hit the VW just past the door. As metal hit metal, the trucker's brakes squealed hard. The VW flipped over twice and finally came to rest at the side of the highway.

In a matter of seconds, which seemed much longer, drivers from two cars waiting for the light to change ran to the crumbled VW. The truck driver had pulled to the side of the highway and he too was now running toward the VW to help. At the same time this was occurring, a Maryland State Trooper, driving out of the State Police Headquarters located across the road, saw the accident and immediately called for help.

It seemed as if all of the men reached the VW at the same time. The State Trooper flipped on his flasher light and ran to the side of the VW, which had come to rest on its left side. As the officer looked through the convertible roof he recognized the driver as Sharon Miles, the daughter of the State Park Superintendent.

Sharon was unconscious and there was blood on her face, head and arms. The State Trooper, Anthony DiCello, who had worked a summer at the State Park, reached for the side of Sharon's neck to feel for a pulse.

"Thank God," he thought to himself as he turned to see one of the North East Rescue Squad firemen standing behind him.

"It's Sharon Miles, Frank," said Trooper DiCello to the fireman. "She's alive!"

"OK Tony, let's get her out."

Just at that moment the ambulance arrived on the scene as the rescue squad firemen moved quickly to get Sharon out of the wreck. Other firemen were busy with the pumper fire engine hosing down the street to prevent a fire from starting.

By now other State Troopers had arrived and while some were directing traffic around the accident, others were obtaining information about the accident. John Miles was driving back from his meeting in Annapolis, the state capitol. He had been monitoring the two-way radio in the Park station wagon and picked up the mike to call the State Police to see if he could help, since he was now only a few miles south of Route 272. John was told that Sharon was in the accident and to head straight for the *Elkton Hospital*. Sharon was seriously hurt.

John asked them to send a car out to pick up Dora and also to notify one of his summer employees, Kirk Daniels.

The State Police car dispatched to pick up Dora and Kirk covered the 10 miles out to *Elk Neck State Park* in short order with headlights on and flashing red light and siren blasting. The officer, Anthony DiCello, knew the Park roads well, and after picking up Dora, drove directly to the springhouse, where Will, Don and Kirk having had lunch, were back at work cleaning the underground reservoir.

In order to save time, Officer DiCello turned on his siren as he approached the springhouse. Will, hearing the siren, climbed topside and quickly ran back to the ladder to call down to Kirk. Kirk was filled in quickly and climbed into the back seat of the State Police car for the drive to Elkton.

Meanwhile, Sharon had been admitted to the hospital through the emergency entrance and two doctors worked quickly to determine her injuries.

As Officer DiCello arrived at the Elkton Hospital with Dora and Kirk they were met at the entrance of the emergency wing door by John Miles. John and Dora embraced and John noticing the worried look on Kirk's face, put his hand on Kirk's shoulder. Kirk managed a faint smile.

John said, "The doctors are working on her right now. We won't know anything for a while." Then turning to Officer DiCello, "Thanks Tony. I appreciate your help."

"Anytime, John" He continued after a pause, "Hell, that's a stupid thing to say at a time like this."

"I know what you mean, Tony," confirmed John as he patted Officer DiCello on the shoulder.

"I'll stick around awhile John. I'm off duty right now and I've got to fill out reports on the accident, so I'll do them here until we know how Sharon's doing."

"Officer DiCello said he worked at the Park a few years ago," said Kirk as he tried to make some conversation.

"Yeah, that *was* a few years ago," replied John. "Sharon was just a little girl and Tony used to take her for rides on the tractor when he was mowing the grass."

Tony, listening to John, forced a smile through his worried face. "Think I'll go over to the cafeteria and bring back some coffee for everyone. I remember tea for you, Dora."

Just as Officer DiCello started to leave, a doctor came into the waiting room.

"Dr. Carey," responded John with an anxious look.

"She's a bit banged up John, but she'll be OK."

Dora and John embraced at the news. Kirk reached into his back pocket for a handkerchief to wipe away a tear and a relieved expression came across his face.

"Seems like this young man has more than a passing interest," said Officer DiCello to John and Dora as he and John shook hands. "I'd better head back to headquarters," he continued. "They might need the car."

"Thanks again for everything, Tony," called John as Officer DiCello started for the door.

"I'll stop by in a few days to see how the patient is."

Turning to Dr. Carey, John said, "Can we see her, Bill?"

"Sure, but just for a little while. I'm going to keep her overnight, then maybe even a day or two, make certain all's well."

"Oh by the way," continued Dr. Carey as he motioned toward Kirk, "if you're Kirk Daniels, then Sharon's been asking for you. Worried about your car, said she got only half of it across the street!" Kirk managed a smile and shook his head slightly at Sharon's humor, even in a situation like this, as he followed the Miles and Dr. Carey toward the emergency room.

Sharon's eyes were closed. From what could be seen, her head was wrapped with a bandage and there were various other bandages on her arms. Additional bruises were hidden by her covers.

Sharon blinked a couple of times and opened her eyes. She gave a faint smile as those in the room moved to her bedside. She managed a weak, groggy, "Hi Mom, Dad. Who is that with you, Kirk?"

Dr. Carey reminded, "Just a few minutes. She's been through a lot," then left the room.

With Sharon lying on her back in the hospital bed, John and Dora moved to one side of the bed while Kirk eased to the other side.

Sharon focused on Kirk, who was at her side now and held out her hand to him. As Kirk carefully took Sharon's hand, she spoke, "Hello there, Star. Sorry about your car."

"The hell with the car," replied Kirk. "How are you feeling?"

"Better now," was Sharon's answer. "I think they've got me all doped up on drugs."

"We'll talk about you being a dope later," joked Kirk as he leaned over and kissed Sharon on the tip of her nose, then whispered, "I love you, Sharon."

Five 5

May 27th was a bright, beautiful and cloudless day. It was the kind of day most appreciated when you are near a body of water and can look out at the glistening waves stirred up by a gentle breeze.

Earlier in the morning, Dora and John had driven to the *Elkton Hospital* in order to pick up Sharon. She had been checked out by Dr. Carey and was released.

As Sharon sat on the side porch of the Miles house looking out at the Chesapeake Bay, her thoughts were interrupted by the sound of an approaching truck engine. Kirk Daniels had driven the dark green dump truck over to the Miles, just after noon, to meet with Sharon. As the dump truck pulled into the driveway Sharon stood up and walked, still somewhat stiff, to the screen door to greet Kirk.

"Stay put," called Kirk as he climbed from the cab of the truck, "I'm not here to see you, just your father!"

"You'd better be here to see me." corrected Sharon.

"Well, since you asked so nicely," returned Kirk, "by the way, how are you feeling?"

"A bit stiff still, but glad to get out of the hospital and home," answered Sharon.

As Kirk entered the porch, he reached to give a greeting kiss to Sharon, but after the kiss, Sharon put her arms around Kirk and for a long moment they just held each other.

"Are you OK?" said Kirk as Sharon wiped a tear from her eye.

"Sure, just being silly I guess."

"I don't think so," said Kirk as he and Sharon walked to the rear of the porch to look out over the Chesapeake Bay.

"What a beautiful day," said Sharon, "and I'm alive!"

"By about three feet," said Kirk with a somber note in his voice "I saw the car!"

"I know," returned Sharon, "Daddy showed me the pictures taken by the insurance man."

"From now on," started Kirk in a stern voice, but Sharon suddenly interrupted.

"Don't scold me," replied Sharon, "I've learned a lesson."

"Well, I just don't want to lose you," explained Kirk.

"You won't, ever," replied Sharon as she turned toward Kirk and held him again.

Just then Dora appeared in the doorway of the house, "Come on you two, lunch is ready."

"OK." was Sharon's reply to her mother, then turning to Kirk she said, "Say Star, how come you didn't bring me flowers?"

"Because I was finishing the cleaning of two campsites in the new Rogue Harbor section. I should have brought you a couple dozen weeds, assorted of course!"

"So that's all I mean to you," kidded Sharon, "a couple dozen weeds?"

"Here, let me hold your chair," said Kirk, ignoring Sharon's last statement and he pushed her chair toward the table gently and noticed the trace of pain on her face as she sat down.

"You didn't answer me Mr. Daniels," said Sharon in a mock tone, "Here I am, bruised, black and blue, in pain, and I'm offered weeds."

Turning to Dora as she brought club sandwiches into the dining room, Kirk said, "I see she's feeling much better today."

"Yes, she does look better," answered Dora, "Dr. Carey wants her to be active, so Sharon can do the dishes and clean up the kitchen."

"Pushing the vacuum cleaner would also be good for her," said Kirk as he ignored Sharon and spoke to Dora in a kidding manner, "maybe dusting too, and some other odd jobs!"

"How about cutting the grass," interrupted Sharon, "I'd be a bit gimpy, but after all, it is exercise."

"Very good Sharon," needled Kirk. "Now eat your sandwich, you'll need your strength!"

"I need help against you two," retorted Sharon, "where's my Daddy?"

"He's over at Black Hills State Park for a meeting on fire fighting," answered Dora, "looks like you'll have to fend for yourself."

"Now I know how Mark Anthony felt, surrounded by assassins" shouted Sharon and she continued, "out, out brief candle, life's but a walking shadow, a..." but she was interrupted by Kirk.

"The "out, out" bit is from Mac Beth, Sharon, don't mix your plays, just walk me to the door. I've got to get back to work." As Kirk finished talking, he stood up from his chair and motioned in the air with his index finger, as if to show that's one for my side.

Kirk climbed into the cab of the dump truck and started the engine. Then as he started to wave and drive off, he saw that Sharon was trying to say something from the porch, so he let the engine settle to an idle, opened the door and placed one foot onto the running board so that he could hear better.

"What did you say?" shouted Kirk above the engine noise.

"Are you coming over tonight?" called Sharon.

"Be over around nine," was Kirk's reply, "Spike is giving me my first sailing lesson this evening." Then Kirk waved and headed the truck back to the road toward the shop where he would pick up some supplies before completing the days work at the Rogue Harbor campsites.

After work Kirk had stopped off at his cabin in order to change into a pair of cut-off blue jeans and tennis shoes for the upcoming sailing lesson. He changed quickly, opened the back door of the cabin stepping out onto the screened porch overlooking the bay and spotted Spike doing some work on the sailboat. Kirk quickly left the cabin and jogged down to the beach and the T-dock where Spike's boat was moored. Spike waved as he saw his student approaching the dock.

"Say, she's a beauty," said Kirk.

"Thanks," returned Spike, "Don helped me put her in the water last night."

"How long of a boat is it, Spike?"

"She's a 26 footer, nice size for the Chesapeake."

"Can I do anything to help?" asked Kirk.

"No, not yet." Then Spike continued, "Tell you what, as long as she's tied here at the dock, I'll give you some background on the boat and tell you what we're going to do, then we can get underway and do some sailing. OK with you?"

"You bet! I've always had an interest in sailing."

"Ever sail before?" asked Spike.

"No, well once, off Atlantic City on Captain Starns' sailboat. That's a restaurant there, and well, they take sightseeing trips, but I didn't do any of the sailing of course." answered Kirk.

"I know the boat you're talking about and that's a good seafood restaurant. I went out on one of those sightseeing trips, but took the speedboat ride." said Spike.

Kirk smiled, "Yea, I took that once, *Miss Atlantic City!"*

"Right!" I had forgotten the name of the speedboat, but that's it, *Miss Atlantic City*," said Spike as he smiled and shook his head, remembering.

"OK, down to work," continued Spike. "As I said, she's a 26 foot long sloop and while I'll write down sailing terms for you to remember and study, we'll keep things at a level where you learn to sail, so that you can get a nice feel for sailing and a natural touch for the boat. A good sense of sailing is what's most important. Knowing the terms can't do too much for you if you're sailing solo, but knowing how to sail with a natural feel will keep you out of trouble. At least, most trouble."

"Out of most trouble?" questioned Kirk. And, both he and Spike broke into a smile.

"That's what you might call at college, Sailing III. Right now we take up basic training," said Spike with a chuckle.

"Right with you Skipper," answered Kirk.

"I like that respect from a crewman, now swab the deck and clean the head." ordered Spike in mock humor.

"I'd sure like to Skipper, but as you said, all those terms come later. For the life of me, I don't know what you mean by that."

"Class begins," said Spike as he set the tone to teach Kirk about sailing. Then Spike continued, "this boat has two power sources, the sails of course and the other is an auxiliary motor. I use a deep shaft outboard motor. It's a 10 horsepower Johnson and has plenty of power to move this boat in and around Marinas, and plenty of power to bring you home in case you completely loose the wind. Larger sailboats have inboard motors, some even diesels. Since most Marinas won't let you sail in and out, the handling of the motor as it relates to this type of sailboat is also important to know."

"So far, so good," said Kirk.

"OK," returned Spike. "Now this boat is called a sloop, because it has one mast but two sails. The large sail is the main sail and the small one up forward is called the jib. OK so far?"

"Yes, if you loose me, I'll ask questions," answered Kirk.

"Good, now this spar which is attached to the mast and runs toward the stern is called a boom. When we make a turn around which is called *coming about*, if you steer the boat into and through the wind, bow first, or a Jibe, if the stern crossed the wind."

"Hold it," called Kirk, "you just lost me!"

"Sorry Kirk," came Spike's reply "The important thing about the boom right now is that it could swing around and knock your block off if you're not careful when you come around."

"That, I understand." stated Kirk.

"Let's see," continued Spike, "I guess that the only other statement I want to make before we get underway and I use the old show and tell method, is this. In sailing, you have to be constantly aware of the wind direction and the face of the wind. You understand what I mean by that?"

"Yes, I do," answered Kirk, "in other words, the power of the wind and the direction it's coming from is a major key."

"That is the key for any seasoned Skipper in figuring his moves." said Spike. "You catch on fast, Kirk."

"I hope so," answered Kirk.

"You'll do OK," returned Spike, "now let's prepare to get ourselves underway. First, let's check the wind. We find that it's coming right at us from the direction of the Bohemia River. So, first we'll ease the boat down to the right corner of the dock and we'll tie the bowline off. Then we can raise the main. I'll do that, while you go forward and cast off the bowline and ease the jib up to move the bow away from the dock. Then you simply trim the jib with these lines over here. These particular lines are actually called sheets. You'll be amazed as to how easily this all works. Of course, we could simply start the auxiliary motor and then set sails after we get out in the bay. But then you wouldn't learn much."

"I'm with you!" said Kirk as he and Spike moved the sailboat down to the right side of the dock and Spike tied the bowline off.

"OK, let's board," said Spike. "Go ahead, cast off and ease the jib up, then come back in the cockpit and trim it tight, so there's no fluttering of the sail. We'll do the same with the main. It's actually called getting the luff out or trimming the sail. Good, OK Kirk, see how smooth she's reacting?"

"Beautiful!" exclaimed Kirk.

"Now come back here and take the tiller," called Spike.

As Kirk came back and sat down, taking the tiller, Spike started forward and stopped about mid-ship. He called to Kirk while pointing to a piece of yarn about three feet above his head on a steel cable that ran from the deck to the top of the mast.

"This piece of yarn is called a Tell-Tale, looking at it will tell you the direction the wind comes from. The cable it's attached to is called a shroud. There are Tell-Tales on both sides."

"Got you!" Kirk sat at the tiller looking all the part of a young ensign on his first day at sea, smiling ear to ear.

By now they had sailed almost to the ship channel and Spike had kept quiet, letting Kirk get the feel of the boat and sailing. Spike smiled to himself as Kirk looked up at the sails, checking for luffing and also checking the Tell-Tales. From time to time, Kirk made small corrections and this also pleased Spike, because it told him that Kirk was serious about learning to sail. It seemed that Kirk had a good feel for sailing and it showed.

"Let's head down toward Turkey Point. Sharon's probably sitting on the porch and she'll want to see my new first mate."

Kirk smiled, raised his right hand, saluted, and eased the tiller, heading the boat onto a new course.

Meanwhile, looking down on the scene from the porch was Sharon. Knowing that Kirk was sailing she had stationed herself there. Even though she was still stiff and hurting from the bumps and bruises of the accident, Sharon had insisted on staying out on the porch to watch Kirk. With binoculars in hand, she had a great view.

"Mom, Dad," called Sharon, "Kirk's at the helm. Just look at him."

John and Dora joined their daughter and John took the binoculars and keyed in on the sailboat.

"He sure is," said John, "looks like a determined Skipper."

"Let me see," said Dora. She was handed the binoculars and likewise viewed the scene of the sailboat making its way toward Turkey Point.

John left, but returned in a moment with his camera case.

"Dora, here hold this a minute while I change lenses and put the telephoto on," said John.

"Oh great idea Daddy," called Sharon, "don't tell Kirk, we'll surprise him. Is there enough light left for a picture?"

"I think so," answered John, "anyway, I've got it down to F-2.8 at one twenty-fifth, that should do it."

While John took a couple of pictures with the camera, Sharon was once again looking through the binoculars.

"Come on you two," called Dora, "let's eat dinner."

As John held the door for Sharon, who was still walking slowly and wincing every few steps through her smiles, they heard Dora say in a matter-of-fact tone, "I appreciate you two volunteering to do the dishes while I change to drive back to town for the PTA meeting."

"Do we have a choice?" asked John and Sharon together.

"No!" Dora replied.

"We'd love to volunteer Dora Dear," said John jokingly.

Six 6

By now, most of Kirk's duties had become routine. He had been working at Elk Neck State Park for just over a month and most often, the hard work of the day was well rewarded through late afternoons and evenings spent on the Chesapeake Bay.

Kirk's sailing lessons continued on through the first two weeks of June. Almost every evening Spike and Kirk would be off in some direction and Kirk had become quite proficient in the handling of the sailboat, both under sail and auxiliary power.

The evening of June 15th was particularly beautiful. There wasn't a cloud in the sky and a full moon was coming up later. It would be a beautiful evening to sail. At the dock, Spike and Sharon were busy setting the boat in order as Kirk walked down the bluff from his cabin.

"Glad to see you've got the cabin-girl at work, Skipper," called Kirk as he approached the dock, "Did she swab the deck yet?"

"Watch that kind of talk, Buster," Called Sharon from the bow of the boat, "Tonight I'm first-mate and if you don't want a mutiny on board, you'll be very kind to the crew."

"Well, if you're the first mate, Ms. Miles, then I'm what?" returned Kirk, who caught himself leaving it wide open for a classic retort from Sharon.

But as Sharon smiled and started to speak Spike interrupted. "You're the skipper, of course!" Spike winked at Sharon and continued, "It's time for you to take the boat out without me along."

"Any objection to your crew selection?" said Sharon in mock anger.

"Crew selection?" returned Kirk. "With Spike saving me from that opening I left you, I love my crew!"

"I know you love your crew," said a smiling Sharon. "But watch out! I'm feeling my old self again, so don't give me any of the Captain Bly stuff or you will have a mutiny on your hands."

"Ms. Sharon Miles, don't get tough with me. You're not a member of any seaman's union and anyway, remember, I can take you two out of three falls anytime," retorted Kirk in a tough-minded manner. He winked at Spike and then continued before Sharon could answer, "Now first-mate, weigh anchor!"

"It's already in the boat," exclaimed Sharon. "How about bringing in those lines as your first command, dear Captain."

"Don't be smart, Sharon," retorted Kirk.

"Think I'll leave you two to an evening of smooth sailing," said Spike as he walked off the T-dock toward his pick-up truck.

"Be nice to me and I'll be nice to you, Captain," said Sharon as she gave Kirk a quick kiss and moved forward to loosen the bowlines.

"OK!" said Kirk as he headed the boat out toward the open Chesapeake. Sharon had straightened out the lines and moved back into the cockpit alongside Kirk.

"You handle the tiller and I'll take the sheets."

Kirk nodded and smiled at Sharon as he started to feel comfortable that they had gotten away from the dock so smoothly. "You do make a great crew," he said.

Sharon smiled back, "I know," and reached to kiss her Captain.

"Well, where should we head?" asked Kirk as he looked out across the Elk River toward Cabin John's Creek.

"How about down to Turkey Point and then we can check our watch and see how late it is."

"OK, but you be the timekeeper. I didn't bring mine."

"Me neither."

"What do you mean?"

"I mean, I didn't bring a watch either, and before you say anything, remember, I'm a newly appointed mate. They don't carry watches, rules of the sea, you know." answered Sharon who looked at Kirk's blank face and continued… "You didn't buy that, did you?"

"Do I look like I washed in with the last tide, Sharon?" questioned Kirk as he slowly shook his head.

"Well look at it this way, the moon will come up and go down, then up comes the sun. Of course with that we'll know the approximate time," came Sharon's answer.

"That, I understand," said Kirk, "The jib's luffing. Pull up on the sheet."

"Yes, Sir," said Sharon as she tightened up the jib and the main. A nice breeze had come up now, and the boat started to heel and reach forward, attacking the waters of the Chesapeake Bay. Kirk and Sharon had settled into an equable sail as the evening darkened, but was being relit by a big, beautiful full moon.

Sharon broke the silence. "Want something to drink?"

"Sure, I didn't know you brought anything."

"Just part of the service. I took a six-pack of Bud from the refridge. Hope Dad doesn't miss it." As Sharon tied off the sheets and made her way into the cabin to get the two cans of beer, she called back to Kirk. "By the way, did you hear the news about C.J.?"

"C.J.?" said Kirk in a puzzled manner as Sharon handed Kirk a beer and settled down again next to Kirk.

"You know, ole Claude, from the *Elkton Drive-In Movie*," returned Sharon.

"Oh sure, C.J.," smiled Kirk. "Guy I bought you from."

"If I didn't have one hand on the sheets and the other on my beer…" started Sharon.

"OK, OK," said Kirk. "What about him?"

"His father fired him," said Sharon matter-of-factly.

"What?!" returned Kirk in a surprised voice. "His father fired him?"

"Close your mouth Kirk, dear," said Sharon, who then continued, "Gave away too many free passes."

"Oh no! We benefited from that too," said Kirk, as he felt sorry for the fun-loving C.J.

"That's not the half of it," said Sharon. "His father worked out a deal with Daddy."

"That family sure seems to work out deals," stated Kirk. "What was this one?"

Sharon continued, "Well, since the budget won't let Daddy hire any more rangers for the summer, C.J.'s father will continue his salary, but he'll work out at the State Park." "That's wild!" exclaimed Kirk.

"Well, his father told Daddy that with C.J. out at the Park, the drive-in will make money again."

"When does he start?" Kirk adjusted the course and motioned to Sharon to correct the set of the sails.

"Tomorrow, I think." Sharon checked the tell-tails for wind direction and took the luff out of the sails.

"Well, I like him, even if he was your old boyfriend."

"My old boyfriend? Well, that was then and this is now. Now I have you!"

"You sure do," answered Kirk and he leaned over and kissed Sharon's forehead.

Kirk saw that they had just passed Turkey Point. "Shall we head over toward Betterton or do you think we should head back?"

"Let's come about and head home, slowly."

"Slowly?"

"Yes. Let's ease out the main a bit and loosen up on the jib. I want to relax in your arms all the way home."

"Where did you learn all about sailing?" questioned Kirk.

"Oh, Spike taught me, about ten years ago."

"I see," was Kirk's only reply, then he reached out and Sharon nestled into his arms.

"How am I going to handle the tiller with you here," asked Kirk as he lightly kissed the back of her head and nuzzled her long, dark, fresh smelling hair.

"Oh, we'll work it out," answered Sharon as she moved closer to Kirk.

Without looking back at Kirk, Sharon spoke softly, "It's a beautiful night, isn't it and I'm so much in love."

"Anyone I know," kidded Kirk and smiled, realizing that the treasure he had discovered this summer would be with him always.

"I don't think so," answered Sharon in mock tones. "But I'll introduce you to him sometime." And then she lightly punched Kirk.

The boat moved slowly along, just over drifting speed. Sharon and Kirk became quiet again, each with their own thoughts, but yet, totally entwined.

Seven 7

Early the next morning a loud knock at the door of Kirk's cabin startled him as he flipped his eggs. "I just broke two eggs because of all that banging," shouted Kirk as he started toward the door.

But before he had taken more than a step, the door slowly opened and a voice said, "That's OK, Kirk. I'll eat them, and cook some more for yourself."

"C.J., what are you doing out here so early?"

"Well today I start work here at the park, and I wanted to make a good impression."

"Obviously not on me. Here, eat these eggs." Kirk handed C.J. a paper plate with eggs and bacon on it.

"Paper plates," said C.J. in a low voice, and he caught the look Kirk was giving him. "No, paper plates are nice, just throw them away, right?"

"Well maybe I'll make you wash yours. I have the feeling this may not be your last meal here." And as he spoke, Kirk went to work preparing his own breakfast.

"Say, these aren't bad," stated C.J. "First time I've had eggs cooked on top of bacon."

"Saves pans," returned Kirk. "Push that bread down in the toaster."

"Well, you haven't said anything about my working here at the park," said C.J., as he poured a cup of coffee for himself and refilled Kirk's cup.

"I heard that your father wanted you broadening your experience by trying your hand as a park ranger," came Kirk's reply.

"That's a nice way of saying that my father fired me," exclaimed C.J. "claims he'll make money now that I'm out here!"

"Don't take it too hard C.J. ole boy. I for one am glad to have the help, cleaning the rest rooms, lifting the trash cans, clearing new camp sites and..."

"Stop! I get the picture. My father has sentenced me to a summer of torture." C.J.'s voice got softer, as he neared the end of the sentence.

"Well, let's not dwell on the good stuff, my friend. Let's you clean the pan while I finish dressing, then we'll start you on your latest career move," said Kirk as pointed toward the sink and handed C.J. the pan used for cooking eggs. C.J. went about cleaning up as Kirk put on a fresh shirt and then reached for the keys to the dump truck. "Let's go," called Kirk as he headed for the door.

As they drove over toward the shop, C.J. was silent for a while, then, still looking forward, he spoke in quiet tones, "You know, Kirk, well to tell you the truth. I'm a little afraid of this..."

"What do you mean?" asked Kirk matter-of-factly, as he made the turn into the shop and brought the truck to a halt.

"Well, as you might have guessed, I'm not really the athletic type and this kind of work..." but before C.J. could complete the sentence, Kirk interrupted him.

"Don't worry about it. I'll help you out. After all, I'm almost a two-month veteran." joked Kirk.

Kirk motioned C.J. to get out of the truck and they walked the short distance to the office, but just before they opened the door, C.J. turned to Kirk and said in a low voice, "I'm also very clumsy."

Kirk just wrinkled his face, pushed C.J. through the doorway and returned, "Remember, they can't fire you. Your father is paying your wages."

"Good morning, gentlemen," called John Miles. "I see you're ready to attack the days activities."

"Yes, we don't work around here, just attack activities," joined Russ Thurman and all the men in the shop had to smile as they looked at C.J. moaning.

"Tell you what we're going to do today," started John as the men gathered around the large lunch table, where this mornings two boxes of donuts had been picked over and the noise of coffee being sipped came to a halt. "Don, you, Spike, Kirk and C.J. will finish painting the inside of the shop. Will, I need you to lead the group for the hike on the nature trail. Russ, you know what to do with the boys on loan from over in Black Hill State Forest and make certain they get all the trash cans in the picnic area. Oh, and be sure they clean those rest rooms well. We've got almost a full capacity weekend coming up."

As John got up, he walked over to the coffee urn, refilled his cup and headed to his office to start on the monthly reports which were due in Annapolis at the end of the week. Russ and Will left the building to do their tasks and Don McLean motioned to Spike, C.J. and Kirk to follow him into the shop area.

"Kirk, help me get the paint, brushes and rollers," stated Don. "C.J., get that six-foot ladder and set it up over in the corner.

Don, Spike and Kirk opened the paint cans, stirred the paint and poured some of the paint into the trays. "Open the ladder, C.J., and place it near the corner," said Don as he slowly shook his head. He knew that C.J. was clumsy, but he was also determined that he would pull his share of work.

Kirk climbed onto the workbench, which ran the length of the wall and this enabled him to reach the top of the concrete block wall. He dipped the roller into the tray and started painting. "Don't get any paint on the floor," called Don. "The boss doesn't want to budget for a shop floor's worth of paint."

In the mean time, C.J. had set the ladder up and decided that rather than dip the paint brush he was using into the tray, he'd just place the gallon can onto the ladder shelf and work from there. C.J. climbed up the ladder and while the ladder wasn't really close enough to the wall, he felt that with stretching, he'd do just fine. He did, well for a while, but then as he looked back to admire his work, C.J. lost his balance. He grabbed for the ladder to balance himself, and in doing so, he knocked the gallon of paint off the ladder shelf. Just before it hit the floor and splattered all over, John walked into the shop to talk to Spike. The look on John's face as the paint can hit the floor told half of the story.

"Oh no," exclaimed John. "C.J.!"

Don and Kirk turned to see what John was so upset about. The look on C.J.'s face told the rest of the story. He stood poised on the ladder for only seconds, although it seemed much longer. The gallon paint can had hit the side of the ladder as it fell and ricocheted out toward the center of the shop. Paint was seemingly everywhere! C.J. peeked at John, saw the look of anger on his face, jumped off the ladder and ran out of the open door of the shop and into the shop yard.

"It was an accident, Mr. Miles, an accident," called C.J. from the middle of the yard.

"C.J., get over here," yelled John.

"You're going to kill me. You're going to beat me, oh no, you're going to fire me. Don't fire me. I can't stand rejection. I'll clean it up," yelled C.J. from the yard.

By this time, John, Spike and Kirk had gathered at the shop entrance, each with a wide grin on his face as C.J. paced around the yard.

"It's OK, C.J." called John. "I'm not going to fire you!"

"What about the rest?" called C.J., as he slowly started to walk back to the shop.

"I won't do the rest, either, C.J.," stated John, and he had to smile again.

In the mean time, the other men, all smiling at each other at what had just taken place, went back to work. John motioned to Don, pointing a finger at C.J., and then the floor. Don nodded understandingly, walked over to C.J. and put his hand on C.J.'s shoulder.

"Son, you have some cleaning up to do," said Don and C.J. slowly nodded.

As John walked back into his office, he called back, "I'll order some of the red barn paint for the floor. Always thought it would look good painted."

The rest of the morning went fairly smooth. The men worked quickly and by lunchtime, the shop looked pretty sharp, that is except for the floor. C.J. had gotten the hang of painting and the only thing he spilled during the balance of the morning was a cup of coffee.

Just as the men started to break for lunch, a station wagon pulled into the shop yard. Sharon Miles stepped out carrying a picnic basket. She waved and Kirk waved back. Kirk motioned to C.J. to follow him over toward a picnic table that was situated under a large oak tree. John, who was just leaving the shop, walked over to Sharon who reached up and kissed her Daddy hello. "Anything in there for me?" asked John, motioning toward the picnic basket.

"Just the kiss," said Sharon. "Mom's expecting you at home for lunch." Sharon then walked over to Kirk and gave him a light kiss. "How you doing, Star?"

"Oh fairly well. It has been an eventful morning," answered Kirk and he winked at C.J. As Kirk and C.J. settled at the picnic table, Sharon opened the basket and laid out a bright red checkerboard tablecloth. She spotted the grin on Kirk's face and the downtrodden look on C.J.'s. "Oh come on, C.J., it's not as bad as it seems," coaxed Kirk. "There's a brighter afternoon ahead. You'll feel better after you eat."

"Think I'm missing something guys. Clue me in or neither of you eat," said Sharon in mock anger as she held the sandwiches away from Kirk and C.J.

"Well," started Kirk, "our friend here had a little accident in the shop, well actually on the shop floor. Seems your Dad didn't want the floor painted, but ole C.J. had other plans, and now it has a partial prime coat."

"Partial prime coat on the floor?" questioned Sharon laughingly.

"I tell you it was an accident. Anyway, Kirk, I warned you that I was a clumsy soul," answered C.J.

"I don't know about you two," started Sharon. "The City Slicker and the Country Bumpkin."

But Kirk interrupted, "Take a big bite of your sandwich, Sharon, and don't talk with your mouth full."

"Good idea, Kirk," chimed in C.J. "Eat Sharon, eat, and let's change the subject."

"Ok, I'll change the subject," said Sharon, trying to hold back a smile, "but I've got to see the floor before I leave."

"Sharon!" yelled Kirk, but before he could say more, Sharon handed him an opened envelope.

"Here, this should be of interest to you," said Sharon. "It's the check you've been waiting for."

"Ah, yes the insurance check for the car," returned Kirk. "Say, you opened this. I could get the Fed's on you for tampering with the U.S. mail."

"Well don't," stated Sharon. "I won't be worth much to you in jail. Agree?"

"Agree," said C.J. quietly and he took another bite of his sandwich.

"That's for me to say," stated Kirk.

"But you agree." C.J. said to Kirk and he turned to Sharon, "he agrees!"

"Was the insurance company fair?" asked Sharon as she took the check back from Kirk and placed it in her pocketbook for safekeeping.

"I'd say so," answered Kirk. "Actually, it's three hundred dollars more than I paid for it."

"That's because convertibles are now gaining in value," joined in C.J. "In fact, if Sharon hadn't wrecked it for you, no telling what it would be worth in a few years."

"Thanks, C.J., I needed that," scolded Sharon. "See what you get for lunch next time."

"Think I put my foot into it," answered C.J. as he looked at Kirk.

"I'm sure it won't be the last time," said Kirk smiling and he slapped C.J. on the back. "Com'on, my friend, let's get back to work." Kirk helped Sharon fold up the tablecloth and he carried the picnic basket back to the station wagon.

As Sharon got into the car, Kirk spoke, "I'm off tomorrow. Think I'll take the insurance check and see how far it will go toward the down payment for a new car. You want to come?"

"Sure. I've got a couple of errands to run, but they won't take long," answered Sharon, who continued. "What kind of car are you looking for?"

"Something small, economical and a hatchback," was Kirk's reply.

C.J., overhearing this as he walked back toward the shop, turned and shouted, "I've got an uncle in the car business. Get you a great deal."

"I don't know about you, C.J.," answered Kirk, as Sharon started the car. C.J. just waved, then said in a lower voice, "we'll talk about it. I owe you for the eggs and stealing my old girl friend."

"I heard that," returned Kirk and he winked at Sharon.

"Well, he really does have an uncle in the auto business," said Sharon. "That's where this car came from."

Kirk nodded, patted Sharon's arm, which was leaning out of the window and said, "Might be a good idea at that. See you this evening?"

"Sure. You want to come for dinner," answered Sharon.

"Thanks, but I think I'll stop off at a pizza place with C.J. when I run him into town. He could use a couple of beers after his first day as a forest ranger. Besides, I've already been to your house three times this week," said Kirk.

"So who's keeping score," returned Sharon and she smiled, winked and started driving out of the shop yard.

As Kirk started walking toward the shop, he was met by Don, who said, "They need you to pick up a couple of loads of gravel this afternoon from Dixon's quarry in Bel Air and take them to Turkey Point. We're to start repairing the access road on Monday, so it looks as if you and the dump truck will be close friends for a while."

"OK," answered Kirk. "I'll pull over to the gas pump, fill up and be on my way."

"Take C. J. with you," said Don. "He's had a tough morning. Did a good job of cleaning up and he'll be pretty tired by tomorrow night, because the paint for the shop floor will be here bright and early in the morning. Besides, C.J. knows exactly how to get to the quarry."

Kirk filled the gas tanks on the dump truck and just as he was finishing, C.J. came over and said, "Clean your windshield?"

"Don't touch a thing," kidded Kirk. They both laughed as they climbed in the truck and started out from the shop yard.

"This afternoon is going to be a lot more fun than this morning, I can tell you that," said C.J., as he stretched his arms and relaxed in the cab of the dump truck.

Kirk smiled, "Well maybe they'll make up for it tomorrow."

"You can bet on that," exclaimed C.J. laughing again.

In the meantime, Russ Thurman, Assistant Park Superintendent, who had been working with a crew of men in the picnic area, came back over to the shop to pick up some additional tools. In leaving the picnic area, he tooted his horn and waved as he spotted Kirk and C.J. rolling by him on the way toward town. Russ walked into the shop to inspect the painting job and was jolted by the design the spilled paint had caused on the floor. Superintendent John Miles walked into the shop as Russ, with hands on his hips, looked at the mess on the floor. Russ looked over at John, nodded and said, “I see you’re doing an all out job of redecorating. It really looks, you know...”

“I know! It was C.J. I hope we can afford him.”

“I thought he was a freebee,” questioned Russ. “Isn’t his father paying his wages?”

“That’s not what I mean.” John pointed to the floor.

Russ nodded his head, patted John on the shoulder and picked up the needed tools and headed back to his pick up truck.

John shook his head slowly and returned to his office to complete the reports.

Eight 8

Kirk was walking back from the central bathhouse toward his cabin. After having breakfast, showering and shaving, he was feeling refreshed and ready to enjoy his day off. An early morning fog was still evident, however, all appearances pointed to a burn-off of the fog and that it would be another warm summer day in the Northern Chesapeake Bay area.

As Kirk approached the cabin he spotted a car's headlights cutting through the fog. The car was actually a Jeep. It pulled up in front of Kirk's cabin and out stepped C.J.

"Well, well, what do we have here?" called Kirk.

"How do you like it?" asked C.J.

"Very sharp. A C.J.-7 for good ole C.J."

"Not exactly Kirk," returned C.J. "It's your Wrangler."

"What?!" exclaimed Kirk. "I can't afford a Jeep."

"Yes you can. You see it's a repo. Only 2 years old and my uncle owed me a favor. Got it for your insurance check, plus the $600 Sharon kicked in," was C.J.'s reply.

"I don't know about you two," was all Kirk could say.

"Say you like it," coaxed C.J.

"Like it? I always wanted a Jeep, but the price, and Sharon giving you money. I've got to speak to that young lady!"

"Well, I think Sharon felt it was a sound investment, especially in you, so just thank her," returned C.J.

"You're right," said Kirk, "And thank you C.J."

"My pleasure. You know, it's only got 14,000 miles on it and no one has used a snow plow on it, so despite the fact that the previous owner couldn't pay, it hasn't been abused."

"The dark blue color is really sharp and the Levi interior really sets it off," said Kirk.

"I know," said C.J. "And look, I'll pick up the fog lights and I can get a great deal on a hard top for it. They'll even throw in a bikini top for free!"

"Sounds just great, thanks again," said Kirk. "Let's go show Sharon!"

"You'd better step into some old clothes, maybe some shorts or an old bathing suit first," said C.J.

"What for?" questioned Kirk.

"Because today is the big day, son!" returned C.J. "What do you think I've got wrapped up in these old newspapers? Lunch??"

"Big day for what?" questioned Kirk, who suddenly remembered what could be inside the bundle of newspapers.

"Oh no, not the salt eel!"

"Oh yes!" exclaimed C.J. "What are you concerned about? Sharon said you were the President of this so called company."

"Yes, that's right," returned Kirk with a thinking smile on his face. "And as President..."

"Oh no you don't," stated C.J. in a stern voice. "You're a working President!" And to make his point C.J. banged his fist on the Jeep's fender.

"Hey, watch out. That's my new vehicle," shouted Kirk as he put his arm on C.J. and motioned him toward the cabin. "Coffee pot's still hot. You can have a cup while I change."

"That's the idea, Mr. President, throw a bone to the hired help and they won't strike on you," returned C.J. as they reached the cabin and walked in. Kirk went on into the bedroom to change and C.J. picked up the coffeepot to pour a cup for himself.

"Want a cup?" called C.J.

"No, I've had two already," returned Kirk. "Just unplug it. I'll clean it later."

Kirk then came out of the bedroom in a pair of old faded blue jean cut-offs, deck shoes with no socks, and as he walked across the room he caught the keys to the Jeep that C.J. had just flipped him.

"Ok my friend, let's go," called Kirk as he headed for the door. "Bring the cup with you."

C.J. followed Kirk outside toward the Jeep. They climbed in and Kirk took a moment to look around. He smiled, looked over to C.J. and winked. C.J. smiled back and gave the hand sign for "Wagon's Ho!"

C.J. took a small sip from his coffee mug and flipped the rest onto the ground. "This coffee's terrible," he said making a face.

"Hey, don't litter the park!" yelled Kirk.

"Then learn to make drinkable coffee," yelled C.J. above the engine as Kirk shifted through the gears.

"I like it strong," returned Kirk.

"Strong is one thing. This stuff could be used to fill pot holes in the road," joked C.J.

"Then don't drink my coffee anymore, ole sport," countered Kirk.

"Let's not get carried away. It's not that bad," said C.J. with a wink.

Just as they slowed down for Sharon's home, Kirk's face broke into a sneaky smile and he said, "Say C.J., you have a sharp knife to cut the eel in bait size?"

"Oh no you don't," shouted C.J. "I've never done this crabbing thing before, and I saw that guy wrap the eel in those newspapers. No siree. No way!"

Sharon had just come out the front door as the two drove up in the Jeep. "You can hear that yelling a mile away," called Sharon. "What's up with you two?"

"Nothing really," smiled Kirk. "Just a labor-management dispute."

"Sharon, I told you I'd pick up these eels, but you know I can't cut them up. You know damn, darn well that I'll throw up," stammered C.J. "Tell him, Sharon. Tell him."

Sharon was laughing, almost holding her sides at the two brave men arguing about cutting the eel into four pieces to tie onto the taut line for bait.

"This is no laughing matter, Sharon Miles. Tell him!" called C.J. as he stepped out of the Jeep and waved his arms in the air.

"OK," Sharon countered. "But you have to help tie it on."

Kirk just slowly shook his head and said in a low voice, "What have I gotten myself into?"

"I heard that Kirk Daniels," said Sharon in a stern voice. "You'll thank me after you see the money we'll make. More than your salary as a ranger!"

"Speaking of thanking, and to change the subject for a moment, thanks for the loan of $600 and helping pick out this Jeep," started Kirk as he got out of the Jeep and walked over to Sharon, but as he continued, Sharon interrupted.

"Hold on there a moment, Star," Sharon said in a stern manner, "That's no loan, it's..."

"Certainly not a $600 gift," interrupted Kirk.

"Oh yes it is. Listen up, Kirk Daniels," started Sharon.

"Wait! Wait! Called C.J. in a loud voice. "I'll settle it. Sharon has a $600 share in your Jeep."

"Yes. That's very good, C.J.," said Sharon as she broke into a little girl smile and reached up to kiss Kirk.

Kirk just smiled, put his arms around Sharon and quietly said, "OK, and thank you, sweetheart."

"Sweetheart, darling! Look, are we going to stand here all day or do we start the enterprise?" said C.J. as he motioned to Kirk and Sharon to get into the Jeep. Then C.J. jumped into the back seat as Sharon and Kirk climbed in the front seats. Kirk reached over, started the engine, backed out of Sharon's driveway and continued down the road to the beach and dock area. They parked the Jeep and walked over to the T-dock and on out to the Miles family's boat.

"Daddy helped me put the taut lines into the boat this morning," said Sharon as they climbed into the boat. "They're all set up for baiting."

"This is still morning, you know," said C.J. as he started to climb in and set the eel package down.

"No, no," countered Sharon. "Keep them on the dock."

"I think she knows what she wants done," said Kirk as he stood in the background. "Today, we should just follow orders." C.J. nodded and climbed back onto the dock as Sharon smiled and held up the pilot's thumb-up sign.

"Today we follow orders," remarked Kirk. "Then C.J. and I commit mutiny, once we get the hang of this.

"And who has the contacts to move the goods?" answered Sharon.

"Just like Kirk said" interrupted C.J. "We're partners to the end!"

"You bet, guys," said Sharon in a snappy voice.

"So, partner, what's next?" said Kirk.

"Glad you asked," returned Sharon. "Kirk, you open the newspapers, take out the salted eel and cut the large ones into four pieces, the small ones, three pieces. I'll feed the line over to C.J. and he'll tie the bait on at three-foot distances and feed it back into the boat. It's that simple."

"I think I'm going to be sick," said C.J. as he looked over toward Kirk and reached for the first of the pre-cut strings to tie the bait on.

"No you're not," scolded Sharon. "You'll do just fine," and then she laughed to herself. "Just think of them as old dead pieces of snake!"

"Oh God, that's it," said C.J. and he started off the dock.

"Sharon!" scolded Kirk. "C.J. get back here. I'll tie them on today."

"I'm sorry," said Sharon, but she did have a sly smile on her face that suggested otherwise. Kirk gave an angry stare toward Sharon and shook his head slowly. "Really, I'm sorry C.J.," repeated Sharon. "Look, you get the life cushions from under the dock and Kirk will help me finish."

"No, I'll help," said C.J. "But you just watch yourself. Know what I mean?"

"Of course," said Sharon, who still had that look on her face, but quickly changed it when she saw Kirk glancing over to her.

Kirk had to smile to himself at this devilish humor of Sharon's. Of course, it was one of the things that captivated him so quickly about her. In the meantime, the three set about the task at hand and it wasn't too long before they had the first hundred yard taut line fully baited.

"Very good," said Sharon. "The other two should go quickly. See, we're a team!"

The task of baiting the lines proceeded quickly as Sharon, Kirk and C.J. moved in rhythmic motions to complete the initial job. The lines, with their floats and concrete blocks for anchors were carefully stowed on the floor of the boat. All three looked up as they heard the horn of an approaching park ranger truck. John climbed out of the truck and walked out onto the dock.

"Hi, Daddy!" called Sharon as she stepped out of the boat and onto the dock to greet her father.

"Hi Kitten," said John as Sharon reached up and kissed her Dad hello.

"We're just about set," said Sharon as she and John surveyed the situation.

"Looks it," returned John, then turning to Kirk and C.J. said, "Fine way to spend your day off!"

C.J. just nodded and slowly shook his head.

"That is if we make a few dollars," said Kirk.

John nodded, smiled, gave a wave and started back toward his truck. As he reached the end of the dock, he paused, turned around and called, "They'll be here at 5 o'clock for the catch. Then we'll have a cookout at 6:30 to celebrate."

Sharon waved in understanding and John waved back and headed toward the truck as C.J. and Kirk climbed into the boat and got settled. "Well, let's go," said Sharon enthusiastically as she jumped into the boat.

Kirk nodded and hit the electric starter for the outboard motor. The engine sprang to life and Kirk throttled back, before calling to C.J., "Cast off, ole man. We're in business!"

"Ok, Pres," shouted C.J. as he took the lines off the cleats and placed them on the dock.

"You don't have to call me Mr. President out here," called Kirk. "Skipper or Sir will do," and he headed the boat south toward the first point. C.J. just smiled, but Sharon made a face and stuck her tongue out.

They didn't have too far to go on this venture out, so Kirk kept the engine speed at about half throttle, just enough to get the sixteen foot runabout onto a plane, so she wouldn't be just pushing water. As they rounded the point, Sharon looked up at the cliff and the long field toward her home to see if her Mother was watching. Then she remembered that at breakfast, Dora told her and John that she was going into North East to do some shopping. Sharon then looked over at Kirk as she heard the engine slow down. She caught Kirk's eye and nodded approval of the spot he picked to drop the first float and anchor of the taut line.

Kirk placed the engine into neutral and said, "OK Sharon, what do we do next?"

"Just slide the concrete block over the side and let it down easy. Then we'll let the line run out over the spool," started Sharon, who thought for a moment, then continued, "toward Turkey point, for the first line."

"So that's what that spool is for," said C.J., as he looked toward the board extending over the side with a free reeling used wire spool on it.

"It helps keep the line straight for letting it out, running it and bringing it back in at the end of the day," said Sharon in a knowledgeable manner. "All the commercial crabbers do it this way. So I've been told."

As C.J. started to lower the concrete block into the water, Kirk motioned to Sharon to take the wheel. Then Kirk placed the line onto the spool to feed it out. Sharon, who was now settled behind the wheel, but sitting on top of the seat back in order to get a better overall view, eased the engine into forward. She then steered a crawling speed in the direction of Turkey Point. Kirk and C.J. worked together in uncoiling and feeding the line through the spinning spool. In no time they had the first baited line in place. Kirk eased the concrete block anchor and float line over the side and in place. He stood up and shook hands with C.J. as they both smiled a confident smile of a job well done.

Sharon smiled and shook her head slowly, "OK you two," she called. "Let's get back to work. We have two more lines to place before we start to harvest our catch."

"What a slave driver," moaned C.J.

"Come on C.J.," said Kirk as he started to get into position to plant the second baited line, "before she starts to beat the drum!"

Kirk then looked over and winked at Sharon, who smiled back and eased the boat 10 yards away from the float. C.J. and Kirk repeated the method used to place the first line and did likewise on the third to complete the large triangle.

Sharon then steered the boat away from the last float and placed the engine into neutral, letting the boat drift a bit.

"Kirk, would you please slide the ice chest out from under the deck?" asked Sharon. "It's time to take a nourishment break!"

"I'm for that," called C.J., who looked at his hands.

"Here," said Kirk as he flipped a bar of soap to C.J.

C.J. reached over the side, wet his hands and washed them, then passed the soap to Sharon.

"Pretty good thinking there, Star, bringing along some soap and towels, said Sharon to Kirk as she passed the soap on to him and reached for the towel from C.J.

"Well, remember, I'm just an ole city boy, not used to roughing it," joked Kirk as he also washed and dried his hands.

Sharon reached down and opened the cooler. She handed Kirk and C.J. ham and cheese sandwiches, plus cans of soft drinks. Then she matter-of-factly handed Kirk her can of diet soda to open.

"This is a fine time to think about breaking your fingernails," joked C.J., as Kirk smiled a quiet smile to himself, opened the chilled can and passed it back to Sharon.

"Why, whatever do you mean, dear Claude?" teased Sharon in a Southern Belle voice, as she placed her thumb over the soda can opening and shook the can, spraying a mist of soda at C.J.

"Your lady friend here," said C.J. to Kirk as he wiped off the small amount of soda that actually reached him. "She's a bit of a smart...you know what," and then took a big bite from his sandwich.

"Well," started Kirk as he thought for a second, and in seeing Sharon squinting her eyes and looking directly at him, chose his words carefully. "Let's say that sometimes you simply ask for it C.J."

"That's all?" said Sharon. "That's all you're going to say to this crew member that came close to practically..."

"Yes, that's all Sharon," retorted Kirk. "Except that sometimes, I agree with him!"

"Well, I like that!" said Sharon in an angry tone.

"Don't give me that mock anger tone," scolded Kirk. "Let's finish up and get to netting some crabs."

"Gee, I love that kind of tough talk," said C.J. as he cocked his head.

"Watch out, crew," said Sharon as she pointed her finger at C.J. "Or you'll have to walk the plank!"

Kirk just motioned with his hand a gesture of clean up the trash, and to C.J. to place the cooler back under the deck. Then he eased behind the wheel of the boat and reached out to touch the electric starter. The engine started at once and Kirk, noticing that they had drifted quite a distance, put the engine in forward and started back toward the first float. He kept the boat at a slow pace and looked over to Sharon to see if she wanted to take over steering while C.J. and he prepared to do the netting. Sharon looked back with a little girl pouting face, her lip accentuating the saddened look.

"I didn't yell at you," said Kirk in a strong voice.

Sharon kept her face in the same expression.

"I love you, I love you, I love you," exclaimed Kirk. "Now kiss me and take the wheel."

Sharon smiled, moved closer to Kirk and said, "Gee, I love that kind of tough talk!" Then she planted a kiss on Kirk and took over the steering.

Kirk moved over to catch the first float, as Sharon slowed the boat even more and placed Kirk in the right position to place the line onto the spool. "I'll just keep quiet for a while," said C.J. nervously, in anticipation of the harvest.

"Good idea," said Kirk. "Move that basket back a little farther, so my reach is right to the center when I dump the crabs," continued Kirk to C.J. So, C.J. placed the bushel basket in a spot he thought was good and Kirk shook his head in a yes motion as he made a practice dump with the net. Sharon, in the meantime, was holding the boat at neutral until Kirk signaled that he was ready to start the run.

"Remember, keep the net very close to the water and enter the water before the crab sees you. Don't stab. Just slide the net down and under the crab so that when he lets go of the bait, he simply falls into the net," coached Sharon.

"OK. Let's hope it doesn't take too long to get the hang of this," said Kirk.

"You'll do fine," said Sharon confidently. "Oh, and don't put the net too deep in the water or the crab will swim right out."

"OK. Let's do it," said Kirk and he took the net from C.J. and moved into position.

Sharon eased the outboard motor into forward, but held the throttle to a crawl. C.J. picked up one of the two back-up nets and held it in the ready, in case Kirk needed it quickly. The line moved slowly through the spool and everyone held his breath, waiting for the first bait to appear. The first bait came into view, just below the surface and Kirk eased the net into the water expectantly, but no crab was hanging on. They all let out a breath and got ready for the next bait, which was three to four feet away. The second one also came and went, as did the third and fourth.

"It's OK. Don't worry about them," called Sharon. "We probably tied them too close to the surface on the anchor line. We'll change them tomorrow." Sharon no sooner got the last of these words out, when a beautiful Blue Point came into view, hanging onto the bait, feeding. Kirk, in one clean sweep, slid the net into place and the crab dropped right in. "All right, Star!" screamed Sharon.

"Nothing to it." said Kirk, beaming. "You might even think I knew what I was doing!" Kirk placed the crab into the basket and got ready again.

"Time will tell," said C.J. soberly. Then his face broke into a wide grin and he yelled, "Man, we're in business! An enterprise!" Sharon smiled a wide grin at C.J.'s emotional outburst, but did not say anything more because she knew Kirk wanted to concentrate.

Kirk, at this point, went about the job at hand in a serious manner and although he was quite pleased with himself for the rhythm he was now performing at, he had no time to relax and enjoy netting, because almost every bait had a crab on it.

"C.J.," Kirk called, as one of the big Blue Points got tangled up in the net.

"OK. Got you," returned C.J. as he quickly handed Kirk a back-up net and worked the crab loose into the basket. Kirk netted two more crabs as they neared the end of the first run. Sharon placed the gear into neutral as Kirk slid the line out of the spool and let it fall easily below surface.

"How'd we do?" asked Kirk.

"You did well," said Sharon

"Kirk ole boy, you did good too!" joked C.J.

Sharon eased the boat onto the second taut line float and C.J motioned to Kirk that he'd set up the line for this run. Kirk shook his head in agreement, as C.J. went about the task of picking up the line just below the float and placing it into the spool rig. As C.J. was doing this, Kirk took a long look into the basket as if to count the catch.

"Don't count them. It's bad luck," said Sharon.

Kirk smiled to himself and looked up at Sharon.

"Well, that's what Daddy always said," explained Sharon. "Don't count them until we get back to the dock, it's bad luck."

"Sounds reasonable to me," said C.J. as he motioned to Kirk to prepare to net the second taut line.

"Ok. I'm ready," said Kirk.

Sharon eased the engine into forward and steered at just a slight angle so that Kirk could have a better view of the approaching bait. C.J. moved into position behind Kirk with the second net held in his hand in case it was needed. Again, the first few bait lines were empty, but the sixth one had two crabs feeding on the eel.

"Easy does it," said Sharon, recognizing that this would require some talented maneuvering so as not to lose both crabs.

Kirk didn't answer, but kept his eye on the approaching bait and nicely slid the net under the crabs. The two let go of the bait at the same time, but Kirk was quick enough to net the first one, then maneuver the net and snatch the second one before it swam away.

"Nice going," said C.J. matter-of-factly, then he handed the back up net to Kirk and took the two crab one from him so Sharon didn't have to stop the boat while they dropped the double catch into the basket.

"I think you've got the hang of it," praised Sharon as she blew Kirk a kiss.

"So far," said Kirk, "This work is fun!"

"The balance of the day's work became almost routine as Kirk, C.J. and Sharon performed in a team-like manner. They made three runs on the taut lines. The last one was also used to carefully bring the baited lines into the boat so they could be used the following day without getting tangled. After everyone was organized and the two bushel baskets filled with crabs were placed in a spot where they wouldn't spill, Kirk slid behind the wheel of the boat and placed the gear in forward, then headed her toward the State Park dock.

C.J. looked at his watch and said, "It's only ten-of-four and I'm bushed!"

"It has been a long day," returned Sharon as she squeezed into the same seat Kirk was using and placed her head on Kirk's shoulder.

Kirk moved over slightly to give Sharon some room and placed one arm around her while steering with the other. He then throttled back a bit as he spotted some small waves coming from a boat which had just passed. Kirk moved the boat nicely, avoiding a bounce, which would upset the extra passengers aboard for the trip toward shore.

As they came within a few hundred yards of the dock, they noticed that John Miles ranger truck was just coming into the dock area. John got out, returned the wave from the boat's crew and walked out onto the dock to greet the new entrepreneurs of the crabbing industry.

Kirk eased the boat into her slip and Sharon jumped out onto the dock and started to reach for the lines attached to the cleats.

"I'll do that," said John and he went about the task of mooring the boat. C.J. stepped out of the boat and raised his arms to stretch. He looked around in a satisfied manner and said, "Man, am I bushed!" and he started to walk off the dock.

"You already said that," returned Sharon. "Now get back here and help unload the catch."

C.J. stopped in this tracks, turned and started to utter something, however, he was cut off by Kirk.

"After that, you can help clean the boat," stated Kirk.

"They're no fun at all, Mr. Miles. Just a couple of slave drivers," said C.J., as he slowly walked back to the boat.

"What can I tell you, C.J.? They're your partners," answered John.

"Here C.J., take this bushel basket and place it on the dock," as he started to reach for the handles on the basket.

"Wait a minute!" yelled C.J. "That thing's full of live crabs!"

"I don't think there'd be a need to hand you an empty one," said Kirk in a disgusted manner. "Now, grab a handle and we'll slide it onto the dock!"

"They might bite, try to get back at us for catching them," reasoned C.J.

"If they do, they'll come after me C.J. I'm the one who netted them," said Kirk in a stern voice. "You're their friend. You feed them."

C.J. started to reach for the handle and the crabs moved quickly around in the basket. C.J. pulled his hand back, looked at Kirk in an apologetic manner and said, "Are you sure they can tell us apart? To them, I'll bet we all look alike."

Kirk just looked at C.J. with a blank stare, but inside he was trying not to break into laughter.

C.J. looked back at Kirk in a pleading manner and said questioningly, "Well, they all look alike to me."

In the meantime, Sharon, with arms crossed, just stood on the dock listening, but she could no longer keep silent. "C.J., the time has come..., the time has come for you to shape up and act like a man. Now get to it and unload that catch!"

"I'll do it, Sharon. But most men don't spend their day off fighting snapping crabs," returned C.J.

"He's right, you know," said John laughing.

"Daddy," snapped Sharon.

"Oh, here comes Harry Campbell's truck. He should be pleased with the catch," said John as he walked toward the parking lot. "You'll have to eventually unload them, though, C.J. Harry didn't come all the way out here just for the ride."

"Now look guys," started Sharon.

"Why don't you go say hello to Mr. Campbell, Sharon? C.J. and I will work it out."

Sharon nodded and started off to greet Harry Campbell, who had shaken hands with John Miles and was walking toward the dock with John.

In the meantime, Kirk quietly spoke to C.J. "Look, I'm not crazy about being bit either, but unloading is a task that hopefully we'll do quite often during the next couple of months. So let's just do it."

"OK. I know. OK." said C.J. as he carefully reached for the handle on the basket and they lifted the first one onto the dock. The second one was likewise placed on the dock and as C.J. stood up, he felt quite proud of himself and winked at Kirk.

Kirk smiled back and quietly said to C.J., so that the approaching trio could not hear, "See? Nothing to it."

Harry was introduced to Kirk, and as they shook hands, Harry turned to C.J. and said, "How you doin' out here, Claude?

"Having the time of my life, Mr. Campbell. Yes sir, the time of my life," assured C.J.

John lowered his head a bit so that Harry would not see the broad smile that had broken out across his face. Kirk and Sharon looked up at the sky in order not to laugh aloud.

"Well, let's load them up. I've got to get back to town," said Harry as he and John carried one basket while C.J. and Kirk carried the other. Sharon stayed behind to give a final check on the boat before leaving it. Then she joined the others by Harry's truck. As Sharon walked up, she called out, "Well, now it's time to celebrate!"

"I'll celebrate later," said C.J. "I'm just going up to Kirk's cabin and fall asleep. Maybe I'll raid the fridge later, but if you all don't mind, I'll just skip dinner."

"Sure, no problem," said Sharon. "C.J., you really did well today."

"Come on, ole pal," said Kirk to C.J. as he placed his hand on C.J.'s shoulder and motioned him toward the path leading to the cabin area. Then he turned to Sharon. "I'll grab a quick shower, walk down to the beach, pick up the Jeep, and be at your place, say forty-five minutes?"

"Fine," said Sharon. "See you later." She smiled as Kirk started to lead C.J. up the path and walked over to her Dad's truck.

"I'll have a frosted mug and iced, cold beer waiting for you. You earned it today!" called John as he climbed in the truck.

Kirk waved acknowledgment as he pointed C.J. up the steps toward the cabin area. "Maybe I'll have some iced tea," mumbled C.J. as he stumbled after reaching the top step. "I'm very tired, you know."

"Yes, I know," said Kirk. "You're still not used to the rugged life."

"I'm basically a city boy, I guess," moaned C.J. as he opened the cabin door.

"That's my line," scolded Kirk as he also entered the cabin, picked up his shower and shaving things and headed back out toward the cabin bathhouse. C.J. didn't answer, but simply walked mummy-like into the spare bedroom and flopped down onto the bed.

When Kirk returned, he entered the cabin quietly in case C.J. had fallen asleep. As he came in and walked across the room toward his bedroom, he peeked into the spare room and smiled as he spotted C.J.

spread eagle on the bed sound asleep. Kirk walked back across the cabin floor and quietly closed the door as he left.

Kirk walked down the path to the beach and boat dock area. As he headed toward the Jeep, he spotted Sharon coming down the road from her house.

"Thought I'd meet you here," called Sharon. "Figured you'd let me drive the Jeep back up the road.

"But I forgot the cap," answered Kirk.

"What cap?" inquired Sharon.

"Well if you're driving," started Kirk slowly, "then I figure I should sit in the back and, of course, you should be wearing the chauffeur cap!"

Sharon responded with a punch on Kirk's arm. "Just hand me the keys!" Sharon got behind the wheel and took a few moments to look around at the instruments, put the key into the ignition and started the engine. She looked over to Kirk and smiled.

"Handles just like the VW," offered Kirk.

Sharon nodded, placed the Jeep in gear and drove on up the road to her home. She was quite satisfied that she had handled the Jeep as smoothly as she wanted to. Sharon started to take the keys out and hand them to Kirk, but he motioned to leave them in the ignition. As they got out of the Jeep and walked toward the back door, Kirk pointed to the large white sail off the Point. Sharon nodded as the sailboat came about and headed in the opposite direction.

John greeted them at the door, handed Sharon a gin and tonic and Kirk a frosted mug of beer.

"You've got the juice of a full lime in there," said John to Sharon.

"Yes, I can taste it," responded Sharon. "It's really good. Just as I like it."

Kirk had taken a long drink of the cold beer, held it and swallowed it in segments. "Wow, does this beer taste great," commented Kirk.

"I can tell," answered Sharon.

"That first one," said John, "on a day like you two had, it's special!"

"That's for sure," responded Kirk, who looked toward the dining room just in time to see Dora come into the kitchen. "Hi Mrs. Miles."

"Hi Kirk. I understand that you've become quite a crabber," answered Dora.

"Well, I didn't miss too many," answered Kirk.

"Oh, Mr. Modest," responded Sharon. "Come on Star, tell us how it really was!"

"Well," kidded Kirk.

"On second thought, don't tell us," interrupted Sharon.

"Sharon!" scolded Dora.

"Oh, Mother, he understands me by now," answered Sharon. "Right Star? Right?"

"But Kirk kept silent, took another drink from his mug and then said, "My little day in the sun and you, Sharon Miles, cast a shadow."

"Oh, that's good," said John and he patted Kirk on the shoulder.

"I'm surrounded by assassins!" exclaimed Sharon.

"Well then," said Dora, "it's time for a station break, Let's eat!"

"Good idea," said John, as he carved the roast beef. "This is just about ready."

"I've set the picnic table out on the porch, thought it would be pleasant out there this evening," said Dora.

"Great idea," answered Sharon. "Come on, Star. Here, you carry the salad."

The Miles and Kirk settled into an enjoyable meal, overlooking the Northern Chesapeake. Both sail and various types of powerboats were making their way and the view from the porch was spectacular. The conversation at the table was as usual, light and airy. As the meal was drawing to a close, Sharon got up and cleared the table. Dora started to get up, but Sharon told her to relax, that she'd take care of it. Kirk, in the meantime, had also gotten up and helped Sharon. Instead of telling him to relax, she winked and handed him some dishes to carry into the kitchen

While they were clearing and stacking the dishes in order to place them in the dishwasher, Sharon turned to Kirk. "Feel like going back on the water? I've got a cold bottle of wine and some cheese."

"Sounds like a good idea," replied Kirk. "I'll call Spike and see if we can use the sailboat."

"Yes. An evening sail sounds great and quite romantic too. Nice touch," responded Sharon.

Kirk picked up the wall phone in the kitchen to call Spike. Sharon had, in the meantime, handed Kirk the family's phone number directory and he read the number off the listing and dialed Spike. After a fairly short conversation, Kirk hung up and turned to Sharon. "Let's go," said Kirk.

Sharon quickly packed the wine, cheese, glasses and napkins and they headed out the front door to the Jeep. It was only a minute or two drive down to the T-dock area. They parked and Kirk reached in the back of the Jeep for the cooler. He looked up to see that Sharon was already at the sailboat and loosening the lines that tied down the main and jib sheets. Kirk placed the cooler just inside the cabin of the boat and hoisted the sails. Sharon, in the meantime, had loosened the lines from the dock and manned the tiller. She tightened up on the main and jib and soon, they were underway.

"You know," said Sharon as Kirk came down from the deck and sat across from her, "we did all that preparation for sailing without saying a word. I think that's really great!"

"Guess we're not a bad team," said a smiling Kirk.

Sharon smiled back. "You want the helm?"

"No, you're doing fine," answered Kirk.

"Turkey Point OK?"

"Sure. Why not head toward Betterton, then swing around toward the Point. I think we'll have a run all the way," came Kirk's reply.

Kirk made himself comfortable and sat with his back resting against the cabin and faced toward the stern. He looked out over the Elk River and toward the cliffs and long field that led to the Miles home. After taking a long look at the beautiful surroundings, his eyes focused on the beautiful dark-haired girl at the helm. He smiled and Sharon smiled back. No words had to be said.

They had sailed for about a half-hour when Sharon motioned to Kirk to take the tiller. Kirk moved toward the stern and took the helm from Sharon.

"Care for some wine now?" questioned Sharon.

"That sounds good," answered Kirk. "Need any help?"

"No, I'm OK," returned Sharon, as she handed Kirk the wineglasses. Sharon then unscrewed the cap and poured some chilled white wine. "I didn't get a wine with a cork," she explained. "Thought this would be easier to handle while we're underway."

"Well, it certainly won't make the papers as the social sail of the evening, but, it's the beginning of a beautiful memory," answered Kirk as he raised his glass to Sharon.

"That's very profound," laughed Sharon as she touched glasses with Kirk. "You guys from Camden certainly have a way with words."

Kirk laughed also. "The Camden days seem so long ago. But so does this Spring." They both smiled.

Sharon passed some cheese over to Kirk. "I brought some fruit also. Want some now or later?"

"I'm fine," answered Kirk. "Do you want to save the fruit until after we come about and head toward Turkey Point?

"Sure. That's OK with me," answered Sharon as she poured the wine again and placed the cheese wedges within Kirk's reach.

"By the way," started Kirk, "How'd we do today? Is the company a success?"

"Why certainly! But we'll be paid weekly, not daily, and Mr. Campbell will supply all the bait," answered Sharon, then she continued. "Our pay is determined by the market price of the crabs in Baltimore. I figure that the split between us and C.J. will net the three of us about equal to your pay as a ranger."

"Not bad," commented Kirk.

"I know," smiled Sharon, "especially since we're only working it on a part-time basis."

"What'll you do during the latter part of August when I have to be back at school for football practice?" questioned Kirk.

"Miss you, write to you, call you, come to see you," answered Sharon.

"I mean," started Kirk, but he was interrupted.

"C.J., my Dad, Uncle Don... Let's not talk about your leaving," said Sharon quietly as her eyes started to fill.

"Hey," said Kirk. "I'll only be in College Park."

"That's too far," returned Sharon as she snuggled close to Kirk. Kirk put his arm around Sharon and kissed her.

They made a smooth turn and were headed away from Betterton and toward Turkey Point. The sun was low and they viewed a beautiful sunset. A gentle breeze was blowing and the boat moved easily through the calm waters.

"I love you," said Sharon.

"Boy, do I ever love you," returned Kirk.

It was a perfect evening sail.

Nine 9

Kirk awoke to the smell of fresh coffee brewing. He sat up on his bed, rubbed his face and eyes and looked from the bedroom of the cabin into the living room-kitchen area.

"About time you came to," said C.J. "Man, are you a heavy sleeper! I could have robbed you of everything you've got."

As Kirk slipped on a pair of pants and walked over toward C.J., who was holding a cup of coffee for him, he answered, "Be my guest. There's not much to steal around here."

"How about the Jeep?" questioned C.J.

"My subconscious is wired to hear the sound of the engine. You would have to push it out of here," answered Kirk as he sipped the coffee.

"Eggs and bacon OK?" asked C.J.

"Sure" said Kirk, "Say, did you sleep here last night? What time is it anyway?"

"It's five-twenty, and no I slept or tried to sleep at home, couldn't get back to sleep, so I drove out here. Figured I could always barge in on you," answered C.J.

"I could have had forty more minutes of sleep you know," stated Kirk.

"Well, this way you don't have to rush," said C.J. as he started to cook the bacon.

Kirk just looked at C.J., with that remark, picked up his soap and towel and started toward the door to go to the centrally located bath house for the cabin area. "Be back in a minute. I've got to shower and wake up."

"Don't take too long. I'm cooking the eggs on top of the bacon!" called C.J. as he poured himself a second cup of coffee.

"Man, we've got the time. Why don't you cook them separately?" yelled Kirk as he walked toward the showers.

"You only showed me one way to cook them?" shouted C.J. from the cabin door. "Now hurry up!"

Kirk didn't answer, but stumbled through the darkness, opened the door to the bathhouse and disappeared inside.

In the meantime, C.J. finished cooking the bacon, drained it and set the table. Then he walked over to the screen door, spotted Kirk walking back, so he started the eggs. As Kirk entered the cabin, the bacon's aroma really caught him. "Man does that smell good. Picked up the scent halfway here."

"I just put the eggs on, sunny side up, OK?"

"Say, you are cooking the eggs and bacon separately," said Kirk. "I might just hire you as my English butler/cook."

"I don't do windows!" commented C.J. as he placed the eggs and bacon on the paper plates.

Both he and Kirk had to laugh at that remark, remembering the television commercial. Kirk then poured orange juice and coffee, while C.J. set the plates on the table. They relaxed and enjoyed good conversation while eating breakfast. Then Kirk looked at his watch. He didn't say anything, just motioned to C.J. and they cleaned up and started for the door.

"Leave your car here. We'll take the Jeep," said Kirk. C.J. didn't answer, but headed for the Jeep and got in. Kirk backed out of the parking space and drove out of the cabin area for the shop.

"I've got a deal on the hard top for the Jeep," said C.J. "A guy wrecked a new Jeep the other day, didn't have the hard top on it at the time. It was up for repo anyway.

"A hard top costs over a thousand," stated Kirk. "So what can I get it for?"

"I think about free," said C.J. matter-of-factly.

"Are you serious?" questioned Kirk.

C.J. nodded, then added, "Of course, you owe me the customary beer."

"With a pizza thrown in," returned Kirk. "Wow, thanks man."

"The smile on your face said that a while ago," said C.J. "You're more than welcome, friend."

As C.J. and Kirk drove into the shop area, Spike was just getting out of his pick-up truck. He waved and they waved back. Spike waited for them to get out of the Jeep and walked over.

"Good morning, gentlemen," called Spike. "You both look bright this morning."

"Good morning, Spike," said Kirk and C.J. "You might say we didn't have to rush this morning." continued Kirk. "We even had time for a hearty breakfast." Then Kirk glanced over at C.J., stared a second, then winked. C.J. smiled back, but before he spoke, the door to the shop opened and John walked outside to greet them.

"Morning boys. Glad you're here early. Kirk, I'm loaning you to Black Hills State Forest for the day. They're rebuilding a road and need the dump truck to haul stones. Better stop at your cabin and pack a lunch." John then turned to C.J., "Son, you're doing public relations work for the park today. You work the guardhouse with Sharon. I'll see you all later. I'm off to a meeting in Annapolis." John headed for the Park Superintendent car.

"He didn't issue any orders for you, Spike. Got the day off?" kidded C.J.

"Not exactly," said Spike as he held the door for Kirk and C.J. "I'm working on a couple of projects in the shop, plus, while it's cool enough this morning, I'll be on the tractor, mowing." Then Spike headed for the coffeepot, picked up the mug with his name inscribed on it and poured himself a cup. "Either of you boys want any?"

"No," said Kirk. "I'll just get the keys to the dump and head over to Black Hills."

"I'll go for another cup," said C.J. and he headed over to pick up his mug. When he looked up at Spike to pour the coffee, Spike had a sly smile on his face.

"I hope I hit the cup," said Spike.

"Spill it on me and I'll put in for workman's comp," said C.J. Spike poured the coffee without spilling it, of course, and by now, the other men were arriving for work.

"Hold it," called Russ, "as long as you're pouring."

"Looks like half-cups gentlemen," said Spike. "I'll put on another pot."

Kirk picked up the keys to the dump truck and greeted the other men. Then he motioned to C.J. and flipped the keys to the Jeep. "Use the Jeep today. I won't be needing it. See you later."

C.J. nodded and said, "I'll pick up Sharon and go over to the guardhouse. You want me to bring you anything for lunch?"

"No, I'll stop off at the cabin area and fix something," answered Kirk as he started for the door.

C.J. walked outside with Kirk and waved as Kirk started the dump truck, pulled out of the shop yard and was off. C.J. took the Jeep and headed in the opposite direction, toward the Miles house, to pick up Sharon.

Sharon was already out of the house and walking down the road as C.J. pulled up in the Jeep. "Good morning, lady," called C.J.

"Top of the morning to you, sir," returned Sharon. "Have you come to fetch me?"

"That's a good way of putting it," answered C.J. "Now climb in and I'll drive you out to our post!"

"Our post?" quipped Sharon. "We're working together?"

C.J. nodded, turned the Jeep around and headed for the guardhouse.

"This is great. It gets boring out there all by yourself," said Sharon.

"Well, I guess they figured I couldn't do too much harm there," said C.J.

"Stop selling yourself short," returned Sharon. "Kirk said you're really doing well now. By the way, where is the Star working today?"

"He's on loan to Black Hills. Seems they're fixing a road and need the dump truck."

"He'll only be here another two weeks, you know," said Sharon as she bit her lip and looked away.

"He's only going to College Park, Sharon," said C.J. "Now look, I don't want this to be the topic of our conversation all day!"

"OK, OK," returned Sharon. "But, I'll still miss him."

"Hell, you'll see him every two or three days," said C.J. in a stern manner. "I'll take you there myself."

"I said OK," answered Sharon. "Pull over there and park. It's out of the way." They got out of the Jeep and opened the guardhouse, which was actually a fair sized building located at the entrance of Elk Neck State Park.

C.J. looked around at the surroundings and said, "Now what?"

"Well since this is a Thursday, it should be a fairly quiet day," stated Sharon. "I guess they want you to get the routine down so that perhaps you can work the booth by yourself."

"That sounds reasonable," answered C.J.

The first hour went by with almost no traffic, just some delivery trucks, plus a couple of cars that wanted the picnic area. Sharon was showing C.J. how to perform the duties at the park entrance, including the paperwork. C.J. caught on rapidly, especially since he had worked in the ticket booth of his father's drive-in movie and had helped with the paperwork there.

It was around ten-thirty when a candy apple red sports car convertible pulled up to the booth. Two very attractive girls about Sharon's age were in the car. C.J. was adding receipts from the previous day, so Sharon greeted the occupants of the convertible.

"Good morning and welcome to Elk Neck State Park," stated Sharon. "What can we do for you?"

"We're looking for Kirk Daniels," said the blonde in the passenger seat.

C.J., who had glanced up at the sharp looking sports car and even more, the attractive occupants, now got up from the desk he was working at and walked over to the doorway where Sharon was.

Sharon, who was startled by the unexpected statement, composed herself quickly and said, "He's not here today."

"Well, will he be back this evening?" asked the girl in the driver's seat. "We could use his cabin for the day and wait for him, couldn't we?"

"Who told you he had a cabin?" said an again startled Sharon, who was losing the composure she had gained.

"Look, I'm Ronnie Volmer, a friend of Kirk's and this is Jean Lyons. She and Kirk dated at Maryland. We're students there," said the girl behind the steering wheel. Some of the guys told us Kirk had a place here and we'd surprise him. We haven't seen him all summer."

C.J., by now, was edging past Sharon in order to handle the situation and save face for Sharon, who was showing a bit of anger as well as embarrassment.

"Hi. They call me C.J. and I'm a friend of Kirk's. He is off the park grounds on a special assignment from the Park Superintendent himself, and he won't be back until late this afternoon. However, I'm certain he'd want you to use his cabin to freshen up and a place to change, while using our beach facilities," said C.J. in his most professional Park Ranger manner.

"Thank you. We'd appreciate that. It's quite a drive here from Baltimore, you know," answered Ronnie.

"Of course," responded C.J. "Now if you'll follow me in that Jeep, Kirk's Jeep as a matter of fact. I'll lead you to his cabin and make you comfortable."

"What happened to his VW?" asked Jean.

"Well, it kind of hit on hard times," said C.J. somewhat laughing and he winked at Sharon, then whispered to her. "That little red-head behind the wheel digs me, you know."

Sharon, smiling to the girls in the car. Took a few steps with C.J. as he walked toward the Jeep and said quietly, "When you return dearie, prepare to die!"

C.J. kept walking and said over his shoulder, "Now, now Sharon, that's murder one. And believe me, it'll all work out."

Sharon stopped walking, and although she wanted to say more, C.J. had started the Jeep's engine. Also, another car had arrived at the booth and she had to take care of them.

The doors were not on the Jeep, so C.J. just waved for the girls to follow. He backed out of the parking space and headed for the cabin area, the red sports car following behind. C.J. parked in front of Kirk's cabin and the girls parked alongside.

"Oh, what a beautiful spot," exclaimed Jean. "You can see for miles."

C.J. smiled and said, "Come right along ladies, the door's unlocked. In fact, there are no locks. This is Kirk's home away from home." C.J. held the door open as Jean and Ronnie walked into the living room/dining area of the cabin.

"Small, isn't it?" said Ronnie.

"And drab too," responded Jean.

"But very comfortable, and as you said, with a great view," returned C.J.

The girls looked around the cabin, into the two bedrooms and then Jean stepped out onto the porch. "This is nice," she said aloud.

"Kirk repaired the screens on the porch and painted the cabin with fresh stain earlier this summer, so compliment him on the great job he did. You know, he's not as handy as some of us, so let's be kind. He tried hard, you know," said C.J. tongue-in- cheek.

"Yes, right," said Jean.

"Good, now, I've got to get back to my post. Can't let the little lady down. She's new and I'm training her," said C.J. as he carried the farce as far as he dared. "Just make yourself at home."

"Thanks," said Ronnie. "Oh, is there a bathroom?"

"That building," said C.J. pointing at the central bathhouse as he walked out the door and toward the Jeep. "Hot showers, too."

The girls followed C.J. out of the cabin and walked over to the sports car in order to get their bathing suits and cooler, which had their lunch in it.

"That girl at the guard post is really pretty," said Jean as they walked back toward the cabin. "I wonder if she's the reason I haven't heard from Kirk all summer."

"She did seem a bit short with us, didn't she?" stated Ronnie. "That C.J., he's cute!"

"Yes, he must be one of the bosses," returned Jean.

The girls had lunch in Kirk's cabin and would change into bathing suits to enjoy the day on the shores of the Chesapeake.

Meanwhile, C.J. had arrived back at the booth, parked the Jeep and was walking toward Sharon. Sharon turned her back on C.J. and walked back into the office part of the park entrance booth.

"Sharon," started C.J.

"I don't want to talk about it. Are the ladies alright?" exclaimed Sharon in a loud voice. "You'd better explain yourself, former friend!"

"Hell, that's easy," said C.J. in a calm voice.

"OK, explain," returned Sharon, hands on her lips.

"Are you angry with me," questioned C.J., hoping to hear the answer - no.

"Angry? No. Mad? Yes!" yelled Sharon.

"A car's coming. You relax and I'll handle them," said C.J., in trying to postpone his reply.

"Why did you send them to Kirk's cabin?" stated Sharon.

C.J. didn't answer, but spoke with the people in the station wagon and filled out their permit to camp in the park for the weekend. He then gave them directions for "C" section and a short impromptu speech on being careful with their campfire. They drove away and C.J. waited for the next blast from Sharon.

"That was well done," said Sharon in a calm voice.

"Thank you," answered C.J. "Did you like the campfire talk?"

"The fireside chat was simply super and if you don't speak about the subject we're all so vitally interested in, you'll never live long enough to give another. Get my drift?" said Sharon in a growing stern voice.

"Well, you see, Sharon," started C.J. as he searched for the right words, the ones that would get him off the hook, "I did it for you, and for Kirk to, so to speak, keep you from having an argument."

"You're selling C.J., but so far, I'm not buying," countered Sharon.

"Yes, I can see that," exclaimed C.J., "And I wish you'd reconsider, because I'm tired of being caught in the middle," said C.J., his voice growing louder as he reached the end of his sentence.

"Oh, that was good," returned Sharon in a calm voice. "You've just begun to be caught in the middle," then she paused, walked outside of the booth, turned toward C.J., and continued in a slow, deliberate voice, "And instead of being angry, maybe I'll just get even. Think about that, Mr. Rat!"

"If you think about this entire situation, you'll understand that what I did was right. What else was there to do? If I let you turn them away and ole Kirk found out about it, which he would, then you'd really be in hot water, Miss Smarty. Think about that," explained C.J. in rapid-fire speech.

"And we certainly wouldn't want to offend that dear little red-head, would we, Mr. Smooth?" answered Sharon.

"Look, Sharon," started C.J., but he was interrupted.

"OK, OK, you're right," said Sharon, her head nodding as she thought.

"I don't like that look on your face," said C.J., as he noticed the change in Sharon's face and voice tone.

Sharon smiled at C.J.'s remark, then said, "I'll be anxious to see what the Star has to say and to see his reaction."

"Bet he's Mr. Cool, Sharon," said C.J.

"We'll see," said Sharon, as she walked back outside to meet an oncoming car. "Five dollar bet?"

C.J. didn't bother to answer, but shook his head in wondering how Kirk would handle a situation like this. "The old girlfriend meets the new one." He said quietly to himself, "I think I'll take notes."

The rest of the day passed without much fanfare. Sharon and C.J. handled the booth smoothly and really didn't say very much about the underlying subject, but it was like waiting for the other shoe to drop. It was about four-fifteen when they spotted the dump truck coming up the road toward the booth. Sharon and C.J. looked at each other expectantly. "Think I'll handle this," said C.J.

Sharon, who by now had butterflies in her stomach, just nodded approval. Kirk pulled the truck to a halt by the booth door. C.J. walked out to greet him and Sharon, who was pretending to be busy at the desk, waved.

"How was it?" questioned C.J.

"Fine. No problems. Might have to go back tomorrow," answered Kirk, who then continued, "And how'd you make out today?"

"Well, it was interesting, at the very least," answered C.J. shaking his head up and down. But before he could go on, Sharon put down the papers she had in her hand and walked over to the door.

"And it could get even more interesting, Mr. Daniels," said Sharon, courage building.

Kirk looked away, then straight out the windshield, then back to C.J. and Sharon. "You know, I feel like I've just come in on the middle of a movie. I've missed something. Help me out."

"Sharon, I told you I'd handle this," exclaimed C.J.

"I know, I know," answered Sharon.

"C.J.," commanded Kirk. "Out with it."

C.J. looked at Kirk pleading for understanding. "You see, Ronnie Volmer and Jean Lyons showed up and I let them use your cabin."

"Did you charge them?" questioned Kirk.

C.J. startled at Kirk's reply to what seemed to him as a ticklish situation said, "No. I just told them they could use it. They brought their own lunch."

"Well, OK, but next time, see if you can pick up a few dollars. You know we can always use the money," stated Kirk as he winked at C.J. Sharon, in the meantime, was standing off to the side, but the look on her face showed that she was a volcano waiting to erupt.

Kirk noticed Sharon's mood and chose to let her vent steam for a little while longer, hoping she'd understand that it was he that inadvertently was placed in a tight spot, not of his own making. He continued to buy time by talking to C.J.

"Well, C.J., it seems that we've got company for dinner. You stop at the park store for, say some hamburgers, hot dogs, baked beans, dessert, you know, and we'll cook on the outdoor grill," said Kirk in a matter of fact tone.

"Sure, OK, if you say so," was all C.J. could reply.

"Good. Pick me up at the shop when you're finished," continued Kirk as he noticed Sharon reaching the slow boiling point. "Why don't you take off now and I'll drive Sharon home to change, so she can join us."

"Bye," said C.J. and he headed toward the Jeep at a rapid pace. Kirk had to smile at C.J.'s fast exit. Stage right, so to speak, and now he had to deal with Sharon's anger at having an old girlfriend drop in. Kirk opened the truck door and climbed down.

"Friend's showing up is no time for anger. I didn't know you then and now I love you, so just help me out," stated Kirk smiling, his arms open. Sharon had to smile and moved easily into Kirk's arms. Both of them said nothing for a long time.

"I just don't want to lose you. I guess I was as afraid as I was angry," said Sharon. "You mean so much to me."

"I thought by now we were pretty sure of each other, but maybe I'd feel the same way if an old boyfriend of yours showed up from Towson State," said Kirk understandingly.

"Well, a couple of guys did show up last week. And, one whom I did date quite often was, himself, upset when I told him I was practically engaged and that instead of being entertained by me, he'd have to use the picnic area," returned Sharon, who continued before Kirk could respond. "Ray also wondered how long I had known you and was shocked that it was only a couple of months. He said it was probably only a summer romance and he'd see me in the Fall."

"I see. Well, to clarify the situation, I had a long talk with your parents last week, the night you went to Elkton to get your hair trimmed," responded Kirk.

"What do my parents have to do with this?" said a puzzled Sharon. "We were talking about one thing and you bring up a conversation with my parents."

Kirk said, "Well, maybe I'm a little old fashioned, maybe it's respect, whatever, I asked permission from your parents to become engaged to you, to marry you."

Sharon sucked in her breath. "Oh, really? They didn't say anything to me. What did they say to you?" she questioned.

"Your Mother was pleased. Your father said he figured I had already made my feelings known, as you had, but was also pleased that I asked," responded Kirk.

"Well, when are you going to do something about it?" questioned Sharon in a snappy voice.

"How about now?" stated Kirk, and he reached into his shirt pocket and pulled out a small jewelry box, opened it and brought out a beautiful single mounted diamond set in a platinum ring. He reached for Sharon's hand and slipped the ring on her finger. "It's now official. Marry me?" continued Kirk.

"We're engaged! We are engaged," stammered an excited Sharon. "Where did this come from? You had the ring in your pocket? This diamond must be a karat. Oh my, how much in debt are you? Oh, I love it! I love you!" At this she was back in Kirk's arms and they kissed.

"It's a pretty ring, isn't it," said Kirk. "Well, I'm not in debt and I guess it's important to you gals, so the diamond is 125 points."

"I'm sorry. I shouldn't have asked those questions," said a more composed Sharon.

"That's OK," returned Kirk. "After all, we're practically partners now."

"I know, but..." started Sharon; however Kirk continued to speak from his heart.

"You see, the diamond, Sharon, it was my Mother's," said Kirk, who had to pause for a second in order not to let a tear form.

Sharon smiled, reached up and kissed Kirk again. "This makes the ring even more meaningful," she said.

Kirk smiled, slowly shook his head and said, "Ole C.J. had a hand in it too. As you might suspect, his father knows the jeweler over in Elkton. He set the stone in your ring. I thought it turned out well."

"It's beautiful," said a gleaming Sharon. "I'm engaged to be married, you know!"

"I know. Have you set a date yet?" kidded Kirk.

"Not yet. Maybe we can discuss it tonight," said Sharon, winking.

"We do have company, at my cabin, remember?" returned Kirk.

"Ah, yes. Fine way to get around it, by giving me an engagement ring and trying to take the wind out of my sails," scolded Sharon kiddingly.

"Speaking of sails, let's borrow your Dad's boat and take them for a ride after dinner. It'll ease my awkward situation," stated Kirk.

"That, my dear, is a good idea. Maybe we can put out one of the crab lines and let the girls try to catch them without being bit," said Sharon.

"That's the gentle Sharon I know so well," responded Kirk. "Close up the booth and I'll drop you off at your parents' so you can freshen up. I know you'll want to look your best!"

"Can I just gloat a little when I show my ring off to Jean Lyons," questioned a sly looking Sharon.

"No, and again, no!" scolded Kirk as Sharon locked the door to the booth and they both got into the dump truck. "You'll be the perfect hostess and not embarrass me!"

"Don't get uptight. I was only kidding," stated Sharon.

Kirk didn't respond, but smiled and drove on toward the Miles' home. As they passed the shop, Kirk asked, "Do you want to stop and show off your ring?"

"No. I want to show my folks first. Daddy isn't due back until after six and I'd hate for the men to see it before him."

"You're right," said Kirk, and he drove on past the driveway leading to the shop. "I won't say anything until tomorrow."

Sharon didn't respond, but leaned over and rested her head on Kirk's shoulder. She closed her eyes briefly, took a deep breath and snuggled even closer to Kirk. In a few moments, Kirk made the turn into the Miles' driveway. He brought the truck to a halt and started to open his door.

"No, don't get out. Mother's not back from town yet. Look, I'll shower and wait for her to come home and drive over in the station wagon. Do you need anything that I can bring?"

"I'm sure we've got enough," said Kirk as Sharon leaned over to kiss him, then moved into his arms as they kissed again.

As Sharon started to get out of the truck, she turned back toward Kirk. "Does C.J. know?"

"Not the date. I was going to get some roses and give the ring to you on Saturday," answered Kirk. "Why?"

"Nothing really. It's kind of nice having this event to ourselves for a while," responded Sharon. "But, you still owe me the roses!"

Kirk smiled. "Ok, and how about if we celebrate over dinner at the Glass Kitchen in Glasgow?"

"Taking me across the State Line to Delaware," mused Sharon. "I don't know about you, Star!" Sharon stepped off the truck and waved as Kirk backed out of the driveway and headed down the road toward the cabin area. Just before Sharon entered her home, she paused, looked at the engagement ring again and shouted, "I'm going to be Mrs. Kirk Daniels!"

Kirk in the meantime, did not stop at the shop, but decided to take the dump truck on into the cabin area and park it there for the night. As he arrived at his cabin, C.J., who was outside at the grill, waved. Kirk was going to toot the horn, but waved instead. He brought the truck to a halt, stepped down and walked over to C.J.

"The girls are over at the shower, freshening up," said C.J. "how'd it go with Sharon?"

"No problem. She'll be over later," said Kirk matter-of-factly. "After dinner, we'll take the girls for a boat ride."

"She didn't say anything? She's not angry or anything?" questioned C.J.

"No, she's just fine," answered Kirk. "Look, I think I'll shower and change," continued Kirk. "The coals look good. We should be ready to cook when Sharon gets here."

"Gave the girls some white wine," said C.J. as he poked the coals in the grill.

"The perfect host," said Kirk, as he opened the cabin door, went in, got clean clothes, soap and towel and reappeared.

"That girl, Ronnie, she really digs me," said a sly, smiling C.J., as Kirk walked past and headed for the bathhouse.

"By the way, congratulate Sharon when she gets here," yelled Kirk, just before he got to the bathhouse.

"What for?" yelled back C.J. He thought for a second or two. Then it came to him. "You gave her the ring?" Kirk waved a yes and disappeared inside to shower. "Man, that's one way of getting out of a tight spot," said C.J. to himself as he reached for the wine bottle, refilled his glass and raised it to Kirk. He took a drink and brought it down as Ronnie and Jean walked out of the ladies bathhouse and back toward C.J. "Now comes Round Two," he said quietly to himself.

"C.J., you have a couple of refills for us?" asked Ronnie as she picked up her glass and Jean's.

"I certainly do," answered C.J. "Kirk's back. He's grabbing a quick shower and will be here in a few moments."

"Shall I get a glass for him?"

"He'll require the bottle," said C.J., who caught himself a second later and continued, "Ah, of beer, yes, Kirk may want a bottle of beer. We'll wait and see." Then he said to himself, "This is going to be sticky and interesting and add panic to the list." He caught himself as Ronnie and his eyes met. He smiled and raised his glass to her. "Maybe I can get the girls drunk before Kirk gets back," he thought. "Drink up ladies. We must go with the flow, maintain a rhythm, otherwise, you'll get drunk," said C.J. aloud. He refilled their glasses. Just as he finished pouring, Kirk emerged from the bathhouse and started toward the group assembled at his cabin.

"Doesn't he look fantastic with that tan?" said Jean as Kirk approached.

Kirk walked up to Jean first, kissed her hello and did likewise with Ronnie, "Enjoy the park today?" questioned Kirk.

"It was great," said Jean, who moved closer to Kirk.

Kirk didn't move away, but asked C.J., "Got a glass for me?"

"He thought you'd want a bottle of beer," answered Jean.

"We have beer in cans," said a puzzled Kirk who was looking into the panic stricken face of C.J.

"Got a glass right here," said C.J. He filled it, handed it to Kirk and moved to refill the glasses. "Rhythm. Got to keep the rhythm," he continued, then said quietly to Kirk, "I'm going to get them drunk for you!"

Kirk smiled at the outpouring of concern by his friend. He turned to Jean and said, "I would have called, but I've been so busy out here at the Park, you know."

"I know," responded Jean. "And would the brunette at the entrance booth be part of what's been keeping you so busy?"

"Refill anyone?" interrupted C.J. "Besides me?"

Kirk, not paying any attention to C.J., said to Jean, "She's pretty important to me."

"I figured as much," answered Jean. "When I didn't hear from you, I knew something was up. How important is she?"

"C.J., let's take a walk," ventured Ronnie and she took his hand. He caught Ronnie's eyes and nodded. They walked toward the cliff overlooking the Bay.

In the meantime, Jean and Kirk continued talking. "Well, we're engaged," was Kirk's response.

"Wow," was all that Jean could answer.

"I met her on my first day here, and I guess we both just knew," Kirk replied.

"I can't believe that the man about campus would or, should I say, could fall like this," was Jean's response, "She must be special. What's her name?"

"Sharon Miles," answered Kirk. Boss's daughter, also. The entire family's great."

"Oh, my. What must she think?" questioned Jean. "Ronnie and I practically barged in on her."

"No problem," answered Kirk. "She'll be over shortly."

Ronnie and C.J., in the meantime, were walking back over toward Jean and Kirk. C.J. had a puzzled look on his face and was trying to read

Kirk. Ronnie walked over to the picnic table, picked up the wine bottle and said, "Refill anyone?" It broke the tension and everyone laughed.

"Congratulations, Kirk," said Ronnie. "She must be some gal!"

"Well," said Kirk, drawing the thought out, "I guess she's not half bad." They all laughed at Kirk's remark. Just then, the sound of an approaching car had them look up and toward the road. "That's Sharon now," stated Kirk and he filled a wineglass and started walking toward the station wagon.

As Sharon stepped out of the car, she gave Kirk a quick kiss and took the glass of wine. She took a long sip and said to Kirk, "I'm a bit nervous. I wasn't too nice to them."

Kirk smiled, put his arm around Sharon and they walked over to the group. "Formal introductions are in order, I guess," stated Kirk. "This is Ronnie Volmer, and say hello to Jean Lyons."

"I'm sorry I was so short with you this morning," was all Sharon could think to say.

"You?" said Jean. "We just barged in."

But Kirk interrupted, "Look, let's all relax. If anyone's to blame, it's C.J."

"Me?" said a startled C.J. "Look, I was..."

"Seriously," said Kirk as he smiled at the surprised look on C.J.'s face, "I'd delegate any actual blame about the situation on me, it's just that I met Sharon earlier this summer and she's been a focal point of my life since." Sharon smiled an embarrassed smile and took another drink from the wineglass. The others also smiled and the tension was broken. "C.J.," said Kirk, "Looks like you're the designated chef for this evening, so I'll be in charge of the refills. By the way sport, you want more wine or would you rather..."

"I'd rather," interrupted C.J.

At that, Kirk excused himself and walked into the cabin for a cold beer. The mood of the cookout was relaxed and light. Sharon made a big hit with the other girls with her wit and easy manner. Kirk took particular pride in how Sharon handled herself and even C.J. had finally relaxed, feeling he had orchestrated a successful evening. Everyone helped out with the clean up, so that particular chore went rapidly.

Kirk took a look out toward the Bay and said to C.J., "Let's leave the coals burn out by themselves." C.J. nodded and took off his chef's apron and cap. He folded the apron and walked over to the cabin to place them inside. As C.J. stepped back outside of the cabin, Kirk yelled over, "C.J., let's take the girls for boat ride. There's plenty of light left for a nice evening cruise."

"Good idea," agreed C.J. "The Bay's as smooth as silk."

They all walked on down the hill toward the dock and Kirk led the way to the Miles' sixteen-foot bow-rider run-about. "This beauty belongs to Sharon's family."

"Wow, she is a beauty!" said Jean.

"Fast too," interrupted C.J., as he helped Ronnie and Jean into the boat. In the meantime, Sharon took off the stern line and stood on the dock by the bowline. Kirk had climbed in and was at the helm. He pulled the choke out a half an inch and pushed the starter button in. The engine came to life and Kirk idled the engine down and motioned to Sharon that he was ready to get underway. She loosened the bowline and stepped into the forward seating area of the bow-rider. Kirk eased the boat away from the dock and slowly brought the power up until the boat set up on a nice plane. He headed the boat toward Cabin John's Creek on the other side of the Elk River. As they cleared the Point and the girls settled back for the ride, Kirk increased the power to about three-quarter throttle. With 5 people in the boat, he felt that full throttle wouldn't give him much more speed, but would just burn extra fuel. Kirk smiled at Sharon, who had settled in the forward bow-rider section and motioned for him to look back at the rooster tail being kicked up by the engine prop. Kirk turned and nodded to C.J., who smiled back and explained to Ronnie and Jean that they were looking at a 3-foot high rooster tail. In just a few minutes, they had crossed to the other side and Kirk then eased the boat to the right and they soon passed White Crystal Beach and continued on toward Betterton. When they reached the Sassafras River, which also flowed into the Chesapeake Bay, Kirk slowed down to maneuver around the traffic coming out of the river. He headed for the docks at Betterton and brought the boat nicely into a slip. A boy, standing on the dock, handed Sharon a bowline and C.J. a stern line. Kirk shut down as the boy tied the boat off.

"Thanks," said Kirk to the boy. "You want to stay here and watch her for me?"

"Yes, sir," came the reply.

"Good. We'll be back in about an hour," said Kirk as he handed the boy two dollars.

C.J. helped the girls out of the boat, while Kirk assisted Sharon. They walked off the dock and up to a tavern, which overlooked the Bay. "Figured we could have an after dinner drink before we head back," explained Kirk.

"You know, Star," said Sharon quietly to Kirk as they fell a few steps behind the others. "You're quite a host. Remind me to tell you how much I love you later on." Kirk just smiled, put his arm around Sharon and squeezed a bit.

They sat outside on the porch, ordered drinks and relaxed in conversation while watching the boating activity as the sun set on Turkey Point. It was a beautiful spot to watch nature's parade of colors. It was about an hour and a half before they got back to the boat. The boy had climbed inside the boat and was relaxing in the forward section. In fact, he had fallen asleep. He awoke at the sounds of the approaching conversation, stretched and stepped onto the dock, ready to man the lines. With everyone inside the boat, Kirk started the engine, and the boy prepared to take the lines in from C.J. and Sharon. Kirk put his hand into his pocket to tip the boy another dollar, because they were later than he said, but the boy wouldn't accept more. The boy stayed on the dock and waved as the boat headed off into the semi-darkness toward Turkey Point. Kirk reached for the buttons on the dash board which would illuminate the navigational lights, then headed directly across the ship channel in order to head back on the other side of the channel. There was plenty of depth outside the channel in this area and Kirk figured he'd miss most of the oncoming traffic by using this course.

In about twenty minutes they were approaching the state park dock. It had been a very pleasant trip, especially with the Bay being so calm. Kirk eased the boat into her slip and C.J. jumped up onto the dock to tie her off.

Soon they were headed back up the hill toward Kirk's cabin. C.J. had Ronnie on one side and Jean on the other, talking and laughing all the way. Kirk and Sharon brought up the rear, arm in arm. "Ole C.J. has moved right in, hasn't he?" said Kirk smiling.

"Proud of your pupil, are you?" returned Sharon, who pulled away enough to punch Kirk in the arm.

"It's just been a matter of getting some confidence in himself," answered Kirk. "He's certainly gained some from the time I first met him."

"Well, a lot of that is due to you. You've pushed him and forced him to do things he never believed he was capable of," stated Sharon.

As they arrived at the cabin, Kirk said, "Want to stop in for awhile?"

"No, it's getting late," answered Ronnie, "I think we'll head back."

"It's really been an enjoyable day, a fun day, even though it started off a bit on the awkward side," said Jean. We thank you."

"It has been nice, Hope to see you this Fall at Kirk's games," returned Sharon.

"Well, take care and drive carefully on the way home," said Kirk. "The road out of the park is full of curves and...," but C.J. interrupted.

"I'll see that they get safely to the Interstate," stated C.J. "Come on ladies, you're safe now. C.J. is in charge!"

"Really?" joined in Ronnie, "I think we'll need someone to watch over C.J.!"

"Thanks for everything," came the cry from the car as the girls climbed in and Ronnie started the engine. C.J. backed his car out and waved to the girls to follow. They waved back through the open convertible.

As the girls followed C.J. out of the cabin area, Ronnie said, "It was really a terrific day, wasn't it? Except, you lost a boyfriend, didn't you?"

"I don't think I really had one in Kirk," said Jean. "You know he dated at least two other girls that I know of, but I tried."

"I'm still trying with C.J.," ventured Ronnie. "He's really cute. I think he'll have to buy us a cup of coffee when we get to town, so I don't fall asleep driving, you know."

"Of course, and be certain he has your phone number," answered Jean. They both laughed as they continued following C.J.

Meanwhile, Kirk and Sharon were on the cabin's porch swing. It was a beautiful evening, slightly warm, but with a nice breeze blowing. "They were really nice," said Sharon as she moved closer to Kirk and snuggled into his arms.

"Why, of course," returned Kirk. "All my friends are nice."

Sharon pulled back for a moment, "Say, Star, how many other surprises like Jean do you have?"

Kirk laughed, "Get back over here."

Sharon hesitated for a moment, "You didn't answer my question, you know."

"I'd say that with me, you're in for a lifetime of surprises, but none like Jean," returned Kirk, then he continued, "that you'd have to worry about."

"Well, OK," reasoned Sharon, and she moved back into Kirk's arms.

After a long kiss and embrace, Kirk quietly said, "Now that we're engaged, when do you want to get married?"

"Tomorrow!" answered Sharon loudly.

"I've got to get a tux, so it would have to be late afternoon," stated Kirk.

"Seriously," said Sharon as she planted another kiss on Kirk, "What do you think?"

"How about January. It would be after the season's over and I figure we're good enough for a Bowl game," stated Kirk, but Sharon interrupted.

"Why not Thanksgiving weekend?" reasoned Sharon. "Our friends attending other colleges could come. We could even spend time in the Bowl city for a delayed honeymoon. Are you guys good enough for the Orange Bowl?"

Kirk laughed. "Seems like you've done some figuring already there lady."

"You might say I started figuring the day I met you, Star," returned Sharon. Kirk smiled and they fell back into each other's arms.

Ten 10

Early the next morning, as Kirk was preparing to leave for the shop, a bulletin from the radio made him pay particular attention. There was a hurricane heading up the coast and the park would be in the storm's path.

The storm had started a few days ago in the Caribbean and reached hurricane force just before passing over Cuba. Most forecasters believed it would move on an easterly course and blow out over the Atlantic Ocean, bringing just rain with light to medium winds in the vicinity of the Chesapeake Bay. The storm track changed, however, and it charged onto North Carolina's outer banks. It now appeared the storm would pass over the entire Eastern Shore Area.

Kirk drove over to the shop to report what he had heard, however, the shop radio was also tuned to a station that was talking about the impending hurricane. As Kirk entered the office, Don handed him a cup of coffee and extended a right hand to offer congratulations on becoming engaged. The other men also joined in and the news of the storm was put aside.

"Boss is just my brother-in-law," needled Don. "You made him your father-in-law. Man, you must really need the job!"

Everyone had a good laugh. Spike went over to the box of donuts, picked it up and walked over to Kirk to serve him, "How about a jelly one?" kidded Spike.

"No, I'll just take a honey-dipped," returned Kirk.

It was a good-natured few minutes as the groom to be accepted the barbs along with the sincere good wishes of the men, who only a few months ago were strangers. The last to congratulate Kirk was John. "Welcome to the family, although it seems like you've been part of it for a while now. As you might suspect, Dora and I are very happy for you kids," then he and Kirk shook hands.

Kirk didn't say anything, he tried, but just smiled. Being brought up in an orphanage had made him a loner. He could not express in words the closeness he felt for this group of men, and especially the Miles family. Kirk looked down, then back up as he finally said, "I thank all of you, I really appreciate the friendship you've extended to me this summer."

An additional news bulletin from the radio interrupted Kirk. It said that the storm was now over Norfolk and indeed was heading up the Chesapeake. After the radio bulletin ended the men started to discuss the situation themselves. John said, "Quiet down, men. Let's gather some chairs and meet in my office. We've got some work to do!"

Don, Spike, Will, Kirk, and C.J. took chairs from the main office area and moved into John's office. Russ Thurman, the Assistant State Park Supervisor, was already in John's office working on the black board. He had drawn a map of the park on it, then divided it into six sections. C.J. and Sharon's names were not listed because they would be readying the shop for families that would remain in the park during the hurricane. John saw that Russ had finished with the map and motioned for him to sit in his chair, behind the desk.

"As you all know," John started, "we're in for a bit of rain and wind. Russ has sectioned out the park for us to take charge of the situation and move as many campers as possible out of here and on the way home. Some have already left. The last time we had a storm of this apparent magnitude, the downed trees gave us years worth of firewood, so I really don't want any campers here, if we can help it."

John picked up the chalk and started to write names onto the map, then he turned from the blackboard and toward the men. "This will take a couple of minutes," he started, "So grab another cup of coffee, if you like, and will someone fill mine?"

Will Romansky didn't answer, but simply nodded to John and picked up his cup, then along with the other men, went into the shop for a refill. John was finishing as the men assembled back into his office. Will placed John's cup back on the desk and eased into a chair. The men sipped their coffee and glanced at the map.

"OK," John began, "Don, you take camping sections A, B, and C. As I said earlier, I don't want any campers left in the park, if we can help it. Tell the people in the cabins to stay in-doors. Will, you take the Boy Scout Group area and send them packing. I don't want any volunteers staying back to help out. We can handle the situation. Be polite, but firm. Spike you've got the Family Pet area. Clear them out. Russ, I think that there's nine camp trailers in that section and while it's a great location to see a storm from, they all hitch up. Then help Don. He'll start in the cabin area. You start in the back of C and work toward him. Kirk, take the gate in case anyone slips by the closed sign, take the dump truck to block the entrance area, in case two come in at once. C.J., go out to the gate and pick up Sharon. You and she can get this place ready in case we do have overnight guests. I'll alert Mr. Kemper out at Turkey Point, after I check out and close the picnic area. Now after each of us finishes up, report back here. I'd like to pull all the boats we can out of the water, so we'll need help down at the T-dock and moorings. I'll want the park boat plus mine on trailers, in case we need them. I'd rather off-load them again into the water instead of having to bale the Bay out of them. Let's see, is there something else?"

Russ broke in before John could speak again. "Supplies for those of us that stay over, plus the campers. You want me to handle it?"

"Yes," was John's reply. "Go over to the camp store first. Tell Roger that he's closed and to leave the key with you. We'll itemize everything we use and settle with him later on."

"He may want to stay. He has no one in North East, besides, he's an old army cook. What do you think?"

"I'll leave it up to you," replied John. Then turning to the other men, "OK, saddle up and let's go!"

Russ shook his head in acknowledgment, finished drinking his coffee in one long swallow. "Cold coffee has a unique taste," he pronounced. Then he walked out of John's office and toward the sink to wash his cup.

"Just leave the cup. We'll clean up," called C.J. as he followed Russ out of John's office.

Russ muttered a simple, "Thanks, kid," and headed out the door and toward his truck.

Meanwhile, with the meeting at an end the other men were also getting set to complete their assigned tasks in preparation for the storm. Spike walked out with Kirk. As they neared the parked trucks, Kirk called out a "take care" and started to climb into the dump truck, but stopped as he heard Spike call out.

"You might want to stop the campers as they leave, so we can tally whose still in the park. It'll make the second check up easier," stated Spike.

"OK, good idea," called Kirk as he closed the truck door, started the engine and followed C.J.'s truck toward the guardhouse.

When they arrived at the guardhouse, Sharon walked outside to greet them. C.J. stopped on the exit side, left the engine running and got out of the pick-up truck. Kirk, however, drove through the entrance side and then positioned the dump truck on an angle, blocking the entire entrance. Before getting out, he took a portable yellow rotating light and placed it on the truck cab roof, then flipped it on. As Kirk climbed down from the truck, Sharon called out, "What's this, an invasion?"

"No, I guess we're trying to prevent one," was Kirk's reply as Sharon came over to kiss him hello.

C.J. said, "OK, you two, break it up. Sharon you're to come with me and prepare the shop for...what we shall call, guests."

"Naw, you clean the place yourself. I think I'll just stay here and make out with ole Star here," joked Sharon. "What do you think, Kirk, m'dear?" as she snuggled closer to Kirk.

"Sounds fair to me," replied Kirk as he held Sharon close and kissed her again. Then he looked over to see C.J. standing with arms folded, giving them a dirty look.

"All right," said Sharon in a disappointed tone, "Let's go, C.J., but remember, I've got seniority over you, so I'm in charge!"

"I was afraid of that. Figured I'd get stuck with the dirty work anyway," muttered C.J. in a voice asking for sympathy.

"Don't pull that little boy stuff on me, Claude. It won't work," was Sharon's reply to C.J. "Now you're really in for it."

"Well, one can only try," answered C.J. in a cheerful tone. "Come on, let's go!"

Kirk walked Sharon over to C.J.'s pick-up truck, kissed her lightly and held the door as she got in. He started to wave, however, the lights of an approaching car caught his eye, so he just gave a thumbs-up and walked over to the front gatehouse to greet the car.

"Hello, and welcome to rainy Elk Neck State Park," said Kirk to the lady driving the car as she rolled down the window.

"Hello young man," came the reply. "Why do you have the road blocked?'

"Well, we're expecting a fairly rough storm, a hurricane, and it's coming up the Chesapeake Bay," stated Kirk. "Now I'd feel a whole lot better if you ladies head straight back to town where you'd be safer than out here."

"Well, we came out to see Dora, Dora Miles, the superintendent's wife, so you'd better unblock this road," came the reply.

"Under normal circumstances, I'd be happy to let you drive on through, however, this certainly isn't normal," said Kirk in his most pleasant manner. But realizing that he was getting nowhere, Kirk thought of something and continued, "Look, I'll tell you what, I'll call down to the house and ask Mrs. Miles if it's all right to come over. It'll just take a moment." Then Kirk walked back into the guardhouse and picked up the telephone.

"About time we got some action," said the lady driving to the lady seated next to her.

Kirk, in the meantime, held his hand over the cradle, so that the dialing of the phone meant nothing and, of course, the number would not be connected. Then, in a loud voice he said, "Hello, Mrs. Miles, I'm sorry to bother you. "Yes, I'll talk louder so you can hear me over the wind. You see, these two lovely ladies have come to the park to visit you for a while. Yes, I can hear you. Of course, I'll tell them. Right, go straight home and drive carefully. Yes, you get back to the storm preparation. Of course, I'm sure that the ladies will understand." Kirk hung the phone back onto the cradle, waited a second or two and walked back outside the guardhouse to the car. Kirk started to explain, but was interrupted.

"We heard you shouting over the wind, young man, and we're turning around and getting out of here. You should have a sign posted at the parks entrance, you know," stated the lady driving.

Kirk was going to tell her that there indeed was a sign, but thought better of it and smiling, said, "Drive carefully. Look out for fallen trees," then he smiled to himself. In just a few seconds, the car had turned around and was heading out of the park.

Meanwhile, the other men were carrying out their assigned duties and also checking to see if the electric was turned off in the laundry and wash rooms to prevent the possibility of an electrical fire. The rounding up of campers was going smoothly. As John had thought, the two boy-scout troops camping in the group section volunteered to stay behind and help, however, Will Romansky thanked them and stated that the rangers could handle the situation. He had them break camp and leave the park within a half an hour.

John drove over to the picnic area, closed the huge gate behind him to prevent anyone coming in that he might miss, and then proceeded to drive through the area slowly, checking it out. The only people in the picnic area were some sailors from the Bainbridge Naval Base, who had been locked-in the previous night. This was a practice John followed, as had several Park Superintendents before him. They simply felt that with the kids blowing off steam and drinking beer, the young sailors were better off staying all night in the Pavilion, rather than being forced onto the highway. John rounded up the 8 youngsters, most of whom were still asleep, and explained the situation. They, of course, volunteered to help, since they didn't have to be back on the base until Sunday night, but John explained that his staff could handle the emergency and perhaps they might be needed on base. They agreed, and followed John out of the area.

After waving goodbye, John headed his truck toward Turkey Point to see Mr. Kemper. As he drove to the Point, John noticed that the high winds had already downed tree limbs. Nearing the Point, the paved highway ended and the road became a dirt lane with grass growing in the middle. With Mr. Kemper's house still a half mile away, John drove past formerly plowed farm fields. The grass had overgrown the fields to where the hay was now more than three feet high and with the high winds whipping through the open fields, it took on a certain beauty. As John pulled into the farmyard, Mr. Kemper came out of the house to greet him. "Hello, John," called Mr., Kemper, as John climbed out of the truck.

"How are you, young fellow?" answered John.

"That's my line," returned a smiling 80 plus year old Mr. Kemper. John also broke out into a wide grin. The two shook hands and Mr. Kemper put his hand on John's shoulder and motioned for him to come into the house.

"Won't be able to stay too long," said John as they entered the house through the kitchen door.

"I know, have had the radio on all morning. Looks like a real blow coming up," answered Mr. Kemper as he set two cups on the table and poured coffee. "You pretty well set at the park?"

"Yes, we sectioned it off and sent the men out to clear the grounds of campers," answered John, who continued, "sent Kirk Daniels out to the gatehouse, figured the football player would discourage people from trying to get into the Park."

"He's a fine young man, you know. He comes out here with Sharon to check on me a couple of times a week," said Mr. Kemper, who smiled, paused and shook his head slowly, then continued while John sipped his coffee. "In fact, last week when they brought the groceries I ordered, I found a bottle of scotch in the bottom of one bag. Black Label too! Kirk motioned to me not to say anything, but I think Sharon knew."

John smiled back as he set his cup on the table. "Kirk and Sharon got engaged to be married yesterday."

"That's wonderful, John. Dora's got to be pleased too. They're suited for one another, you know," answered Mr. Kemper. "The kids set a date yet?" questioned Mr. Kemper.

"Well, they both graduate next May, but I don't know if they can wait that long," answered John. Before he could continue the conversation, an announcement about the hurricane on the radio interrupted them.

"I guess you better be heading back," said Mr. Kemper as they got up from the kitchen table. "I appreciate you're coming out here."

"Wanted to see if you'd come to our house and ride the storm out with us," was John's reply.

"Thanks, but I'll be fine. Spent many a storm out here, and I thank you," Mr. Kemper replied. Then he and John walked back into the farmyard. They both looked up at the darkening sky, then knowingly toward each other.

"Take care of yourself," said John as he got into the pick-up truck.

"Don't worry about me none, you'll be busy enough, son," replied Mr. Kemper. "I'll see you after the storm. Give you a cup of coffee, with some royal in it!"

"I'll probably need it then," answered John as he started the truck and drove out of the farmyard.

As John headed back out and looked over the waving grass, his thoughts went back to a time when he was much younger and the fields were full of crops, before Mr. Kemper retired from farming.

Mr. Kemper, instead of going back into the house, decided to take a walk toward the lighthouse at the Point. He still had a lively step and covered the three hundred yards in a short time. The white lighthouse, outlined by the ever darkening sky would be an artist's delight, however, the beauty of the scene this day was outweighed by the impending dangerous hurricane. As Mr. Kemper neared the edge of the high cliffs that overlooked the headwaters of the Chesapeake Bay, he stepped carefully, checking the footing beneath him. The height from Turkey Point to the beach below near the lighthouse was just over one hundred feet. As he looked out over the water from this vantage-point, he could see for miles down the bay. While no ships were in the channel, a lone cruiser about forty foot long was making its way against the ever-growing white capped waves that were being kicked up by the wind. It was headed up the North East River, which was to Mr. Kemper's right, as he peered out at the boat. He felt sorry for the man at the helm, having to fight the elements on such a day, but he was not concerned for the man or the boat's safety. While watching the scene, Mr. Kemper noted that the boat had been eased to a speed where she maneuvered through the waves with little or no pounding to the hull. The boat was obviously headed to either McDaniels Yacht Basin or Bay Boat Works and would be there in a good harbor within an hour. He watched the boat until it passed out of sight around the Point. Then he took a long look around at the entire scene from Turkey Point, up the Elk River to the left. where the Bohemia leads into it, then, at about the eleven o'clock position, toward the Sassafras River, then back down the Bay and finally slightly to his right where the North East River flowed into the Chesapeake. By this time, large raindrops had started to fall, so Mr. Kemper started back down the path toward his farmhouse. He felt confident about the house, after all, it had been there for more than one hundred years, and of course, had withstood many a storm during that time.

In the meantime, the park rangers had completed their tasks and had gathered at the T-docks on the Elk. Spike had driven the Ford tractor down to the docks in case it was needed. Will, who had gotten there first, moved both the state park boat trailer and John's trailer into position, was now out onto the dock and walking the state boat toward the ramp. Spike simply hooked the trailer onto the tractor and grabbed the bowline from Will in order to guide the boat onto the trailer. Spike walked back to do the same with John's boat. Don arrived and walked out onto the floating T-dock. He checked the entire dock, especially the pilings to make certain they were solidly anchored to the bay's bottom. While at each piling, he also checked to see that floating dock would ride up the piling all right, Russ pulled up in his truck and motioned for Don to get in the truck. Don ran over, opened the door and got in.

"Looks like the rain is joining the wind," said Don as he rolled the window down three or four inches and reached into his shirt pocked for the cigarette. He then pushed in the lighter on the truck's dashboard.

"Yeah, the storms' just reaching the Baltimore, Washington area. I figure we start to get the main force in about three hours," answered Russ, who started to open a notebook. "How many boats are tied up at the docks?"

"I think about ten to twelve are left from the two-week campers," answered Don.

"Let's check them out with the book to see who owns the boats," said Russ.

"OK, but I was going to move some of the boats to other slips," was Don's reply as he motioned toward the docks. "We don't want them banging into each other."

"Good idea," said Russ. "Guess we can't get the ones without covers out of the water."

"I'll have them moved closer to shore, away from the deeper water, in case they sink," was Don's reply, then he continued. "I think there's only three or four without covers."

Russ nodded his approval, then picked up the mike to call John. Don finished his cigarette, put it out in the ashtray and got out of the truck. He walked over to where Spike and Will were finishing up by dragging the park rowboats behind the tractor to where the beach and forest met. There they chained each of the ten boats to a tree. Don explained what they had to do next. Spike drove the tractor back to the front of the dock. Don and Will followed behind. Russ parked the truck off to the side and joined them on the dock. He said, "I got in touch with John on the radio and he's on the way back to the Park now. He saw ole Bill and will check out the gate with Kirk, plus he'll stop at the office, then join us. So, it looks like you've got another hand, me!" Russ then buttoned up his raincoat and looked up at the ever-darkening sky.

"Spike came up with a good idea," said Don as he and Russ walked further on the dock. "We could leave a man down here with a civil defense pump in the back of the pick-up and if any of the boats look like they're in trouble, we'll just pump them out."

"OK," returned Russ, "but make sure Spike or whoever is on duty knows to drop the hose in case the bay comes up too far. We can always go find them after the storm if they break away or just sink." The men went about the remaining tasks at the dock and planned to go back to the shop/office when they finished.

In the meantime, John stopped at the gatehouse to check in with Kirk. Headlights were needed now because between the darkening sky and the deep forest foliage, although it was only around noontime, the visibility was, as is it were, dusk. Kirk spotted the headlights, pulled on his raincoat and started out to greet the oncoming vehicle. He stopped while still under the cover of the building as he recognized that it was John's truck and waited for him to pull up.

"Everything's quiet?" called John as he rolled the window down.

"Yes, pretty much," said Kirk as he stood back under cover. "Rain's really coming down now."

"Storm's been holding over Baltimore for the past half-hour, according to the radio, but it'll cover the forty miles in no time once it gets started. Looks like we're on the leading edge right now," remarked John. "I'll send some lunch over and relieve you later on," he continued.

"Fine, I'm OK out here," returned Kirk.

John nodded, rolled the truck window back up, gave a high sign and drove off toward the shop. As he drove, John went through a mental checklist to determine if all the preparation work was completed. The two points he pondered were to have water placed in the civil defense barrels in case the pump failed, plus a C.D. generator engine to use for electricity, just in case. He pulled up in front of the shop, only to see C.J. waving him toward an open overhead door. John pulled into the shop.

"Couldn't get the boss wet!" called C.J. as John stepped out of the truck.

"Got everything under control?" asked John as he surveyed the area.

"I think so," answered C.J. as he pulled a clipboard up to read, that he was holding. "I tried to jot everything down. Let's see, we've got three families that stayed behind: one with kids from Rocky Mount, North Carolina; plus two retired couples, one from Tempe, Arizona and one from Largo, Florida. I thought Largo was out on the Keys, but they said regular Largo was near Tampa, nice people. Also," as C.J. continued, before John could speak, "Sharon filled the C.D. barrels with water and I moved the

C.D. engine out into the field away from the building, fumes you know, and stretched the cord back into the shop, in case we need electricity."

"Good," said John as he smiled at the efficiency C.J. had shown. "By the way," he started to say but was interrupted by Sharon who had just entered the shop from the office area.

"Of course he filled it. There's also a spare water-tight five gallon can near it for refilling, in case we need it."

"Well, it looks like everything's in good shape," was all John could say.

"I guess we're as ready as we can be," began Sharon. "We have a pot luck dinner planned for this evening. Between what we have and what the campers want to use up, we'll have a banquet."

"That's a good idea," remarked John. "This way, in case we do need to hold out for a couple of days, our supplies will go further."

"Smart daughter you've got, right dear ole Dad?" kidded Sharon.

"I've never had a doubt on that accord," stated John as he spun Sharon around and gave her a smack on the tail. "By the way," John continued as Sharon felt her rear end and gave a clenched fist to her Dad in jest, "I'm heading up to the house to see if your mother needs anything. Come with me and make some lunch to take out to Kirk. He won't have time to take a lunch break."

"OK," Sharon replied. "We have everything in hand here." Then checking her watch, she said, "Wow, it's twenty after two. He must be starved!"

As Sharon and John started to get into the truck, the men who had been at the dock came into the shop. John walked over to get a report on their progress and was pleased to find that so far, everything had gone smoothly. Russ walked John back to the truck and motioned for C.J. to pull the overhead door up.

"You should have heard the conversation old Donald was having with a camper when I caught up with him in B section," stated Russ, as John got into the truck. "The camper wanted to stay and ride out the storm, as he put it. But Don told him that this would be no place for an adventure, that falling trees can't see where they're falling and that one tree the size of those in that section would squash him, just like you'd step on a rotten grape!" All of the men and Sharon had a good laugh. "But that's not the half of it!" Russ continued. "The guy still wanted to stay, but Don finished him off by saying that he'd already checked the guy out, so he'd have to leave in order to keep the Park records straight. Madder than hell, he was, but he left!"

The men continued laughing as John backed out and started toward his home. Don, in the meantime, had gotten a cup of coffee and just stood there looking at the men with a silly look of quiet accomplishment on his face.

"I'd say that you men could use some good hot food. Come on in the office," said C.J., and he motioned Don, Russ, Spike and Will to follow him.

As they entered the office area, the people who stayed behind got up to say hello to their hosts. C.J. did the introductions. "Gentlemen, let me introduce Mr. and Mrs. Denney. They're from Tempe, Arizona, and Mr. and Mrs. Gienetti from Largo, Florida. We had another couple with children, but they just made a telephone call to friends in Philadelphia and will wait out the hurricane up there. Mr. Denney and Mr. Gienetti have certainly made themselves useful, took some of the caulk and repaired those leaking window sills and the ladies prepared a hot lunch for you."

"Well, we sure appreciate the hot lunch. Been a long wet time since breakfast," responded Spike. "And you gentlemen did a job we've been meaning to get to. We thank you." The conference table that served many purposes in the shop office, from actual business to catch-all, now had a bright red and white checkerboard tablecloth on it with place mats, stoneware and napkins all set for the luncheon.

As the men picked spots and sat down, Will remarked, "This looks like we're sitting down to Thanksgiving Dinner!"

"It's just the things we keep in the travel trailer," said Mrs. Denney. "Now you boys just relax and we'll serve you. We've all eaten, so just dig in!"

Mr. Denney took a spare chair and sat down with his coffee cup. "Come on and sit over here Dick," called Mr. Denney to Mr. Gienetti.

Dick Gienetti motioned OK and filled his coffee cup, then joined the others. The men talked, joked and generally enjoyed the lunch break. Mrs. Denney and Mrs. Gienetti went about the task of serving the luncheon, pouring extra cups of coffee and clearing away the dishes. They joined in the conversation and really seemed to enjoy themselves, despite the now howling winds and heavy raindrops that were beating out a mighty tone on the metal shop roof.

C.J., who had eaten lunch with Sharon and the overnight guests, was walking between the crowd gathered at the conference room and John's office where he was listening to radio reports about the hurricane.

"You can forget about the storm reports, C.J.," called Don. "The hurricane is just outside the door!"

Meanwhile John and Sharon arrived at the Miles' house. The rain was really coming down now and John pondered a moment before opening the truck door and running to the house.

Sharon glanced over and asked why John was hesitating. "You ready to make a run for it, or do you want to turn on the windshield wipers and wait out the storm here in the yard?"

John smiled at Sharon, "No, it might be more comfortable in the house," he said as he reached for the mike on the two-way radio. "I'd rather have Kirk out here during the storm. No one in their right mind will be on the road to the Park, and if they are, they can go to the shop. Don's new specialty is handling those special cases." Sharon laughed as John brought the mike close to his mouth and pushed the transmission button. "Park Super to main gate," John spoke. He wasn't much for special codes and preferred to talk in clear, plain English. "Keeps down misunderstood messages," as he told his men.

In a few seconds a static-filled reply came back, "Kirk here, John."

"If everything looks ship-shape out there, then come out to the house. A hot meal awaits you, young man," replied John.

"On my way!" stated Kirk in a firm voice.

"Well, let's go," said John to Sharon. "Your Mom's got the door open." With that, Sharon opened the truck door and dashed for the house, John trailing her by a few feet.

Kirk, back at the gatehouse, took a long look around to be sure everything was secured in case a window broke. He then left the building, making certain that the door was closed tightly. Kirk then stepped up into the dump truck fired up the engine and headed toward the Miles' home. He slowed and glanced to his left as he passed the shop. While it was only a little after three, the storm-darkened sky made it seem much later. Kirk noticed, as he drove by that the lights were on in the shop. "At least the hurricane hadn't knocked out the electricity," he thought to himself, "not yet, anyway."

Kirk drove into the Miles' yard and parked next to the pick-up truck. He dashed out of the truck, swinging the heavy door to a tight close and ran toward the open door of the house as Sharon greeted him. "Did you get wet, Star?" said Sharon as she held a towel for Kirk.

"No, I ran between the raindrops," came Kirk's reply, but he took the towel and wiped his face. "Man, that wind and rain is something, and even a little fun. I've never been through a storm like this before," he continued.

"Old Mother Nature can kick up her heels when she wants to," smiled John who came into the foyer as Kirk was toweling off. "How'd things look as you came in from the gatehouse?"

"The gate is secure, the shop looks OK, still with electricity, but the electric lines are really whipping in the wind. Some of the young trees are nearly bent in half too. One old tree in the scout section looks like it's down."

After John listened, he said, "You want a beer or a cup of coffee?"

"I'm still on duty, you know," answered Kirk.

"And you may be through much of the night," replied John.

"With that," stated Sharon, "I'll get Kirk a beer!"

Come on into the dining room. Dora has some hot soup and sandwiches for us," said John. Kirk and John walked into the dining room. John motioned for Kirk to sit down as Sharon came in from the kitchen and handed both men bottles of cold beer with frosted mugs nested upside down over the opened bottles.

Dora came in holding a serving tray with four bowls of hot clam chowder, plus a bowl filled with Trenton Oyster Crackers. "This should warm you up," she said as she placed the bowls on the table.

"It does look good," came Kirk's reply. "I love these Trenton Crackers too. Bookbinders in Philadelphia and a couple of seafood restaurants in Atlantic City serve them."

"Do you want me to get the sandwiches?" asked Sharon.

"No, just relax and enjoy your soup. I'll get them later," was Dora's reply.

The meal was quite relaxing, despite the howling winds and noisy driven rain pounding on the roof and sides of the house. Since Dora had made the house storm ready, especially realizing that John and Sharon would be tied up preparing the State Park to receive the brunt of the hurricane, the meal afforded John his first relaxing period in many hours. With the television tuned to a Baltimore station forty miles south, and the radio in the kitchen tuned to a local station from Havre de Grace, information about the storm was always being updated. John also checked with the shop office by the two-way radio from time to time.

After the meal, John walked through the kitchen and was going to open the door and step out onto the screened porch that overlooked the Chesapeake Bay. He pushed back the curtain on the door to see if the rain was whipping over the porch itself. At that moment, Dora walked into the kitchen, carrying the last of the luncheon dishes. "Don't you dare," said Dora in a stern voice. "The last thing I need is a hurricane charging into my kitchen." She set the dishes down and punched John in the arm.

"I was only looking," was John's reply with a sheepish smile on his face. He then took Dora in his arms, hugged her and gave her a kiss. "You did good, getting the place ready for the storm," he continued and kissed her again.

Sharon and Kirk were in the living room watching the television as John and Dora came in. The announcement from the Baltimore station was that the eye of the storm has passed over the city and the back end of the storm was now being felt.

"The eye should be overhead soon," said John. "You girls, I'd like you to stay here. Kirk will check out the dock area and I'll give the balance of the Park a once over and stop by the shop, before coming back here." Since he could do no more for the moment, John sat down in his easy chair and closed his eyes. The sound of the television, plus his concern about the well being of the Park wouldn't permit him to fall asleep, but he rested. Sharon had moved to the sofa and Kirk was stretched out on it with his head resting in Sharon's lap. Dora had also come into the living room and was sitting in her chair watching the television reports. She likewise had been hard at work and this was the first time she paused for a moment to relax.

About a half-hour later, John eased up out of his chair. He walked over to the living room's picture window, pulled the string on the curtain rod and opened the curtains. He had noticed that the sound of the wind and the rain had died down and wanted to verify it. John then walked to the foyer and opened the front door. It did indeed seem that the eye of the hurricane was overhead because here was an eerie calm, yet the ever-present feeling that all hell was about to break loose again. By this time Kirk had also gotten up and walked past John to the front yard, where Sharon joined him. Dora stopped at the front door.

"I'll head on down to the boat dock," said Kirk in a matter of fact tone.

"OK, but don't worry about bailing out any of the boats. We'll take care of them later. I don't want you down there when the storm shows us her back-side," said John and he walked back into the house to get his truck keys and a jacket.

Sharon walked Kirk to the dump truck. He climbed in and started the engine, after what seemed like a long time. "Wires must have gotten wet," he called from the truck as John paused by the driver's side of the dump truck, before getting into his pick-up. Kirk headed down the road toward the beach and dock area. He noticed through the rear mirror that John had gotten his truck started and was headed in the opposite direction toward the shop and main Park area. As Kirk approached the dock area, he noticed that the water had risen at least four feet above a normal high tide.

Most of the boats without covers were half full of water, although there seemed to be no noticeable damage. Since the outboard engines had all been removed, the main concern for damage, if the boats did become full of water, was of course, no longer present. A quick check of the Park rowboats, which were tied to trees, showed that they too were all right. With the eye of the hurricane still overhead, Kirk pondered whether he should bail out some of the boats when a cabin cruiser came into view from the Point to the left. It didn't seem to be under power, but it was still too far away to see if anyone was on board. Kirk started to walk back to his truck in order to call in what he saw when a pick-up truck came down and rode into the dock area. Kirk walked over as Spike and Will got out.

"Figured you might start to bailing, so we brought the C.D. pump," said Spike. "Help us take it on down to the dock and we'll have them clear in no time."

Kirk smiled at the thoughtfulness of Spike and Will, but was worried about the cabin cruiser as it continued into the main beach and dock area cove. "Take a look out there. That boat seems to be just drifting," said Kirk as he pointed.

"It certainly does," said Will. "You and Spike can take the pump to the dock and get it set up. I'll take the pick-up and get the Park boat."

Kirk and Spike, with Will also helping, picked the civil defense pump up and unloaded it from the truck. Kirk and Spike then got on either side of the pump and started off with it toward the dock. Will motioned toward the hose and off loaded it right there. He didn't want to waste time by carrying it all the way to the dock. Will then backed the truck around and headed back up the road to the big field just a hundred yards away. He swung the truck around and into position, then hitched up the boat trailer and was on his way back to the dock area in no time at all. While he was backing the trailer down the boat ramp into the water, Kirk motioned to Spike that he would help Will. Spike gave a high sign and continued bailing the boats with the C.D. pump. Kirk bounded off the dock and onto the boat ramp. Will, by this time, had the trailer far enough into the water to float the boat off. He got out of the truck and walked back to the trailer. "Take your shoes off and climb aboard. Stick the sea cock in so the damn thing doesn't sink on us and start it up before I release you off the bow eyelet," were Will's quick fire orders. He took a breath and continued, "I'll pull the truck and boat trailer up into the field and be back in a minute."

"Aye, aye, Sir," was Kirk's reply and he saluted, still holding one work shoe in his hand.

"That too," laughed Will, catching the shoes tossed to him by Kirk.

The electric start engine came to life right away. Kirk had given it a quick choke and quickly gunned the engine, then idled it back as Will released the boat off the trailer.

Kirk backed around, holding the bow to the incoming waves while Will drove the truck, with the trailer attached, out of the water and up the road to the field. In a short time he was back. Spike had stopped bailing long enough to come over as Will came down the hill to ask if he would need additional help. Will said that he and Kirk would be able to handle the situation. Kirk, in the meantime, had maneuvered the park boat out to the end of the dock. Will and Spike walked rapidly out to the end of the dock area and Spike steadied the bobbing boat as Will jumped in. Will gave a "Wagon's Ho" sign and they were off. Kirk brought the throttle up to about half speed because anything more would only pound the hull and soak both he and Will. The cruiser was now about half way into the cove and within about fifteen minutes, it would have smashed into the beach area. The wind driven waves would soon have taken a damaging toll on what looked like a thirty-foot plus cruiser. They cut an angle to meet the cruiser in the shortest distance. You could see she was a classic wooden boat.

"Let me take over here," shouted Will above the now growing wind. "You're younger than I am, so you can climb onto the cruiser."

"OK," was Kirk's reply and he throttled down while he and Will changed places. Kirk then moved into the bow section of the sixteen-foot bow-rider to prepare to board the cruiser. As he started to get ready to make the jump, he turned back as Will shouted above the wind and the outboard engine noise.

"Make a quick check in the cabin for the key. Break the cabin door if it's locked, gently of course, and if you find a key, try to start the engine. If you can't find a key then get a line so that we can tow her to an anchor point," came Will's instructions.

Kirk gave a high sign as Will maneuvered to the cruiser's stern. With a leap, Kirk had one foot on the top of the transom, then into the cockpit. He moved rapidly, checked the ignition first, but found no key and tried the cabin door. It wasn't locked. Kirk looked around quickly to determine if there were any hooks in view with keys attached. He came back out of the cockpit, held his hands up in a sign of no luck.

"Make certain you check the drawers and also the fuse box panel!" shouted Will.

Kirk waved and disappeared back into the cabin. The first place he checked was the fuse box, sitting on a hook to the right was, in fact, two keys. Kirk grabbed both and in a flash was back into the cockpit. After a quick high sign to Will, he was seated in the captain's chair. The first key didn't fit. Kirk surmised that it was probably an extra key for the door. The second key fit and Kirk turned on the ignition. Then with his fingers mentally crossed, he eased the choke out half way and maneuvered the throttle about half way also, then let a few seconds pass and pushed in the button with *starter* printed just below it. The engine turned over, but didn't start. The battery seemed strong by the sound of the cranking, so Kirk gave a quick pull of the choke all the way out, hoping not to flood the engine as he did so. She kicked to life! Kirk moved the choke back in a bit and settled the throttle to about 800 RPMs, let her settle a few seconds and eased the choke back in almost to the board, dropped the RPMs to 500 and slipped the gear into forward. He had been so intent the past few moments that he didn't have time to look over at Will. As he did, Kirk caught the wide smile of Will and the quick salute of a job well done. Will motioned for Kirk to follow him, and started off toward the point below the Miles' house. Kirk figured that the way Will was heading, they were going to take the cruiser deep into the next cove and anchor her in the safest harbor possible under the circumstances. While Will moved along as fast as he dare go. The wind and waves were building, as the back side of the hurricane started to show herself, and as the eye of the storm moved northward. Kirk stayed a safe distance back and even planned to take a wider turn around the Point in order to reduce the hardship on the classic wooden boat's hull. He was moving along at around 1200 RPMs now and as he started around the Point, Kirk eased her up to 1500 RPMs. Will had cut the Point much shorter and was further into the cove, checking out a suitable spot for anchorage. The best spot seemed to be near the beach called *Boy Scout Beach.* This group camping area had its own beach. But even more importantly at this time, the diving platform, which was anchored with heavy concrete, might prove very handy. Since the cruiser had obviously broken loose from her mooring, Will didn't know if there was an anchor aboard or how much additional line, if any. He pulled the park boat up to the diving platform, went forward into the bow riding section and quickly took a line, jumped onto the deck and tied the boat to the dock. Although Will had placed the engine in neutral, he didn't shut it off for fear that it wouldn't start again. Kirk in the meantime, saw what Will was doing and slowed to about 600 RPMs and headed slightly deeper into the cove before turning back into the chop. Will motioned that he wanted Kirk to bring the cruiser in on the shore side of the platform and Kirk waved back in a sign of understanding. As Kirk eased the cruiser up to the platform, Will could see that the anchor was still neatly in place on deck. It was obvious that the line, which held her to a mooring, had broken loose. Just a piece of well-worn hemp was hanging to the cleat on the port side. Will stood there for a second, trying to figure if he wanted to use the anchor rope to tie off onto the platform, or to just take the boat deeper into the cove and simply anchor her. At just that moment, Spike appeared on the beach waving his hands and holding up rope. He figured that perhaps the cruiser would have lost her lines and that Kirk and Will would need help. As Will waved back, out of the tree line and onto the beach came John, also carrying rope. A broad smile came on Will's face as suddenly the problem at hand was solved.

"Keep idling," yelled Will. "I'll go get them and we'll tie her off!"

Kirk gave a high sign and eased away from the platform, around to starboard and took the cruiser deeper into the cove once again. Will, in the meantime, jumped back into the park bow-rider and headed for the beach. John walked out to waist deep water to meet Will, because the waves now striking the shore would swamp the sixteen-footer. As Will pulled near, John slipped the ropes he was holding high, so as not to get them wet, and into the bow section.

"Glad to see you guys," said a smiling Will, as he steadied the boat against the waves. John eased himself into the boat. "You want to tie the bow to the platform and then a stern line to a tree on shore?"

"That's exactly what I wanted to do," answered Will. "After looking at the rotted bowline though, I wasn't sure that the anchor line would hold either."

John just nodded in understanding, then, as they reached the diving platform, John tossed the ropes and jumped onto it. He then reached for the bowline of the park boat and tied her off.

Kirk turned the boat around and had a front view of the action taking place on the diving platform. He eased the cruiser back to 500 RPMs and slowly maneuvered back into position. As he slid up to the platform, John boarded the bow of the cruiser and Will quickly handed him a line. John tied it off, and handed the line to Will who set about placing a spring line, now that he had the luxury of extra line. He handed the second line to John to tie off on the opposite side of the bow. John, in the meantime, had also placed forward fenders overboard on both the port and starboard bows. Then he headed for the cockpit with the last of the ropes for the stern line. As he did that, Will checked the lines on the platform one last time and jumped into the Park boat so that he could maneuver into position to pick up the stern line and bring it toward shore. As he pulled up, John tossed the coiled rope gently to Will, and then jumped into the bow section of the Park boat. Will eased the boat backward toward shore in order to keep the bow facing the waves. John prepared to go overboard again with the line. Spike moved closer to the shoreline to help. Kirk, in the meantime, kept the cruiser at an angle to the waves and was also maintaining the tension on the forward spring lines as best he could. John eased over the side and motioned to Spike, who had started toward the water to stay on the beach. John brought the long rope out of the water and Spike grabbed a hold of it and pointed to a tree, just up the beach for the tie-off, which would maintain the wave angle Kirk and the spring line had set. Will, in the meantime, had gone back to the platform area to pick up Kirk when he shut the cruiser down.

Kirk cut the engine took a long look around the cockpit to be certain all was battened down, eased out of the captain's seat and for the first time, noticed he was wet to the bone. He shivered slightly, feeling the cold now, but reached for the ignition key, opened the door to the cabin and placed the key back on the hook in the fuse box. He quickly checked to be sure all the windows were shut tight, came out into the cockpit, shut the door and went forward to check the bowlines, before jumping onto the diving platform. He then jumped into the Park boat with Will and after waving to Spike and John, they were off and headed around the Point and back to the T-dock. It had been a long two and half hours and neither Will nor Kirk said anything on the way back, except their eyes met once and they simply smiled at a job well done.

As they approached the dock, they could see that John and Spike had already arrived around by truck. Spike was backing the tractor, which was hooked to the trailer, into the water to receive the Park boat. Will brought the boat in quickly. If he hadn't, the waves would have made it impossible to maneuver. It slid into the trailer with a bump. Will cut the engine just as Kirk, who was in the bow, set the hook of the trailer onto the boat's bow eyehook. Spike immediately pulled them out of the water. He drove about 50 yards up onto the beach, near to the road and the large field and toward the Miles' house. Will and Kirk got out of the boat as John and Spike came over to shake hands with them. Before Spike got back on the tractor, he walked to the rear of the trailer, reached into the boat and pulled the seacock. Out poured two buckets of water.

"Did you ever think to check the fuel tanks?" questioned Will to Kirk.

Kirk nodded yes. "There might be enough to turn the engine on, and maybe even rev her once or twice," answered Kirk with a wide grin. "I was close to just anchoring her deep in the cove." They all had a hearty laugh.

"You did well," said John. "You two saved what looked like a real classic boat."

"Kirk deserves most of the credit. That young man is cool under pressure," answered Will. Then turning to Kirk. "You're one fine young man!" Then he shook hands with Kirk.

"I'm one wet young man," said an embarrassed Kirk. "Hell, it was a fine team effort!"

"Let's go up to the house," said John. "Dora and Sharon have something hot and, what we all need, some dry towels!"

The men climbed into the trucks and drove the short distance to the Miles' house. As the truck doors opened, so did the door to the house and Dora stood in the doorway for the men to make a quick dash, like a stampede the unorganized rush was made.

Dora had a handful of towels and as each man passed through the doorway, they each received one. Sharon stood just behind her mother with a large sheet towel, waiting for Kirk.

"Why'd you let them beat you to the door?" was Sharon's remark as Kirk crossed the finish line.

"You know, age and all that," said a smiling Kirk as he took the towel from Sharon.

"I see, thought you'd just lost a step over the summer," replied Sharon.

"Yeah, I guess you're right," said Kirk matter-of-factly. "I let you catch me!"

Sharon punched Kirk in the arm then turned away with a little girl hurt face, but Kirk spun her back toward him and put his arms around her and they kissed, then they joined the others who had headed for the kitchen where Dora was passing hot coffee.

"I'd put some brandy in the coffee," said Dora. "Wards off colds and evil spirits."

John was the first to do so, and simply handed the bottle to Spike to do likewise. Spike held the bottle for Will, then poured for himself. Spike looked over at Kirk, who had just come into the room, but Kirk said no. He started to walk toward the refrigerator to get a cold beer, but Sharon handed him a large mug, then poured a beverage from the teapot. Kirk shrugged his shoulders as the other men smiled at Sharon's take charge manner, then tasted the beverage in the mug, and made a 'yuck' face, but he quickly smiled at Sharon. "Boy this is good! What can I tell my friends here that I'm drinking?"

"It started out as a hot toddy, but hand it back so I can pour the poison in," said Sharon in mock anger. "Drink it all up!" She said in her Dr. Frankenstein voice. Kirk grabbed his throat. Everyone had a good laugh.

John, in the meantime, moved into the den-office-spare bedroom and picked up the two-way radio. He placed the call to the shop. "C.J., Donald, Russ, come in. This is semi-official."

"C.J. here," came a reply.

"Everything OK down there?" questioned John. "The lights just went out," said John half to himself.

"Really? We have plenty of light here."

"Give me that," came another voice. "Russ here, John. Our lights just went out also. We've been following the boat rescue through Dora and Sharon. All OK there?" said Russ in an official sounding voice.

"Fine. Will, Kirk and Spike did a good job. Boat's OK too," responded John.

"According to the radio, the storm's passing at a good speed, but we're going to bunk in here anyway for the night. I'm sending Don home though. OK with you?" was Russ' come back.

"Sure. I'm sending Will and Spike over. Kirk can sleep here in my den. Over and out," returned John, who reached for the flashlight in his desk drawer. He checked his watch. It was now almost 9:30 p.m. "It's been a long day," he thought to himself, and he suddenly felt tired.

John took a deep breath, trying to ward off the fatigue, which had set in, pulled himself up and walked into the kitchen. When the lights had gone out, Kirk reached for the Coleman lantern, which Dora had placed nearby, so John entered a brightly lit room. Dora, Sharon and Kirk were clearing the dishes, while Spike and Will sipped coffee from the man-sized mugs Dora had purchased long ago for the occasions when the men would stop by to see John.

"Looks like everything's under control here," said John.

"Yes. Do you want another cup of coffee?" replied Dora.

"No, I don't think so," answered John. "It might keep me awake." Then John smiled at the thought, because almost nothing would keep him awake on this particular night.

"How's everything at the shop?" questioned Spike.

"They're OK," answered John. "Looks like they rode the storm out without any real problems."

"If it's OK with you, Will and I are going to head over there. We're kind of bushed. I think they've got bunks for us," said Spike.

John nodded approval. "Kirk can sleep in the den, since the wind and rain are dying down, I'm about to do the same. I might be asleep before you hit the truck door."

Will and Spike left and drove on into the darkness toward the shop. Dora and John checked the house over once more before heading for their bedroom. Finally, John checked the light switches to make certain that they were in the "off" position so that the house wouldn't all of a sudden light up like a Christmas tree should the electricity come back on during the night.

Sharon and Kirk had moved to the living room after Kirk shut off the Coleman lantern. "My hero," said Sharon in a teasing manner, as they settled on the sofa.

"It's been along day," said Kirk as Sharon snuggled into his arms.

"Yes, I know," answered Sharon as she maneuvered to let Kirk's head rest on her lap. She stroked his hair and then bent forward and kissed his forehead.

"I'll be asleep in a couple of minutes if you keep that up," said Kirk in a sleepy voice.

"Oh don't worry, I'll pour some water on your face when I'm ready to turn in," answered Sharon as she kissed Kirk again and took a deep breath of contentment.

"I'm almost asleep you know," muttered Kirk.

Eleven 11

"Com'on Star, rise and shine," said Sharon as she opened the draperies in John's den. "It's a beautiful morning. Look!"

"Wait," came Kirk's reply, "I've only got half an eye open. How did I get into your dad's den?" continued Kirk.

"Here, have a cup of coffee," said Sharon as Kirk sat up on the Castro convertible sofa that doubled as a bed when the Miles had guests overnight. "Somehow I guided you here last night and tucked you in," continued Sharon and she winked.

"Sorry I missed it," said Kirk as he took a sip of coffee.

John peeked his head in the doorway. "Breakfast in five or six minutes, say, you look as tired as I feel," he said to Kirk.

"You must feel very tired," moaned Kirk, "but don't worry, I'll be there coach." John left to go back into the kitchen and help Dora set the table.

"Speaking of coach," started Sharon, she paused, and took a long look out the window, not saying any more and not really looking at anything.

"Look," said Kirk, as he pulled his pants on, "let's think about the fact that I've got three whole days before I leave for College Park, not that I've only got three days."

"You're right, of course, but they'll still pass too quickly," answered Sharon.

"Look pal, here's the bottom line, I love you, I love you, I love you, now, let's go have breakfast. Besides, we have a lifetime together that's just begun," was Kirk's reply.

"Wow, that's sort of semi-romantic. Gee, I love that kind of talk," mused Sharon as she turned away from the window and met Kirk's open arms. She gave a great bear hug to Kirk and said, "And I love you!"

Sharon and Kirk joined John and Dora in the kitchen. Dora had prepared an old-fashioned breakfast of fresh eggs over-easy, country ham, grits, fresh baked biscuits that could be dipped in the red-eye gravy that John made from the ham drippings and black coffee, plus, of course, fresh orange juice. The fresh O.J. was a favorite in the household and whenever possible, John visited the street market in Baltimore to purchase fresh oranges by the crate.

While everyone certainly enjoyed breakfast, the meal was, nevertheless, rushed a bit, as John was anxious to see what damage had been done to the park. It was just past 7:00 when John picked up his two-way radio and walked out onto the back porch to get a glimpse of the Elk River. He took a long sip of coffee from the cup he brought with him and surveyed the area. While it was plain to see that several small trees were down and that some debris was floating on the water, the brightness of the day seemed to make any damage look less than perhaps it really was.

Dora joined John on the back porch, "it doesn't look too bad," she said.

"You're right, but I'll bet that the waterfront properties caught hell. The tide came up about six to eight feet above normal, by the looks of the field across the Elk River," answered John.

"Kirk is just about ready," said Dora, "he's finishing up a piece of country ham."

John laughed, "for a boy from New Jersey, he certainly does enjoy a Southern buffet."

Dora smiled, gave John a kiss and went back into the house. John flipped the switch to on, brought the radio close to his mouth, depressed the transmission button and spoke, "Super to base, anyone awake yet?"

"Already had breakfast and was going to give you a wake up call," came Russ' familiar voice.

"If I had known I was going to get extra service, I certainly would have slept in," was John's comeback. "What's it look like down there?"

"Doesn't look bad at all John," answered Russ, "Mother Nature did some tree trimming plus a few trees are completely down from what I can see. Spike checked the cabin area, it's ok."

"I'll be over in a couple of minutes. Send Spike and Will down to the boat area with the C.D. pump. Kirk will meet them and maybe we can clean up that area first," stated John, who then continued before Russ could reply. "By the way, don't send the people staying there back to the trailer area yet, let's check it out first."

"OK," said Russ, who continued, "ole C.J., he really took charge John, he's alright, he really surprised me."

John smiled to himself, "OK Russ, over and out." John then walked off the porch and around the house, looking it over, before heading back to the house. He handed his coffee cup to Dora, reached for the key hook which was located next to the wall phone in the kitchen, took the keys to the pick-up truck, motioned to Kirk and both men headed for the front door. Sharon and Dora walked them to the door, as did the Miles' dog, who dashed out and ran to John's truck.

"I'll call you later," said Sharon to Kirk, then she reached up to kiss him good-bye.

John, likewise, gave Dora a kiss, then put his arm around Sharon, "Better get to the gatehouse early, we'll keep the picnic area closed for the day, so if anyone is crazy enough to come out here, let them use the beach on this side of the park."

John and Kirk left the house and walked toward the parked trucks. "Head for the boat area, Spike and Will are coming down to help you clean up that area," stated John. "We'll check on the ownership of that cruiser after lunch."

Kirk nodded, then climbed up into the dump truck, fired her up, backed out of the yard and headed down the road toward the boat and beach area. John opened the door and the dog jumped in. John headed the other way and as he neared the shop, saw that Spike and Will were backing out of a parking space and driving out of the shop yard. They passed and waved a high sign to each other, but neither stopped. John parked the truck and made the short walk toward the office door of the shop, but the dog walked off back toward the house, as he had done many times before.

Once inside, he greeted the overnight guests, accepted a cup of coffee from C.J. and walked into his office. Russ was already in the office sitting behind John's desk. There were papers in neat piles and Russ was working on a set of reports. He looked up as John came in and smiled the knowing smile of one deep into paperwork. John didn't say anything, but picked up Russ's empty coffee cup, walked back to the doorway, caught C.J.'s eye, and handed him the cup to be refilled.

"It was a good time to catch up on the reports," remarked Russ.

"I appreciate it, they've gotten a bit behind, and..." replied John, but he was interrupted by Russ.

"And, we certainly wouldn't want Annapolis giving us hell over paperwork," joked Russ.

They both laughed. C.J., in the meantime, brought Russ' coffee to him and simply placed it on the desk within easy reach.

John motioned for C.J. to sit down and he sat on the edge of the desk. "Hold up on the paperwork for a moment," said John to Russ. "I've got something to discuss with you, plus I want to get your input on another subject." Then, turning to C.J., he said, "Listen up young man, because some of this deals with you." John then smiled to himself as he saw the worried look on C.J. Russ, in the meantime, stopped writing, but was still holding the pen in his hand.

"Russell, it looks as if I've got the pleasure of losing you," stated John to a now serious face and somewhat puzzled Russ. "You've been promoted to Superintendent of Sandy Point, congratulations!"

Russ didn't say anything right away, he simply continued sitting for a second or two, but stood up to receive John's handshake. C.J. also extended his hand of congratulations.

"I don't know what to say," were the words finally spoken by Russ. "Wow," he continued, "this is really great, but leaving here after nine years of working with you is tough." Russ dropped back into the chair, looked at C.J., then up to John and simply smiled. "It's all thanks to you John...I..." but John interrupted.

"Right from the first, you took to the park, to each task that came along. You learned quickly. You've worked hard, you've earned the promotion," said John, who then continued after a slight pause, "and speaking of learning rather quickly, well more quickly than slowly," and John had to pause again, this time because his wide smile started to turn into a bit of a laugh. "C.J., my boy," and John couldn't help adding a little W. C. Field's to his voice, "C.J., I'm adding you as a permanent ranger!"

"You're not kidding are you, Mr. Miles? I thought he was going to fire me, Russ. When your own father fires you, you never know what to expect," then turning back to John, "do I get this in writing. No one will believe me," stammered C.J.

Both Russ and John were laughing now, and C.J. was half laughing also.

"You do get an official letter from Annapolis, and I'll even assign a truck to you, maybe I'll even teach you, or maybe Spike can teach you to operate the dump truck, after all, Kirk leaves us in a couple of days," said John in a semi-official voice.

"Well, congratulations are certainly due to you, C.J., you're off your old man's payroll and onto the State of Maryland's, benefits and all!" said

Russ and he shook hands with C.J. Then C.J. also received a hardy handshake from John.

"All of this takes place officially, the day after Labor Day. I've known about it for almost two weeks now, figured that after the tough day and a half of the storm, that the good news would sit well with you," stated John.

"It sure does," started Russ "I guess that finishing all these reports will be good practice, so to speak," continued Russ and he smiled again.

"You're right, so to speak," returned John, "and you've only three weeks to train your replacement," John paused as Don walked into the office, "speak of the devil."

"Speak of what devil?" said Don. "I'm going to check on the cabin area, if no one's assigned to it, stopped at the picnic area John, on my way in, tree limbs all over the place, I wouldn't open it today, maybe best to wait until Saturday for a re-opening."

"I've already checked the cabin area," said Russ, "sit with me and I'll teach you how to do some of these reports," and Russ motioned to Don to join him.

"Sure wish I could help you Russell ole boy, but hell, I can hardly read and write," answered Don in a good ole boy voice, and he started back into the shop.

"Wait a minute Don," started John, "we're making some changes that you should know about, Russ is leaving us, promoted to Super at Sandy Point and C.J. is becoming permanent."

"Congratulations Russ, that's just great, you deserve it, man, you too, C.J., he's a lot brighter than he looks you know," said Don and he jokingly nodded at C.J.

"The other move, Donald, is you to Assistant Park Superintendent, effective the day after Labor Day," said John as he extended his hand to Don, who immediately had his hand shook by C.J. and Russ.

"Well, you didn't do bad, John, two out of three moves are good, but me, as your assistant, I don't know what to say, thanks, I'll do my best man!"

"You'll do just fine," said John, "besides, I need someone to beat the hell out of C.J. when he messes up!"

"Maybe my old man will hire me back," kidded C.J..

"Not a chance," responded John, "we own you C.J., there's no escape!"

In the meantime, Will and Spike had joined up with Kirk at the boat docks. Three of the boats without covers had apparently sunk or at least were filled to the gun-walls with water. At present, the tide, which had come in six to eight feet above normal, was out just as much, and the boats were resting on the sand bottom, filled with Chesapeake Bay. Kirk had not started to bail these boats with the bucket he had brought from the house, because they'd be easy to handle with the C.D. pump, but was out near the end of the dock working on a boat whose cover had been torn by the wind.

It was almost three-quarters full and Kirk leaned in carefully with the bucket and started to bail it out. He had almost emptied the boat and climbed in the now steady boat to finish when he spotted Will and Spike driving down to help. He stood up for a second, waved and went back to bailing.

Will and Spike off-loaded the C.D. pump and took it out onto the dock where they started on the first three boats that were lying on the bottom. The engine kicked over and soon water was being placed back into the bay. The men didn't speak much, but worked quickly. Once the boats on the dock were secure, Will and Kirk carried the C.D. pump over to the already beached park rowboats.

Spike, in the meantime, had walked up the road to the big, open field where he left the tractor. He drove it back down to the beach/dock area and as a rowboat was emptied, he untied it from the trees used as storm moorings and, hooked them on behind the tractor, dragged them the short distance to the normal water's edge.

He simply put the anchor out forward, although with the tide out, they were going nowhere. Spike said to Kirk and Will that they could come back after lunch, when the tide would be in, launch the row boats and place them back into their slips at the dock. They decided not to try and launch any of the boats that had been placed in the field, because it would take too much time. But, they would put it off until later in the day or even tomorrow, because there was simply too much to do getting the park back in shape again.

It was near noon when the initial job in the boat dock area was completed and while the men were tired from the heavy work that had been their task since early morning, they were in good spirits as they got into the trucks and headed toward the shop.

While Will and Spike turned into the shop, Kirk, in the dump truck, kept driving past the shop to the gatehouse to meet Sharon. He pulled up to the exit side of the gatehouse and stepped down from the truck. Sharon had spotted the truck coming and was standing, waiting for Kirk as he drove up.

"Hi lady," was Kirk's greeting. "Want to get married?"

"Best proposal I've had all day," chimed in Sharon.

"Not much business, huh?" returned Kirk.

"Well," started Sharon, she paused with hands on her hips.

"Well what," said Kirk as he took Sharon into his arms, "as they say, we've got to stop meeting like this, people will talk you know."

"The 'well', is in question to the question about getting married," Sharon paused a moment to think, "I think that makes sense, anyway, when?"

"That does make sort of sense," said Kirk, "well, I was thinking of after football season, as you know, but quite frankly I'm not sure I can wait that long, taking into consideration your views, which I respect, and the local and state rape laws, get the point?"

"I know, it's tough, but just think if I had given in at, say my prom night with C.J.," started Sharon. "Look, if you want me, I'm yours!"

"Thanks for delegating your guilt to me," Kirk said in a disturbed-voice.

"I'm sorry. Look!" said Sharon, and she fell back into Kirk's arms, "Oh, how I love you!"

"I love you too, I just don't know how any man could feel about a woman as I feel for you," returned Kirk. They kissed and Kirk just held Sharon.

"Thanksgiving weekend, you've got one more game after that," said Sharon, "but most of our friends should be OK for the Saturday, at the U. of M. chapel?"

"It's a date," said Sharon. "Let me look at a calendar, I don't even know the date I'm getting married on." Sharon ran into the office, checked the calendar, "It's the 28th of November," she shouted from the office. "Some honeymoon, probably at the local motel!"

"Don't think so small, with the team we have this fall, we should take the ACC and maybe wind up in the Orange Bowl," said a confident

Kirk. "It will be just a delayed honeymoon, but in the meantime, on our honeymoon night, I'll do..."

"I know, God knows what to my body," interrupted Sharon.

"I really wish that we could do away with smut talk," needled Kirk, "at least long enough to have some lunch, what do you think?"

"That's some change of subjects, there Star," responded Sharon, "it goes from me to ham and Swiss on rye. I don't know about you!"

"You know about me, if anyone does, I think you do," answered Kirk.

"Yea," was all Sharon responded, with a grin from ear to ear, then she reached up and kissed Kirk. "Let's have lunch," Sharon said, after a short pause.

"I can go over to my cabin and make up something, since you really shouldn't leave here," said Kirk, "or do you want to get a break away from here?"

"None of the above," answered Sharon in a sharp tone, "I packed...ham and Swiss on rye, plus a salad. Which do you want?" continued Sharon as she walked into the gatehouse.

"A nice light salad will do just fine," kidded Kirk, but in a serious, monotone voice.

"Great, do you want mayo or just mustard on your ham and Swiss," answered Sharon in a nonchalant voice, as if she hadn't heard Kirk.

"Mustard will be fine," said a smiling Kirk and he caught the brightness of Sharon's eyes as she handed him the sandwich from the cooler she brought from the house.

They sat on the top of the two desks in the gatehouse and started to eat when Kirk eased off the desk, lifted the lid of the cooler and reached for the plastic pitcher. He also picked up the two plastic cups that likewise were sitting on ice.

"Lemonade in frosted sort of mugs," responded Sharon when she saw Kirk look at her in puzzlement, "I figured that a Coke wouldn't quench my thirst out here."

Kirk didn't say anything at first, but just filled the glasses, then took a long drink of the lemonadc, "You're right, that does hit the spot."

They sat, eating in silence for a few moments, then Sharon said, “Did you ever wonder why we don’t have arguments?’

“Not really,” answered Kirk, and he took a bite of his sandwich. “What are we supposed to fight about, anyway?” continued Kirk after a few chews.

“Well, it’s just that a lot of couples I know are having little spats all the time and so far we haven’t had any real disagreements. I just think that’s strange, and, really nice, also,” stated Sharon in a satisfied tone. “My folks are another couple that don’t argue,” and Sharon pondered for a moment, then continued, “and you’re right, my folks don’t disagree on many subjects and when they do, they seem to talk it out.” Then Sharon turned toward Kirk and pointed a finger at him, “Listen, Kirk Daniels, let’s make a pact right now to talk things out and not yell at each other. All right?”

Sharon looked at Kirk, the finger now limp. Kirk reached out, grabbed Sharon’s finger and said, “Right, here we’ll shake on it!”

They both had to laugh and Kirk got up, moved over to Sharon and put his arms around her. They kissed and then Sharon jumped off the desk as a car approached the gatehouse.

While she was outside talking to the people in the car, Kirk cleaned up after the luncheon, checked his watch and walked outside. He paused long enough to catch Sharon’s eye, pointed to his watch and headed toward the truck. Sharon, had nodded an understanding, then went back to the discussion with the people in the car.

Kirk drove back to the shop where he met with the other men. Plans were continuing, as was the work in cleaning up after the hurricane. The cabin area had not been hard hit. While there were quite a few tree limbs down, the old tall trees had withstood yet another assault from Mother Nature. Utilizing all the men in task force teams along with several trucks and the two tractors, one with a front-end loader on it, made the clean up move along at a rapid pace.

After the cabin area was finished, camping areas A and B were tackled. A few of the younger and shallow rooted trees were down, however, the first task was to clear the roads and paths, the fallen trees could be cut with chain saws in the normal course of the working days to come.

The plan for this day was to work until 7:00 P.M. While the twelve-hour work-day seemed as though it would be quite long, John had arranged with Dora for a light snack to be served to the men at 4:00. It was an enjoyable pick-me-up of tea sandwiches and fresh fruit, along with ice-cold lemonade.

Dora brought along a large checkerboard tablecloth and spread it over one of the picnic tables at a campsite in section B that overlooked the Elk River, which was almost two miles across at this point. Dora's snack was a hit with the men and it truly served its purpose. For a half-hour, it was also a most relaxing and peaceful place to be.

John checked his watch. "Russ, I'll check in with you later. As long as everything is moving along here, I'm going to take off and see Bill Kemper. I sure wish he had a phone out there, just want to be certain he's OK."

"Right," answered Russ, "we'll handle things here, say hello to ole Bill for me."

"OK," was all John replied, then he walked with Dora to her station wagon. He kissed her and opened the car door, "I should be home around 7:3O for dinner. I'll just check back at the shop for a minute when I leave Bill."

"I know you and your 'just-check-in' stories," kidded Dora. "Why don't you call me when you get to the shop, I'll call back when dinner is ready." With that, Dora got into the station wagon and started the engine.

John had to smile at Dora's knowing him so well, she also, had that quiet knowing smile, winked at him and drove off. John walked over to his truck. Russ met him there.

"We'll bring the thermos and table cloth back to the house."

"Just drop it off at the shop, I'll stop there after I see Bill," responded John.

Russ nodded in acknowledgment as John got into his truck and started off out of B section, John stopped at the gatehouse as he left the park. He told Sharon to close up at 5:00, however, she said that Kirk would pick her up when he finished, John then continued his trip out of the park and then left, onto the road to Turkey Point. He stopped twice to remove large branches that had fallen across the road.

The road narrowed to one dirt lane. While no damage could really be done to the farmer's fields, now turned to hay, the heavy rains, nevertheless, had beaten down the grass. John thought of tooting the horn as he got near the house, but remembered that Bill might not hear it. John smiled, as he thought of recent times when he had to talk louder to Bill, who had a hearing aid, but didn't like wearing it, because, as Bill would say, "Damn thing makes too much noise."

John pulled into the farmyard, parked the truck, got out and headed toward the house, but stopped as he heard Bill calling from the direction of the Turkey Point lighthouse. He spotted Bill, gave a wave and continued walking toward the point. It took just a few minutes to cover the hundred yards.

"Well, I see you and everything else weathered the storm," came John's greeting, as he and Bill shook hands.

"Well, you're right, I'm still here--too damn ornery even for Mother Nature to catch up with," came Bill's reply. Both he and John had a good laugh.

"Take a walk with me to the point," continued Bill, "it's so beautiful and ever-changing. The Mrs. and I used to come out here every evening. I still do. You know, John, I even pretend she's still with me when I come out here and watch the sunset." Bill looked away for a minute, then wiped a tear from his eye, looked back at John and smiled an innocent, somewhat embarrassed smile at John.

John put his hand on Bill's shoulder and patted the gentle, yet rugged, old man. They walked and stood at the overlook on the point saying nothing, each with his own thought, but also enjoying the simple beauty of Turkey Point.

"I've got a fresh pot of coffee on, John, and old Jack Daniels is waiting at the house for us. I don't think we should keep him wondering if we're ever gonna get there," said Bill, after a while. He gave John an affectionate pat on the shoulder, as one would to a son, and motioned for them to walk toward the house.

Neither one said anything but they started back on the trail toward the old farm-house. They'd walked about forty yards when John stopped dead in his tracks. A black snake, about four feet long (but when John would eventually tell the story, would grow a couple of feet), crossed their path. Bill walked on forward. He was stopped by the snake, which had also been startled, and stopped in his tracks.

Bill knelt down beside the snake and stroked its head. The snake seemed quite content, and unafraid. He even seemed to become relaxed.

"He's an old friend," said Bill, "He's a pilot snake, from the King snake family, not a black racer, the racer's are usually nervous."

"I hope you don't mind if I take your word for it," said John. Bill smiled, knowing that John, while really not afraid of snakes, still didn't care to be around them.

"Come on," said Bill, "that Jack Daniels will be, as you younger people say, more meaningful now!" John nodded.

They walked the rest of the distance and John, who had reached for the door first, started to hold it for Bill. "Don't be polite with me, go on in there," came Bill's retort, "the day you give me the respect due me, is when you lay me next to Edna, and not before!"

John didn't say anything. He just smiled to himself and entered the house first. They walked from what was called the mudroom, into the kitchen. Bill didn't stop to talk, but reached for two man-sized coffee mugs and put them on the table. He then reached into the cabinet and took out a fresh bottle of *Jack Daniels Tennessee Sour-Mash Whiskey*, broke the seal, and poured about two or three ounces in each mug.

After he set the bottle onto the table, he went to the old wood-burning stove and picked up the well-worn pot, poured coffee in each cup, then opened a fresh can of evaporated milk to be used as cream.

"It's tradition to lighten it, you know," said Bill with a smile and a twinkle in his eye, "wouldn't want it to sting!"

"You can never fault tradition," answered John as he added cream to his Coffee Royale.

The men touched coffee mugs in salute and took a drink. John actually took a sip, however, Bill took more of a swig, held it a bit and swallowed the Royale in a couple of segments. He looked over at John with an approving smile and smacked his lips.

"Best way to enjoy high-coffee time," came Bill's statement and he took another sip.

"Looks like the storm didn't do very much damage out here," said John, after taking a sip of coffee. '"From what I could see driving out, just a few trees down."

"That's about it. Hell, I battened down things, pulled the shutters in and went to bed," answered Bill. "The noise of the wind, plus the hard rain on the roof just put me to sleep. Guess I'd be useless in an emergency," continued Bill after a sip of coffee.

"Bet you'd be there if needed," returned John.

"How's the park. Get hit bad, or about the same as here?" questioned Bill.

"Well it didn't seem as bad as they predicted."

"Maybe she blew out of steam when she came up the Chesapeake," reasoned Bill, "I have seen some blows in my time, and this turned out to be only a medium storm."

"Of course, on the other hand, we're more prepared these days," pondered John as he finished his coffee. John got up and reached for the coffeepot.

"Let me put some Jack in first," said Bill as John held the pot, "That way you can be the mixer."

John waited as Bill poured some Jack Daniels in his cup and nodded as Bill held the bottle over John's cup. Bill added some cream from the can as John replaced the pot on the stove.

"How about coming over to the house for dinner tonight," said John as he settled back down.

"Thanks, but I've got a couple dozen crabs for tonight John, picked them up this morning in the creek that leads into the cove" was Bill's reply. "But I'd be pleased to come in a couple of days."

"You've got a date," answered John, "two days from now we'll pick you up."

Bill nodded, smiled and took another sip of coffee, "This one's stronger than the last, who poured the whiskey," continued Bill in a kidding manner.

"I just poured the coffee," answered John in an innocent tone.

"Then it's your fault, coffee's gotten weak. Thanks," returned Bill laughingly.

"I've got to leave soon," said John, after they sat for a few minutes, "want to stop at the shop before heading home."

"Well, just keep the truck in the ruts and if you reach North East, then you've missed the turn-off to the park," answered Bill.

"I might just miss the turnoff," said John, "my forehead is getting stiff!"

"Just tell Dora that you had a drink with two old friends," said Bill as he and John got up.

"Is my truck still in the yard, or did it leave without me?" kidded John.

"That's it, worry about yourself, those damn crabs will probably bite me, I think I'm in slow motion," was Bill's retort "I'll probably steam my hand by mistake. You pour powerful coffee!"

"Next time, make the coffee 5O%, pouring Jack first is unfair," said John, feeling the J.D.

"Well, least I can do is open the truck door for you. Don't worry about a thing, I'll tell Dora it was all your fault, forced an old man to drink and walk," answered Bill. "I could break a hip or something, you know about old people."

"By the way," said John from the truck cab. "I've got an extra CB-base unit now, and I'm bringing it down, it'll keep you in touch with the shop and the house, in case we need you."

Bill gave a high sign as John closed the door to the truck, started the engine and drove out of the farmyard. He was feeling the Jack Daniels and laughed at himself as he kept the truck in the ruts until he was past Bill's farm and onto the hard surfaced road back toward the State Park. To say the least, John was feeling the coffee!

Bill, in the meantime, went back into the house to heat up the stove. He took down his crab pot, put in the sticks he kept to keep the crabs off the bottom of the pot, added water and some vinegar, then took down the can of Old Bay Seasoning to put on the layers of crab.

It was a little past 7:00, when John pulled up to the office. Russ was just locking up, but re-opened the door to the office as John climbed out of the truck and walked toward him.

"Everyone's headed home, all a bit tired, I might add," said Russ. "How'd you make out with Bill," asked a now smiling Russ, "OK, I think?"

"Bill, ole Jack, and I did fine, and all is well at Turkey Point," responded John.

Russ followed John into the office and flipped on the light switch, "Guess you didn't notice it was dark in here," kidded Russ, they both laughed.

John picked up the phone and called Dora. She said that Sharon and Kirk were already at the house. Dinner would be ready in 20 minutes. They talked a few minutes more then John hung up and joined Russ in the shop.

"Everything looks ship-shape around here," stated Russ.

"Let's take the rest of the day off," said John who looked at his watch.

"I'm with you," responded Russ, "too much work is bad for the soul!"

"You just make that up?" asked John as he ushered Russ out into the shop yard and locked the door.

Russ didn't answer, but smiled as John's questioning face smiled at him.

"See you in the morning," was the only response Russ gave and he gave a high sign as he opened the door to his truck and got in.

John waved back, got into his truck and headed out of the yard and toward his home. The trip took just a couple of minutes and John gave a salute to Sharon as he pulled to a stop.

"Hi Daddy," came Sharon's greeting as she met John at the truck door and opened it for him.

"Hi Sweetie, where's Kirk?" was John's reply as he gave a kiss and hug to his daughter, then put his arm around her as they headed for the house.

"Kirk's out back, husking the corn for dinner," was Sharon's answer. "They found the owner to the cruiser, the boat was out of Betterton. It'll be picked up tomorrow. The owner wants to give a reward. Will says that it should go into Kirk's college fund.

"It was duty beyond the call," stated John. "I guess the man is grateful he doesn't own just a pile of lumber that washed up on the beach. Will, he's just Will, I would have been surprised if he wasn't giving his share away."

"Hello Darling," was Dora's greeting as John and Sharon came into the house and on into the kitchen where she was putting the finishing touches on the roast beef. "Are those eyes bloodshot from the strain of the past couple of days, or the past couple of hours with Bill Kemper?"

"I'd say 50-50," was John's reply and he gave Dora a hug and kiss. "I hear you, probably more like 70-30. I guess you don't want a drink before dinner," said a now smiling, coy Dora, being satisfied at the past comeback.

"No, but wine with dinner would be nice," returned John, "what are we having, so I'll know what to choose?"

"The roast beef you took out of the freezer this morning, remember, or does the kitchen smell like baked fish?" needled Dora.

"Just wanted to see if you knew," answered John, "I know what I pulled out of the freezer this morning, it's this evening that I forgot!"

"Somehow that makes sense, I don't know how, but somehow," responded Dora and she pointed to the already opened bottle of Simi Cabernet Sauvignon sitting on the counter.

"Why don't I wash up," said John.

"Good idea," answered Dora, "dinner will be served in about five minutes."

"Parents," exclaimed Sharon, "I'm going out back to help Kirk."

"If you think that parents are a problem, Sharon," called Dora, "wait until you have children and see how you handle dotting grandparents!"

It wasn't long before everyone was seated at the dining room enjoying dinner. They kidded John a bit more about his late afternoon coffee break with Bill Kemper. They discussed the promotions at the park which involved Russ, Don, and C.J., the condition of the park after the storm and finally, Kirk's last couple of days before heading to College Park in preparation for his final year playing football for the University of Maryland.

As usual, it was an enjoyable meal in the Miles' household, as Kirk played out John's usual role as host and served the meat, plus poured the wine.

After dinner, Sharon and Kirk decided to take a walk down the road that led to the beach. They didn't say much during the walk down, they just held hands as they strolled, each with their own thoughts, yet, of course, those thoughts were quite along the same track. They paused at the boat dock, held each other for a moment, then walked onto the dock. The wind had died down, as had the waves on the bay, and the boats tied in their slips at the floating T-dock were once again at rest. Kirk and Sharon walked to the end of the dock and gazed out at the now darkening bay.

“Feel like taking the boat out?” said Sharon. “The bay looks inviting.”

“Sure,” answered Kirk as they walked toward the stern. There, he first checked the gas tanks, then satisfied that there was enough fuel on board, he loosened the stern lines. Sharon, in the meantime, had jumped into the forward section of the bow-rider and was ready to take the forward lines off the docks when Kirk gave the signal. Kirk reached into his back pocket, where he kept his key case, opened it, got the ignition key and started the engine. He nodded to a watchful Sharon and she placed the lines on the dock, then maneuvered back through the open windshield of the bow-rider, closed it behind her and settled next to Kirk.

In just a few seconds, they had backed out of the slip and were slowly moving out into the bay. Kirk kept the boat at just a crawl as he eased past the boats that were on moorings, then brought her up on a plane at about three-quarter throttle. They headed southeast, across the bay in the direction of Betterton

Sharon tapped Kirk on the shoulder, then put her hand on the dashboard near the toggle switches. He nodded “Yes” and she hit the switch that turned on the boat’s running lights.

Kirk kept to the right of the ship channel, then as they neared Turkey Point they started across toward the opening of the Sassafras River and the city dock at Betterton. Kirk placed the boat into a slip. Sharon used parts of the anchor line to manage a temporary mooring. They stepped up onto the dock and walked toward the town.

“What do you think?” asked Kirk as they approached the town square. “Do you want to have a drink? Should we stop and pick up some wine and cheese and head back out?”

“Let’s stop at the convenience store. It’s faster, get some cheap champagne. The charmat bulk process stuff, some cheese, and go off to some quiet cove and make-out,” came Sharon’s reply.

“Gee, I love that kind of smut talk, why are we walking so slowly?” returned Kirk.

Sharon simply punched him on the arm, “That’s love, not totally smut!”

Don’t bruise me, I’ll have enough of those in a few days, and remember, I could take you in two out of three falls in a wrestling match,” kidded Kirk. They entered the store, went to the dairy cooler and started to look for a cheese that would suit them.

"Look, the muenster comes in little cubes, what do you think?" questioned Kirk.

Sharon nodded and picked up a package of the Muenster cheese. They then walked over to the upright cooler that contained wine, beer, and soda. Kirk didn't say anything, but simply slid open the door and reached for the Alamden Champagne. As they paid for the wine and cheese, Sharon spotted a coffeepot and resting beside it were paper cups for the coffee.

"We're going back out in the boat, could I have two of the cups?" asked Sharon.

"Better take some napkins, too," said the clerk as he put the things in a bag. It didn't take long to walk back to the boat, since most of it was downhill. They reached the boat, Kirk stepped in, took the bag from Sharon, then helped her in. Normally she'd just jump in, however, a cruiser about 3O-feet-long was making its way past the docks and kicked up some waves. She untied the lines as Kirk started the engine and eased back out into the river.

It was only a couple of minutes before they had cleared the Betterton point and were on their way. Kirk kept the boat on the right side of the channel and did not cross to the other side as he would normally do. As they passed White Crystal Beach, Kirk said, "Captain John's Creek?"

Sharon, snuggled next to Kirk, simply nodded an approval. In a few minutes, they pulled into the wide-mouthed cove known as Captain John's, which is located almost directly across the Elk River from the state park. Sharon went forward and dropped the anchor over the side into the shallow water. Kirk put the engine into reverse and hauled up on the anchor. Sharon then tied the anchor line off on a cleat.

Kirk uncorked the bottle of champagne. Sharon picked up the two paper cups and held them for Kirk. Before setting the bottle down and taking a cup of the vintage charmat bulk process champagne from Sharon, he reached over and kissed her.

"We're some class act, Star," kidded Sharon, "champagne, cheese, moonlight, and love."

"It can only get better," responded Kirk, and he kissed her again.

They snacked on the cheese, sipped champagne, and snuggled in each other's arms while looking up at the moon and starlit evening. For a long time, they just enjoyed each other, saying nothing. Nothing had to be said.

"I like your morals, and yet somehow, I don't like your morals," came a mumbling from Kirk as they lay in each other's arms.

"I know," was Sharon's reply, "but just wait," she continued, "you'll have more woman to handle than you'll know what to do with. I've been storing it up."

"I don't doubt it one bit," returned Kirk, "I'm just glad it's me that will be the benefactor." Then he eased back into Sharon's waiting arms.

It was past 11:00 when they finally weighed anchor. Kirk motioned to Sharon to stay put and he went forward, brought the anchor in and then came back, hit the electric starter and crept out of Captain John's so as not to disturb the three cabin cruisers lying at rest for the night. Kirk brought the boat up on a plane and took her across the Elk at about three-quarter throttle. He settled the boat down before entering the area of the parked boats near the dock and quietly placed the Miles' boat into her slip.

Sharon gathered up the empty champagne bottle, cups, and cheese tray, while Kirk tied that boat off for the night. They placed the garbage into the trash can at the end of the dock and started up the hill toward the Miles' house.

"You should have raped me, you know," bolted Sharon as they walked arm-in-arm.

"I thought about it many times, but then how could I respect you in the morning," said Kirk in a matter-of-fact tone, smiling at himself for his fast response.

"Haven't you got the respect in the morning a bit backward," questioned Sharon.

"I don't think so, as you say, with all that, you know bottled up, you might just turn a simple rape into practically an orgy. Give me a break!" kidded Kirk.

"Somehow, I don't know how, but what you just said makes some type of sense," reasoned Sharon, "you know," she continued, "I think about raping you every night!"

"How do I do," questioned Kirk, "do I put up resistance?"

"You respond very well, that's why I say your remark makes some sense," answered Sharon.

"I hope you don't tell our children about this conversation, till they're old enough," stated Kirk.

"Don't think we'll have to. I imagine they'll be passionate and hot-blooded on their own," remarked Sharon. "After all, they'll have us for parents!"

"Yeah," came Kirk's reply, as they walked around to the back porch of the house. Kirk stayed at the bottom of the steps while Sharon moved up one step in order to look Kirk straight in the eyes. She faced him, put her arms around him and they kissed for a very long time. Love was being spoken, but nothing was said.

Twelve 12

During the next day and a half, Kirk was kept busy at both the park and over in the picnic area as he tried to complete projects before heading back to the University of Maryland. John had instructed Kirk to take C.J. along on the trips to North East for road gravel and teach C.J. how to use the dump truck. Kirk told John that maybe Spike, Russ, Don, or any of the other men would be better qualified to teach C.J., however, John responded that perhaps while all the other men did know more about construction and the like, Kirk knew more about C.J. and would be patient with him. Kirk understood and undertook the crash, better make that immediate informative course, to teach C.J. the wherewithal on the operation of the dump truck. He came out of John's office on the morning of his last day and motioned to C.J. to follow him outside.

"You want a fill-up of coffee before we leave for North East?" asked C.J.

"Might as well take it along. How'd you know we were going to town?" questioned Kirk, and he knew as he looked around the room at the smiling faces. Kirk had to smile also, then he slowly shook his head as C.J., who was also looking around overfilled Kirk's coffee cup and spilled coffee on the table. "I know it's a long ride C.J., but mine holds just one cup," called Kirk across the room. Then Kirk walked over to C.J., took the cup and sipped some off the top.

C.J. cleaned up the mess, then picked up a couple of donuts and followed Kirk out the door, but before closing the door behind him, he poked his head back in. "This'll be a picnic!" Kirk, now just a few feet from the truck, heard the laughter coming from the shop and turned to see C. J. hurrying towards him. "Coming right along, Kirk ole boy, coming right along. Here, I've got a donut for you."

"What are they laughing about?…As if I don't know?" asked Kirk as he turned to face C.J.

"Don't worry about a thing. I've watched you drive the dump and last night I dreamt about it. Just five speeds forward and a two-speed axle, believe me, it'll be a piece of cake, you know. I asked for this truck, and asked John if you could show me," answered C.J. as he motioned for Kirk to get into the truck, his hands waving Kirk toward the truck door.

Kirk had to smile at his friend. "I'll take it out of the yard and down the road a while, out of sight of the shop, then you can drive it on into town," he said, then climbed into the truck and fired up the engine.

C.J. jumped into the passenger side. "I was counting on you taking it out of the yard but the 'down the road a while' should include past the gatehouse. I wouldn't want to hit it on my first pass, would we!"

Kirk didn't say anything, but looked over at C.J.'s face, which was quietly asking for help. He simply smiled and shook his head. "OK ole friend," then he pulled out of the shop yard and onto the road that leads to the park's exit, toward the town of North East. He motioned to C.J. to follow him through the gears as the truck picked up speed.

C.J., knowing that there wasn't much time, paid close attention as Kirk told him that the truck was no big deal, that he also had to learn how to handle the dump as well as other equipment which was new to him, just a short three months before. C.J. shook his head in acknowledgment, but he still lacked a bit of what Kirk had been teaching him all summer, self-confidence.

As they neared the gatehouse, Kirk slowed the truck to a stop, right in the middle of the road. He placed the truck in neutral, set the brake, opened the door and climbed down. C.J. opened the door, likewise jumped down and met Kirk at the nose of the truck.

"Lift the hood?" questioned C.J. "what's wrong?"

"Nothing is wrong. Let's take a walk," said Kirk, and he started walking toward the gatehouse, which was about 50 yards away. C.J. had a puzzled look on his face, but followed. In a couple of minutes they were standing in front of an exit lane by the gatehouse.

"This exit lane and that entrance lane," said Kirk pointing, "they are larger than that dump truck. Go drive it through this lane and I'll meet you on the other side!"

"It'll never fit," answered C.J. looking helplessly at Kirk, "Not with me driving."

"It will fit," said Kirk in a loud, commanding voice. "Do it now!"

C.J. started for the truck mumbling to himself in a low voice, "It'll never fit."

"Remember to take the brake off and drive slowly. You can do it," called Kirk.

C.J. stopped, turned to Kirk, threw his hands in the air, and said, "What's the worst thing that can happen?" He walked a few feet more and turned again, "I'd duck out of the way if I were you," he said in a low, matter-of-fact manner. Then he headed for the truck, stepped up into the cab, held a thumbs-up signal out the window and took a look around, drew in a deep breath and reached for the gears.

A loud, grinding noise brought C.J. straight to attention, "the clutch, simply forgot to push the clutch in," he said laughing nervously to himself. Then he yelled out the window to Kirk, "It's OK, relax, just relax, I'll get over there in a minute or two," then ducked back into the cab to start over.

Kirk waved back and smiled to himself as he shuffled his feet, also a bit nervous for his friend's first solo trip in the truck. Kirk tried to look calm for C.J.'s sake. "Take your time, we're in no hurry," he called back.

C.J. this time pushed the clutch in, put the truck in gear and fought his nervousness as he eased the clutch out while at the same time pressing the accelerator. The truck started moving forward at a crawl, but that was fine with C.J., and Kirk too. C.J. then lined up the truck and headed for the exit lane of the gatehouse. Kirk looked toward the windshield of the truck and noticed that C.J. had a wide grin on his face. He knew that C.J. was all right.

"It's going to fit," exclaimed C.J. out loud as he passed through the exit lane. He drove about twenty-five feet more and applied the brakes pushing the clutch in as he came to a stop. He slipped the truck into neutral and waited for Kirk.

"Thanks for waiting," said Kirk as he opened the door and climbed in. "I thought you forgot me. OK, let's head for town, but remember, I want to live to play football and to get married this fall. So don't kill us!"

"Relax kid, you're in good hands with C.J. Now be quiet while I do this again and get started," said C.J. as he systematically started the truck off down the road. He looked over at Kirk after a moment and Kirk simply smiled. The ride to town was rather slow, but neither C.J. nor Kirk seemed to mind.

As they reached the outskirts of North East, C.J. slowed the truck and started to pull to the side of the road and bring the truck to a halt. Kirk, who had dosed off a bit during the slow ride startled awake as the truck left the highway and came to a stop on the shoulder.

"What's the matter?" asked Kirk as he looked around to see where they were.

"Well, we're just about here, that's North East ahead. I had to do last five miles alone you know. You slept through it all," scolded C.J.

Kirk smiled, "You see what great confidence I have in you, and just about there is not there, so drive on through town and over to Union Gravel."

"You're crazy," yelled C.J. "Hell, I could take out half of North East with this truck. You drive, please."

"No, C.J., you are at the helm and there you'll remain," stated Kirk.

Just as C.J., now slowly shaking his head, started to put the truck in gear to drive on, a station wagon pulled off the road just in front of them. Both C.J. and Kirk spotted Sharon in the station wagon. They got out of the truck just as Sharon opened the car door and stepped out. They walked toward each other.

"Got a problem?" called Sharon as they moved toward one another.

"No, C.J. just wanted to be certain of the directions to Union Gravel," answered Kirk as he protected C.J.'s pride.

"I see," responded Sharon, but she, like C.J., had lived in the area all her life and she knew what Kirk was doing. "Well, just thought I could help."

"You can help make lunch more pleasant, how about the diner at around 11:45?" asked Kirk as he walked Sharon back to her car.

Sounds fine, see ya later C.J., you look great behind the wheel," called Sharon as C.J. headed back to the dump truck.

Kirk gave Sharon a quick kiss, closed the car door as she got in and then he walked back to the truck. As he opened the door and climbed in, he called, "OK, Wagons Ho!"

"I still wish you would drive, you know. I just want to be on record," said C.J. as he put the truck in gear, released the brake, started back onto the highway.

"I know my friend, but you are doing fine, everything will be OK, but just in case, I'll keep one hand on the door handle, so that I can jump free," joked Kirk.

"Thanks a lot," laughed C.J., "but you can relax, I've decided not to crash the truck!"

"I'm relieved, the state of Maryland thanks you on behalf of the truck and I'm certain that this fine town will give a parade in your honor, instead of hanging you," stated Kirk. "You're a credit to something or other!" Both C.J. and Kirk laughed, but more importantly, C.J. was relaxed and even confident as he drove through town, turned right onto Route 7 and after a two-mile stretch, pulled into the Union Gravel Company yard.

"Pull up over by the office," said Kirk, as C.J. slowed the truck, "Come on inside with me, so that you can sign the receiving ticket for this load."

C.J. brought the truck to a halt, climbed out of the cab and followed Kirk into the office.

"Hello, Kirk, thought you'd be down at football practice," said Frank Desher, owner of Union Gravel. "Who's that with you? Claude, is that you boy? Heard that John was working you out at the park."

"Yes sir, Mr. Desher, it's me," answered C.J.

"He's permanent now, Mr. Desher. C.J. is a full-fledged State of Maryland employee," stated Kirk. "He'll sign the forms from now on."

"Well I'll be," responded Frank Desher. "Good for you boy, that's just fine."

"I'll be coming by from now on," stated C.J. "The dump truck is my assignment for now. Kirk's teaching me, he leaves for the University tomorrow."

"Well, OK. I'll fill out this delivery ticket for the road stone, load your truck, then you sign here on the bottom and take the yellow sheet with you," said Frank Desher.

"I'll go with him Mr. Desher, show ole C.J. where to park the truck for loading," said Kirk and he motioned C.J. to follow him outside.

"Just tell me where you want this ole rig, son. I'm feeling pretty good," said C.J., as he walked crisply toward the truck.

"Back it into that shoot, sport, and they'll load you," said Kirk smilingly.

"That's not wide enough for a dump truck," said C.J., "Are you crazy?"

"It will fit. Do it, NOW. We have a lunch date," said Kirk firmly.

C.J. climbed into the truck, started the engine, and drove over to the gravel shoots. He started backing the truck very slowly, intently and followed Kirk's direction as he eased to a halt in exactly the right spot.

"You did just fine," said Kirk to a smiling C.J., who had flung the door open and jumped triumphantly to the ground and made a Zorro "Z" with his finger.

"Alright!" exclaimed C.J., "the man has arrived, to save the day!" he sang.

Kirk had to laugh at his friend, then looked over to the man that was ready to load the truck and nodded. In a few minutes, they were all set. C.J. had walked into the place to take care of the paperwork and Frank Desher followed him outside.

"Good luck to you, Kirk," said Frank, "score some touchdowns for us, won't you!"

"I play defense, try to keep the other team from scoring!" replied Kirk.

"Yes, well, do what you can boy, we'll be counting on you," answered Frank. He shook hands with Kirk and walked back toward the office. Kirk smiled and slowly shook his head, then glanced over to C.J.

"Do what you can boy!" joked C.J. "Do what you can!"

"Com'on," said Kirk, and he motioned C.J. toward the dump truck. They got into the truck and C.J. started the engine.

"Now is the time to drop into the low-speed axle, right?" questioned C.J.

"Right," answered Kirk, "Let's head over to the diner and meet Sharon."

C.J. nodded, eased the dump truck forward and left the yard. They traveled back down Route 7 toward North East's center and after a few minutes, turned right onto Route 272. Nothing was really said during the trip, because C.J. was concentrating on handling the truck correctly and since he was doing well, Kirk did not bother him. Finally, after the turn onto Route 272, Kirk said, "Just ease into the back part of the parking lot, out of the way."

"OK," said C.J. "I'm doing alright, yes?"

"You sure are," answered Kirk. "You've caught on really fast."

"How's this?" asked C.J. as he brought the truck to a halt in the far corner of the lot.

"That's good," answered Kirk, "Set the brake and also leave her in gear."

C.J. nodded and did what Kirk said then looked over at Kirk who just gave a thumbs-up sign. Then both men climbed out of the truck and headed toward Sharon, who had already parked on the Route 40 side of the diner.

"Hello lady," called Kirk as they got closer, "Want to buy a struggling college boy some lunch, huh, lady?"

"Well, only if you marry me," answered Sharon.

"OK, you've got a deal," responded Kirk with a crooked grin, "But I want dessert, too!"

"I'm dessert, honey," said Sharon in a Mae West voice.

"God, some people will do anything for a meal," joined C.J. "Look, I'll ease both of your commitments. I'll buy!"

"Mind your own business C.J.," scolded Sharon, "But we will let you buy, after all, you are a working man now."

"Mind my own business," said C.J. almost under his breath, "Listen Lady Miles," continued C.J. in a louder voice, as they walked up the steps of the diner restaurant, "If I want to be yelled at, I'll let you know," then he winked at Kirk.

Before Sharon could answer, Kirk reached for the door and ushered Sharon into the restaurant. He held up three fingers to the hostess and pointed to a booth. She shook her head "Yes" and as Kirk and Sharon slid into one side of the booth with C.J. sitting across from them.

"Would you like the waitress to bring water, sir?" the hostess asked Kirk as she placed menus in front of everyone.

"No, just ask her to bring three glasses of iced tea," answered Kirk.

"My, my, a real take-charge guy," said Sharon as she punched Kirk's arm lightly.

"Yes, I'd like iced tea," said C.J. in a voice to himself, "I don't want to be difficult."

In what seemed to be just a couple of minutes, the waitress appeared with the iced tea.

"Two pieces of lemon for you Kirk," and she placed the iced tea in front of Kirk, Sharon, and C.J., then continued, "Let's see, a club sandwich for Kirk, and what would y'all like?"

Sharon looked on in disbelief, controlled disbelief, and C.J. seemed confused also that the waitress knew so much about Kirk's preferences. C.J. was quickly trying to get the mental computer going to somehow protect Kirk, but it wasn't working fast enough. "Oh Lord," C.J. thought to himself, "Are we in trouble."

Kirk noticed C.J.'s look of astonishment, then glanced over toward Sharon. "I think everyone wants a club sandwich Kathy. By the way, where's that bum of a husband of yours? Playing Navy at ole Bambridge?"

"Three clubs," answered Kathy. "Yeah, he's on day-shift now."

"Tell him I said hello and I won't forget the tickets to the U. of M.-Navy game, although I'm suspect about who he'll be routing for." said Kirk. "By the way, this is my fiancée, Sharon Miles, her Dad runs the park, and my friend, C.J. As you can see, C.J., she's spoken for, he's a ladies man!"

"Hi," said Kathy, "Kirk sure has spoken of you, and C.J. I'll put the order in."

As Kathy walked away, Sharon took her right index finger and made a check mark in the air, "One for you, Star, you really had me going for a moment."

"You can't be serious," needled Kirk, "I've stopped here for lunch when I'm in town, she and her husband are friends. I'm surprised." Then he had to smile.

"I know that, you know, I knew that all along that it was OK," said C.J.

"I saw the panic in your face C.J., OK," scolded Sharon, "panic!"

"Let's just relax over lunch, simply a matter of false conclusions," stated Kirk.

"Yes Sharon, let's relax, I'm having a tough day," said C.J., "A tough day."

"I tell you that you're doing fine and you tell Sharon it's a tough day," started Kirk.

"I need sympathy," said C.J, "It's part of my make-up, if you will."

But before Sharon or Kirk could respond, Kathy brought the club sandwiches, "That was fast, the cook must have seen Kirk come in," and she set down the meal.

As she took a bite of her club and chewed for a moment, Sharon said, "It's OK, C.J., you can still come to the party tonight. I want to know where you are. It'll make it easier to kill you!"

"I don't want to be killed, I don't even want to be threatened. So cool it girly, just cool it, and eat your parsley," instructed C.J. in a kidding manner.

Before Sharon could respond, Kirk said, "Yes, eat your parsley, I want you to have sweet, fresh breath, for when we kiss, parsley is good for..."

C.J. broke out laughing, put his hand over his mouth, but couldn't control himself. "I'm sorry, it just seemed funny at the time, and now!"

Sharon didn't say anything. She gave Kirk a "how could you say something so insensitive" look and then turned to C.J. with the start of a sweet smile that changed to a "I am going to kill you" glare.

"It seems," stated Kirk, as he gathered his thoughts, "that I am, as usual..." and he took another bite of his sandwich, chewing slowly in order to let his words sink in and have C.J. and Sharon wait for his next words.

"I just hope we don't get the innocent victim bit," said Sharon before Kirk could finish chewing. "You've used that one before. I'd be your script writer, however, since I'm the receiver, I'm anxious to hear your reply."

"I'll just bet you are," said Kirk. "But," and he took another bite.

"Kirk, please chew more rapidly, you know, we are waiting," said C.J. in an English accent, then he quite properly picked up the last of his sandwich.

"Let me say this, Sharon," said Kirk as he finished and wiped his face with the napkin. "I love you!" He put his napkin down and caught Kathy's eye, who picked up three dessert menus and came over to the table.

"Beside a fill-up on iced tea, do you care to have dessert?" Kathy asked.

"Blueberry pie fresh?" questioned Kirk.

"Chef baked it this morning," answered Kathy. "But I'll warm it for you in the oven. And vanilla ice cream, right? How about you two?"

"Iced tea is fine for me," said Sharon. "I don't want to have blueberry breath!"

"I'll follow Kirk's lead, and could you cut a wide slice?" C.J. pleaded, using his most appealing style.

"Shhh, quiet," answered Kathy. "You'll get me into trouble." Then she winked and left the table for the counter where she took out an uncut blueberry pie and went to work. There was a moment of silence as the three waited for the conversation to start again, when Kathy appeared again with the iced tea pitcher. She refilled the glasses. "The pie should be heated now, I'll scoop them with ice cream. I cut C.J.-type pieces," said Kathy and she patted C.J.'s shoulder.

"Do you think that the "I love you" will get you out of trouble?" questioned Sharon.

"Only for a lifetime," answered Kirk and he reached over and kissed Sharon.

"This is getting sickening," said C.J., as Kathy returned with the pie.

"Shut up and eat your pie C.J.," scolded Sharon. "Do what she says," said Kirk, "Eat your pie and pay the bill."

Sharon had to smile as she lifted her glass and took a sip of iced tea. They finished, and as C.J. picked up the check and reached for his wallet, Kirk said, "I'll get the tip." C.J. nodded and headed for the cashier.

Once outside, Kirk walked Sharon over to the station wagon as C.J. headed for the truck. Kirk gave a quick kiss to Sharon, told her to drive carefully, and walked toward the back of the diner to meet C.J., who had already started the truck and maneuvered it near the exit to Route 272. Kirk jumped up into the truck and C.J. pulled out onto Route 272 heading east toward the park. The engine was groaning under all the weight that she was hauling and C.J. looked over to Kirk for reassurance that all was OK.

"You're doing fine," commented Kirk, "Just ease back as we start down the hills so that you maintain control, it'll complete our trip." C.J. didn't answer, but looked over and smiled. He looked confident and pleased with himself that he was doing so well. He was also grateful for a friend like Kirk who coached him in a matter-of-fact manner, simply expecting him to learn well. They covered the ten miles from town a bit more slowly than even the slow trip to town because of two things: the load and C.J.'s carefulness. However, neither Kirk nor C.J. seemed to mind and the trip was enjoyable.

"What's that, a fox?" shouted Kirk excitedly as they climbed the last hill near the picnic area entrance.

"I don't know, I think it was a dog," answered C.J.

"Keep climbing the hill, I'll jump off and see," said Kirk as he opened the truck door, stepped out onto the running board and leaped off the slow-moving truck.

"I'll stop at the park entrance," shouted C.J. "Come back Shane," he yelled, remembering the line from the famous Alan Ladd movie.

In the meantime, Kirk stayed on his feet as he jumped and began back tracking to see if it was a dog he had seen. It didn't take long because coming out of the brush, as Kirk approached was a small, white and brownish poodle-looking dog. Kirk knelt down as the dog came near and scooped her up into his arms. He hugged her and said "Hello little girl, are you lost or did someone dump you out here?"

The dog, feeling Kirk's genuine warmth and calm, reassuring voice, wagged her short stub of a tail and licked his face and neck. Kirk smiled and hugged her closer to him. He looked up to see where C.J. had stopped and to his astonishment saw that the dump truck bed was up and the load was being dropped onto the road near the sign that welcomed people to Elk Neck State park. C.J. had jumped off the truck and was wildly waving his arms. He was yelling something, but Kirk was too far away to make out what it was.

Kirk came closer to the disaster area and C.J. had met him half way. "I know what you're thinking," said an excited C.J. "I don't know what happened. It happened, if you know what I mean," and he pointed over his shoulder at the pile of stone sitting in the middle of the road.

"Say hello to the dog," said Kirk in a matter-of-fact voice. "By the way, I don't think John wanted the load dumped in that particular spot."

"Hi doggie, I'm glad you're not a fox," answered C.J. "Do you know what I've done? Do you?" said a now shouting C.J.

"Well, from initial appearance," stated Kirk, "I'd say we screwed up!"

"Nice doggie," said C.J. as the dog licked him. "What do you mean 'we'?"

"I was with you. It wouldn't have happened if I hadn't jumped off," said Kirk.

"Oh God, now I've gotten you into trouble," responded C.J.

"This is my last day, kind of a humorous way to go out," mused Kirk. "Well, pick up the mike and radio for a front-end loader to come out."

"How 'bout a snow plow, just move it off the road," responded C.J. "OK, hell, could we simply leave it and refill the road here?"

"We could erect a monument to the occasion," returned Kirk. "The road, it doesn't need refilling. You want me to call in?"

"No, I'll do it," answered C.J., and he walked over to the truck and just before reaching for the mike, said to Kirk, "This is one hell of a mess, you know!" Then C.J. threw his arms up in disbelief.

"It sure is, Ollie," returned Kirk as Stan Laurel would say to Hardy.

C.J. ducked into the cab of the truck, took a long breath, and picked up the mike. "This is C.J. to base, Come in plcasc," he said.

After a pause of only seconds, but what seemed longer, a voice came back, "Base to C.J., What's up?" The voice was John's.

"Well...you see, I hoped Russ or someone else would have answered, if you know what I mean," responded C.J.

"Russ, Spike, Will, and Don are here, who would you like to speak to?" asked John. "But remember, we can all hear the base station."

"I know," responded C.J. "I think Don might understand."

Don walked over, took the base mike from John, shrugged his shoulders, and said, "Don here C.J., where's Kirk?"

"Well, you know he had to chase down the dog but it's OK, 'cause he's out by the pile petting the little fellow, girl," said C.J.

"What pile C.J., and where are you?" questioned Don, as the others gathered closer to the base unit so that they wouldn't miss any of this unfolding event.

"I'll tell you where we are, if you don't get angry or mad, and Kirk didn't have anything to do with this, besides, it's his last day, so why don't you give us a break and simply drive the front-end loader out here? OK, guys? Fellow workers?" asked C.J.

"Are they on the way?" asked Kirk as he drew closer to the cab.

"They'll be right over," said C.J. to Kirk as he leaned out of the truck, then he leaned back into the cab and spoke in a lower voice, "Listen, Don, you know that pile of stone that was on the truck? Well it escaped from the bed prematurely and right now it's kind of dispersed onto the roadway by the park entrance sign. Somehow the dump truck bed came up," said C.J.

The men listening started laughing, but did not want C.J. to hear them and then moved away from the base mike. "Give us ten minutes," responded Don. "Stay put, move the truck in front of the pile so that no one hits it."

"Well, we're already in front of one side," answered C.J. Don didn't answer C.J., but smiled to himself and then looked up to see the other men laughing. "I guess he has a point," reasoned Don.

"Spike, Will," started John, but was interrupted by Don.

"I don't believe any of us wants to miss this, John," stated Don.

"OK," answered John. "I'll stay here, I'd rather not know."

"Wish we had a camera," said Don, "historic picture out there."

"We do," said Russ, "I was taking a few photos of the park for my collection. You're right, this'll be a classic." Then he headed for the door.

The others followed, with Spike walking over to the tractor which also served as the front-end loader. A convoy of trucks headed out of the yard and toward the park entrances. Don and Russ each took their pick-ups and Will followed with the park's second dump truck, in case it was needed. Spike brought up the rear. John walked out into the yard to watch the parade start down the road and simply smiled, shook his head slowly and went back inside.

In the meantime, C.J. climbed out of the dump truck, looked at Kirk in an almost pleading manner and shook his head. He walked over to pet the dog again. "Don't worry," said Kirk reassuringly. "It'll be ok, they're all good men."

Both Kirk and C.J. looked up as the sound of truck engines drew near. Don drove slightly past them, then backed up his pick-up by the other side of the stone pile, turned on his headlights and flashers, then got out and walked up to Kirk and C.J.

"Interesting place you picked to dump the load," he said, and winked at Kirk as C.J. bowed his head and looked off toward the woods. Will and Russ had, in the meantime, parked on the other side of the road. Spike, who, of course had to drive slower, was just coming into view.

"Well done," said Russ, "this is one hell of a mess." Then he motioned to C.J and Kirk to climb up onto the pile of stones so that he could get a picture.

"Wait for Spike," kidded Will, "a shot of them standing in the loader would be most memorable," and then motioned Spike to drive up to the stone pile.

"This isn't funny you know," said C.J. in a loud voice.

"Oh yes it is" said Russ. "It's funny as hell. I love it. Now do as Will said, get into the basket. Spike lift them to the top of the pile."

Kirk, who saw the humor from the beginning, stepped into the basket, still holding the dog and beckoned C.J. to follow. Kirk had that wide grin of triumph on his face. C.J., who was starting to calm down, also climbed in. He had a nervous smile on his face but it was also turning toward glee as Russ lined up the first of several shots with his camera. Everyone got into the act, standing on the pile with C.J. or in the front-end loader getting their picture taken.

"I'm out of film," said Russ, "but it was worth it. Let's clean up the mess."

"Is anyone going to comment on what I did?" questioned C.J. as he simply stood by.

"What you did," said Don, "was break up an otherwise uneventful day," and he gave a mock punch on the arm to C.J. "But next time, we'll kill you!"

The men all laughed and went about the task of reloading the dump truck. In just a short time everything was cleaned up and the trucks headed back to the shop. Kirk insisted that C.J. continue to drive the dump truck as he held the dog on his lap. C.J. slowed to a crawl as he made his way through the gatehouse entrance, then picked up speed again and headed into the shop yard. The other men had arrived before C.J. and Kirk. They were standing by the shop entrance with John as the dump truck pulled up. C.J. parked the truck, then along with Kirk, climbed out and walked toward the group of men. The men clapped!

"You want to leave the load in the truck or should I dump it?" questioned C.J. to John, and he waited, so to speak, for the other shoe to drop.

"Well," started John, "why don't we leave it where it is for now."

"You want to hear the story about what happened?" asked C.J. "You see..."

But John held up one hand, "No C.J., I'll wait for the pictures!" All of the men had a good laugh and John put his arm on C.J.'s shoulder. "Don't worry about it," he continued, "it's no big deal." C.J. felt relieved, his smile was genuine and even he managed a nervous laugh.

"Let's clean up the balance of the work here and then clean up for Kirk's barbecue," said John, who turned to Kirk, "I guess the dog was to blame?"

"No, he or rather she just contributed to the start of another interesting event," announced Kirk, who after a moment continued, "here, pet her, she doesn't bite." John reached out and patted the dog on her head and rubbed her ears.

"Decided what you're going to do with her?" he questioned as he held the shop door for Kirk.

"Figured that Sharon and I would take a ride to Turkey Point and introduce her to Bill Kemper, her new master," answered Kirk. "What do you think?"

"It's a great idea, I'm sure he'd like the company," said John as they entered his office. "It'd be a problem though, if she ran away." Kirk put the dog on the floor. She wagged her stub of a tail, looked up at him, then went through the door into the main shop as Will and Spike called her. They had fixed a paper plate with a sandwich broken into small pieces and set it down on the floor for her.

She went right to work, stopping just once, looking up with a short, quick wag of her tail, then right back to the plate. In no time, the sandwich was gone, then she moved over to a small bowl, filled with about a half cup of milk. She certainly enjoyed the meal and the attention.

Kirk and John had moved from his office to the shop to view the banquet. "I don't think she'll take off, John. She was dumped out there."

“Maybe you're right, that does happen out here,” answered John who then turned his attention to the men.

“Let's wrap it up, see you all at the house around six.” Kirk called the dog and she followed him outside and toward the jeep, stopping once to relieve herself, then happily running to catch up with Kirk. He lifted her up into the seat next to him and started the jeep. C.J. came out of the shop just as Kirk started to back out of the parking space and waved for Kirk to stop.

“I'll come with you, clean up at your place, then you can drop me back here to maybe pick up my car as we go to the Miles’. Do you have a clean pair of jeans for me?” Then noting that the dog was in the front seat, C.J. continued as he leaped into the back of the jeep, “I see you already have someone riding shotgun, I’ll hop in back. OK, let's go!”

“Are you comfy?” questioned Kirk as he started forward and out of the shop yard toward the cabin area. After shifting to second, he reached over and patted the dog.

“I'm fine back here, you were speaking to me, right?” questioned C.J.

“No, I was checking with the pup,” answered Kirk. “You can grab hold of the roll bar.” Kirk kept a close eye on the dog as they drove along, fearing that she might be frightened, but she was quite controlled and her only movement was to lie down on the seat. They pulled into the cabin area and Kirk brought the jeep to a halt in front of his place. He got out and the dog came across the seat and out the driver's side. She followed Kirk to the cabin. C.J. brought up the rear, tagging along.

As they entered, the dog scouted ahead of Kirk and C.J. She went quickly through each room, then out onto the screened porch sniffing things and the air as she checked out the cabin.

Kirk, in the meantime, went into his bedroom, sat on the chair near the bed and took off his shoes, dropping them one by one in a tired fashion. He then took off his clothes and slipped into a pair of khaki Bermuda pants, stuck his feet into rubber flip-flops, grabbed a towel and soap, plus his shaving kit and headed out of the bedroom toward the door.

C.J., who had stayed overnight with Kirk many times and kept some spare clothes in the so-called guest room had done the same as Kirk and met him as they headed for the shower room in the central bath house. The dog, who had finished checking the place out, likewise met Kirk and C.J. at the door and looked up wagging her tail, fully expecting to go along with them.

Kirk had to smile. He knelt down to pet the dog, but she met him half way, putting paws onto his chest and licking his face. “OK, you can go along,” said Kirk to the dog, then as he opened the screen door to the cabin, he called over his shoulder to C.J. "Better bring an extra towel, I've got a hunch we're going to need it."

The dog scooted out the door, stopped to be sure that Kirk was following, and ran back to him as if to say, "Hurry up!"

C.J. had retreated back to the closet where the towels were kept for the extra towel, and was now bringing up the rear. "It's not necessary for you two to wait for me, even though it's polite. I'm coming," kidded C.J.

Kirk covered the 40 yards to the shower room in no time, and held the door, first for the dog as she rushed in and went exploring, then for C.J. to shut him up with his so-called complaining. C.J. nodded approval as he entered.

"What's that lady doing in the men's shower?" said C.J. firmly as he pointed to the dog.

"Oh, just waiting for you to bathe her," returned Kirk as he headed for a stall.

"Now hold on, there son. You don't expect," started C.J., but he was interrupted.

"We're going to my going away party, plus, I sort of saved you from getting into a lot of trouble today, you know," answered Kirk. "Wash the dog!"

"In a way you and your friend here, started the trouble, that's a wash out, to coin a phrase. You've got me on the party bit though," said C.J. as he motioned to the dog with a snap of his fingers to follow him into the shower stall. The dog cheerfully followed C.J., "What am I in for?" he asked in a low voice.

Kirk took a quick shower, dried off and put his Bermuda shorts and flip-flops back on and was at the sink shaving when the stall C.J. occupied opened and out stepped a tail-wagging, clean dog. She shook herself and sprayed everything in sight, including Kirk. He reached for the extra towel and with shaving cream still on the right side, knelt down and dried the dog off.

"You look almost cocoa in color with some white mixed in," said Kirk as he finished, put the towel down and continued shaving. He looked down for a second and found the dog looking back up as if to say, "Well, what's next?" He reached down, picked up the dog and put her onto the counter top, then he continued shaving. She sat and watched, then stretched over and took a drink from the running water in the sink.

"Coco, that's a good name for her," said C.J. as he emerged from the stall, draped with a towel wrapped around himself. "Do you mind if I use your razor?"

Kirk rinsed off his razor and set it down on the counter top next to the shaving cream, rather than put it into his shaving kit. He motioned to C.J., who acknowledged and then reached for the after-shave lotion. After what seemed to be a long pause, Kirk said in a loud voice, "Coco!" The dog raised her ears and wagged her tail. "Coco," he said in a lower voice, "good girl." C.J., in the meantime, started shaving as Kirk finished up and started toward the door. "See you back at the cabin," said Kirk.

"I'll bring your kit," responded C.J., "looks like the dog, Coco, is going with you."

"I don't see why not," answered Kirk as he looked down at Coco. "After all, you dragged the poor thing into the shower and bathed her!" Then he opened the door and motioned for Coco to go on ahead. She started toward the cabin as Kirk started to chase her, but he had to stop as one of the flip-flops came off of his foot. Coco stopped, and charged back toward Kirk, who was trying to balance on one foot, while holding a towel and wash cloth plus put the loose flip-flop on. Coco grabbed at the rubber flip-flop, took it from Kirk's hand and dashed off toward the cabin once again.

Kirk started off after the dog. "Hey, come back here!" But it was no use. The little tail-wagger was waiting by the cabin door, happily holding her treasure. Kirk took off the other flip-flop. "Might as well have two dirty feet," he said aloud, and headed for the cabin.

In a few minutes, C.J. came though the door and was surprised to see Kirk sitting on a chair with one foot in a bucket of water. "Man, you sure do like clean feet. I never saw anyone wash them twice in just a couple of minutes," then he had to smile as he surmised what had happened.

"Let's not get too deep into this subject," answered Kirk. "I'd hate to have to throw a bucket full of dirty foot water at you!"

"You've made me reach a level of understanding," returned C.J., "so let's simply get dressed and hurry over, so I can explain to the party guests all about your clean feet!"

"That does it! Prepare yourself for a pail of H2O!" shouted Kirk. At that, C.J. picked up the dog and held her close to his face.

"Cease, before dampening us. And, show some class!" he shouted back.

"Show some class?" questioned Kirk. "Where did that come from, some film you showed at the drive-in?"

"I couldn't think of anything else to say. It sounded sort of Shakespearean, you know, sort of English-like," reassured C.J.

"OK, I'll show some class and not wet you down, besides, I don't want to loan you any more clothes," answered Kirk, "so, let's get going."

C.J. headed for the door with Coco tagging right along. She was first at his heels, then maneuvered around in front of him so that she would be first out the door. “Pushy little kid, aren't you,” commented C.J. as he opened the door and started for the jeep. Coco was already at the side of the jeep when C.J. arrived, waiting for him to lift her into it.

Kirk, in the meantime, took a look around the cabin as one would, being certain that he hadn't forgotten anything, then followed C.J. out the door. He eased into the driver's side only to have Coco jump in his lap. Kirk petted her, then slipped the key into the ignition and started the engine. C.J. reached over and picked up Coco and held her on his lap as Kirk first backed out of the parking space, then headed out of the cabin area toward the Miles house.

In just a few minutes, Kirk was pulling into the yard. Sharon came off the front porch to meet them. She walked up to Kirk's side of the jeep, reached in and kissed him hello, even before he cut off the engine. She also received a lick on the face from Coco who scooted across from C.J.'s lap to Kirk's. Sharon reached in and carefully picked up the bright, tail-wagging poodle. She continued to hold her as Sharon's dog come to greet Kirk. There was a quick hello to Kirk, then complete interest in the new arrival with four legs.

After tail wagging in both dogs showed that they'd get along all right, Sharon set Coco down on the ground. The two dogs jumped and played as everyone, including the four-leggers headed for the back yard, which had been set up for Kirk's going away party.

“Welcome to your party, said John as he extended his right hand. Kirk shook hands with John as Dora wiped her hands on a towel after setting the salad bowl on one of the picnic tables and came over to hug him.

“We'll miss you Kirk,” said Dora as she gave Kirk a long bear hug.

“I can't tell you when I've been happier than with you and John as parents,” said Kirk quietly to Dora. “You can't imagine how much you mean to me.” He hugged Dora again as Sharon came over with an ice-cold can of beer. “Then, there is a certain feeling I have toward your daughter,” he said as Sharon came up to them holding out the can of beer for Kirk.

“Yes, there is,” started Sharon with a twinkle in her eye. “And that feeling will probably make you a grandmother several times over!”

“Sharon,” said Dora in a scolding manner, “show some Newport class!” and she smiled.

“Yes, Mother,” answered Sharon, “I'll watch the Great Gatsby from beginning to end,” then she hugged Dora.

Kirk, in the meantime, moved over toward the men gathered at a picnic table, which was serving as a portable bar. He raised his beer can in salute and shook hands all around.

"When does practice begin?" asked Don. "You certainly will be ready for them."

"Day after tomorrow," answered Kirk, "I'm sure all the guys have been working out over the summer, so the coaches won't ease into training!" Then Kirk finished his beer and tossed the can into the trash barrel, which was five feet away.

C.J. who had maneuvered behind the picnic table-bar, designated himself as bartender and reached into the ice-filled tub to hand Kirk another beer, "Make that four cans," said Kirk, "the chef looks thirsty!"

"Coming right up young fellow, may I see some ID?" kidded C.J. as he started to hand Kirk the cans of beer and then pulled them back

"The only ID you'll get from me is Indigestion when I belt you in the stomach, Mr. Bartender," stated Kirk in a serious tone, but with a wide grin.

"Well, all seems in order there, spirited young man, here are the beverages of your choice. Enjoy, enjoy," said C.J. in a W.C. Field's voice. "By the way, would you like some popcorn or potato chips to stuff down your gullet, perhaps a Maryland crab leg, shell and all?"

"No, how about a Philadelphia soft pretzel?" questioned Kirk.

"No can do, you need Vine street car and bus fumes to give that extra bit of flavor, now, what can you expect from a clean air park?" reassured C.J.

"Well, how about," started Kirk, but he was interrupted by Sharon.

"Ok you two," started Sharon, "come off the stage and introduce your little dog to her new owner. Bill's just coming out of the house."

"I didn't know he was here," said Kirk, "how'd he get here?"

"I picked him up earlier," answered Sharon. "Let's go find the puppy dog."

"You want me to help?" questioned C.J.

"What, and take you away from this self-imposed role as bartender?" returned Sharon.

"Is she putting me down?" asked C.J. as he stood with his hands on his hips.

"No, just putting you on," laughed Kirk, "you make a great bartender."

Sharon, in the meantime, had walked over to the back porch and met Bill Kemper as he walked down the steps. Kirk also walked over and reached out to shake hands with Bill as the old gentleman looked up and smiled at Sharon and Kirk. He gave Kirk a hardy handshake and hugged Sharon.

"You two make a fine looking couple. You'll be happy a very long time," said Bill. "Be sure you always respect the other's feelings, love and respect." Before Sharon or Kirk could reply, Sharon's dog and Coco came running along."

"We've got someone we want you to meet," said Kirk as he reached down and picked up the tail-wagging poodle. "This is Coco and she needs a person like you to give her some love and a good home."

Bill reached over to pat her and was greeted with a couple of wet kisses from Coco's tongue. Kirk then placed her in Bill's open arms and he hugged her. By now, most everyone had gathered near Bill. Seeing him hug and talk quietly to the dog brought hands up toward the eyes to wipe away the moisture, "I thought this was your party, Kirk," said Bill and he sat down on the bottom step with his new daughter dog.

"Let's all grab a seat. Looks like dinner is about to be served," said Dora who walked over to the barbecue pit where Will and Spike were already taking the steaks off the grill and setting them in piles on the large tray resting on the picnic table next to the grill. Russ was busy making the corn on the cob, which he was cooking in a large tub over a make-shift fireplace made of cinder blocks. And right next to Russ, Don was working over a similar fireplace steaming the Maryland blue-point crabs that they had caught earlier in the day.

"Everything's just about ready," said Don to Dora, "look out for the steam."

"Smells like you've used plenty of Old Bay seasoning on these crabs," mused Dora, "John had better check the beer supply!"

"Now we could always serve iced tea," needled Don.

"Of course we could," returned Dora in a kidding tone.

"Looks like I'm just in time. The chefs look like they could use a little liquid refreshment," said Kirk as he opened the beer cans and handed them to Spike, Will, Russ, and Don.

"The oasis comes to us," said Don, "forget the iced tea for a while," he said with a wink to Dora. "You do good work," he remarked to Kirk. Kirk just smiled, held his beer can in salute to Don and raised his can for a swallow of what the author Gene Shepard once called "the Mother of us all".

"To Gene Shepard," said Kirk, "and to people like you that he calls friend."

Don raised his can back in salute, "To Gene," then after taking a long drink from the beer can, Don continued, "You caught his show on beer, I see."

"Yes," said Kirk smiling as scenes of the show Gene Shepard did on beer flashed through his mind.

"I had seen that show before, sure wish he was on TV again on a regular basis." Kirk then put his can down and helped Russ with the corn. "This is supposed to be a party for you, go sit down," said Russ as he motioned to Dora to take Kirk away. "By the way, thanks for the help and beer."

"Come on Star, as Sharon would say," needled Dora as she pointed Kirk toward the table where Sharon was already sitting with Bill Kemper. Kirk walked over and sat down next to Sharon, who had already placed a steak on his plate. "Nice of you to join us. In town long?" kidded Sharon.

"No, just for the night, lady. Want to get married?" asked Kirk.

"Maybe tomorrow, I'd hate to get married in the dark, besides who would marry us tonight. Those Maryland quickie marriages went out years ago," said Sharon.

"That's not exactly true," returned Kirk, "I understand that a hotel bell captain has nearly the same power as a ship's captain and that they perform marriages right in the hotel room, using a genuine Gideon Bible."

"Do you believe this man?" said Sharon to Bill, "smart, just plain smart."

"Well, he is a slick-talking city boy you know," laughed Bill. "Be careful 'cause they can make anything seem to make sense," he continued.

At that moment, John and Dora joined them and sat down. "Anyone need anything?" asked John, "Like now, before I get comfortable, Sharon" he kidded.

"Yes, beat this young man next to me with a stick, or a log, he propositioned me, claims hotel bell captains have the same power as ship captains," complained Sharon, but with a smile and twinkle in her eye, "Mr. Kemper heard him."

"Well, in a manner of speaking, he's right you know. I'm entrusted with that same type of power as superintendent of this park," said John and he took a bite of corn.

Sharon looked over to see Kirk smile that innocent smile and he just shrugged his shoulders as if to say, "See, I told you". Then Kirk took a bite of steak.

"Mother, can you believe these men?" asked Sharon. "Smart-minded men."

"Of course," answered Dora, "I've known your father for twenty-five years."

In the meantime, Bill, who was completely enjoying himself, was also sharing his steak with Coco. In fact, she had climbed up onto the picnic table bench seat next to Bill. He looked over at Dora to see if it was all right and she just smiled an "OK". As he started to give her another piece, he received a wet kiss. The meal continued with light-hearted talking and laughter on into the evening.

John had placed colorful lanterns around the yard and as the sun set, the colored lights took their turn in making the atmosphere festive. Other than the sound of people enjoying the evening, the only other source came from the two bug zappers kept in the yard. The blue light of the zappers obviously attracted the unwanted guests and "zap" they're gone! The two blue-lighted zappers certainly seemed to work because no one was waving off insects or slapping themselves in order to kill insects.

Don got up from his seat and took his plastic knife and banged it against a half-filled can of beer. Everyone stopped talking and looked at him. "I've seen them do this at weddings and meetings," started Don, "it sounds more official there, however, I did get your attention and I guess that's the point." He shifted his feet and body a bit. "With Kirk going back to college," Don continued, "John, Dora, and what's-her-name wanted to throw a farewell dinner, except ole what's-her-name is going to marry the guy, so he really isn't going, so to speak. Now, if you follow me, I'll eventually make sense. I know what you think, but I've only had five and a half beers!"

"In other words," said Russ as he stood up, "Don, like all of us wanted to show Kirk how much we care, by joining in on his last night at Elk Neck."

"And," said Spike picking up the tempo, "to present Kirk with gifts so that he can think of his friends back here at the State Park."

"First," said Will as he stood up and walked over to Kirk's table. "We have," and he reached into the grocery store bag that served as a sort of gift wrap, only to pull out a gallon-sized mayonnaise jar filled with all kinds of things. "Some Elk Neck beach sand on the bottom, some clay from Turkey Point, stones from the C.J. disaster, mud from the cove. Sorry it dried out. Some assorted garbage to remind you of those hot days on that detail, the remains of the first tube of suntan oil you shared with Sharon, a peach pit from the park trees. Spike ate the peach. Let's see, oh, some nails, screws, old wood shavings, etc., from the shop along with last night's shop floor dirt. This remembrance, we offer to you with the instruction that you really should, under no circumstances, open this jar."

"This really underwhelms me and I'll cherish it, for several days," remarked Kirk with a wide grin, as everyone laughed heartily "I don't," but Russ held up his hand and interrupted Kirk.

"We're not quite finished yet. The script says your humble speech comes later," said Russ, "And now, for the next presentation, here's C.J.!"

C.J. came from behind the so-called bar where he had also eaten his dinner. "Thank you for that fine intro, Russ, I appreciate all the kindness that went into the 'Here's C.J.!' I wish we had it on tape!" Then C.J. reached into his pocket and pulled out a crumpled piece of paper and went over near a lantern for more light to read by.

"We have for you Kirk, ole boy, phew, a damn bug flew into my mouth, ugh, wait a minute, I need to wash him down." and C.J. took a swig of his beer. "Here, let me move into some darkness and read this," he continued.

At that, John came over to hand C.J. a flashlight. "Want me to hold this for you?" asked John as he flipped the switch.

"No, I'll be fine, thank you and stop trying to share the stage with me," kidded C.J. "Now, where was I?" asked C.J., unfolding the paper again.

"Washing down a bug," quipped Don, "now, get on with it, son!"

"OK, stop laughing everyone. This is a solemn occasion, losing this sort of fine young man, back to the evil devil's own cities," started C.J. "First, I have for you, and don't bother to take notes, I'll give you this official sheet of paper, Schultzie's Bar & Grill of North East awards you with a full pitcher of beer, for each five hot sausages purchased on a 'one free with five sausage' basis. Confused? I'll explain later. Next, a free haircut at Frank's salon shop, then four passes to the *Elkton Drive-In Movie.* I thought you and Sharon would want me and a date to join you. Don't look at me that way, my father knows I took these passes. Next, a lunch for four at the diner, including hot blueberry pie for dessert. Finally, a free car wash if you purchase one or more gallons of gas at Gene's Mobil. Also a free lube and oil change, but only if you own a Jeep CJ-7, lucky you!"

Dora got up next as C.J. Carefully folded the paper and gave it to Kirk, noting quietly to him that he did, indeed, have another more legible copy.

"Kirk, Don's wife Pattie, and Russ's wife Vicky, got together and embroidered this practice-jersey for you." Then with Pattie and Vicky holding the shirt, Dora read "Elk Neck State Park, summer home of Kirk Daniels." Kirk got up and held the shirt against his body to show it would fit.

"I know, it's corny," said Vicky in an embarrassed manner.

"Not at all," quickly responded Kirk, "I love it, and all the work that you and Pattie put into it, thanks, this is my home!"

"Ok, Star," said Sharon as she got up and went around in front of the table. "My turn to speak. First, I never knew that one's life could change so drastically over a summer. For that, I thank you," and she smiled a smile just for Kirk. "Now, on behalf of all the folks gathered here tonight in your honor, we honor you with this Hamilton quartz watch inscribed simply with 'With Love, Your Elk Neck Friends."

Kirk got back up, took the watch from Sharon and kissed her lightly, then he looked out at the friends gathered there and had to look down for a second and wipe away a tear.

"I guess now is the time for a bright, snappy speech," he started, "but, to echo Sharon, I never dreamed that life could change so, during a single three-month period. This summer has been filled with things that bring about life's memories, some that I'll certainly cherish all of my life. For the watch, I guess someone noticed that my old cheapie was on its last few ticks. I thank you for the watch, mostly thank you for your love."

Kirk smiled as everyone clapped. Then John came over and shook hands with Kirk as the other men likewise lined up to shake his hand. C.J. was the last and also held out a cold beer for Kirk.

"Well friend, it's been quite a summer for me too, mostly thanks to you," stated C.J. and after shaking hands with Kirk, he gave him a great big, bear hug. "You're the brother I never had," continued C.J. in a quiet voice.

"C'mon Star, let's take a walk down to the beach. They don't need you to clean up after your own party," said Sharon as she joined Kirk and C.J. So C.J. nodded his head, gave Kirk a pat on the shoulder, then went over to join the other men as they worked to quickly clear off the picnic table and put out the charcoal fires. At the same time, the gals were bringing the leftover food back into the house.

As they walked down the road to the boat dock and beach, Kirk and Sharon could still hear the conversations coming from the back yard. John was telling Bill Kemper that he'd run him back over to his house on Turkey Point with his new daughter dog whenever he was ready. And Don was yelling at C.J. for dumping a bucket of water onto the coals, rather than just carefully pouring it over them. C.J. remarked that the most important thing had occurred, the fire was out!

Kirk and Sharon, holding hands, smiled at each other over the commotion, as they walked on out of voice range. "What a beautiful night," said Sharon as they reached the beach and walked out onto the dock, "and yet it's also a sad night, knowing that this is our last night together here at Elk Neck." Then before Kirk could speak, she put her arms around him. "Hold me," she said softly and felt the comfort, as Kirk's big arms brought her even closer to him.

"This won't be our last night together at Elk Neck, just the last night for this summer season," stated Kirk, who kissed Sharon on the end of her nose. Then continued, "do you realize that perhaps the next time we are together on this very dock, it'll be as husband and wife?" he said in a cheery voice.

"That's a nice thought, a very nice thought," reasoned Sharon as they walked farther out on the dock and climbed into the Miles' boat. Sharon walked on through the boat, up to the bowrider section and sat down. Kirk sat next to her, put his arms around her and they kissed, "I love you," said Kirk quietly.

"Oh, how I love you," answered Sharon as she moved closer to Kirk. They kissed again and held each other tighter, neither wanting the evening to end.

It was indeed a beautiful night and the sight of two people that much in love filled the evening with all that is right, as though someone had written a love song just for them.

Thirteen 13

The sound of heavy rain and thunder woke Kirk early in the morning. He reached over to pick up the alarm clock, saw that it read 5:45, placed it back on the night stand and fell back in bed, satisfied that he could sleep for at least another hour before getting up to pack for the trip back to the University of Maryland. Each time he'd drift off, a loud clap of thunder woke him.

"Sounds like incoming rocket blasts doesn't it," came C.J.'s voice from the other cabin bedroom.

"God, is that you talking?" asked a sleepy Kirk.

"Yes, my son, after all the beers at the clean up from your party, I couldn't make the flight back to town, so John told me to sleep it off at his place or yours. I chose yours," said C.J. in a firm God-like voice.

"Go back to sleep," said Kirk, "but before you do," he added, "please cut out the noise, a quiet shower will do."

"I'm trying to get it over with one big storm, to keep you dry later on but I'll tone it down a little, it's keeping me up, too," answered C.J.

Kirk didn't answer, but slowly shook his head and laid his head back into the pillow. Just as he drifted off, a scratching noise woke him again. He got up and walked toward the living room to figure out where the noise was coming from, thinking that perhaps a raccoon had somehow gotten into the cabin.

"Did you hear that?" asked Kirk of C.J., as he passed the guestroom, but he peered into the room only to see that C.J. was sound asleep. Kirk continued to the door, opened it and in walked Sharon's dog. "What the devil are you doing out? Look at you, you're soaked," said Kirk as he reached for a towel to dry him off. The rubbing and drying felt so good that the dog was falling all over himself and likewise into Kirk.

"Will you stand still, man you're like a bowl of Jell-O," said Kirk as he dried the dog's head and ears. Then the dog reached up, grabbed the towel and started to play tug-of-war with Kirk. He even let out a few playful growls and he tugged harder with a matching tail wag beating faster as he shook the towel.

"Would you calm down, don't you know what time it is?" said an exasperated Kirk and he let go of the towel. Kirk then went back to his bedroom, sat down on the edge of the bed, looked up toward the ceiling with a "why me?" look and started to lay back down, but this also was interrupted as the dog leaped onto the bed and started for the soft pillow. “Oh no you don't,” said Kirk, “you go to the foot of the bed,” and he pushed the dog down by his feet.

Finally, Kirk laid back down and fell soundly asleep, with a curled-up dog laying at his feet. Actually, he was crowding Kirk, but being as tired as he was from the previous evening, Kirk simply crashed back into the pillow. The rainstorm continued, but much softer than before!

At about 8:30, both Kirk and C.J. were awakened by the crash of the screen door slamming. The dog jumped off the bed and greeted Sharon as she carried a grocery bag into the kitchen area. “’C’mon you sleepy heads, I've brought breakfast for you bums!”

“Good morning, said a sleepy Kirk as he sat on the edge of his bed and pulled on a pair of pants. “Your very wet pup spent most of what seemed like night crowding me out of my bed.”

“When I didn't see him this morning, I figured that he was over here. He was on the porch, but I guess the rain storm sent him running for dryer shelter,” answered Sharon. “Eggs, scrambled or sunny side?”

“Yes, my bed,” exclaimed Kirk, “sunny side up will be fine.”

“This is a strange conversation to be a part of,” said C.J. as he came out of the spare bedroom.

“Who said you're part of the conversation,” answered Sharon in a kidding, stern voice. Pour the orange juice C.J.” Then in an extra sweet voice she said, “How many slices of bacon would you like, dear?” She gave him a kiss on the cheek.

“Four slices would be fine, darling,” answered Kirk, and he winked at C.J.

“A rasher of bacon for Kirk, and C.J., you may also have a rasher,” said Sharon in her sweet voice.

“Four slices is all I want,” said C.J. “I don’t really want a rasher.”

“A rasher is four slices, C.J.,” said Sharon, “and that's straight out of Home Ec.! Besides, I’m cooking a dozen slices, a rasher for each person.”

“I think each of us should eat just three of the four slices,” said Kirk, as he poured three cups of coffee, an egg and some bacon will be needed to satisfy the sniffing nose of our friend here,” and Kirk patted Sharon's dog on the head. The dog wagged his tail, agreeing to the last statement.

C.J. set the table, then picked up one of the coffee cups and walked over to the side door, opened it and stepped out onto the porch that overlooked the Elk River. He took a long look out across the two-mile wide river and came back into the kitchen. “You know, that farm across the Elk is really beautiful. The house almost looks as if it's out of the old south, those columns and the way it looks something like Jefferson's home.”

"I'm going to buy that farm someday," said Kirk matter-of-factly. "I fell in love with that place the day after I fell in love with Sharon."

"Oh, well put!" exclaimed Sharon. "You may have a piece of my bacon for that."

"Man, some guys will stoop to anything to con an extra food ration," needled C.J., "if I said something nice, all I'd probably get..."

"Is a slice of unbuttered bread!" interrupted Sharon.

"Let's eat," said Kirk in a cheerful voice as he placed a paper plate on the counter, cut up an egg, broke up three slices of bacon and set it on the floor by the table for the dog.

"I've got the coffeepot," said C.J. as he anticipated Kirk's next move and motioned for Kirk to sit down at the table.

Sharon, in the meantime, served the bacon and eggs. Kirk picked up the extra slice of bacon, which Sharon had placed on his plate and put it back on her plate. Sharon smiled and Kirk winked back. C.J. placed the coffeepot back on the stove and joined them.

"Well," said C.J., "this is it, the last meal. 'FINE', as they say in the movies."

"Shut up C.J., or I'll scratch your eyes out," answered an annoyed Sharon.

"It may be the last meal here, but it's not our final meal together, so let's not be sad about it. Sharon's going back to Towson State and C.J.'s taking over the cabin," said Kirk matter-of-factly.

"What's that last part?" questioned C.J. "The cabin take over?"

"You're right," said Sharon as she sipped her coffee, then got up to get the coffeepot for everyone's refill.

"After all, I'll be down there near you," reassured Sharon as she refilled Kirk's and C.J.'s cups.

"Fine, fine Sharon," said an anxious C.J., "what's with the cabin?"

"Simple, with you becoming permanent, and with this cabin already refurbished and set for heat with the pot-belly stove, John figured you might want a place for your own if you wanted to winter out here," answered Kirk. "The central bathhouse is kept open all winter anyway, so you'd have hot showers. You'd just need to heat water for cabin use."

"That's just great, fantastic!" raved C.J. "Kirk, you'll always have a place to stay, visit, when you come back, in the guest room!"

Kirk laughed. "I'd turn the key over to you, if we had one. What time is check-out?" kidded Kirk.

"You'll have to be out by noon, or face the penalty of doing the luncheon dishes," stated C.J. " We have strict rules!"

"Well, rules are rules," answered Kirk, "and, I don't like to do dishes."

"Good, I'll help you pack and send you on your way," kidded C.J.

"Some people have ice water in their veins," said Sharon as she again reached for the coffeepot, refilled her cup and Kirk's, then looked at C.J.'s empty cup and put the pot back on the stove.

"Oh that's very nice," complained C.J. and he got up to fill his own cup.

"What kind of a way is that to act, just because I evict this man-friend of yours, well, what have you got to say?"

"That was very good," said Kirk, "just the right voice tone."

"Well, thank you," started C.J. "I try to remain modest about..." But he was interrupted as Sharon reached over and flipped his coffee cup over onto the table. C.J. jumped up, scaring the dog, as the coffee started running off the table onto his lap. The dog also jumped.

"Sorry, it was just a terrible, terrible accident," said Sharon in a theatrical voice, as she put her hand to her forehead.

"That does it," started C.J., "OK fella, you and this women are going to leave, peacefully or perhaps I'd better call the cops!"

"One, C.J., you really do ask for abuse," answered Kirk as he sipped his coffee and patted the dog to calm him down.

"Is there more?" questioned C.J.

"Two, you don't have a phone to call, the cops, however, you could walk out onto the porch and yell for them," needled Kirk.

"Out numbered again," said C.J. to himself in a soft voice.

"Poor baby," said Sharon as she got up and started clearing the table. Kirk started to help, but she motioned "No" to him. Kirk then planted a kiss on Sharon and headed back into the bedroom to finish packing. The dog tracked along to help.

"Need help?" called C.J.

"Not now, help Sharon," answered Kirk.

"Need any help Sharon," said C.J. in a voice tone that requested a "No" answer.

"0f course C.J.," answered Sharon sweetly, "you can clean your messy frying pan and your new coffeepot and..."

"I get the picture, lady," said C.J. "And I thought you were classy."

"I was only kidding and I was going to help," said Sharon in a mock angry voice, "but now you can FORGET IT!"

"Hey, relax, I said you were classy... right," pleaded C.J.

"Well, OK," answered Sharon, "let's finish up the K.P."

Soon Kirk emerged from the bedroom with two suitcases, set them down and went back for two more.

"It's nice to hear that you two are getting along so well, actually entertainingly so," remarked Kirk.

"Take that junk outside and throw it into your jeep, be on your way, stranger," said C.J., "and take this woman with you, be gone."

"Oh, that was very good, C.J.," said Sharon in a sweet voice, "and don't worry about the opening game tickets against Virginia."

"I get it, load and clean, lady," said C.J. softly, then in a booming voice, "like I said there handsome stranger, let me ferry these heavy bags to your vehicle for you and do...do come again!"

Kirk laughed, picked up two of the suitcases, motioned for C.J. to grab the other two and walked toward the door which Sharon had already opened. They headed for the jeep and Kirk put his two down and opened the tailgate. C.J. handed Kirk the ones he was carrying and Kirk placed those in first. "I'll put the other one on the back seat," said Kirk. C.J. opened the passenger side door and held the front seat up at an angle, while Kirk finished the loading. Then they took the doors off and slid them in back.

"Well C.J., it's been an interesting summer, and a great one. The best I could ever imagine," said Kirk and he put an arm around Sharon while holding out his hand to C.J. C.J. shook hands with Kirk, then put his other hand on Kirk.

"You're the best, man, the very best," said C.J. and his voice quivered a bit, "I don't know how I can ever thank you Kirk," he continued, "what you've done for me this summer." A tear came to his eye and he lowered his head a little to hide it.

Kirk took his arm from around Sharon and gave C.J. a big bear hug, "You're the brother I never had C. J.," Kirk said quietly and patted him. C.J. smiled, stood back, wiped his eye, unashamed, and said, "I'll catch up with you in a couple of weeks, after you've got some practices under your belt, in the meantime, I'll get to work and let you two say goodbye." C.J. then headed for the truck.

"Well kid," started Kirk... but he was interrupted as Sharon put her arms around him, kissed him and held him for a long time.

C.J. saw this and did not blow his horn, but simply waved as he pulled out of the parking space and headed for the shop.

"I love you too," was all that Kirk said. He held Sharon tightly. It seemed like they held each other for a long time, neither saying anything. Nothing needed to be said.

Finally Kirk pulled away slightly, kissed Sharon's forehead and gave her a peck on the nose. Then he kissed a tear on her cheek. Sharon smiled, but it was forced. She tucked her head under Kirk's chin and held him again.

"I know you've got to go and I know it's only a few days before we see each other, but, I don't like being away from you even that long Kirk Daniels," said Sharon quietly. "We just need to get married sooner, that's all," she continued. "How about next weekend?"

"Sounds great, but I don't think I can get away before Thanksgiving," said Kirk, as though he was mentally checking out his calendar, "my weekends are a bit overbooked this fall."

"I'll hold you to it, Star," said Sharon, this virtue of mine is getting too tough to live with. I want you so badly."

"Well, being with you isn't always easy on me either," answered Kirk.

"I know," said Sharon matter-of-factly, "I'll make it up to you, believe me."

"I'm counting on it," said Kirk, as he kissed Sharon again and got into the jeep. "I'll call you tonight," he said as he started the engine.

"That's not necessary, I know you'll be busy with the other players, getting reacquainted and all," answered Sharon.

"I'll call you, tonight," said Kirk firmly as he put the jeep in gear.

"Thank you," answered Sharon, "I love you!"

Kirk smiled and winked at Sharon as he backed the jeep out of the parking space and headed out of the cabin area.

He looked in the rear view mirror to get a last glimpse of Sharon and he saw that she had walked on past the cabin to the bluff overlooking the bay. While standing there a few minutes, Sharon's mind drifted back to the first day she met Kirk as he walked around the back of her house and onto the porch.

She smiled as she thought. "If that wasn't love at first sight, I don't know what is, and thank God, he fell in love with me!" Then she turned away from the bay and headed toward the station wagon she had driven over with the breakfast.

In the meantime, Kirk had stopped off briefly at the gatehouse where Spike was holding down the fort, and told him he'd send tickets for some upcoming games so the men could all see some games. And then he was off, heading out of the park and toward the town of North East.

As he drove, he could not help but think of all the events that had occurred during the past three months. He smiled about his first meeting with Sharon and involuntarily shook his head a little as his thoughts raced through the events that had lead up to this moment. "It wasn't a whirlwind courtship," he thought, "it was a tornado" and, of course, his thoughts drifted to his initial meeting with C.J., at the drive-in movies and how their friendship grew to where you thought they were lifelong friends.

The Miles' family naturally came into view in his mind's eye and how much Dora and John had come to mean to him. He was now driving through North East; a town he didn't know existed three months ago, but now, knew quite well and liked especially the people.

As Kirk turned onto Route 40 and headed toward Baltimore, he spotted a Maryland State Trooper car and waved to the officer, who recognizing Kirk's jeep from trips to the State Park to see John, waved back.

The balance of the trip was routine. He crossed the Susquehanna River, and as always, noted the beauty as he looked to his left over toward Turkey Point. In driving through the Harbor Tunnel, he wished he had kept the doors on, rather then placing them in the back because of the fumes, however, once out of the tunnel all was well.

After paying the toll, Kirk headed onto the Baltimore/Washington Parkway and then to Interstate 495 and finally to Route 1 and the University of Maryland. He pulled up to his dorm, got out of his jeep and took a long stretch.

"Hey, where'd the jeep come from," called a voice out of second story window, "that sure beats the old VW."

"The VW had the misfortune of meeting a truck and lost but no one was seriously hurt. A friend of mine and my fiancée helped me get the CJ-7," answered Kirk.

"I was going to ask if anyone was hurt," returned the voice. "What fiancée?"

"I anticipated all that, Tony. Now get down here and give me a hand, like the gentleman you strive to be. I'm tired of hollering to a second story. The young lady, we'll talk about later, over a beer," answered Kirk, as he put the doors on the Jeep and got the luggage out.

By now Tony and two other football players had come down to see Kirk's new Jeep and to help carry the gear upstairs.

"Hi Bill, Jack, let Tony carry the heavy one, looks like he bulked up even more than he was supposed to," said Kirk.

"Mama's cooking," answered Tony, "and don't get smart with me or you won't get invited to one of Mama's Italian feasts."

"Like Kirk said," joined Bill, "you've bulked up in all the right places, and you look even faster than before." At this, everyone had a good laugh, especially Tony.

"Yeah, I'm faster," answered Tony, "especially if they use a sundial to time me. Kirk had the right idea, get out of Baltimore for the summer. Not me, maybe I could've gone to Elk Neck too, but I wanted to stay in town and drive the Good Humor truck. Between Mama and the ice cream,

God, the coach will kill me. And I've hardly eaten in two, well, almost a day, since breakfast this morning and I feel starved," then he grabbed the largest suitcase and headed for the dorm motioning with his head for the others to follow.

"The list says you're in 341 Kirk, got one of the corner rooms all to yourself." said Jack, who continued, "Guess that goes along with being co-captain of the team."

"Either that or my old roomie complained about me," answered Kirk. "Here we are, 341, do you have a key Kirk or should I simply kick the door in?" asked Tony as he stood back and let Kirk pass.

"Let's try the door first," answered Kirk, " I'd hate to have to make a run to Rickles, so early in the school year for a replacement door."

Then Kirk turned the knob and the door opened. He gave Tony a look of "get inside" and everyone passed Kirk and went into the spacious corner room. They set the suitcases down by the closet.

"Funny, mine was also open," said Tony matter-of-factly with a grin on his face. "Oh look, the key's on the dresser."

"Maybe they're all open," answered Kirk as he picked up the two keys, put one in his pocket and gave the other one to Bill. "You keeping everyone's spare key like before?" questioned Kirk.

"Yeah, I guess so. I've still got the board on my closet door," said Bill and he put the key in his shirt pocket.

"Anyone want to join me at the gym?" asked Kirk, "I want to work out at the weight room."

"Yeah, sure," came an answer from Bill and the others nodded 'yes'.

"Good, see you guys downstairs in five minutes," stated Kirk. They met and walked to the gym, which was not far from their dorm. It was cool inside, compared to the summer out of doors, but not cold, so they'd be able to keep their strength up without the mugginess that sometimes zaps the strength to do heavier weights.

"Just a nice, easy workout, boys," spoke Tommy O'Brien, an assistant coach, "the hard work begins tomorrow morning, let's not hurt ourselves."

"Hi Tommy, good summer?" asked Kirk.

"Not as good as yours, so I hear," answered Tommy.

"No one could have had as great a summer as I did," remarked Kirk.

"When are we going to meet the lady?" questioned Bill.

"In due time. I want to make certain you guys behave yourselves before I introduce her. She's not used to zoo animals," kidded Kirk.

"Oh that's nice," a voice came from the far side of the gym, "look who's talking."

"Hey Ducky!" yelled Kirk. "Good to see you man," and Kirk walked over to shake hands. "She's so special. Well, we're engaged is all I can say."

"Congratulations my boy," said Ducky, who is actually Donald Walters, a wide receiver on the U. of M. football team. "When do we get to meet the young lady?"

"Day after tomorrow, she's a senior at Towson State and was the boss's daughter at Elk State Park. It took about five minutes or less and I was a goner. She's something else, Duck," answered Kirk.

By now the other fellows had walked over and heard the last part of the conversation. The good-natured kidding went on for a few minutes, then they settled down to doing stretching and getting set for their workout.

Kirk had taken a 25-pound weight, raised it over his head, holding on to it with both hands, then brought it down and through his legs, while bending his knees in a low attitude. He did 10 repetitions of this to loosen up his back and then went over to the slant board with the same weight. He laid his chest on the upright slant board and put the weight behind his neck, then did 10 reps of pushing his back and shoulders back, again to loosen his inner back muscles.

After this he picked up another 25-pound weight, brought his feet close together and bent low to touch the floor, then up to the waist and back down, not bending the knee. This time Kirk likewise did 10 reps and handed the weights to Jack, who was standing next to Kirk. The other fellows were working on their own routines and again Tommy O'Brien told them to take it easy.

"I'll work your routine with you," said Jack Macklin, who was Maryland's six-foot two-inch, 240-lb. fullback.

"OK" came Kirk's reply, "I am going to use lighter weights today."

"Me too," answered Jack as he started to loosen up with the 25's.

"I'll hit the bike before the sit-ups," spoke Kirk, and Jack simply nodded. Kirk rode the Lifecycle bike for about three minutes when Jack came over.

"You haven't put the level in," said Jack, "the 'L' is blinking."

"Yeah, I just hit the manual button, it keeps a steady 340 that way. I don't want to go through the level segment yet," answered Kirk.

"That's a good idea," said Jack.

"It's a nice way to ease into it," and he hit the manual button also. "These lifecycles are really great," he commented.

When they finished with the bikes, they went over to the sit-up boards, Jack put his on the fourth level and started the crunch sit-ups. Kirk put his on the second level and started.

"Show off," said Kirk and Jack simply smiled. They each did a quick 50 and then turned over on their backs to do 50 knee-to-chest exercises. Jack dropped his board to level with the floor and Kirk left his at the same level.

They then walked over to the leg extension machine and decided to do two sets each for the balance of their exercises, except the incline press, in which they agreed to do three sets. For the leg extensions they did the first set at 90 pounds and the second set of ten at 70 pounds. Then they flipped over on their stomachs and eased into a program designed to strengthen their hamstring and calf muscles.

"Keep it light," said Jack quietly. "I'll do the first set at 40 pounds and the second set at 30," came Kirk's reply. After that, they walked over to the leg press machine. Kirk went first and set the weight at 360, but he pushed the seat back four notches. Jack nodded approval, as did Tommy O'Brien, who had wandered over.

After the leg work was finished, they started on the shoulders and chest by first sitting at the Master machine and doing a shoulder press at 150 pounds. Then, after the two sets they moved to the bench press. Kirk had placed the pin in at the 300-pound point, but Jack pulled it out and put it back in at the 270 pound level. Kirk smiled and did a set of 10, then it was Jack's turn to do a set. "You'll need some strength to lift a beer later," kidded Jack, who then did his first of two sets.

When this was completed, it was on to the fun machine, the Body Master incline press machine. Kirk placed the pin in at 300 pounds and this time both Jack and Tommy agreed. Kirk did a set of 10 and then got up from the seat and Jack took his place. They did the second set at 250 pounds and the third set at 220 pounds. The last exercise for shoulders was on the first Master machine, only the seat was placed facing the machine with the seat back pushed up a notch in order to get a straight-up push, as though you would have the bar directly overhead, a military press, so to speak.

The first set was done at 200 pounds and the second at 150 pounds. Flies followed by the back pull and then onto the lat machine. Then using the lat machine, Kirk and Jack did triceps using sets of 7 and working progressive weights on a single set of 80 pounds, 60 pounds, and 40 pounds. From there, they took a drink of water and headed for the free weights.

"Let's do 4 super sets using medium weights," said Jack as he picked out a set of 40s and handed it to Kirk. "I'll feed you the 35, 30, and 25, try six of each, and be smooth," continued a kidding Jack.

Kirk went to work bringing them all the way up. This enabled him to keep the pressure on the bicep muscle without breaking the plane, or relaxing the muscle. When he finished using the 40s, he dropped them in place and Jack handed him the next weights while rolling the others out of the way.

They went through the first set then Jack let Kirk rest a minute before handing the weights to him for his first of four single sets.

"I almost get tired looking at you guys work, especially with those Mickey Mouse weights," said Tony laughing as he picked up a pair of 100s and started to work out. "Man you must have grown soft over the summer!"

"We'll see who's in shape and out of shape tomorrow when the real work begins and who can handle the initial wind sprints by the clock," yelled Tommy from the Lifecycle bike he was riding. Kirk didn't say anything, but just smiled at Tony and winked at Jack.

"Sometimes I open my big mouth too soon," said Tony quietly, but Tony's quietness is usually at loud speech volume.

"Sometimes!" came a chorus from all around the room.

"OK, OK, I hear you guys, now let's finish up and get something to eat. I'm getting hunger pains, got to keep up my strength," said Tony as he finished a set and dropped the 100's to the floor.

The balance of the workout was light-hearted with jokes being offered up and laughter coming between the grunts and groans of the lifting. It has almost 2:30 when they finished, by doing a few sets of negatives, headed for the showers and a few minutes in the whirlpool.

"Well, where do we go for something to eat?" asked Tony as they emerged from the gym into the warm afternoon. The Goal Post Restaurant?"

"Sounds good to me," said Kirk. "But won't this spoil your dinner, eating lunch so late in the afternoon?" as he slapped Tony on the shoulder.

"Why should it? Hell, we don't have to eat dinner 'till around 6:00," answered Tony. "By then, we should be hungry enough to split a cow!"

Everyone had a good laugh as they walked toward the Goal Post, an off-campus beer and burger restaurant which was a popular student hangout. As they entered, Bill took down a large sign, which was hanging on the window to the right of the door and handed it Tony, motioning to him to read the sign. Tony held the sign up, read it and called out to the owner, who was in the corner talking to the new waitress and waiter about their new jobs.

"Welcome Freshmen," said Tony, in a booming voice, "doesn't say anything about returning students. Did I miss something, Vic?"

"No, come in Tony, you guys know that freshmen come in early for orientation, the other signs go up later," answered Vic. "Right?"

"It doesn't say 'Welcome Returning Football Players' guys who have been lifelong, three-year customers who tell younger students and freshman football players exactly where to come and partake of good food and ale. We feel unwanted," said Tony.

"Here, have a beer on the house," said Vic, as he reached for the mugs and tapper of draft beer. "Good luck, be nice," he continued as he placed the mugs on a tray for Tony to take to a table where the others had settled, "I've got to get back to my training."

"You think a beer will buy us off? And us, seeing that you get free football tickets for you and the Mrs., I'm only inquiring," kidded Tony as he picked up the tray and winked at the students in the corner.

"Enjoy lunch on the house," said Vic, "dessert you pay for, and I get invited to Mama's feast!"

"Why not, you're family, Vic, and thank you," answered Tony.

Vic nodded and sent one of his waitresses to get the order. As the fellows looked at the menus, the Korean cook came out of the kitchen to greet the returning players. He walked over and took the menus away from them, smiled and motioned for the waitress to refill the mugs.

"I'll make the burgers like you want," he said.

"Hey Park, how you doing man," said Jack. "Are you head cook yet?"

"Chef," laughed Park, "I went to school, might quit this dive!" Park caught Vic's look, smiled and said, "But for now, I'll cook for you," and he hurried back to the kitchen.

The waitress served the beer and soon the meal was brought out. The conversation was light and lively, each telling about their summers, but mostly listening to Tony talk about his experiences with the Good Humor truck and the streets of Baltimore. There was laughter all around.

Finally, Jack said, "Well Kirk, we've all spoken and you've listened, so tell us, the lady and the job, it must be some story."

"The lady is Sharon. You'll all meet her in a couple of days. I met her the afternoon I arrived, took one look and fell in love. She is, to say the least, incredible, sharp, witty, fun to be with, long, dark auburn hair, a figure that won't quit and the future mother of my kids. On Thanksgiving weekend we'll be married and you're all invited. Outside of that, the job was just great, working at Elk Neck State Park, being right on the Chesapeake Bay and Elk River, it was like having a paid vacation. Absolutely great people to work with, a family, if you know what I mean. It was a great summer!" exclaimed Kirk.

"Sounds routine to me," kidded Bill, "but how did this lady fall for you, no one else to look at? Maybe she'll come to in time."

"My good looks, charm, let's see, what else," needled Kirk.

"I don't know, hell man, you're only 22. Marriage?" questioned Tony.

"You can answer that one for yourself in a couple of days," answered Kirk.

They finished eating the late lunch, or as Tony would say, snack, and headed back to the dorm, that housed the players. Once there, they went their separate ways and said they'd get together later for the team dinner. Kirk went to 341 and started to unpack. He, at first, felt somewhat uncomfortable having the larger corner room, however, he smiled to himself, "he'd have to make the best of it" and continued unpacking.

Jack stopped over to see if Kirk had enough hangers. Kirk said he'd need a few more and Jack returned with a handful of wooden hangers and two cans of beer. Jack then settled down in one of the two lounge chairs and opened the beer. He handed one to Kirk, who settled into the other chair for a few minutes of rest. Jack and Bill had been roommates during their first two years at the University, but Jack lived off-campus last year in an apartment with three other fellows.

"No apartment this year?" asked Kirk as he took a long sip from the can.

"Naw, it's not all it's cracked up to be. I'm a little neater than the other guys and while I didn't say too much, the slobs got to me every once in a while, say once a day. Studying is another thing, too," answered Jack matter-of-factly, and he got up from his chair and walked over to the window. "Not a bad view. Wouldn't mind this room myself," Jack continued, "want to sub-rent?"

"I'll only need it 'till the end of November," answered Kirk, who by now had moved his chair nearer to the bed and had propped his feet up on the bed. "Here, throw this in the trash can," and Kirk handed Jack his beer can.

"How could I get the room though?" questioned Jack as he tossed the beer can into the trashcan from about eight feet away.

"Simple, easy, you have a good season and I'll do the arranging, bad season, forget it," answered Kirk with a wink.

"You know I'll be here through the summer and maybe even longer to get the degree. I'm short about ten credits come May," said Jack.

"Well, don't worry about the credits, just make sure you finish, since you've come this far. Hell, life is ahead of us," remarked Kirk.

"How about you, you're out in May?" questioned Jack.

"Yes, but I loaded up the first two years and took some summer courses when I worked the area for Good Humor." answered Kirk.

He got up, stretched and said, "I'll catch you later. I'm a bit overextended, even tired, think I'll grab a little nap."

"OK, see you later," and Jack left the room, closing the door behind him. Kirk, who was dressed in cut-offs and t-shirt, simply kicked off his running shoes, propped up a couple of pillows on the bed and stretched out. As he started to get comfortable, he thought for a moment, got up and set the alarm clock so that it would go off in two hours, then he settled back down and in no time was fast asleep. Neither the noise in the hall or outside bothered him.

"Come on pal, let's get to it, we're due at the dinner in 45 minutes," boomed Tony as he flung open Kirk's door.

"Did I oversleep the alarm?" questioned Kirk mostly to himself. He then pushed the alarm button to the off position. "Thanks for the wake up," he said to Tony, half in jest, "think I'll grab a quick shower and shave."

"Catch you later," said Tony and he left.

Kirk reached for his towel and shaving kit and headed out of his room and down the hall for the showers. After showering and shaving, Kirk stopped by the hall phone, then called out to Tony who was in his room but with the door open just a few feet from the phone, "Tony, let me borrow your credit card, I need to make a call."

"Need to make a call, need to, the lady friend I suppose," kidded Tony as he reached into his wallet and pulled out his telephone credit card.

"Yes, I need a Sharon-fix," answered Kirk and he started to dial the number. In a couple of minutes Kirk said, "Hello Dora, Kirk here, is that reasonable-looking daughter of yours there?"

"That reasonable-looking daughter is also on the line," came Sharon's voice.

"Think I'll hang up and let you two work it out," kidded Dora, "take care Kirk, John is also yelling hello."

"Say hi to John and take care," answered Kirk. "Well, lady, how are you?" Kirk continued to Sharon.

"I'm fine, be down in three days to set up the apartment with my roomies," answered Sharon. "And after you left me all alone, I had a good cry. The tears were completely your responsibility, you know."

"Sorry about that, I'll make it up to you," answered Kirk.

"You better believe you will," stated Sharon, "I deserve it, darling."

"That you do." answered Kirk who continued after a pause, "Look I've got a guy here listening to every word I'm saying and I don't think he'll leave until I introduce you to him. Tony's is the next voice you'll hear." then turning to Tony. "Ok, say hello and goodbye to Sharon."

"Sharon," yelled Tony who paused for a second listening to Sharon, "OK, I'll talk lower," then turning to Kirk with his hand cupped over the speaker, "Very bright girl, wanted to know if she should stay on the phone or go outside and listen. I'm coming in loud." Then back to Sharon, "We're all looking forward to meeting you, any other good looking girls over there? You'll arrange things, all right! What?" Then looking straight at Kirk, "turn you back to the Star."

Kirk half smiled and then gazed up toward the ceiling in an "Oh no, Sharon, you shouldn't have," look.

"Sure thing, catch you later Sharon," answered Tony, then handing the phone to Kirk, he continued with a wide grin, "my silence can be bought!"

"Hello again," said Kirk, matter-of-factly. "We've got to head over for a team dinner, but obviously, I wanted to speak to you."

"I needed to speak to you," came Sharon's reply "By the way, I said something wrong, didn't I, about calling you Star."

"Don't worry about it, I'll get some good-natured razzing, that's all," was Kirk's reply. "No big deal."

"Put Tony back on for a second please," said Sharon.

"Sharon wants you for a second," called Kirk to Tony. Tony came back out of his room and took the phone from Kirk.

"Yeah Sharon, this is Tony, got me a date already?" joked Tony.

"Listen to the following, Tony," started Sharon, "one word about my pet name for Kirk and 1). no dates, and 2). you're dead meat, got it, your life is behind you!"

"I've got it. By the way, I like blondes," answered Tony, then handing the phone back to Kirk, "that lady has a way with words, Star."

"You and Tony have a nice conversation?" questioned Kirk in a kidding manner.

"Let's say he understands the real world," answered Sharon. "Now back to us, I know you've got to go, I love you and have a great evening."

"I love you too, talk to you tomorrow," returned Kirk and he hung up.

"About ready?" asked Tony as he followed Kirk back to his room.

"Just give me a moment," answered Kirk who continued a moment later, "It seems like you and Sharon have become friends already."

"Friends, huh, you're right about one thing, she's a winner!" noted Tony.

Tony and Kirk left his room, headed down the steps and spotted Bill and Jack waiting out in front of the dorm. "We're off," said Kirk and they started walking toward the dining hall. They walked in silence until Tony opened with, "Spoke to Kirk's girl, Sharon, on the phone. I don't know how he did it, but she's something else. Can't wait to meet the lady, plus, for your information guys, she's got the keys to a whole stable full of fillies. This is going to be one hell of a year!"

"Calm down fellows," started Kirk, "we're not going to be the social directors for you guys, maybe she'll arrange a date or..."

"No way, Star," stated Tony, "Sharon mentioned parties, etc., we'll handle this phase of the operation with Sharon herself."

"What's with the name Star?" questioned Jack.

"Nothing, just an inside joke, nothing, forget it," returned Tony who opened the door and ushered the gang into the dining hall. As Bill, Jack, Tony, and Kirk entered the dining hall, they spotted other players and coaches. Greetings came from all sides and the most popular spot initially, was the huge shrimp bowl and keg of beer. The players, of course, were kiddingly warned about drinking too much of the beer and that the workouts tomorrow would be difficult. Everyone understood, but had a great deal of fun.

It was past 12:00 when Kirk closed the door to his room and fell into bed. It had been an extremely long day and Kirk was just plain tired. In no time at all, he was fast asleep.

The next morning came early because Kirk had forgotten to pull the curtains closed and the bright sun woke him. He glanced at the clock on the nightstand and it read 6.30. Kirk rolled over, pulled the sheet up over himself and tried to get back to sleep. He tossed a couple of times and came to the realization that in thinking about the day's activities with the first practice, he was simply too excited to go back to sleep. With that, he slid out of bed and put on his shower shoes, grabbed a towel, washcloth and soap, then headed down the hall for a shower.

As he entered the bathroom, Kirk was not surprised to see at least half a dozen other players, apparently they were also getting an early start on what would be one busy day.

"Good morning, gentlemen," called Kirk as he put his things down and walked into a shower stall. "Is everyone bright this morning?"

With that, a rumble of groans came and a washcloth was tossed, just missing its target, the rear, unsuntanned area. "Someone missing a washcloth?" called Kirk in a matter-of-fact voice and he tossed it onto a stool. After showering, but not shaving (he'd do that after the practice), Kirk dressed in team t-shirt, shorts, and running shoes. He met a group of players heading over to the dining hall and joined them for a very light breakfast of juice, cereal with a banana, and one cup of coffee. The real meals would come later, when the practice was over.

The atmosphere during breakfast was bright, loud, and confident. This was a fine football team, one that was, in pre-season polls, picked to win the Atlantic Coast Conference.

At 8.30, the players as a team, moved from the dining hall to the spacious locker room for a meeting. The coaches each talked for a couple of minutes about the schedule of practices and workouts, both as a unit and individual specialization teams. All of the fellows arrived in good shape, so the hard work of honing the group of young men into a team that would play the difficult schedule of conference and non-conference games began at once!

The morning workout consisted of stretching, calisthenics, running drills, and a review of the playbook. After a light lunch, the players returned to the practice field and went through some plays, as well as a review of the playbook

The intensity of the drills would come during the next few days as the practice sessions built the team into a well-oiled machine. The routine was a difficult one, but one that each young man relished. The hard work was fun, and tired, sore muscles were virtually ignored. There was a goal ahead and these determined individuals would meet it.

Each evening, Kirk spoke with Sharon on the phone and she could certainly tell through his voice that, while things were going well, when evening came, he was dead tired. She wouldn't keep him very long during the calls, even though she'd like to, but simply listened to the details of his days, brought him up to date on hers and stated the most important part of the call. It was then that they'd hang up. He walked back to his room and stopping to chat a few minutes with someone else and she, pausing a few minutes before joining the rest of the family, each really wanting so much, to be with the other, to be together!

Fourteen 14

During the few days while they were apart, Sharon packed suitcases, boxes and bags with things to take back to school. John and Dora kidded her, of course, about the accumulation and wondered if they could fit it all into the station wagon or if they'd have to call a moving company. Sharon took it good naturedly, everyone knowing that the station wagon would haul the freight south to Towson.

Sharon left home after breakfast on Monday. John loaded the station wagon earlier in the morning and she'd keep the car a few days, before returning home on Saturday. Kirk, according to the plan, would drive to Elk Neck late on Saturday and take Sharon back in the Jeep, leaving the station wagon with Dora. It was also planned that they'd wait dinner for Kirk, who would be expected around 7 or 8 o'clock and that C. J. would join in to welcome the battered, bruised U of M middle line backer back to Elk Neck. That was the plan!

Sharon arrived at her apartment, just off campus, around lunchtime. Helen Ellsworth and Joanne Parker, Sharon's roommates, spotted her as she pulled up. They came down from the second floor apartment to greet her. Helen's boyfriend, Rick VanDuser was visiting and, of course, was enlisted to help unload the car. He really didn't mind, but was smart enough to make certain that the gals also helped. Things were put down in Sharon's room. She'd unpack later. And off the four of them went for a quick lunch.

It was just past three o'clock when Sharon arrived at the U of M practice field. The field was basically off limits and only those with official passes were permitted an up close view. Since Sharon wasn't really expected, Kirk hadn't arranged for a pass yet. "Hello," Sharon said to the older gentleman who served as the guard this particular day, "I'd like to go down to the practice field and see one of the players."

"I see," said the guard, who put his hand to his chin and looked her over. "And I suppose that you're not a spy from another college who's just trying to get past me. And you'll probably tell me that you're not some groupie, but some important lady by the name of Sharon Miles!"

"Well, my name is Sharon Miles and I'd like to see Kirk Daniels," said a somewhat startled Sharon, "Do you know me?" inquired Sharon.

"We've been waiting for you to show up somtetime, and yes, everyone here sort of knows the young lady Kirk has fallen for," answered the guard. "He's quite a catch you know, and from the looks of you, you're quite a catch yourself young lady!"

"Thank you. Do I need a pass or something?" questioned Sharon.

"Young lady, my OK is all you need on this campus," assured the guard. At this time, Sharon, who was dressed in a Towson College tee shirt and shorts, started walking the 40-yard distance to the edge of the practice field. As she walked, she looked at the jersey numbers, trying to find #55.

"Look at the legs on that," came a quip from one of the players.

"You're a dead man Joey, if that's who I think it is," called Tony as he motioned to Kirk to look.

"She does have great legs doesn't she, Joe," called Kirk, who waved to Sharon and held up 5 fingers, as in give me 5 minutes until the end of practice. Sharon waved back.

"So that's your lady," said Bill as he moved over to Kirk.

"The future mother of my children," kidded Kirk, "you know Billy, she looks better every time I see her," he continued.

"I can understand why," quipped Tony. "God, Kirk, she looks better than she sounds over the phone. "Hi, Sharon, I'm Tony," he yelled from across the field and waved.

"I can tell from the sound of your yelling," called a smiling Sharon and she waved back.

"She's a winner, that lady, a winner," said Tony to Kirk.

"I know, she is something else," answered Kirk and he continued, "and I haven't seen her in four days."

"Let's finish up, com'on guys, just a few minutes more and I'll free you for the evening," called Tommy O'Brien.

It was just a few minutes more when the practice session ended and the men were, as Tommy said, set free for the evening.

"I'm sweating, dripping wet," said Kirk as he walked over to Sharon, but stayed a foot or two away so that he didn't get her soaked.

"Who cares," said Sharon as she moved closer, put her arms around his neck, reached up and kissed his sweaty face. "God, have I missed you, sorry guys" she said as she backed down and continued to look at Kirk's face, "but I'm in love with your linebacker!"

"Like I said," stated Tony, "the lady is definitely a winner!"

"Will you marry me if he doesn't," continued Tony, "my mother would understand, even if you're not Italian!"

"She's taken Tony, for this life and the next," stated Kirk who walked off the practice field hand in hand with Sharon.

"I assume, Mr. Clean," kidded Sharon as they walked along, "that you'll take the better part of the evening taking a shower and shaving. I'll give you fifteen minutes," and she squeezed his hand.

"I was going to say ten, thanks for the extra five," needled Kirk.

"I thought all this regimentation would have settled you down," answered Sharon, "it must be the company you've been keeping," she continued, as she winked at Tony.

"There are others like you, over at the stable, right?" questioned Tony.

"Your mother's going to enjoy the funeral. A great send off, if you keep this up, Tony, get off the stable," stated Kirk as they came to the locker room door.

"He simply doesn't understand my earthiness Sharon," answered Tony.

"But I do," remarked Sharon as she put the back of her hand to her forehead in a Hollywood actress mood. "Now, all I need is to find someone Mother would approve of!"

Tony just shook his head. "It's hard to keep up with you, Sharon," he said and he held the locker room door for Kirk and some of the other players, "How do you manage Kirk?"

"Piece of cake," stated Kirk matter-of-factly, then he smiled at Sharon and continued, "See you in fifteen minutes."

"You said ten," answered Sharon, "piece of cake, huh," she continued.

"She's going to kill you," said Tony to Kirk as he closed the door and they walked down the tunnel leading to the locker room.

"No way, I could take her in two out of three falls," remarked Kirk kiddingly referring to the wrestling term.

"Yea, well you've got ten minutes and don't cut yourself shaving," answered Tony who thought for a minute, "we all having dinner together?"

"You all are eating together tonight," stated Kirk as he undressed and entered the shower room, "Sharon and I are going out with each other!"

"This means none of us are invited," said Tony in a loud voice, so that everyone in the locker room could hear.

"You have a clear picture my friend," answered Kirk and he quickly washed his hair, rinsed off, and headed for the sink to shave.

"I suppose you're going to take her to Tags Restaurant in Laurel, like all the rest," called Tony loud and clear from the shower.

"That was uncalled for Tony, she's not anything like any of the rest," called Kirk as he finished shaving and toweled off.

"Sorry," came Tony's reply. "You're right man, she's top choice, a real lady."

"No problem," called Kirk, but after a pause, "Don't go to Tags tonight!"

Tony laughed. "I know you want to show her off. Don't blame you."

"Some other time guys," said Kirk to Tony, Bill, and Jack, as he dressed. "This evening, I just want to be with her alone, OK?"

"We understand," said Jack, "catch you later. Enjoy man."

"Oh we will," answered Kirk as he took one last look in the mirror and then looked at his watch. "Twenty minutes, wonder if she waited," continued Kirk and he waved a goodbye as he headed out of the locker room to join Sharon.

"Twenty-two minutes seems like an hour when you're waiting," said Sharon as Kirk exited from the door and walked over to her.

"Are you sure your watch isn't running a little fast," kidded Kirk as he put his arms around her. "I was working toward ten minutes."

"I'm not certain about my watch," answered Sharon, "but my motor's definitely running fast." Kirk and Sharon just held each other for a moment and then Kirk said, "Com'on let's get out of here. We'll grab dinner at Tags, up in Laurel."

"I hear that's the place players take everybody," said Sharon.

"You're not everybody," answered Kirk sharply.

"Don't get defensive," stated Sharon, "I was only kidding. I've been there before and seen the football players with their dates. Maybe even you!"

"Why didn't you say hello," said Kirk, now smiling and somewhat embarrassed at the way he had spoken to Sharon, "I'd have met you earlier."

"You weren't ready for me and maybe we'd have been spoiled, besides, my Daddy wouldn't have approved of you. I was there with my parents, it's their favorite Italian restaurant, even though, I think the owners are Greek," answered Sharon.

"How could they not have liked me," said Kirk as they approached the jeep and he started to hold the door open. "I'm the father of their future grandchildren. Climb aboard, my lady!"

"No, let's take the station wagon, it's more conducive for making-out after dinner," answered Sharon and she flipped Kirk the car keys. "We can also talk of grandchildren then," and they walked over to the station wagon. The drive to Tags was basically a straight drive up Route 1 toward Laurel. It was not only a local favorite, but out of town salesmen and even people from both Baltimore and Washington came there. The food was good and plenty, the atmosphere was warm and friendly, and you felt at home. Kirk and Sharon didn't say much on the drive to Tags. Mostly Sharon just nuzzled close to Kirk and thought of how wonderful life was. Kirk, likewise, was into his thoughts and he also reflected about how much this girl sitting next to him meant. He couldn't envision life without her now.

"You can probably get away with parking at the Howard Johnson Lodge if Tags' lot is full," stated Sharon as they came near the restaurant.

"I know but they don't care for that," remarked Kirk, "we'll see." As they drove into Tags' parking lot, Kirk spotted a parking space and pulled into it.

"You are lucky," said Sharon, "almost in front," as she slipped on a wraparound skirt.

"I am lucky," answered Kirk. He leaned over to kiss Sharon as he put the gear into neutral. "I sure do love you lady," he remarked. They got out and made the short walk to the restaurant door. Kirk held the door for Sharon and followed her in.

"Well Sharon, how are you, how's your folks," was the greeting she got from the hostess. "Who's that with you. Oh my God, Kirk of Maryland!"

"Hello Louise," said Sharon and she pointed to her ring finger, "He is with me!"

"You're engaged, oh my God. Paul come here," said Louise as Paul, one of the owners appeared out of the kitchen. Paul walked over and held out his hand. "Hello, Kirk. How does the team look," said Paul as he and Kirk shook hands.

"Oh, I think we'll do all right," answered Kirk, who continued, "You know Sharon Miles, and I guess her parents from Elk Neck State Park."

"Of course," answered Paul, "they're old friends, and we've known Sharon since she was a little girl. Welcome darling, it's nice to see you again."

"They're engaged to be married, Paul. Look!" and Louise pointed to Sharon's ring.

"This is wonderful," said Paul, who shook hands with Kirk again and kissed Sharon. "This calls for a celebration. You're our guests tonight. Anything you want," then turning to the other patrons in the restaurant. "Friends, help me congratulate two wonderful young people on becoming engaged. Kirk Daniels, a fine young man and football player at Maryland and his beautiful bride-to-be, Sharon Miles, who we've known since she was a little girl. Her Dad is the main ranger at Elk Neck State Park. Her

Momma's a fine schoolteacher and she, the darling, is a college student at Towson. You're after dinner drinks are our pleasure, in their honor." At this, Louise showed them to a table and Paul, as well as the other diners, clapped for Kirk and Sharon.

"You'd better be good to her," said Louise, "I know you boys at Maryland."

"I promise Louise, with all my heart," said Kirk and he winked at Sharon.

"That was wonderful and embarrassing," said Sharon quietly to Kirk as they sat down.

"I know, I didn't expect it either," replied Kirk. "You know, we're a wonderful couple. We really are and I'm so proud that you chose me."

"Well, I don't know about using the term 'proud,' but I'm thankful we found each other. Besides, when I saw you, you were a dead duck and didn't know it, Star," answered Sharon with a wide grin.

Just then Louise showed up at the table, "No beer for Daniels, champagne, the good stuff, Korbel. Not that cheap Cold Duck you people usually drink," and she put down four glasses and filled them. When they were just about filled, Paul came over and offered up a toast to Kirk and Sharon and they all took a sip of champagne.

"You want off the menu or should we just cook for you Kirk," asked Paul.

"Please, we'd enjoy it more if you selected Paul, and thanks for everything," said Kirk as he and Sharon handed Paul the menus.

"We'll keep it light. You're in training. Some soup, salad, veal, pasta, you know, nice and light," answered Paul and he walked back into the kitchen.

"Do you want some more champagne," said Kirk as he noticed Sharon's empty glass and reached for the bottle from the champagne bucket. "I'm half intoxicated from all that's happened in the past few minutes, but why not," came Sharon's reply and she moved her glass close to Kirk.

"Yeah, it was unexpected," remarked Kirk as he poured Sharon's and then filled his glass, "shows what they think of you and your family."

"And you," answered Sharon matter-of-factly. "This is for us!" Just then a waiter came over with cups of minestrone soup and bread. He checked the champagne bottle, poured the remainder in Sharon's and Kirk's glasses and took the bottle away. Kirk smiled and nodded approval as the waiter left. Sharon picked up the soupspoon, tasted the soup and nodded her head, 'yes,' as Kirk broke off some bread and put it on her bread plate.

Louise, who had just seated a couple near them, stopped off to see if everything was OK. "Why did you give her the end piece, saving the middle for yourself?" she questioned.

"Louise, if I hadn't given her the end piece, she'd be yelling at me. She'll get the other end piece too," explained Kirk.

"In that case, all right," answered Louise, "I'm glad he looks out for you Sharon. We have to keep them in line you know," and she patted Kirk on the shoulder.

"He does and I do," answered Sharon, "I look forward to a lifetime of caring for him and being cared for by him."

Louise smiled, patted Sharon and walked back toward the door to greet arriving guests. As she left, the waiter came back to check on them and seeing that they hadn't finished the soup yet, he departed. "That was a nice statement lady," said Kirk softly as he finished his soup.

"Just the plain truth," returned Sharon, "I'm in love with you, Star!"

"Well, as you certainly well know, I'm in love with Sharon Miles," answered Kirk.

"Of course you are," stated Sharon as she held her glass up, clicked it against Kirk's in salute and drank the last of the champagne, "How could you help yourself," and her devilish smile broke into a wide grin. Before Kirk could come up with a smart remark, the waiter was back with the salad.

"Caesar salad for two," said the waiter, "Would you like some fresh ground pepper," he continued as he set the salad plates down and headed for the large pepper mill. Both Sharon and Kirk nodded yes as he came to them and ground the pepper over their salads.

"With a Caesar, you're stuck with kissing me tonight," kidded Kirk as he picked up a fork full and crunched on the tasty salad.

"Oh well, I'll just have to make do," said a smiling Sharon. "You know, I was rather surprised that the waiter ground the pepper over the salads," she continued as Kirk stopped just short of putting the next fork full in his mouth and held the fork in mid-air with a puzzled look on his face. "Yes, I can see by that look on your face that you also thought that the peppy'a should have put those finishing touches on the salad. Perhaps he was at some other restaurant performing his duties," continued Sharon with that look on her face knowing she had gotten Kirk. She lowered her eyes and started to eat her salad.

"The peppy'a?" questioned Kirk, "Is that a new word or just a relatively new word, peppy'a," he said softly again.

"Emm, I'm still chewing," said Sharon and then she put another fork full in her mouth. "Just catching up to you," came the explanation to Kirk as he watched her put the next fork full in, without answering. "Maybe the peppy'a will show up and pepper your veal," remarked Sharon and she continued as she started to pick up another fork full, "You know, the peppy'a, the man who goes from restaurant to restaurant grinding pepper. My, come on man, where have you been all summer, cooped up in the woods!"

Kirk was about to respond, but with nothing too bright, and he was glad to see the waiter come back with their dinner.

"Veal piccata," said the waiter as he placed the plates in front of Sharon and Kirk. "We also have a nice order of linguine, not too heavy, saves room for dessert. Would you like fresh ground pepper?" Kirk looked at Sharon and had to smile.

"Of course," answered Sharon, before Kirk could speak "and I see that you're the acting peppraier!"

"Only for this restaurant," answered the waiter, "I'm exclusive here, you know."

"How's everything?" said Paul as he approached with a bottle of wine and two glasses. "Some very nice Fune Blanc, SoBon Estate, a good Dry Sauvignon Blanc California," continued Paul and he uncorked the wine and poured some for Kirk to approve as he also laid the cork beside the glass.

Kirk took a small sip, looked up at Paul and said, "I'm not too good at this, but it tastes great. What do I do with the cork?"

"Most people aren't too good at tasting, my young friend, however, you did fine. It tastes good and that's the key," stated Paul who poured a glass for Sharon and continued, "As for the cork, a quick whiff will usually tell you if it's vinegary. Ah, but this particular cork belongs with the champagne cork she put into her pocketbook, a special cork!"

"Thank you, Paul, it is a special cork, a very special night from you that we'll never forget," answered Kirk as he looked at Paul, then Sharon.

"It is so wonderful that words can't describe," remarked Sharon. "Thank you, seems not an important enough word," she continued after a short pause.

"Your faces show everything and they also show love for each other, never loose that look," stated Paul. "Besides," he kidded, "the next time you come, I'll overcharge you to make it all up," and he laughed as he walked away to greet dinner guests that Louise had just seated.

"So now you're somewhat an expert on wine," needled Sharon as she picked up her glass, motioned a salute to Kirk and took a sip.

"Of course I am," returned Kirk. "What I do know is that this is a very good tasting white wine and the veal is incredible!"

"Oh, it is good," answered Sharon. "It's so good, it's hard not to gobble it down."

"I know," remarked Kirk, who reached for the breadbasket.

"Have some more bread, it'll slow you down, that's what I'm doing!"

"When did the bread theory come about?" questioned Sharon.

"I just thought it up, for you, maybe the linguine would be better," answered Kirk.

"Speaking of the linguine, why do you use the soup spoon to twist the spaghetti and not just a fork, like this," Sharon remarked.

"Because I'm from Camden and we're more organized, more professional Italian food consumers. Remember, I lived in an Italian neighborhood," answered Kirk.

"Really, it takes both hands to eat from what I see, for me, it takes only one hand to eat, much more simplistic," kidded Sharon.

"Why did the waiter bring another soupspoon after the soup," answered Kirk, with a smug look on his face, as in I've gotcha now! Sharon, not to give in just yet called for Paul to come over and she explained the argument...discussion, and asked for his opinion.

"What do you want from me," Paul replied with his hands in the air. "Gimme a break, I'm Greek!" and at that off he was again.

"See, it's settled," laughed Kirk as he finished eating and took a sip of wine.

"It is not settled, Mr. Daniels, we simply need a non-Camden Italian to settle this. If not today, then look to the future for the answer," came Sharon's reply.

"Tony, his mother, that's who will settle this for you Miss Miles," remarked Kirk and he finished his wine.

"Is she originally from Camden?" asked Sharon, in a non-trusting voice.

"No, she is not from Camden," answered Kirk, then in a low voice, with a little boy smile on his face, "she's from Philadelphia."

"A mile wide Delaware River separates the two cities and I suppose that Tony's mother is even from South Philadelphia. Right?" challenged Sharon.

"Well for the most part, you're correct," mumbled Kirk.

"You crook, slime," stated Sharon, but she was interrupted by Paul.

"No, we don't have lime pie or sherbet, but we have many other desserts," stated Paul who thought for a moment. "How about some fresh strawberries with heavy cream or whipped cream and, if you like, I'll put a wedge of lime on it, just for you, huh, nice and light."

Sharon thought for a moment and was about to answer. "The strawberries sound great, it will be nice and light, plus the lime is just the perfect touch," stated Kirk, who added after a pause, "thank you, Paul."

Paul smiled, patted Kirk on the shoulder and went over to the waiter who was preparing to clear the table and gave him the dessert order. The waiter then came over to the table removed the dishes, silverware, breadbasket and wineglasses. Then swept the crumbs into his hands with a napkin. He then straightened the tablecloth, reset the coffee cups, and gave them fresh napkins and spoons for dessert and coffee. He then stepped back a foot to survey the table and, satisfied, he said, "strawberries and lime, I like lime too. Do you want cream or whipped cream?"

"Sharon will have whipped cream and I'll have the heavy cream," answered Kirk.

"Is that, an old Camden tradition," kidded Sharon.

"English I think however, I just like the taste of cream," answered Kirk. Sharon didn't answer back, but just looked at Kirk and smiled in thinking of all the things she loved about him.

"Penny for your thoughts," said Kirk after a few seconds and he also smiled. Sharon didn't reply, but just shook her head gently and reached for her water glass. At this the waiter was back with dessert, then he went over to the beverage station and returned with the coffeepot.

"We also have decaffeinated, if you like," he said as he put the creamer on the table.

"Sharon?" questioned Kirk.

"This is fine," she said, "I prefer the high test over the unleaded."

"Same for me, thank you," was Kirk's reply.

"How about an after dinner drink?" asked the waiter.

"I don't think so," responded Kirk, the champagne, wine and the delicious strawberries, with lime will do just fine, thank you," and he looked over at Sharon, who simply nodded affirmatively.

"What do you think?" questioned Sharon to Kirk as the waiter walked away.

"Think about what," answered Kirk as he took a sip of coffee.

"The strawberries and lime, do you like that combo?" she asked.

"I don't and I'm not about to try it," answered Kirk, who thought for a second and continued, "The strawberries and cream are delicious. The lime I put over here," and he showed Sharon that he had hid it on the saucer, just in front of him where no one could see it. "I'll squeeze it, after I'm finished, to make it look used," and he winked at Sharon in satisfaction of the deed.

“That was relatively smart,” stated Sharon, who thought for a second and continued, “I don’t have a better idea, so I’ll follow your lead, just this once, that is,” and she likewise hid the lime slice.

“I know that is tough for you kiddo, but try to follow my lead later on when I take you in my arms,” stated a devilishly smiling Kirk.

“Just be careful I don’t throw caution to the wind and forget my virtue,” said Sharon quietly, “my fate may be well in your arms.”

“Oh, we’ll work it out, somehow,” answered Kirk and then after a second or two, “Oh, I’ll help you off with your clothes!” Then Kirk put the finishing touches on his strawberries and finished his coffee. Sharon was about to respond, however, the waiter was back with the coffeepot.

“More coffee?”

“No,” answered Sharon this time, before Kirk could respond. “We have to leave shortly so that Kirk can tear my clothes off!”

Kirk, of course, was embarrassed and although you couldn’t tell very much because of the darkened dining room and because he had a deep tan, but he blushed a solid red.

“Ah, young love,” remarked the waiter, “I understand and of course there is no charge, with our compliments, say good-night to Paul and Louise and you young folks are off, to perhaps, Elkton to get married.”

“Thank you,” answered Kirk, who had regained some composure, “Everything was terrific!”

As Sharon got up, the waiter quickly moved to hold her chair, “Our pleasure,” he said. Kirk reached into his pocket and took a ten dollar bill from his money clip and placed it next to his coffee cup, although the meal was free, he wanted to tip the waiter who normally counted on tips as a major portion of his salary.

The waiter held up his hand in protest as in, “this is not necessary!”

But Kirk responded, “please, we appreciate everything that was done for us.”

As Kirk and Sharon made their way toward the door and Louise, Paul spotted them and joined Louise, “It was wonderful having you two,” stated Paul.

“It’s a night we’ll always remember,” said Kirk, “our thanks to you wonderful people.”

“I second the thought,” added Sharon, “everything was perfect,” and at that Sharon gave a hug and kiss to Paul and Louise. Kirk gave Louise a kiss and shook hands with Paul. They started for the door, and Kirk was already there holding the door for Sharon. Paul called Sharon back for a moment and slipped a ten dollar bill, tightly wrapped, into her hand so that Kirk could not see what was happening.

"Give this to him later on, my dear, I'll take care of Carlos and tell your folks hello," said Paul. Sharon squeezed Paul's hand and looked at Louise, who simply smiled as Sharon headed for the door, which Kirk was holding.

"Everything OK?" questioned Kirk as they started walking across the parking lot.

"Sure, ah, they just wanted to be remembered by my folks," answered Sharon, and then she spun around unfastening the wrap around skirt and flinging it in the air as she hummed the stripping song!

"Smut," called Kirk as he caught skirt, "an act of clear smut!"

"And you're in for a lifetime of it. Lead me to smutland!" exclaimed Sharon as she spun around and threw her arms around Kirk's neck and kissed him. "I'm glad you love me, it makes life so grand!"

"I love you, I love you, I love you. Now don't bother me for three minutes while I get your smashed little body into the car," answered Kirk.

"I'm drunk on love," yelled Sharon as they neared the car, "and also a little smashed on champagne and wine," she said quietly as Kirk held the door and Sharon climbed into the station wagon. "Are you going to take advantage of me," she said as Kirk closed the door and walked around to the other side, unlocked the door and got in.

"I would have," answered Kirk with a slight smile and twinkle in his devilish eyes, "except you didn't have the presence to open my door as you usually do, that means you're too smashed and wouldn't be a challenge."

"Give me another chance, let's re-enact the last five minutes, I'll do better next time. This was just a rehearsal," explained Sharon.

"Just one take is all you get tonight," answered Kirk as he started the car, backed out of the parking space and headed onto Route #l. "Now put your shapely legs up on the seat so I can cover them with the skirt. Rest your heavy head on my shoulder and pass out until I get you home," continued Kirk as he drove.

"You somehow manage to say the nicest things," said a sleepy voiced Sharon, "will you tuck me into bed when you get me home?" she added.

"Perhaps you're not as shot out of the saddle as we all once thought," answered Kirk as they left the Laurel area and continued heading north on Route #1. Sharon didn't answer but moved slightly as she snuggled closer to Kirk and rested her head on his shoulder. He simply put his arm around her as they drove on, thinking to himself how wonderful things were at this point in his life. He was a senior at a major university, attending college on a scholarship, playing the game he loved so much and now, reaching the zenith in having such a wonderful girl to love. Even through the tough, early days of his childhood, he felt blessed, his future on track. Kirk looked over at the sleeping Sharon and smiled.

It wasn't too long before Kirk pulled up in front of Sharon's apartment. It was just past ten o'clock as Sharon stirred with the car coming to a halt. Kirk shut off the engine. He gave a squeeze to her shoulder as he started to take his arm from around her.

"Not so fast Star," stated Sharon and she held onto his arm, "I'm not ready to go in yet," and she started to move closer to Kirk, "The time I was asleep doesn't count, you know, remember, you were one of the pourers!"

"I refuse to have the blame delegated to me," stated Kirk in a firm, but kidding voice and he continued after a slight pause, "However, I would stay and tuck you in and work on taking advantage of you, except I've got an early practice tomorrow morning my dear!"

"I know, I should have stayed more sober and driven you home, you've got another hour of driving," answered Sharon as she quickly kissed Kirk and opened her car door to get out. "Don't walk me up. I'll see you tomorrow."

"I'll drive up after practice and pick you up," said Kirk before Sharon closed the door.

"No, I'll get a ride, don't worry about it but arrange a pass this time," she kidded and she closed the door and headed toward the apartment.

Kirk waited for a moment or two, to be certain that Sharon was inside, then he started the car and was off to College Park.

The drive back was, as they say, uneventful. Kirk was a bit sleepy and kept the car radio on more loudly than usual to help keep awake. He listened to a Country station. It's not that a guy from Camden usually tuned in to Country. Between the previous years spent at the U. of M. and his most recent tenure at the Elk State Park he had, shall we say, acquired a taste for the folk guitar and the music that went along with it. Passing cars though, would not have been impressed as Kirk sang along with the radio and improvised on the Hank Williams Classic, *Long Gone Lonesome Blues*, as he turned the commercials down and warbled his way through. Hank, though, would probably have appreciated the effort Kirk tried to put forth.

It was nearly eleven thirty when Kirk parked the station wagon near his jeep and walked to his dorm. As he got to his room, he could hear the phone ringing and quickly opened the door, raced to the phone and gave a rushed, "hello!"

"I just wanted to be certain you arrived home in one piece and to tell you I love you and to get straight to bed," Sharon said in a familiar voice.

"Thanks for calling, but I do need to go down the hall and relieve myself of some champagne, wine and stuff," answered a kidding Kirk.

"Oh, I really do not think that we need a detailed plan of your life during the next few minutes, my dear, just do your thing and GO TO SLEEP!!" answered Sharon, "now, say you love me and hang up!"

"I love you, bye," Kirk replied and he hung up the phone and headed out of his room and down the hall!

Just before seven o'clock the next morning Kirk was startled awake by the phone. "Oh my," came his first words as he picked up the phone, "can you hear me through the cotton in my mouth, hello," he continued as the alarm went off and he laid the phone down to shut if off.

"I'm back, good morning whoever you are, I'm going to kill you!"

"My, what a cheerful person you are this morning," came Sharon's voice.

"You, I'll just damage a little, if I kill you, you'd only get even with me," replied Kirk, "let's see, thanks for making sure I'm awake. I love you and bye!"

"I love you, too, now go straight to the potty," said Sharon, as she hung up.

Kirk had to smile as he also hung up. Stretched as he sat on the edge of the bed, got up, reached for his shaving kit, towel and soap, then again, made the trip down the hall.

Some of the other members of the football team were already in the showers and others, like Kirk were just half-awake and staggering in. Not much was said as the fellows came in and out of the shower room. The conversation would take place in a little while over breakfast.

Kirk, Tony, Bill and Jack left the dorm at about the same time and walked over to the cafeteria together. Tony was the most curious and asked for a blow by blow description of the previous evening.

"You mean they picked up the tab for entire meal, everything?" questioned Tony after Kirk detailed how well he and Sharon were treated.

"That's about it," came Kirk's reply and as they walked a few feet further, he continued, "they really think a lot of Sharon and her folks."

"Yeah, Tony," stated Jack, "you've got to be second generation customers to be treated like that. And you've always been a slob when you've gone there so you don't stand a chance of a free on the house meal!"

Tony didn't say anything for a moment, then he lit up with a bright smile and said, "Well, my kid will be second generation!"

"That's a very bright, meaningful and quite correct statement," kidded Bill, who was first at the cafeteria door. With the long sweeping arm movement of a doorman, Bill ushered the others in. "Of course, we all hope they're still in business a quarter century from now, for your sake that is," and he followed the chuckling guys. Well, Tony didn't think it was as funny as the others were.

It almost seemed that as each group of players hit the cafeteria line, all of the food disappeared. Some of the guys couldn't get everything on one tray, so they pushed two along. This was not an everyday occurrence, because when there was a tough field practice, the guys ate lighter, however, this morning was a classroom meeting and the playbook would be the center of attraction. The real work would begin after a light lunch.

In the meantime, Sharon was cooking breakfast for Helen, Joanne and herself at the apartment. It was a typical girls nest with a routine having been worked out for bathroom time, however, one functional decoration, shall we say, was strategically located mirrors so that the girls could do their hair at any time. This was Sharon's mother, Dora's idea. Even to the point of having mirrors on opposite walls in the hallway and in the bathroom so that the girls could see the back of their head when they combed it out. Dora had used this very system years ago and it helped keep peace between roomies!

At breakfast the girls chatted, but mostly listened about last night's dinner with Kirk at Tag's Restaurant. Sharon talked about it in a matter-of-fact way. It's not that she didn't brag a little, but these girls were close friends. She didn't want them to think that she was putting them down for not having parents like hers or a fiancée like Kirk, who usually got a little better service than someone who just walked into Tags off the street.

After breakfast Joanne and Sharon were going to ride down to College Park. Sharon would be practice teaching in that area and she wanted to check out some apartments for herself and, of course, after Thanksgiving, new husband, Kirk.

During the last cup of coffee, the girls browsed through the Washington papers, searching the want ads for apartments. The conclusion was that this was almost a hopeless task because the available apartments in the College Park Area seemed quite expensive.

"I don't know if the trip will be worth it?" questioned Sharon, almost to herself, but out loud enough to solicit an opinion from Joanne and Helen.

"It won't hurt to look," answered Joanne as she put her cup down and got up to put two more pieces of bread in the toaster. She noticed the look from Helen and Sharon as she put the toaster button down. "I'm still hungry, I'll eat it dry, with just a little strawberry preserves."

"I thought you were watching your weight. Remember the diet plan we all talked about," replied Helen.

"These aren't the crumb buns Sharon always brings home, you know," answered Joanne. "If the crumb buns were here we'd all be stuffing ourselves."

"Can someone help me with my problem," said Sharon, "to change the subject."

"Of course we can. And what is your problem dear," answered Helen in a motherly tone. She put her hand on her chin as if she were really paying attention, then her eyes got big and she continued, "I do have the solution to your little problem," and she paused to take a sip of coffee, "it's really simple, just have Kirk and his clan help. The U. of M. must have a bulletin board or something with rooms, apartments, etc., right?"

"You may have something there," reasoned Sharon "us poor little ole girls from the sticks don't think as fast as you city girls."

"Then it's settled," said Joanne as she took the toast out of the toaster and went to the refrigerator to get the strawberry preserves. "We can all go shopping, have a light salad for lunch and drop the problem in Kirk's lap his afternoon when we all meet him and the guys!"

"Silly as it sounds, it is a good idea," answered Sharon.

"You two go, Rick and I have some things to do," stated Helen, "Maybe we can catch up with you this evening, in College Park or Washington."

"I'll check with Kirk to see if he's free tonight and call you," answered Sharon who continued after a pause, "He wasn't too clear about it last night."

"Maybe it was you that wasn't clear, Miss Wino," kidded Joanne.

"Oh that's very nice," answered Sharon, "but I think you're right!"

"Let's change and get going," said Joanne as she cleared the table. The stores don't open at the mall until ten, besides, I want to shower and wash my hair," came Sharon's remark as she got up to help.

"Washing your hair takes forever," answered Joanne. "The stores'll be closed by the time you finish drying that long mane, just pull it back."

"Do you hear this," asked Sharon looking directly at Helen, then turning to Joanne, "did you hear your voice. What a terrible thing to say to a friend."

"Cut the hearts and flowers, get your shower, and I'll help Joanne with the dishes and straighten up around here," Helen remarked.

"I will hurry, Joanne dear," Sharon replied in Betty Davis style, and she was off down the hall.

In less than an hour Sharon came bouncing out of her room, dressed in a yellow summer dress and wearing sandals. Looking strikingly beautiful with her long dark auburn hair flowing over her shoulders, as if she just stepped out of a magazine ad. "That's got to be close to record time," she shouted.

"For you, a record," responded Helen in dry humor tones.

Just as Joanne was putting on a pair of tennis shoes, there came a knock at the door. "Can someone get the door?" asked Joanne.

"I can't find my pocketbook," said Sharon, she had gone back to her bedroom for the great pocketbook hunt.

"I'm in the bathroom," Helen's voice came through the door. The knock came a second time, louder, this time.

"I'm coming, but I've only got one shoe on," yelled Joanne as she came down the steps and opened the door.

"You've probably got a good reason for answering the door while wearing one shoe and carrying the other, Miss and or Mrs. But let me tell you, little lady, I'm a member of the Maryland, yes that's right, State of Maryland Government, and we know Kirk Daniels' fiancée, a one Sharon Miles resides here. And we want to see her. I do mean, now," came the intense speech from C.J.

"I should slam the door right in your face," answered Joanne, who paused for a second. Satisfied that her answer came out OK, continued, "First of all, what's a Miss and or Mrs. Second don't try to push me around with that State of Maryland Government stuff because I'm from the Commonwealth of Pennsylvania and the Roxboro section of the City of Philadelphia, get it Philadelphia. And third, Sharon Miles is a friend of mine and not 'a one Sharon Miles'. And fourth, you're not a 'we' want to see her, but a 'you' want to see her, so now what words of toughness have you got left in your verbal arsenal, huh?"

"You know I could take you in two out of three falls," answered C.J., remembering what Kirk had once said, as he tried to look tough.

"Who's there," Sharon called from upstairs.

"Some government guy that I'm going to bounce out of here," answered Joanne.

"If that voice from above belongs to Sharon Miles then get down here lassie, or I'm in trouble with your shapely friend here," called C.J.

"That's the first nice thing you've said" answered Joanne before Sharon could reply.

"God that's a familiar sound," called Sharon as she started down the steps and then spotting C.J., ran down the steps and gave him a big bear hug.

"This is a strange way of greeting a 'G-man', Sharon. Are you trying to score points to save Kirk's neck?" commented Joanne as she started back upstairs.'

"Joanne, meet your date for this evening. Say hello to C.J.," answered Sharon as she and C.J. followed Joanne up the steps.

"It's a good thing you made that shapely comment, buster," said Joanne over her shoulder as she reached the top step, "or else you could be dead meat."

"Buster!...Buster!" exclaimed C.J. as he reached the top step, then motioned to Sharon, "climbing steps keeps you in shape, couldn't find a ground floor apartment?"

"Second floor apartments are better for girls," came Sharon's answer as she guided C.J, into their living room, then winking at Joanne, "It's nice to see you two getting along so well this early in your relationship."

"We're getting along just fine," answered Joanne as C.J. started to speak, "He challenged me to best two out of three falls" she paused and looked straight into C.J.'s eyes "Right? Going to beat up on a poor little helpless girl?"

"Well, I didn't mean," started C.J., who brightened up, "OK, best four out of seven. I'm a fair man!"

Joanne just looked at C.J., but had to break into a smile.

"One thing you should know," Sharon said to C.J., "Joanne knows karate quite well."

"What does quite well mean?" said C.J. as he got up from the sofa. "Where are we going, I just got here," he continued as he followed Joanne and Sharon back downstairs.

"Are we going to the front lawn for a match. I was only kidding. Does Joanne really know karate, Sharon?" asked C.J.

"She's so good, we don't need a watchdog," said Sharon matter-of-factly.

"Oh that's very nice. Thank you for that resume comment," stated Joanne.

As they came outside and onto the front porch, C.J. said, "I won't be as easy as you think, lady. Kirk toughened me up this summer. I plan on living the day out."

"Since you're supposed to be my companion for this evening, which means you carry cash or credit cards and are purchasing groceries at this evenings restaurant, today you live," answered Joanne, who turned to Sharon "my car or his?"

"That's a great idea," stated Sharon, "C.J., you drive and Joanne will come home with me."

"I am a bit confused. Help me out, ole pal," said C.J.

"Kirk has the wagon. I'll bring it back here tonight with Joanne. For now, we're going to stop off at the mall in Laurel, shop, let you buy lunch, and then we'll let you continue chauffeuring us to see Kirk, after which, we can all enjoy a ride into Washington for dinner, if he's not too tired," came Sharon's reply.

"From the sound of all this I neatly round out your plans," quipped C.J.

"You're right, but we are pleased you're here. We all love you," remarked Sharon.

"Let's not get sickening," stated Joanne as they reached the sidewalk, "which car is yours, the Mercedes," and she laughed.

"Yes, I'm driving the Mercedes, little lady," answered C.J. and he produced the key.

Joanne, not to sound too taken back at this particular second, caught herself and said, "Why the red bumps on the key?"

"This key is for the alarm system as well as the door," and C.J. opened the door.

"I'll get in the back and let you two continue this stimulating conversation," stated Sharon as she opened the door and climbed in.

C.J. held the door for Joanne and went around and got into the driver's seat. As he put the key in the ignition he said, "As I said, I'm driving the Mercedes, it's my fathers car. I've got a Toyota 4x4 pick-up with a cap, not the best vehicle for hauling a crowd of more than one, so we switched for the day."

"Either way I can see that you're a man of class, especially with me sitting next to you, and of course, what's her name in the back," quipped Joanne.

"Oh lucky me," kidded C.J. as he headed south on route #1.

"How many days are you off," said Sharon to C.J., "just today?"

"And tomorrow," answered C.J. "I figure that ole Star, as you call him, can find some place for me to bunk in for the night, unless, of course I get a better offer" C.J. paused, recognized the silence and restated a little louder, " unless I get a better offer!"

"We heard you the first time," Joanne replied as Sharon smiled, but kept silent, "we were just ignoring you."

"I see," answered C.J. "You've cut my options to one."

"You never had more than one," remarked Joanne, "that's a red light."

"Of course the light is red, that's why I'm slowing down," stated C.J., "and may I say that your last remark was rude, cruel and quite frankly, one that you'll regret ever saying. I feel hurt, saddened."

"Are you making an attempt at delegating guilt, not that I mind, but you should know that I no longer accept guilt," repeated Joanne.

"This has been very entertaining, gang, but we're here and all good things must come to an end, C.J. dear, please pull into the Laurel Mall and remember when the time comes to pick up the luncheon check, the black widow lady rode in the front," remarked Sharon.

"Of course, on the other hand" stated Joanne, but C.J. interrupted her.

"Everyone can relax. I've decided that today should be a non-battle day. I'm happy. I'm seeing my two best friends and I've met a very interesting, lovely young lady," stated C.J. as he brought the car to a halt in a parking apace. "I'll spring for grilled cheese sandwiches all around," he shouted as he got out of the car, and laughed,

"With white wine I hope," was Joanne's reply.

Everyone had a good laugh as they strolled from the parking lot to the indoor Mall.

"Isn't this the mall that George Wallace was shot in, when he was running for president a few years back?" questioned C.J. as he looked around.

"No, he was shot in the Plaza Mall in the center of town," answered Sharon.

"Where do you want to eat lunch?" asked Joanne.

"How about Friendly's," answered Sharon who turned to C.J., "what do you think?"

"Fine with me, they have great ice cream," was C.J.'s reply.

They walked over toward the Friendly's Restaurant, the girls stopping along the way to window shop and after a few minutes they were seated in a booth, with Sharon and Joanne sitting across from C.J.

As the waitress handed them menus, Sharon said to C.J., "one of the things we thought about doing was looking for an apartment, but we don't know the area well enough, got any ideas?"

"Give me a minute. You mean for you and Kirk?" questioned C.J.

"Yes, but I might move in earlier. I'll be practice teaching in the College Park area beginning in October," replied Sharon.

"Well, maybe I do have an idea," said C.J. as he thought out loud, "let's give our order first."

"Why don't you order for everyone C.J., my dear, since you're financing lunch," said Joanne in a lovingly kidding voice.

"Let's see, Friendly's," started C.J. without looking at the menu, "We'll start with corn chowder all around, cups of course and those cheeseburgers served on toast, with French fries and a milk shake for me, a vanilla Frappe, you call it. Girls, Frappes or iced tea?"

"Iced tea," Sharon answered and Joanne nodded her head 'yes', as the waitress looked her way. "This sounds like one of those, through the lips and straight to the hips meals, C.J.," continued Sharon.

"Don't worry about it," replied C.J. "We'll walk it off, besides the corn chowder here is great, and not heavy. Since you're having iced tea, you'll need an ice cream cone for dessert. I can go along with that."

In just a couple of minutes, the waitress was back with the soup. She also put several packs of crackers in the middle of the table and was off again.

"Not bad," stated Joanne as she tasted the soup, "I've never had corn chowder before. In fact it's good!"

After taking a couple of spoonfuls of soup, C.J. stopped for a second, reached forward, opened a pack of crackers and said, "I do have an idea."

"Really," came Joanne's quick reply, "I can't wait to hear this."

"Don't underestimate C.J.," stated Sharon, "give him a problem and he's like Sherlock Holmes and Dr. Watson rolled up in one."

Just as C.J. started to speak, the cheeseburgers and French fries arrived. The waitress was also back in a flash with the beverages. Before C.J. could pick up his Frappe filled glass, Sharon had it and took a drink through the straw. She gave C.J. the high sign and he smiled.

"Well, what's the great idea?" questioned Joanne before she took a bite of her cheeseburger.

"I can't tell you, but I'll take you there and show you," was C.J.'s reply as he munched on his French fries, "you'll have to see it to really appreciate it. Trust me," and he went about happily enjoying his lunch. The girls, especially Joanne eyed C.J., with his "trust me" statement, however Sharon had known C.J. for years and knew that something was brewing and he'd spring his plan at the proper time, so she just continued enjoying lunch and motioned to a skeptical Joanne to do the same.

After lunch, they stopped at the counter and got the ice cream cones that C.J. had promised and took a walk in the mall. The girls stopped along the way looking at various stores and after finishing the ice cream cones, went into some of the stores to so some shopping. C.J. told the girls that he was going to walk over to the pet store and to meet him in that area when they were finished. Then they went their separate ways. No sooner had the girls moved out of sight C.J. headed for a phone. He made a call to finalize his plan for Kirk and Sharon. "This is going to take longer than I have change for," he remarked to the listener, "call me back at this number," and C.J. gave the pay phone number to the party on the other end.

The phone rang and C.J. quickly picked it up. The conversation did take quite a while, as negotiations took place. "I can't promise that they'll like it," C.J. stated at one point. He was reminded by the caller that the so-called deal, which was just hammered out, was the best bargain in the entire Washington DC area. He was reminded by the caller not to bring other friends his way, because he couldn't afford dealing with C.J., who closed the call with, "thanks Uncle Frank, I owe you one." He hung up and walked to the pet store. C.J. had spent about 15 minutes in the pet store and was playing with an Airedale puppy in a closed pen area when Sharon and Joanne wandered in. He spotted them, picked up the puppy and handed her back to the attendant. Sharon and Joanne petted the Airedale for a second or two before the puppy was placed back in his cage.

"That little girl won't last long, she's bright as a new silver dollar," stated C.J. to the attendant as he came out of the cage area, a barking Airedale wanting back.

"Especially since she's an Airedale," came the attendants reply, "we don't get many of those."

"Are you girls finished?" asked C.J. as they left the pet store and started walking in the mall. "If so, then let's be on our way to College Park."

"We are through for the day and here, fill those empty arms," was Sharon's reply as she handed C.J. some packages to carry. They walked out of the mall and over to the car, where C.J. put all of the packages into the trunk. It wasn't too long before they were off and headed south again, on Route #1 toward the Washington area.

In a few minutes they passed the University of Maryland campus. C.J. slowed the car and started to turn into the Cherry Hill Mobile Home Park, Sharon and Joanne looked at each other, but didn't say anything. C.J. drove to the office, parked, and everyone got out of the car and walked toward the office. The door opened and a man of medium height and weight came out, perhaps in his early sixties and wearing a U of M baseball cap.

"Hi Uncle Frank," called C.J. as they approached him, "say hello to Sharon and Joanne. Sharon's the potential customer. Joanne, well you know."

At this Joanne punched C.J. in the arm, "the 'you know', huh," she stated.

"Hello girls," answered Uncle Frank. "Let me show you around and I'll tell you all about C.J.'s scam...plan, yes his plan," and he smiled.

"You may be a dead man before this day's at an end," said Sharon quietly to C.J. "dead meat, if you know what I mean!"

" Or more likely a hero, and I will accept a grateful apology," answered C.J. "I told you to trust me, right?"

"Well, let's see," stated Uncle Frank as he surveyed the mobile home park, "as you can see, this is a convenient place to live, has a pool, clubhouse, washers and dryers, a nice quiet place to call home. Now, let's go look at what C.J. made me cook up for you," and he motioned for everyone to follow. They walked a short distance and stopped at one of the large Mobile Homes. "This is a twelve foot wide and fifty foot long unit," stated Uncle Frank as he reached in his pocket for a ring of keys and finally found the one he was looking for. "It has about everything you'd ever need and is a two bedroom model. Just look it over and tell me what you think. I'll keep quiet." As they walked up onto the small porch, Uncle Frank unlocked the door and stepped back to let Sharon, Joanne, and C.J. enter first.

"It's beautiful," stated Sharon as she surveyed the living room, which was located to her right, at the front and then took a few steps to her left and went into the kitchen area. "There's even a dining room table back by the kitchen," she continued and motioned to Joanne to look back there.

"Wow, the place looks like a small palace," remarked Joanne.

"Take a look in the back. There's two bedrooms and this place even has one and a half baths," stated Uncle Frank. "It is, you might say, a pretty complete two bedroom apartment," continued Uncle Frank, after a pause.

"Well, what do you think, is this a stroke of genius?" asked C.J.

"That all depends, Mr. Semi-genius," answered Sharon, who continued after again gazing around the mobile home, "who could afford a place like this?"

"Sharon, please when you asked me for some ideas on an apartment, you never mentioned price." stated C.J., who then turned to Uncle Frank and asked, "Did I mention a specific price to you on the phone?"

"Let's all go back into the living room and sit down and relax. I need to relax when a family member is taking advantage of me. It helps the bitter pill go down easier. You know, Sharon, most people really believe that I'm in business for a profit, not C.J., of course, but most people," answered Uncle Frank, as he lead the way back to the living room and sat down in an overstuffed chair.

Sharon, Joanne, and C.J. followed. Joanne and Sharon sat down on the sofa, while C.J. dropped into the other chair, which was a rocker recliner. Joanne at this point figured it was best to keep quiet, so she just sat back and said nothing. C.J. was also quiet at this point.

"Uncle Frank, can I call you Uncle Frank," stated Sharon, who paused for a moment, while trying to formulate her next sentence.

"It's OK," answered Uncle Frank, "I know you're trying to make me feel better, but you don't have to, it'll be OK."

"You should be on the stage, Uncle Frank," said C.J. quietly.

"That's not nice to say," interrupted Sharon.

"They've got to pay the heat and electric bill, C.J. I don't include that as part of the bargain. They want heat, they want electric, and they are the ones who pay. Your mother's sister is my sister, but these kids must pay, that much agreed, agreed," stated Uncle Frank.

"That sounds fair," answered C.J., who paused for a moment, then continued, "they can move in on the first of November and they'll move out by the end of June."

"Can I interrupt to find out what the last few minutes was all about," questioned Sharon.

"Of course," answered C.J. "You can have this trailer from the first of November through the end of June, while Aunt Mildred is in Florida. The rent is free. Uncle Frank owns this thing, but you have to pay utilities and you must provide me with sleeping quarters when I visit you and or Miss Sharpie here. Of course, unless I get lucky and stay at her place." Joanne didn't offer a comment, although she'd like to, but figured she'd save it for later when they were alone, instead she just smiled at Sharon and shook her head.

"I don't know what to say," stated Sharon "this is a dream come true!"

"For openers, you can take the word of the semi-genius, thank me for having an Uncle Frank, and see to it that he gets into a football game at the reasonable price of no charge," responded C.J.

"For now, Uncle Frank, thank you," said Sharon and she got up and kissed him.

"If you want to show the young man, Mildred will be home later this afternoon. We don't let her drive at night. We make her do all the shopping and driving during the daylight. It helps keep the area inhabited. Bring a bottle of something. She likes that Bailey's for those nippy nights," remarked Uncle Frank.

"We'll be back this afternoon, after Kirk's finished with football practice," came Sharon's reply, as they all filed out of the mobile home. "Thanks so much Uncle Frank," said Sharon again as they reached the bottom step and patio. "This is too good to be true!"

"It's my pleasure, it's his pleasure," kidded Uncle Frank as he playfully punched C.J. on the arm.

They all walked back toward the office and said goodbye. C.J., Joanne, and Sharon got into the car and started back out of the Mobile Home Park. It was a short drive to the University of Maryland Campus and not much was said. Sharon sat in the back seat and just thought of what had happened. She smiled to herself and couldn't wait to tell Kirk. C.J. drove over to the football field; however, practice was over, so he just found a parking space near the locker room so that they could spot Kirk.

"Do you always work deals like that?" questioned Joanne, as they got out of the car and started walking toward the locker room door.

"Always," answered Sharon, before C.J. could even muster a thought, "ask Kirk about how C.J. got him a fairly new Jeep at cost, after I totaled his VW. See C.J. doesn't understand full list. I don't think he even understands a deal unless he's engineered it!"

C.J. didn't respond. He figured Sharon spotlighted him enough. After all, C.J. was somewhat modest, well, he felt as if he was somewhat modest!

"What college did you attend?" questioned Joanne, as she looked C.J. straight in the eye. Harvard Business or Wharton School at Penn?"

"Actually, the University of Delaware for a while," responded C.J., who pondered for a moment and said low and rapidly, "Before they threw me out!"

"Threw you out? Flunked out? You seem too bright for that," said Joanne, matter-of-factly. There must be a story behind this."

"Well yes," started C.J. slowly, "No, I didn't flunk, I was bounced out, so to speak and there is a story behind it, some other time, OK."

Joanne nodded "yes", but before she could say anything C.J. opened the outside locker room door and walked in. Joanne looked at Sharon.

"He'll tell you, no big deal. He's a great guy," offered Sharon.

In the meantime C.J. found his way down the hall and opened the actual locker room door and went in. "Press, *The Times*, you know. Where is a one Kirk Daniels, young man," he said to the first player he saw.

"Over there with the Trainer," came the reply as he pointed to Kirk. C.J. walked over to where Kirk was sitting on the training table talking to the team doctor and the trainer. They were examining his left knee.

"Don't worry kid, it's a long way from your heart," said C.J. as he approached the table and gave Kirk a gentle slap on the back.

Kirk looked up, stuck out his hand for C.J. and said, "Just needs a band aid,"

"Yeah, we know," interrupted Sandy Klein, the trainer, "it's only pain! What tolerance."

"Gentleman, say hello to my brother, goes by C.J.," stated Kirk, "C.J., you're shaking hands with Sandy Klein and Doctor Warwick."

"Pleased to meet you C.J., we didn't know Kirk had family," stated Sandy.

"Became my brother this summer. Isn't it great when you can choose your relatives," continued Kirk as he winked at a wide smiling C.J.

"Yes it is," replied Doctor Warwick who shook hands with C.J. and continued, "You must be a special young man." Then looking back at Kirk he said, "You've got, at least, until tomorrow, off. We'll see about the balance of the week."

Kirk made a face at the announcement, not pleased at all with missing practice, but he, of course, understood. The season opener was three weeks off and it was important to be healthy for that game. "I can still use the gym though, with the weights," stated Kirk.

"Just as long as the knee stays out of the gym. The rest of you can work out. Let's be noticeably healthy, OK," answered the Doctor.

"I understand," Kirk replied as the doctor walked away.

"It's no big deal now," said Sandy, "He wants to keep it that way."

"You've got little or big problems?" questioned C.J. as Kirk got off the table and walked over to his locker.

"It's no big deal and they're right, but we've got a hell of a team this year and I don't want the others to think I'm doggin it," replied Kirk.

"No chance," Tony's voice came from his locker, a short distance away. "He's one of the hardest workers in camp, next to me, of course," continued Tony as he spoke to C.J. and stuck out his hand as he walked over. You must be Kirk's friend Jeep. Glad to know you man!"

"It's C.J.," corrected Kirk.

"Same thing," reasoned Tony who turned to the rest of the players and in his normal booming voice continued, "This here's Kirk's buddy Jeep, be nice to him. Daniels says he knows cars and women!"

Bill was the first to come over and shake hands with C.J., "nice to meet you, Jeep" and after a pause he continued, "the name, from the Army?"

"Not exactly," said C.J. as he looked at a smiling Kirk, "It's a recently acquired handle. It's nice to meet you, Bill."

"You won't get used to Tony, his mother broke the mold, we think, over his head! He's a great guy. Give you anything he's got except the shirt off his back," kidded Kirk, who thought for a second "unless it needs washing."

"That's very nice," commented Tony

"Is it true?" questioned Kirk, "Am I lying?"

"No," replied Tony, who thought and continued "still though..."

"I'm heading for the shower, be done in fifteen," said Kirk to C.J.

"I'll head outside and tell the girls," C.J. replied.

"Tell the girls as in more than Sharon," questioned Tony as Kirk was walking into the shower and C.J. was leaving.

"Peggy won't be on the Towson campus for another week and a half," said Kirk as he adjusted the shower water.

"What Peggy, who's Peggy," yelled Tony as he followed Kirk into the shower.

"You're going to get wet," said Kirk, as some of the water splashed Tony.

"Who cares about wet. Who is Peggy?" questioned Tony again.

"Apparently she's, as Sharon put it, someone Mother will approve of. Sharon, for some reason, probably pity for you, phoned a girl friend of hers and asked her if she'd like to have a date with some big time football star. Could she possible mean you?" Kirk replied.

"That's me," beamed Tony, "that Sharon's a winner. I had faith in her, you know!"

"I know," answered Kirk, "now let me get my shower in peace."

"No problem, I'll just talk to Sharon until you come outside," responded Tony.

With that Tony looked down at his wet tennis shoes and squashed out of the shower, picked up his gear and headed for the door. Kirk just smiled and continued on with his shower, a little more rapidly now, because of the time he had wasted talking with C.J. and Tony.

As Kirk was toweling off and then getting dressed, C.J. reappeared.

"Tony is talking to Sharon about someone named Peggy, so I thought I'd wander back in. We're going to Washington for dinner, my treat, at Hogates down on Maine. It's a fun place," said C.J., who thought for a second and continued, "you can walk all right?" he questioned.

"Yeah, I just can't tackle anyone for a couple of days," laughed Kirk.

"We just have to make one stop at the Cherry Hill Mobile Home Park to see my Aunt Mildred. I don't know if Uncle Frank will be there or not. They're brother and sister you know. Sharon and a little later, you and Sharon will be sort of house sitting Aunt Mildred's place while she's in Florida for the winter. You see Uncle Frank is insisting that you pay the heat and electric, but I know he keeps some lights on while she's away and he has to keep the heat on, so that the pipes don't freeze. You know, you're actually doing him a favor by keeping an eye on the place," rambled C.J. as Kirk continued getting dressed, "I'll work it out."

"Did I miss something," questioned Kirk, "I feel as if I've tuned into the second segment of a mini-series on TV. Bring me up to speed."

"Sharon will give you the details. But quickly, she asked me to help her find a place near here for practice teaching and for the two of you. I sort of worked things out with my Uncle. He owns the place," answered C.J.

"Well," said Kirk as he took a look around, "let's go see Aunt Mildred!" Kirk and C.J. left the locker room and met Sharon and Joanne.

"We were just talking about my meeting Peggy," stated a smiling Tony.

"Peggy, one of the girls from the stable," kidded Kirk.

"That's no way to describe Sharon's hand picked lady that my mother's going to approve of, Daniels," said Tony defensively, "right Sharon?"

"Right," answered Sharon, "I'm trying to teach class to Tony, but it'll be tough!"

"Enough said, let's go see Aunt Mildred," responded Kirk, "and, my dear," Kirk continued as he pulled Sharon along, "detail me on what you and ole C.J. have done about living quarters. See ya later Tony," and they walked to the car, following C.J. and Joanne.

"There's not much to tell. You see I asked C.J. if he knew anyone who could help us find a place. And you know C.J., he was on the phone in a second and the next thing I knew, he's negotiating with his Uncle Frank and we've got a palace on wheels, so to speak. It doesn't move though," answered Sharon, "you're not angry are you," she questioned, thinking he might be upset by not being consulted.

"You must be joking. Of course I'm not angry. If C.J. has set something up, it's been done all right," answered Kirk and he stopped Sharon and put his arms around her, kissed her and continued, "Let's catch up with C.J. and Joanne," as he put his arm around her and they walked over to C.J.'s car.

"Everything OK?" questioned C.J. as he held the front door for Joanne. "You're not upset with me are you," he continued in a low voice.

"Pleased, grateful for your help, yes, angry, hell no," answered Kirk as he held the back door for Sharon and then climbed in. They left the campus and made the short trip to the Cherry Hill Mobile Home Park without saying much. C.J. concentrated on driving. Joanne relaxed next to him and Sharon nuzzled close to Kirk. They entered Cherry Hill Park and drove over to Aunt Mildred's home. Uncle Frank was just coming out.

"It's OK, I talked to the old lady and she agrees with the deal."

Then he headed for his office.

"Watch that old lady stuff, you're my oldest brother," yelled Aunt Mildred from the small porch by the front door.

"I'm also your youngest brother, your only brother," he answered,

"Uncle Frank, shake hands with Kirk Daniels," said C.J. to Frank, who stopped in his tracks and came back to meet Kirk.

"I'm sorry, excuse my manners," said Frank "It's nice to meet you Kirk."

"My pleasure," answered Kirk, "I know you're busy, we'll see you later."

"Come right in children," called Mildred, "I'll make tea."

They all filed into the mobile home and C.J. made the introductions. Aunt Mildred went about making tea and showed Sharon where the cups were as Kirk, C.J., and Joanne settled in the cozy living room.

"What do you think?" questioned C.J. to Kirk.

"It's incredible, beautiful," answered Kirk as he looked around.

"We'll give you the grand tour, after tea," responded Sharon as she placed the teacups on the coffee table and returned to the kitchen for the plate of cookies.

Mildred did the honors and poured tea for everyone and Sharon passed the cookies. There wasn't any conversation at this point as each person fixed the tea the way they wanted and gathered up a couple of cookies. Finally Mildred broke the silence, "Well, this is cozy. I didn't realize this living room could hold this many people. Are you all comfortable?"

"Yes," came the answer, almost in chorus as each responded.

"Good. Well I understand from Frank that you two are going to house sit for me while I'm in Florida," said Mildred.

"Not exactly," answered Sharon who paused a second, looked at Kirk who smiled and winked at her, "I'll move in first, while I practice teach in the area and Kirk will join me in late November, after we're married."

"I see, well, whatever you young folks do is fine with me," answered Mildred.

"Everything is worked out with Uncle Frank. Kirk and Sharon will take good care of the place for you," said C.J. in a reassuring voice.

"I'm certain they'll take care of the place," responded Mildred firmly, you can see that the moment you meet them" and after a thoughtful pause she continued, "and you didn't take care of one important detail with negotiations young man," said Mildred in an almost scolding manner.

"What's that, Aunt Mildred," responded C.J. as the others sat in silence and listened, while sipping their tea.

"The heat and light bills, Claude," answered Aunt Mildred.

"Claude," said Joanne out loud, then caught herself and quickly took a bite of cookie, but looked back at C.J. with a smile, even though he had an exasperated look on his face.

"Don't worry, I told your Uncle Frank that he had to keep the heat on anyway, same thing with the electricity, the cheapskate. You know, I'm half owner in this glorified trailer camp, so my vote counts around here, anyway, forget those bills, he'll pay," stated Aunt Mildred.

"Thank you Aunt Mildred," responded Sharon right away.

Kirk joined in with his thanks a few seconds later, after he washed down his bite of chocolate chip cookie with some tea.

"That's super of you Aunt Mildred," stated C.J. who did not realize that she was half owner in the Park. He didn't bother to tell her that he was going to do battle with Uncle Frank on the heat and electricity bills, figuring that she should enjoy the spotlight for this nice gesture. After tea, Aunt Mildred told Sharon to show Kirk the rest of the home, the grand tour, so to speak, and of course he was impressed.

"We thank you for the hospitality, Aunt Mildred," said C.J. after Sharon finished the tour with Kirk, "we're going down to the Hogates Restaurant, in Washington for dinner. Do you know the place?"

"Of course I know Hogates, been at both the old place and the new location, down on the waterfront. In fact, I understand from my parents that I was also at their stand in Ocean City, New Jersey, many years ago, many years ago," answered Aunt Mildred.

"I didn't know they had a place in New Jersey. Kirk's family is from Camden, near Philadelphia," responded C.J.

"They had a place in Ocean City before World War II and moved here years ago," answered Aunt Mildred who continued as everyone got up to leave, "Have you children been to Hogates?"

"No," came the reply from Kirk, Sharon and Joanne.

"Well, you'll enjoy it, great food and a wonderful view of all those expensive yachts. Make certain you get a table by the window. Did you make reservations, Claude?" questioned Aunt Mildred.

"No, I thought," stated C.J., but Aunt Mildred interrupted.

"No matter, this time of the year, in fact most of the year, those popular D.C. restaurants are crowded. You run along and I'll phone Hogates for you," stated Mildred.

"Thanks, Aunt Mildred," responded C.J.

"Thanks, and we'll take good care of your home," said Sharon.

"I know you will. We'll see each other before I leave for Florida," Aunt Mildred replied as everyone went down the porch steps toward C.J.'s car. They left the Park and headed south on Route #1 for just a few hundred yards, then onto the I-495 beltway toward the Baltimore/Washington Parkway.

"We'll take the New York Avenue exit, then onto I-395. I'm pretty sure there's an exit for Maine. From there, we just wing it, cause I always get lost, but somehow stumble into the waterfront," stated C.J. as they made the exit off of I-495 onto the Baltimore/Washington parkway.

"With Joanne up there helping you navigate, how can we miss," stated Sharon.

"Of course," came Joanne's reply, "sometimes I can hardly find the bathroom!"

"What class," kidded Sharon, "maybe you and Kirk should change places."

"It's the truth," answered Joanne, "pull over C.J. and I'll change."

"No, that's OK," stated C.J. "I think we'll be all right, I think."

"There's a sign for New York Avenue," shouted Joanne, "how am I doin'?"

"A rocket scientist couldn't have done better," was Kirk's reply.

"That's very good," stated Sharon, "don't patronize my dear friend."

"I wouldn't think of it, just trying to be encouraging," answered Kirk,

"You're all doing a great job, for now," stated C.J., who continued, "the help is needed when we are on I-395 and I start looking for Maine Avenue."

"We know, that was only a test and the real navigation problem lies ahead. We'll be up for it. Just look at Joanne, at the ready," stated Sharon.

"Keep this up and I'll be forced to have a drink to calm my nerves," responded Joanne. "Let me know when to look for Maine."

"We're still on New York, it'll be a few minutes," said C.J. as he moved into the left lane and prepared to make the turn onto I-395.

"I see the sign for 395. So far this is easy," said Joanne.

"On that note, I'll take a few z's," said Kirk as he sat back in the seat.

As they drove on I-395, South, below the maze of government buildings, C.J. eased into the right lane, preparing to exit when he saw the sign for Maine Avenue. "OK, there's Maine and look over to the left, see those buildings, that's where we want to be."

"Just swing around and go in that direction, we're bound to get over there" stated Joanne matter-of-factly.

"That may be easier said than done. We've got to get on the other side of 395 first," answered C.J. as he tried to figure out a route.

"I'm certain you'll work it out," remarked Joanne who was silent for a moment then continued, "the worst that can happen is we get a little lost, drive around a little, then find the restaurant."

C.J. didn't answer, but as he approached 9th street, he looked to his right and thought that the street crossed 395. He turned right, as they crossed over 395. Kirk commented, "Looks like you knew what you were doing all the time, my friend."

"Well, I was close to knowing," answered C.J. as he made a right turn and drove in front of the waterside restaurants. "There's an underground parking lot near the restaurant," he continued in a low voice to himself.

"There's an entrance," said Joanne.

"No, it's right next to the restaurant," answered C.J. as he approached Hogates. "Ah, there it is," and he turned left and went down the entryway, stopping at a ticket machine and gate. C.J. hit the button. The power window opened and he reached for a ticket. As the machine released the ticket, the gate went up and C.J. proceeded slowly, making a left turn. Then he spied the door with *Hogates* written above. "We'll park over there near the door. Would you hold this ticket? We'll get it validated for the parking fee," said C.J. to Joanne and she took the ticket. C.J. parked the car and everyone got out and headed toward the Hogates door. They entered and climbed the one floor to the restaurant level.

"Wow, this looks great," said Kirk as he surveyed the scene. "Look at the seafood display," he continued as they all walked over to the large refrigerated case that displayed all the fresh seafood the restaurant was serving that evening.

"This place is beautiful," joined in Sharon. "It looks like fun."

"It is a fun place," said the man behind the counter. "The restaurant is straight ahead, so check in at the reception desk to check on your reservations, then over there, to your right, is the cocktail lounge. We have a great buffet for you to enjoy, while you're having an adult beverage."

"Thank you," said C.J. "I've been here before, but it's been a while. I'm C.J. this is Joanne, Sharon, and Kirk. I work up at Elk Neck State Park, a Forest Ranger," he continued.

"I'm Sam. Glad to know you folks. A state man, huh? I was a Fed for awhile, C.J., Army!" Everyone had a good laugh. C.J. left for a second and walked over to the reception desk, gave his name, told them that a reservation for four had been called in. Then reassured, he came back and joined the group at the display case. "Well, all is set. Aunt Mildred arranged for a table by the window overlooking the Marina and we can relax in the lounge for a while," stated C.J.

"Have a good time," said Sam, "stop before you leave."

"Thanks, Sam," said C.J. as they headed toward the lounge.

"There's a table by the window," said Kirk as he entered the lounge area and looked around. He walked over to the table and everyone followed. As they each took a seat, C.J. looked around for a waitress, but one was already on her way.

"Looking for me," she said cheerfully.

"That we are," said C.J. as everyone settled into their seats.

"What can I get you?" asked the waitress.

"Well, let's see," started C.J., "Joanne, Sharon, Kirk, you having a Bass Ale?" Kirk nodded, "I'll have a Bass Ale also," said C.J.

"Gin and Tonic for me," stated Sharon.

"The same for me," added Joanne.

"Two Bass' and two Gin and Tonics," said the waitress, who finished writing and then added, "please visit the buffet over there; it's loaded with goodies."

"Thank you, Kathy," answered C.J. as he got up to visit the buffet.

"Should someone wait behind to save the table?" Sharon asked solicitously.

"No problem, I'll take care of it," stated the waitress as she placed cocktail napkins.

"How'd you know her name was Kathy?" inquired Joanne as she and C.J. walked toward the buffet "You know her?"

"Only by the name on her badge," answered C.J.

"This looks good," said Kirk as he handed out plates all around.

There was plenty to choose from, three different types of cheese squares, chicken wings, Mexican something with Taco chips, nachos, some veggies, swedish meatballs and those little hot dogs. It was quite a nice spread of food for cocktail hour. Everyone returned to the table with a plate full of food. Kathy had already placed the drinks and Ale on the table, but waited for them to return to bring Kirk and C.J. frosted glasses for the Ale. She poured the Bass, checked if all was all right and departed.

"Nice touch," said Kirk as he picked up the frosted glass, "Cheers!"

"Cheers," returned C.J. as he also lifted the frosted glass of Ale.

"Some of those boats look like live-a-boards," said Sharon as she looked out the windows. That one looks like those barge homes, see it?"

"They live on a barge," questioned Joanne as she looked out the window. Trying to figure out which one was the barge.

"They're fixed up like a regular apartment," answered C.J. "A friend of my father has one up in New Jersey at a place called the Barge Club, or something like that. It's a restaurant with a Marina and the restaurant is on a turn-of-the-century work barge, quite a neat place to eat. But anyway, the Harbor Master lives on a beautiful barge. It's near New York on a river that flows into the Hudson, but in Jersey."

"With all the explanation, have a drink, tip that mug!" kidded Kirk.

"Cheers," said C.J. as he did take a sip of his Ale, paused for a second and continued, "by the way, the barge is the blue and white one on the third row, over there. See it?"

"The one without the pointy front, right?" answered Joanne.

"Is this girl bright," kidded C.J. and he winked at Joanne.

"This is quite an enjoyable spot," stated Kirk as he looked around the Marina. It looks so peaceful and inviting, with all the boats at rest.

"It does," responded Sharon. "Makes you wish one of the boats was yours."

"Someday," answered Kirk and he smiled at Sharon.

At that moment, the waitress stopped back to see if all was well or could she bring them another drink.

"I think we're OK, Kathy. We should head on into the dining room so they don't give our table away," was C.J.'s reply.

"In that case," said Kathy laughingly, "it's time to pay up," and she put the check on the table.

Kirk started to reach for it, but C.J. grabbed it up, "I'm the working man now," he said as he handed Kathy the check and money. "Your job is to keep Maryland's opponents from scoring touchdowns and to complete the education bit, so that you can buy me dinner!"

"Oh, do you play football at Maryland?" questioned Kathy, with a cute smile as she picked up the check and money from C.J.

"Oh, he does," joined in Sharon, "and he's taken but there are about fifty others that you can choose from."

"Sorry," stated Kathy a little embarrassed, "I didn't mean to..."

"That's OK, he is kind of cute," responded Sharon who thought for a moment and continued, "and I'm sort of protective."

"With good reason," answered Kathy and she left to get the change.

"They're talking about you like you were a piece of meat," challenged C.J.

"No," answered Sharon before Kirk could respond, "Like a hunk!"

"In that case, I'm not offended," stated Kirk sort of proudly, "Let's all head for the dining room while I relish the moment."

"If we weren't in such a public place, I'd kick you Kirk Daniels," stated Sharon.

"You build my ego up, then you want to tear it down. What's the fairness in that, m' lady? Maybe I should head back into the lounge," kidded Kirk as he put his arm around Sharon and gave her a kiss.

"One step toward the lounge and you're a dead man," returned Sharon, and she squeezed Kirk's hand, then held it tight.

"Hi, the C.J. party? Table for four by the window," said C.J. to the hostess as they entered the dining room.

"Yes, sir, right this way," was the answer and the hostess picked up four large menus and motioned for them to follow her. They arrived at a table by the window, again overlooking the Marina, but a few gangways down. It was just getting to be dusk and the lights of the Marina were coming on, like a Christmas garden scene. The Marina was taking a different view and feeling as darkness approached.

As they got settled, the waiter came over, placing water glasses, and seeing if they'd like another drink. But before anyone could answer, another waiter brought the famous Hogates cinnamon buns, hot and with an inviting aroma.

"Boy, do these smell good," said Sharon as she broke off one of the buns and placed it on her bread plate. Kirk handed Sharon the butter dish.

"What do you think, Kirk, another Ale or should we order wine?" questioned C.J.

"I'd rather just have a glass of iced tea now, maybe coffee a little later." was Kirk's response, "What do you girls want?"

The girls agreed and the waiter left to get iced tea all around.

"What a menu," said Joanne, "everything looks so good."

"You're right," answered Sharon as she scanned the menu. Kirk took a quick peek at the menu, placed it down, took a drink of water and looked back out the window, waiting for everyone to make their decision.

"You've made up your mind already?" questioned C.J.

"I sure have, the soup sampler, and the Mariner's platter," replied Kirk.

"Let me see," said C.J. as he looked at the menu seeing what Kirk was talking about, "That does sound good. Me too!"

"I'd call that three," responded Joanne, "gives you a taste of everything."

"Make it four," said Sharon as she closed her menu.

Just then the waiter came back, placed the iced tea glasses all around and took out his pad for the order, but before he could speak, "Tell you what," said C.J. in a knowing manner, "I'll order for all of us!"

Kirk, Sharon and Joanne almost had to snicker as C.J. did the ordering for everyone. The waiter seemed somewhat impressed with C.J.

There was laughter all around, during the meal and everyone had a great time. Joanne and C.J. hit it off, which especially pleased Sharon and by evening's end, it seemed that Joanne and C.J. would be more than just friends. The capper of the evening though came as C.J. asked for the bill, only to find that Aunt Mildred had made arrangements. Dinner was on her! They were going to stop off and have a nightcap near campus, but in checking the time, Kirk had to get back for some rest before the early morning practice. They stopped by the fish counter, talked a few minutes with Sam, and headed back down the steps to the parking garage. The drive back to the University of Maryland campus was a little faster, since C.J. knew exactly where they were going. They parked C.J.'s car at Kirk's dorm and Kirk gave Sharon the keys to the station wagon so that she and Joanne could drive on back to Towson. Before they left though, Sharon and Kirk took a short walk. C.J. and Joanne also took a short walk, the opposite way.

"Fifteen minutes," called C.J.

"Right," said Kirk who looked into Sharon's eyes, "twenty-five minutes!" he called.

Fifteen 15

The next couple of weeks were quite hectic for Kirk and the rest of the Maryland players as they rounded into a solid unit in preparation for the football season's opening game. The team consisted of nine starting seniors on the offensive team and eight on the defensive unit. There was almost a veteran look on the team and the confidence level was that of a team picked to win their conference. All of the polls had the University of Maryland ranked in the nation's top 20 and one poll even had them picked to finish in the top 10. It would be an exciting year for both Maryland players and their fans.

How the team finished in the national ranking would depend on a number of things in which the players had no real say. For example, other teams around the country could out perform them within their own conference and get better press enthusiasm. Individual player performances could also bring more notoriety to a particular school. And then, there was the ever-present possibility of injury to key players, which could upset the balance of a team. But, with all that aside, the team was ready, and just as important, they were a healthy group.

Kirk had been able to make a visit to Elk Neck and spend some time with the men he had worked with during the summer. He had grown quite fond of the forest rangers, who befriended him and made the summer so pleasant. When he spoke of the summer to fellow football players, he often referred to it as a "paid vacation of hard work, tempered with extreme fun".

The weekend visit also was enjoyable from the aspect of spending time with the guy that had, in one short summer, become his best friend, well, perhaps his next-best friend. The best friend status, of course, belonged to one Sharon Miles. And then, there was Dora and John, as far as Kirk was concerned, they were his family. He promised Sharon though that she could share them with him. But, even though the weekend was not only enjoyed, it was also a welcomed diversion from the intense practices.

Kirk's mind was back at the U. of M. practice field. He really couldn't wait to get back, complete the practice sessions and scrimmage. Then get on with the season. This was understood by all those at Elk Neck and they tried to make the weekend visit as pleasant as possible.

Kirk drove back to campus on Sunday afternoon and spent the evening with fellow players, relaxing, but also getting back into the intense relationship that built talented players into a well-oiled machine. Sharon had stayed on at Elk Neck for a few days. Classes didn't start for a week and even though she wanted to be down at Towson, or more particularly at College Park with Kirk, she knew he needed the preparation time away from the distractions that she might inadvertently cause.

She settled for the nightly phone call and became a good listener. Sharon didn't keep Kirk on the phone too long. She could always sense the anxiousness in his voice as he let down after the day's practice and was comforted by his "I love you too" sign-off, which made both of their evenings.

On the team, Kirk plays middle linebacker. His position is on the defensive unit and he lines up behind the defensive line. His basic job is to keep the offensive player carrying the ball from gaining ground and to protect against the short pass. When people find out that he played football, they usually asked him how many touchdowns he had scored. His usual stock answer is, "My job is to keep the other team from scoring."

He does, however, have two touchdowns to his record. One in which he blitzed into the opponent's backfield, stripped the ball loose from the ball carrier and ran 37 yards for a score. The other touchdown was an intercepted pass against Penn State, which resulted in a 46-yard dash to the end zone. That score turned out to be the winning touchdown and the game ball was presented to Kirk. Sharon has the ball for safekeeping.

Kirk is also co-captain of the team. He's really proud of that because it shows the confidence of the coaches in his ability and leadership. His leadership role on the team has emerged during the past couple of years.

Kirk came to Maryland as a shy freshman, a former star in high school, yet now, among stars from many high schools, as well as standout college stars. He worked hard to gain a starting position. While he had played both offense as a full back and defense as a linebacker in Camden High School, it was his defensive talents that gained him a full scholarship at the university. Kirk liked playing offense, but loved playing the middle linebacker position. As they say, "He loves to hit and has a nose to be where the ball is." There is also the interesting transformation of the happy-go-lucky Kirk Daniels to the serious, intense Kirk Daniels, the football player. He is all business when the day of a game arrives. Usually the night before the game is when it starts, he has trouble sleeping and the next day's game plan is pictured in his mind for most of the night. While some of his fellow players yell, hit lockers and such to get their game face on, and still others get so nervous that they get sick, Kirk simply goes into himself about the task ahead and works to get the job done.

The schedule of teams to play would be interesting and also tough. A tough schedule, if you win, is great because you do receive extra TV and press coverage and as we discussed earlier, that often helps in the national rankings. On the other hand, well, we shouldn't discuss the other side of the coin just now. The team looks terrific, so let's be optimistic!

First, Maryland will travel to Syracuse, New York and play Syracuse University inside the famous Carrier Dome. Syracuse is always tough, especially at home. Next, Maryland has their home opener against long-time rival, The University of Virginia. This should be a good game because Virginia usually has some surprises to offer, but the players and coaches like having Virginia where they are on the schedule. It's the first conference game and they look for it to be the successful start toward a championship year.

The third game of the year will be a doozy! It's off to Baton Rouge, Louisiana, for a Saturday night battle at Louisiana State University's Tiger Stadium. L.S.U.'s Tiger Stadium had been dubbed 'Deaf Valley' because of the noise level. The Fighting Tigers won their conference last year, not an easy feat when you consider the teams that make up the S.E.C. That game will also be on national television! "Let's play the first game, complete it, and then, to the next game. One at a time, don't think ahead" is the advice the coaches preach. Easy advice!

Well, after Baton Rouge, it'll be home to play against the Wolfpack of North Carolina State. State had eight wins, two losses, and a tie last year and finished second in the conference. They are always tough!

After N.C. State, the U. of M. travels to Florida and a game against last year's number one team in the country, the University of Miami. The game will be played in the Orange Bowl and will also be on national TV. There is a bit of a schedule break in the sixth game of the season as Maryland plays host to Wake Forest. It gives them time to lick their wounds. However, Wake Forest is often a surprising team and a spoiler, and it is Maryland's homecoming weekend.

The seventh game of the year will also be played against a North Carolina team. This time, Maryland faces Duke University. While Duke was only four-and-seven in the win, loss column last year, they are expected to be a strong challenger this year.

The eighth game of the season will be spent playing on North Carolina soil. Maryland will travel to the beautiful community of Chapel Hill to play against the University of North Carolina. The U. of N.C. finished just behind N.C. State that last year in the Atlantic Coast conference and their aim this season is for a title!

The following game will be most important, not only because it's against Penn State, but because the team could at that point be fighting for a national title, if...Good thing this is a home game.

The tenth game of the season will be an away game, about 50 miles away, in Annapolis against the Naval Academy. This game pits two local Washington, D.C. area teams against each other. While it's really not an away game in terms of location, still, it's on enemy turf and most of the tickets sold will be Navy fans. Navy will play hard to beat the local boys and will use this game as a stepping stone to their next game, against their arch rival, Army. That game will be played on neutral ground in Philadelphia.

Maryland's last game of the year is a conference battle against the Clemson Tigers. Clemson won the conference last year and did not lose very many players. The ACC championship, along with a strong post-season bowl game may well be on the line on that afternoon. As the coaches say, "One game at a time, don't look ahead."

The players had gathered in a local pub, the Goal Post. They were relaxing after a long day's practice. Opening day was less than a week away and the conversation was more business-like than usual. It ranged from talking about the schedule as a whole, to individual game night or exciting cities they would go to and, of course, it came back to the task at hand, having a good showing and getting that all-important first victory under their belts.

"I wish we were starting at home, rather than up at the Carrier Dome," came a remark from one of the players after he sat his bottle of beer back on the long table the fellows were settled around. "I'm sorry," he remarked afterward, hoping not to bring any of the other guys down.

"Don't worry about it," started Kirk as he reached for a handful of peanuts. "Let's look at this first game in another light though," he continued, noting now that he had everyone's attention. "I think that the mental part of this thing is easier on us than Syracuse. All we have to do is go up there a day earlier, have a couple of practices, get used to the field and play a football game. They, on the other hand, have all the distractions of a home opener, people wanting tickets, photos, everyone wanting to speak with you. It's a helluva mess to be quite frank. I, for one, am glad for the peace and quiet of the Carrier Dome!"

Everyone had a good laugh, especially knowing that the dome was anything but quiet. It did, though, serve to lighten things up for the guys.

"Great speech Star," Sharon's familiar voice came from behind Kirk. He stood up, reached out, put his hand on her shoulder and gave her a kiss.

"You want to sit down?" asked Kirk, surprised that Sharon was there, but quite glad to see her.

He started to look for another chair, but stopped as Sharon said, "I'd rather just take a walk!"

"A walk it is, see you guys later, I know you all understand," kidded Kirk.

"Bye Kirk, bye Sharon," came a chorus from the guys. "Hand me Kirk's beer," called Tony. "He'll be using chewing gum now!"

As Kirk and Sharon left the Goal Post, they walked a few feet away from where no one in the place could see them and stopped. Kirk gently put his arms around Sharon and just held her for a moment. He touched her long, dark auburn hair, looked into her face and eyes, and still, saying nothing, brought her close again.

"God, do I ever love you," finally came from his lips.

"I love you so much," replied Sharon. "I got in this afternoon and couldn't wait 'till tomorrow to see you!" and she squeezed in close to Kirk.

"I'm glad you came, actually, I thought you would be here tomorrow!" answered Kirk.

"I was, but tomorrow is too long, it's been long enough," stated Sharon. "I know, well, it's starting and I'm so glad to have you here to share my last season with me, it means a lot to me," replied Kirk.

"It means just as much to me," returned Sharon, "I'll be able to share how well their dad played football, with our children. Don't make me lie!"

"You kids are going to be all right," came a voice from a nearby porch. "You're in love. It shows. I don't mean to eavesdrop, but you were, sort of, in front of my house!"

"That we were," answered Kirk, "and we will be alright. I just love the devil out of this lady. We're getting married this winter."

"Good luck kids," the voice from the porch replied as Kirk and Sharon walked on.

"Thank you," they called back and they put their arms around each other as they strolled toward the campus to enjoy the time they had together before the team completed drills and left for Syracuse. They would have this evening and tomorrow, then Sharon and Kirk wouldn't see each other until after the game.

The Miles would see the season opener. John, Dora, and Sharon will fly up to Syracuse from BWI, Baltimore, Washington International on U.S. Air, take in the afternoon game and fly back to BWI the next morning. John enrolled the traveling trio in the frequent flyer program, figuring that they'll catch the LSU, North Carolina and Miami games, in addition to this weekend's contest at the Carrier Dome of Syracuse University. The other away game would be an easy drive to Annapolis, against Navy.

The last practice on the U. of M. field went well and the team was anxious to get on with the trip to Syracuse. They would fly up on a charter U.S. Air flight, have a work session in the Carrier Dome, spend the night and do the deed the following afternoon. Sharon was sitting in the stands during the final practice and although a lot of what she saw looked like ongoing confusion, her eyes hardly roamed from watching her guy's number 55, go through the plays. She waited outside the locker room for Kirk after the practice.

When he emerged, Sharon started toward Kirk, but was cut off by several young boys who ran up to him and the other players seeking autographs. Kirk glanced over at Sharon and shrugged his shoulders, being somewhat embarrassed at the attention and the fact that the kids would want his autograph.

He was patient and signed the books, programs, and pieces of paper that were placed in front of him. While some of the guys just jotted down their name, Kirk took the time to ask each boy his name and wrote, "To_____, Best Wishes, Kirk Daniels." Kirk, through his tough upbringing understood what the signature meant and wanted to personalize the autograph. The one he cherished had been done that way by former heavyweight boxing champion Jersey Joe Walcott also of Camden. That photo is framed above Kirk's desk. Jersey Joe was always an inspiration to Kirk and he, like the former champion, didn't want to disappoint the kids.

"I'm impressed," said Sharon as the last of the boys walked away and she walked up and gave him a kiss. "Can I also have an autograph?"

"On a check, photo, or marriage license?" questioned Kirk.

"OK," was Sharon's response.

"In what order," kidded Kirk as he took Sharon's hand and they strolled toward the cafeteria.

"Well, I don't need a check signed, I have a photo of you, but I'd like one in your uniform, signed to me, of course, and the last offer. How about November, you autograph for me and I'll autograph for you," answered Sharon and she squeezed Kirk's hand. "How do you feel, tired, hungry?" she continued as they approached the cafeteria and Kirk held the door for Sharon.

"All of the above," was Kirk's reply, then after a pause, he continued, "not actually tired, but strung out, over-extended and quite anxious."

"That's understandable, you've got a lot on your mind, and, I guess, you'll be a little uptight until the Syracuse game is behind you," said Sharon matter-of-factly as she picked up a tray, napkins and silverware.

"We can share the same tray, I'm not very hungry," she continued.

"Well, I don't like to be uptight around you," answered Kirk as he looked over the desserts and chose the largest cut of blueberry pie. "Why do they put desserts first, rather than at the end where they belong?" he mused.

"So that you don't get to the end of the line, look at the full tray and skip dessert, they want you purchasing the full fare," answered Sharon as she chose a large chocolate chip cookie. "Keep your eyes off my cookie!"

"I think I'll just have the roast beef salad, then save room for supper," stated Kirk smiling.

"Hi Kirk," the voice from behind the counter said, "how's it going, man."

"Hey Raymond, it's A-OK. Say hello to Sharon," answered Kirk.

"Hello Sharon. So this is the lady the girls whisper about," kidded Raymond.

"Nice to meet you, I think, Raymond. What whispers?" answered Sharon.

"Hey, you invaded the campus and ran off with one of the most eligible guys, and from the look of your ring finger, you're not throwing him back," stated Raymond. "You having the roast beef salad too, Sharon?"

"Yes, on the salad and yes on the 'not throwing'," answered Sharon.

"Good, on both parts," responded Raymond who reached out and took away the roast beef salad from Sharon. "The one already on the tray is yours," and he took the salad to the back counter, put twice as much roast beef on it and handed it back, Kirk's!"

Kirk gave the thumb-up sign to Raymond and they moved on down the line. "Do you want iced tea?" Kirk questioned as he reached for a glass for himself.

"Sure," came Sharon's reply and Kirk picked out another glass of iced tea.

"Let's go over there," said Kirk spotting a table in the corner.

Kirk and Sharon went over to the corner table and took the things off the tray. Kirk then put the tray on a service table that had other trays on it and came back over to Sharon and sat down.

"To continue our conversation before that rude man brought up my invasion and then forced me to claim the secondary salad, while he piled mounds of roast beef on yours," stated a smiling, kidding Sharon. "You're not to worry about being what you call, uptight, around me. First, I understand what your concerns are, and second, your concerns are not a burden to me. I share them. I hope you'll always let me share them, so that, well, in a way I can, I can help, even if it's only to be a good listener for you. All right?"

"All right. How was I so fortunate to find someone like you? You really do make things worthwhile for me," stated Kirk.

"Of course I do, you lucky devil," responded Sharon in a lively manner and she clinked her iced tea glass against his. "It was a lucky day for both of us when you came up on my back porch. From that day forth, I was determined you wouldn't get away!" They finished their lunch and walked over to Kirk's dorm. From there, Sharon and Kirk took the jeep, with the top down, to nearby Silver Springs. There were a couple of good antique stores and Sharon wanted to look for an oval mirror for her folks' anniversary. Dora collected antiques. John, for the most part, let her do the decorating, except that is, for his combination den/study/office. That was a comfortable man's room!

With the wind, traffic sounds, and engine noise, nothing was said on the drive to Silver Springs. Kirk found a parking space on the street in front of the antique store and eased the jeep into the space. They unlocked the seat belts and Kirk walked to the meter. He reached into his pocked for some change, but Sharon beat him to it, putting the coins in and turning the meter on. "There, we've got an hour, plus the ten minutes that were left," said Sharon and she reached for Kirk's hand.

" Is this the place you want to go to first?" said Kirk as he noted that there were three antique stores, two on this side of the street and one directly across the street.

"I've seen their ad in the paper several times and from the look of the place, it's an antique shop and not a used furniture store, posing as an antique store," answered Sharon. "One with my antique knowledge must be careful!"

"As you well know, my antique knowledge adds zero to yours," remarked Kirk who looked at the colonial-styled store which was painted in dark green with the lettering painted in an antique gold. The front window of the shop had a colonialized-bar window with many windowpanes in it and the display included a beautiful old rocking horse and carousel horse.

The balance of the window display had paintings and some small pieces of cut glass, all tastefully placed to show some of the things they sold. "I'm impressed," he started and then read aloud what their sign stated. *The Lion Hearted. Art and Antiques, Fine American and English Furniture, American and European Paintings, Antique Silver and Jewelry, Complete and Authoritative Appraisal Service.*

"OK, let's go in." Kirk held the door for Sharon as they entered.

"Good afternoon," said a very attractive, gray-haired lady in a white, summery-looking dress, "I'm Cathy Starns, can I show you anything, or are you just browsing?"

"Hello," answered Sharon as Kirk simply nodded a greeting. "Yes, we're looking for an antique oval mirror, it's to be a gift for my parents' anniversary."

"Are your folks decorating with mostly American or English pieces?" questioned Cathy.

"A lot of what they've collected or have had handed down through the family is from England," answered Sharon, who paused for a moment, then continued, "really, it's mostly my mother who likes the antiques, my dad kind of goes along. The den is his!"

"That's often the case," remarked Cathy. "However," she continued, "the husbands are the ones who take credit and show off the pieces to guests and friends."

"You know, you're right!" answered Sharon.

"Well, let's see if we can help you out," stated Cathy. "What size oval mirror are you looking for and what room will it be in. Do you want one that is more plain to accent or should it stand on it's own, in a place, say like in the foyer or at the end of a hall."

"Wow," stated Kirk, "there's a lot more to this than I imagined."

"I don't think they, well, mom wants one that overwhelms the room, but not one that is too small, and it would go over an antique table in the foyer. There is an old coat rack that was in an office in Chicago that my grandparents had and my grandfather said, made it through the Great Chicago Fire, plus an old umbrella stand that my folks picked up on a trip to England. But I think they got it in Edinburgh, Scotland," was Sharon's reply.

"And what about the table?" questioned Cathy.

"It's really decorative, if that's what you want to call it. I never liked it when I was young, but now I can see the individual craftsmanship that went into making it. My grandparents brought it over with them, when they came to this country to live, in the twenties," answered Sharon.

While this conversation was going on, Kirk began wandering around the shop looking at the different pieces on display. "Don't break anything," kidded Sharon, "I don't think you have enough on you to cover the broken article you have purchased!" They all had a laugh as Kirk promised he'd be careful.

"Well, from what you describe, you'd like a medium-sized, oval mirror without too much of a decorative posture, so that it wouldn't clash with the table, but accent it," responded Cathy. "When is their anniversary?"

"Well, it's not until November, actually the 13th, but I thought I'd better start looking, because it might be hard to find," answered Sharon.

"You're right. I don't have exactly what you want right now. And exactly what you want is what you should buy, nothing less." stated Cathy, who pondered for a second, then continued, "I have a supplier, two wonderful old ladies that acquire things for me and several other dealers, who are in London right now. I'll contact them. They're not due back in the States until mid or late September, but I'll know long before then what they have."

"That sounds great," responded Sharon, "I'm glad we came here."

"Yes, while the ladies are only one of our suppliers, they love being put on the hunt for something special! I'll relay all the information to them and see what they come up with," stated Cathy.

"Should we check back with you around the middle of September?" questioned Sharon.

"Either that or leave me your phone number or address," answered Cathy.

"Well, I'll be changing apartments, moving from Towson to College Park," started Sharon, "I don't have the exact new address yet." She paused for a second and started to continue when Kirk spoke up.

"I'll write down my address and the phone at my dorm. That'll do for now and you touch base with Cathy after you've moved," said Kirk.

"That's fine," responded Cathy and she gave Kirk pen and paper.

"Do we need to leave a deposit?" questioned Sharon.

"No, don't worry about it," answered Cathy.

"Let me ask the big question, how much is something like this going to be, and if it's too much, do you have terms?" Kirk asked boldly.

"That's hard to say," stated Cathy, "if I had to guess, I'd say five hundred dollars. These particular ladies are not expensive. As I said, I'll relay all the information, including that it's an anniversary present from two thoughtful young people with a limited budget. Normally a mirror like that can sell for seven or eight hundred dollars. Visa, MasterCard, etc., or if you wish, some other arrangements can be made to suit your needs.

"This is terrific, Cathy, I'm really glad we came here, you've set my mind at ease, because, as you must suspect, we really don't know very much about antiques," stated Sharon as they prepared to leave the shop.

"It's my pleasure," answered Cathy, who paused and then continued, "maybe we'll develop a long-term customer in you and your young man."

"If it's furniture, say chairs and things, they'd better be sturdy," answered a laughing Kirk. "My friends are big, clumsy fellows!"

"Kirk plays football for the University of Maryland," stated Sharon to Cathy. "I'll make them all stay outside until they're housebroken!"

"Good idea," reasoned Cathy, "my husband graduated from Maryland, has season tickets," continued Cathy. "I'll have to attend a game and see you play."

"Let us know which game you're attending," stated Sharon, "we'll get together."

"Fine, it has, really been a pleasure," answered Cathy. "We'll start the hunt!"

"OK," responded Kirk. "Did you see that old fire truck?" he said to Sharon.

"Later, maybe if you're a good boy," was Sharon's reply as they made their way to the door and out of the shop.

"We still have 15 minutes on the meter. Of course, 10 of those were a bonus. Do you want to look around or go?" questioned Kirk as they stood on the sidewalk.

"Let's head back, we got what we came for. I'd rather just spend some time with you. After tonight I won't see you until Saturday," was Sharon's reply.

"Any place special for dinner?" questioned Kirk.

"In your arms," answered Sharon as they climbed in the jeep.

Kirk shook his head as he started the engine and backed out of the parking space. "I know just the spot, it's called the Holiday Inn. We can send down for some groceries," he said as he started down the street.

"Don't tempt me." answered Sharon, "I'm weak right now!"

Kirk smiled, "That's right, put the burden of your virtue on me," he called over the noise of the engine. Then noticing that people walking on the sidewalk were turning to see who was talking loudly, realized that his voice was carrying over the engine noise.

Kirk broke into a loud laugh, as did Sharon, who also realized what the people were staring at. Kirk reached over and put his hand in Sharon's who squeezed tight and just looked at her man.

Nothing more was said because of the noise of the open jeep and they drove back to Kirk's dorm where they parked the jeep and walked over to Sharon's parents' station wagon. It was quite warm and the air-conditioned car would be much more comfortable.

Just as they reached the car and Kirk was opening the door on the passenger side for Sharon, a loud voice called from an upstairs window. "Are you two going to dinner?" yelled Tony.

"Yes, we two, are going for dinner and you can have dinner with Kirk tomorrow," called Sharon as she got into the car without waiting for a reply from Tony.

"That's what I thought," shouted Tony, really to Kirk who just smiled and waved so long to Tony. "Tell her to keep a check on the stable for me," he added, then disappeared inside as Kirk got into the car.

"Have you made a decision?" questioned Sharon as they were driving off campus.

"Sure, the Holiday Inn," answered Kirk with a sheepish grin.

"Whatever your pleasure," came Sharon's response. "I'm yours to do with as you see fit," and she moved over close to Kirk and put her head on his shoulder, nuzzling in to be near him.

"We'd better go to the Ming Palace for Chinese food. You'd never forgive me," kidded Kirk as they drove along.

"That's not true." answered Sharon, "I'll forgive you, but, of course, I'd have to tell my mother and she'd never forgive you. My father, on the other hand, might understand. Take your chances as you wish."

"Let me fill you, or more properly, half fill you with Chinese food first, then I'll think about the raping, looting, and pillaging," answered Kirk as they pulled off of Route 1 and into the Ming Palace parking lot.

"I can hardly wait for the meal to be over. I just love all the smooth talk" kidded Sharon as she unlocked her seat belt. Kirk had to smile at the conversation that took place in the last couple minutes. After parking, he opened his door and started to go around to open Sharon's door, but she had already opened it and was getting out as he arrived.

"You keep away from me you pervert," she said aloud as she spotted two policemen coming out of the restaurant. "He drove me to this far-eastern den of sin and speaks of looting, raping, and pillaging, officer, arrest this man!"

"You're right ma'am, the food in there is almost sinful and as for the other, you're an awful pretty lady, can't say I blame him." Then reaching out his hand to Kirk, the officer continued, "Hi Kirk, how's it going?"

"Just great Jimmy. Hello there Howard," answered Kirk as he shook hands with both men. "This is my fiancée, Sharon Miles. Her dad's the super' up at Elk Neck."

"Hello Sharon, nice to meet you," they replied, then to Kirk as they headed for the restaurant entrance, "Carry on," in a military sounding way.

"Those fellows are U. of M. campus police," said Kirk matter-of-factly as he held the door for Sharon and they entered the Ming Palace.

"I figured as much. I'll bet you can't get arrested in this town, can you?" questioned Sharon in a kidding manner.

"I don't break the law," stated Kirk in a low voice. Then to the owner in a louder tone, "Hello Bing, how are you this evening?"

"Just fine Kirk, thank you for joining us tonight," answered Bing, who took two menus from the stand, then stopped, before showing them to a table. "You want off the menu tonight?" he questioned.

"No, some wonton and then please, just cook for us, Bing. Let me introduce my fiancée, Sharon," was Kirk's reply.

"Very nice to meet Kirk's fiancée, Sharon," stated Bing, who then took them to a table near the corner, "more private, plenty of room," he stated.

"Thank you Bing," answered Kirk as he held the chair for Sharon and then sat down.

"Can I get you a drink, scotch for you Kirk?" asked a smiling Bing.

"I'm not old enough to drink scotch," answered Kirk, "how about a strawberry daiquiri for Sharon and I'll have a gin and tonic."

"OK," was Bing's reply, "but remember, when you reach 30, you must change," and Bing left the table laughing. He then motioned and a waiter came quickly to Bing, who spoke in Chinese. The waiter left in the direction of the bar. Sharon had a cute grin on her face as she said, "Another of your haunts!"

"Yes, I like the combination Chinese-Hawaiian decor. What do you think?" stated Kirk, but Sharon reached over and covered up his mouth with her hand.

"Don't think. I'll decorate, you'll love it," stated Sharon.

No one spoke for a couple of minutes as the waiter came over with their drinks. Then filled the glasses with ice water and brought a plate of noodles to munch on as well as two small bowls, one with sweet and sour sauce, plus one with hot mustard. Just then another waiter came with a plate of spare ribs.

"This is an appetizer. Wonton is next," stated the waiter.

"Thank you," was Kirk's reply, then to Sharon, "dig in!"

"First a toast," started Sharon, "to a successful and healthy season!"

"Here, here on both counts," said Kirk in a low voice, then he touched Sharon's outstretched glass with his.

The spareribs were delicious. Messy, but delicious. When they were nearly finished, the waiter appeared with a couple of wet towels for each of them, plus some fresh napkins. "As we said, delicious, but messy!" Just after the plates were cleared, the waiter brought the wonton soup. He noticed as he placed the soup plates down that the water glasses had been used during the sparerib eating contest because of the leftover barbecue sauce fingerprints. Without saying anything he removed the glasses and replaced them with new ones.

The main course arrived soon after Kirk and Sharon finished their soup. Bing stopped by as the waiter brought the covered plates. Bing removed the covers and placed the piping hot dish in front of Kirk and Sharon. "Lobster, shrimp, and scallops, fried rice, Chinese vegetables," said Bing.

"It looks great," said Kirk, "thanks so much!"

"It tastes even better," said Sharon, "just outstanding," she continued as she, having been served first, couldn't wait and dug in!

"Oh very good," was Bing's reply and satisfied that all was well, he left, but spoke in Chinese to the waiter, who in just a few seconds brought hot tea and cups for the party of two.

"This reminds me of the meal we had at Tag's," said Sharon after a few minutes, "a gourmet whirlwind in dining."

"We have been treated well," responded Kirk as they continued enjoying the hospitality of friends who Kirk met almost four years before with one of the coaches. While the waiter kept a watchful eye to see if anything was needed at Kirk's table, they left him and Sharon alone for the rest of the meal.

Kirk and Sharon were involved in small talk, mostly about school, friends, the mobile home, and past meals. They didn't discuss the upcoming football season. Sharon knew that Kirk would have enough football talk from coaches, teammates, fellow students, and the press. So, she felt that the other conversation would, not so much take his mind off football, but simply, help relax him.

It worked. Perhaps not quite the plan Sharon had laid out, but maybe because Kirk so enjoyed being with Sharon that the subject matter was unimportant. Kirk knew, of course, that Sharon was staying away from the football subject on purpose. He appreciated her thoughtfulness and went along with it. He even talked of antiques, loud enough for the next table to hear him, and winked at Sharon who knew he was kiddingly trying to impress the neighbors.

At the end of the meal, Kirk started looking for the check, but none was coming as Bing stated that this meal was on their friendship and because Kirk came with his lovely bride-to-be. However, Bing made it clear that when Kirk came back with those beer-drinking, white rice hungry fellows called the Maryland football team, he'd even charge them for the ice water and noodles, double for fortune cookies. And he laughed.

Sharon and Kirk said their "thank yous". Kirk estimated what the bill may have been and left an appropriate tip for the waiter.

"That was really wonderful," said Sharon as they strolled hand in hand through the parking lot and over to the station wagon. "You know

Daniels, I think it's going to be fun married to you. God am I glad you found me," and they stopped, kissed, and held each other before Kirk opened Sharon's door.

"I'm the lucky one," stated Kirk as he held the door and Sharon got in. "I found the most important thing in my life on a back porch!"

"Yeah, come to think of it, you are lucky. I'm a good catch," kidded Sharon.

After they left the parking lot, Sharon moved closer to Kirk and rested her head on his shoulder. "I love snuggling next to you," said Sharon softly.

"I love having you there," answered Kirk as he reached over and kissed Sharon's forehead and touched her hair with his chin.

It was an otherwise quiet ride back to the U. of M. campus with Kirk and Sharon sitting close to each other and feeling very comfortable about their love and future life together. It was such a good feeling.

That night Kirk slept well and wished he could have continued the enjoyable sleep past the 6:00 alarm, but there it was ringing a deafening tone. He got up, went to the washroom and returned after showering and shaving to pack some clothes for the trip. While suits were not necessary, a sports coat and tie were. Blue Jeans, etc. were not. During the luncheon and other team functions, the fellows would wear the team jackets, with the school crest on it.

The players brought their bags down and team managers took them over to the bus as the players, went for breakfast at the cafeteria. It was then onto the bus for the ride to BWI and the U.S. Air flight to Syracuse, which would not be a regularly scheduled flight, but a charter. The plane would not only carry players and coaches, but also bring other officials from the U. of M.

The ride to the airport took less than a half an hour and just after stopping near the *U.S. Air* sign on the departing flight level, the players, coaches and balance of the entourage got off and entered the terminal. The plane was at the ready, fueled, catered, and set to leave the gate. It wasn't long before the pushback and taxi to the runway. Then it was off to Syracuse. While they were well into the flight and enjoying a snack and diet coke, Coach Wyneski walked back toward where Kirk and Tony were sitting.

"How's it going Kirk?" spoke the coach quietly.

"OK, a little anxious to get the first game under my belt, you know what I mean," was Kirk's reply.

"Did you know that Johnny Conklin didn't make the flight?" asked the coach as he sat on the chair arm behind him.

"No, what's the matter, he OK?" questioned Kirk as Tony just sat and listened.

"Chicken pox. Never had them as a kid," answered Coach Wyneski.

"Wow, that's rough. When's he coming back?" questioned Kirk.

"Not in time for tomorrow's game," replied the coach.

"Who's kicking?" questioned Tony, who now also joined the conversation, with a low voice.

"Well, Doug Sanford's going to kick off and, of course, Billy Davis will still do all the punting, but Doug isn't sharp on extra points and field goals," said the coach, waiting for the light to come on in Kirk's head.

"Kirk's always practicing. He'd do it," kidded Tony with a wide grin.

"You are kidding," replied Kirk. "I haven't kicked in a game since high school, and I'm a straight-up kicker, not soccer style."

"You're accurate and that's what we need for tomorrow," stated the coach.

"You're serious, aren't you?" questioned Kirk with a worried look on his face.

"Look, you're cool under pressure. You're always practicing. Now's your chance. We won't press it. We'll go with Doug if you think we should, but Doug wants you to do it. I know it's tough, but who figured on chicken pox," stated the coach as he let up for a minute to let Kirk sort it out.

"We'd better score a lot of TD's," Kirk replied after a few minutes thought. "I don't want to attempt a field goal past the 15. 15, that's what, 7 behind the line and 10 for the end zone. That's 32 altogether!"

"Well, I'll tell everyone you've got extra duty and we'll take it from there. You'll do just fine and thanks Kirk," was coach Wyneski's reply and he put a firm pat on Kirk's shoulder before heading back up the aisle. Kirk didn't answer, but just made a long sigh and took a deep breath.

"Hell, you always wanted to play some offense, now's your chance, what's the worst that can happen. Don't think about it," kidded Tony.

"I should be OK on the Pat's," reasoned Kirk who thought for a minute and continued, "just keep my head down, let the fans tell me if the kick's good. That's what my coach always preached in high school."

"Did you ever kick field goals in high school?" asked Tony as he took a drink of Coke.

"Yeah, I tried three and made all of them, but they were all inside of the 20 and we scored big at Camden. The games weren't on the line," Kirk replied. "I'd be shaking if tomorrow's game was on the line and I'm it."

"So would anybody else," was Tony's matter-of-fact answer, then he looked around and got up out of his seat. "I'm gonna find the head.

You're making me nervous," and he walked down the aisle toward the back of the plane.

Kirk picked up the can of Coke from his seat table and took a drink. He was glad for a friend and teammate like Tony who could ease the pressure. Tony often seemed high-strung, but when the game started, he was all business. Kirk's thoughts then switched to Sharon as he sat back in the seat. He smiled as he thought of her seeing him line up to kick an extra point. And he decided not to tell her that he'd kick in addition to his regular duties as a middle linebacker, he'd let her just see him out there. Then he closed his eyes and just thought of Sharon and fell off to sleep.

"Hey, wake up," came Tony's voice, "we're about to land. I don't want to do this by myself."

Kirk opened his eyes and looked out the window. They were on final approach and seemed to be just about a hundred feet above the ground. He looked back at Tony, who after four years of this still wasn't certain he liked flying and smiled. Tony gave a quick smile back.

The plane landed without incident, of course, and taxied to the gate. Once there, they got off the plane and headed for the waiting buses. Their luggage was quickly off-loaded to join them. A truck would take the equipment directly to the Carrier Dome Stadium. It wasn't too long before the buses were headed for the Syracuse Marriott.

At the Marriott, the players would get settled, two in a room and then have lunch in a banquet room before setting off to the Carrier Dome for a light practice. Tony and Kirk roomed together. It had been this way since they first met as freshmen. They were quite the opposite personalities, but got along just fine and looked after each other.

As Kirk and Tony were standing in a special line off to the side for their room arrangement and key, Tony nudged Kirk to look at who just walked through the door. "Isn't that C.J.?" asked Tony.

"It sure looks like him. I'll walk over," said Kirk, who left the line and walked through the lobby toward the hotel's front door. "What are you doing here?" said Kirk as he shook hands with C.J.

"Took a few days off for vacation and decided to drive up," was C.J.'s reply as he shook hands with Tony, who handed a key to Kirk.

"We're in #243, in the back, lunch is in 20 minutes, in some room, we'll find it. Hey C.J., how's it going, man," stated Tony.

"I'm A-OK," was C.J.'s reply "You guys look relaxed, confident."

"Oh great!" returned Kirk, "It doesn't show!"

"As they say in Jamaica, 'No problem'," stated Tony.

"You've never been to Jamaica," said Kirk.

"I know, but that's what they say," answered Tony, who after a pause, continued, "Where are you staying, got a room yet?"

"I thought I'd check around, find someplace cheap," answered C.J.

"No place cheaper than our room, right Kirk?" stated Tony.

"He's right, we'll get a roll-a-way," answered Kirk.

"Yeah, let's go to the room, call housekeeping and get a bed for our equipment manager," stated Tony, who thought for a minute, "there will also be an extra place at meals, since Conklin didn't make the trip. C.J., you're in business!"

"Thanks guys, but don't you think I'll be noticed?" questioned C.J.

"You let us handle it. Come on, let's find the room," stated Tony, who started walking through the lobby toward the sign pointing to *GUESTROOMS*. Kirk and C.J followed him.

We'll find the room and you can bring the car around to the back and unload your stuff," stated Kirk as they waited for the elevator.

"This is great!" said an excited, smiling C.J.

Tony just smiled back and put his hand on C.J.'s shoulder as the elevator door opened, then playfully shoved him in. Kirk followed, hit the *two* button and the elevator doors closed to take them to the second floor. "It's over here," said Kirk as they checked the direction of the room numbers and walked down the hall to #243. Kirk put the key in and they went into the room.

"Very nice. Plenty of room for the roll-a-way," he continued as he surveyed the room that had two double beds, a chair, sofa and desk, plus a writing table and dresser.

"Look, what we have," called Tony as he lifted the cushions from the sofa.

"Well, we won't have to get a roll-a-way after all," stated Kirk as he looked over toward Tony, who had the cushions on the floor and the sofa bed opened almost all the way.

"It's got the sheets, blankets and all," stated Tony as he flipped the cushions onto the opened bed.

"Pillows...check the dresser and closet. They've got to have extra pillows for the sofa bed somewhere," reassured Kirk as he started opening drawers.

"They're here," said C.J. as he showed Tony and Kirk two pillows that he lifted off the closet shelf. "I'll leave them here for now."

"OK," started Tony as he looked around the room, satisfied that all was well, "Let's get some groceries. I'm starved."

"You're right. The suitcases will be up after a while and C.J. can bring his car around after we eat. That sound OK C.J.?" said Kirk.

"Fine with me. Sure the meal is OK?" answered C.J.

"Who's gonna argue with us?" stated Tony as they walked out the door and headed for the elevator.

"Let's take the stairs," said Kirk as they neared the elevator, "it's only one flight," and he opened the door to the stairway and started down.

"Where are we supposed to go?" questioned Tony as they came out of the stairwell onto the main floor. "Hey Coach," called Tony to Coach Wyneski who was walking down the hall toward the lobby. "Which way to the grub? Follow you?"

"Follow me," answered the Coach, "And eat light Tony, we want you fast. Looks like you've been hitting the dessert tray too often."

"Me, no coach, I'm OK. Rapidamente. Quick as a quarterhorse," returned Tony. "By the way coach, shake hands with C.J., he's our equipment manager. Kirk's good luck charm. Conklin's meal replacement!"

"All those. That's a tall order for one guy," answered the coach as he reached out to shake hands with C.J., "what's really up?"

"That's our story and we're glad you're on our side Coach," stated Kirk as he put his hand on the Coach's shoulder. "Where do we sit?" Kirk continued as they entered the banquet room.

"I'm at the coaches' table," stated Coach Wyneski, "and the three of you are far, far away," then before leaving them and walking over to join the other coaches he continued. "Bring that luck to the game, C.J.!"

"He'll need some kind of tag, press, coaches, something, cause he doesn't have a ticket yet," stated Tony, "OK?"

Coach Wyneski, who had started walking away, called over his shoulder without looking around, "I'll handle it!"

C.J., Tony, and Kirk didn't answer, but smiled at each other and looked for a table on the other side of the room far from the coaches!

After lunch, the players went back to their assigned rooms, unpacked suitcases, changed into relaxing clothes, and met at the hotel lobby door for the bus trip to the Carrier Dome Stadium for a light practice. The Astroturf carpet would not be unfamiliar to them because they played on a similar rug at home, however, the coaches, in addition to wanting the players to have a light practice to work off steam, also wanted to let the players get used to the indoor stadium.

Many of the players hadn't played at Syracuse before, because last year's game was at Maryland, so feeling at ease indoors was important. The only thing they couldn't assimilate was the noise level. While this would be difficult, the team had worked on other signals to compensate for the noise.

The practice went well. The players seemed to have fun and there was an air of relaxation among them, although they all wished that the game was being played right now!

After the practice, a team meeting was held in the locker room. At the conclusion of the meeting the coaches were satisfied that the team was as ready as they were going to be. A relaxing evening was in order and this got started on the rowdy bus ride back to the Marriott hotel. It was just passed 5:00 when the bus pulled up to the hotel. The players off-loaded and started to walk into the lobby.

"I'm still worked up. I feel like taking a walk," stated Tony.

"We'll join you," said Kirk as he motioned to C.J. to come along. "Dinner won't be until 6:30, so we've got time."

The three started off on a walk, but before long, more than a dozen players had joined them. "Don't get lost," called one of the coaches in a loud voice. No one answered and there was no real conversation during the walk, which took them around the hotel and through some office complex grounds. They did draw some attention, though, as they walked along. People getting out of work stopped to look at the 15 or so large men passing by, but no one spoke to them. Perhaps they thought they were a gang or an invading group of mercenaries. Maybe they were, at least they had some special plans to invade the Carrier Dome the next day and come out victorious!

They got back to the hotel a few minutes after 6:00. The players went to their rooms to wash up before coming back to the banquet room for dinner. Kirk, Tony, and C.J. went to room #243, turned on the television and relaxed for a few minutes before they joined the rest of the team.

"Are you going to call Sharon?" questioned Tony. "Want us to wait in the hall?"

"Not now, after dinner," was Kirk's reply.

"Do you want to see the game show or the news?" asked Tony as he flipped the channel on the television.

"Forget it," answered Kirk, "let's head down!"

C.J., who was sitting on the sofa with his feet propped up on the coffee table, got up, put his sports coat on, and was ready to dine. As they left the room, Kirk started back to shut the television off.

"Leave it on," stated Tony, "my father says always leave the TV on when you leave a hotel room. Makes anyone wandering the halls think someone is in the room. Cuts down on break-in's!"

"Good idea," answered Kirk, as he stopped, then joined the others in the hall. As they walked toward the stairwell, Tony said, "You're not saying much C.J., you must be hungry."

"I did work up an appetite during that walk," answered C.J. The trio walked to the banquet room and headed for the same large table they had before, away from the coaches, but near the other players.

It seemed that most of the young men were as hungry as C.J., because not much was said during dinner. Also, many of the players preferred to have private thoughts at this time as they mentally prepared for tomorrow's game. It was just about 8:00 when the players filed out of the banquet room. Most of the guys were tired and would head to their rooms to relax, while others would gather in groups in someone's room and talk for a while.

Kirk checked his watch and told Tony and C.J. that he was going back to the room to call Sharon. Tony stated that he and C.J. were going over to Bill's room and to join them if he ever got through with the call.

C.J. and Tony stayed behind and talked with some of the other players as they left the banquet room, and Kirk went back down the hall to make his phone call. He pushed the elevator button without thinking, then thought, damn, it's only one flight up to the room and started for the stairwell, however, the elevator door opened almost before Kirk could take a step, so he walked in and pushed the button for the second floor. Once in the room, he chose the phone by the desk rather than the phone by the bed, and dialed Sharon's number.

"Hello," came John Miles voice on the other end of the line.

"Kirk here John, how's it going," answered Kirk.

"Fine here, all the men are pulling for you tomorrow. We'll plan on seeing you for a few minutes after the game," returned John.

"That's great! Tell those lovable gold bricks to keep their fingers crossed. The kicker is down ill and I'm the PAT/field goal kicker," was Kirk's reply.

"You'll do just fine," was John's fatherly response, "I've got to get off now, before my darling daughter rips the phone from my hand!"

"Take care, John. Have a good flight," answered Kirk.

"Finally," said Sharon in an exasperated, joking tone.

"Behave yourself," was Kirk's reply, "otherwise I won't make this an 'I love you' call," he continued.

"In that case, I'll behave myself," answered Sharon, who then continued, "how's everything in Syracuse. You feeling OK?"

"They told me on the plane that Johnny Conklin is down with chicken pox and I'm kicking PAT's field goals, and to tell you the truth, I'm nervous about it. But, I'll get by," stated Kirk, who decided to share this with Sharon before the game.

"My hero, see, I'm right to have called you Star," kidded Sharon.

"I hear you," was Kirk's reply. "By the way, C.J. drove up."

"Yeah, he said he might surprise you. I hope the game's not sold out, but he'll find a way to get in," answered Sharon.

"He already has. He's our equipment manager, Tony and mine, plus Tony has designated him my good luck charm. He'll watch the game from the sidelines. By the way, we have a sofabed, guess who's bunking in with us, and eating Conklin's meals!" was Kirk's reply.

"Good ole C.J." stated Sharon. "He really cares, you know."

"I know," answered Kirk. "He's one great guy. We'll take care of him."

"I love you," was Sharon's response.

"I love you too," answered Kirk. "Wish I was with you right now."

"Me too," returned Sharon. "I'll be thinking of holding you in my arms as I fall asleep tonight," Sharon continued in a low, quiet voice.

"Is this conversation turning to smut?" asked Kirk in a kidding manner.

"Not really, there's plenty of time for smut. This was loving holding. You know what I mean," responded Sharon.

"Well, OK," kidded Kirk, "I'd love to be holding you right now," he continued on a serious note.

"Where are Tony and C.J.?" questioned Sharon, "not listening, I hope!"

"No, they're down at Bill's room. I'll meet them there for a while, then hit the hay," answered Kirk.

"Well, I'll say goodnight to you. Good luck tomorrow. Dream of me, loving you. Don't worry about the game. I'll be proud of you no matter what happens. Maybe I should rephrase the last part," said Sharon thinking she said something wrong and she was silent for a moment.

"That's OK, I know what you mean and I love you for it," answered Kirk as he stood up from the chair and prepared to hang up.

"Good night, darling," replied Sharon. "I love you."

" Good night, sweetie," answered Kirk and he hung up.

Sharon walked back into the living room from the kitchen and smiled as John and Dora looked up. "He sounds great. I hope all goes well," she stated as she sat down next to her mother on the sofa.

"He'll do alright, it's the other 50 or so guys I'm worried about," kidded John as he got up from his Lazy Boy chair, "I'm going to arm myself with a beer. Anyone want something?"

"No," came the reply from Dora and Sharon.

"I'm going to bed," started Sharon. "See you all in the morning."

"Good night," answered John and Dora.

John stopped before leaving the living room for the kitchen, "Set your alarm for 5:00. OK, 5:30," John corrected himself as he smiled at the face Sharon made.

` In the meantime, Kirk had joined C.J., Jack and Tony at Bill's room. They all talked for a while, actually there were about a dozen fellows crowded into the room and there was about half that many conversations going on at the same time.

It was just past eleven, when the players started leaving for their own rooms. Kirk, Tony, and C.J. headed for 243. "Give me the key," said C.J., and he took the key from Tony and rushed down the hall, "after all, I am the equipment manager!" Kirk and Tony chased C.J., but he arrived at the door before them.

"Oh God, let me open the door before they crush me. Wait, listen, don't hit me. I've got to drive home. I'm the good luck charm!" yelled C.J. as Kirk and Tony closed in.

They stopped just short of C.J., who had crunched up waiting for the crush of the two heavily armed football players. He had one hand on the doorknob and the other on the key. When he didn't feel the hit, he opened one eye carefully. "Hi guys, come on in" and he opened the door only to be pushed in first.

They flipped the TV on and relaxed a little while longer before calling it a night and sacking in. C.J. laid awake for a while, thinking about the wonderful friendship he had with Kirk and how Kirk included him in all these things as an equal, without question, and how Kirk's friends also took him matter-of-factly. C.J. smiled to himself, as he turned over and flipped his pillow over too. "Well, he is my brother. I never had one, but I do now," and he drifted off to sleep.

Breakfast was scheduled for 9:30 and most of the players slept in. Fact is, most would have preferred to sleep a little longer. Kirk was first up and took a long shower. The hot water felt good and practically took his mind off the game this afternoon. With the hot water pouring onto his neck and shoulders, he tried to change his thoughts to Sharon; however, thoughts of the game constantly crept in. While he was shaving, Tony stirred and came to the bathroom door. "I'll be out in a minute," said Kirk as he splashed water on his face and quickly brushed his teeth.

"That's OK, I'll use the hall, or better yet the balcony," kidded Tony who, though still in his shorts and without a top, opened the door to the hall. "Hey, they put a paper at our door," and he picked up the Saturday paper and brought it in.

"Aren't you superstitious, reading the paper on game day?" questioned C.J., as he sat up on the edge of the sofabed, yawned and stretched.

"Only if my name's in the obit section," answered Tony as he opened the paper to the sports page. "You might think we're in Syracuse, from reading the damn sports page. They got us as six point underdogs!"

"That's good." said Kirk as he exited the bathroom and gave a sweeping hand and arm movement so as to say "The bathroom is yours".

"Don't take too long," said C.J. from the edge of the sofabed, "or else you'll have company" and he had to laugh as Tony came back to the bathroom door and stared at him.

"Why do you say that," yelled Tony to Kirk as he started the shower water.

"Because this puts even more pressure on them than just the home opening date. I almost feel sorry for them," answered Kirk.

"Man, you've got logic on your side, no matter what," yelled Tony.

"You do have a point, you know," said C.J., as he thought for a second.

"Not really, I'd reverse the whole thing if we were at home and a six point favorite. Tony worries. I don't want him worrying," remarked Kirk.

After C.J. finished in the bathroom, the trio went back to the banquet room for a buffet breakfast. Some fellows ate, some could not, as each individual started to prepare himself for this afternoon's task.

"There's a change from last night," said C.J. quietly to Kirk as they stood at the buffet drinking orange juice before picking up a plate and digging in.

"I know, I try to be loose for the guys, but my stomach's starting to do somersaults. I may start to go silent as we get close to game time, nothing personal, just bringing the game into focus. And even though you're on the sidelines, I won't talk to you. I need to keep my mind on the game," answered Kirk as he filled up his orange juice glass a third time.

"I understand," said C.J. "I can feel the tension building in the room, I'll keep out of the way. Wish I had a priest handy!"

"I don't think a priest will help. We've simply got to out play them. Most often people in the stands don't understand what's really happening on the field. The other team, they're busting their tails. We're doing the same. Sometimes the defense wins the individual battles on a series of downs and sometimes we take it on the chin. As the game wears on, one team may have the rhythm and takes charge of the game. Sometimes it's a battle to the end. And as the game nears the end, you're hurting, tired. But, you can't let your teammates down, so you reach back, even if nothings there, you find something and play your heart out for your coaches and your teammates. It's the most incredible feeling. And when the game is over, win or lose, you're drained. Happy you've won; devastated you lost, but drained. I'm not much different on the outside, win or lose. I respect the guys we just played, try to talk with them. Hell, the offensive right tackle played with me at Camden High. He got an offer from Syracuse, me, Maryland."

"I never thought of much, except having a great time in the stands," stated C.J.

"I know, and that's OK. I just hate to see the fans get on a guy who's just given everything he has and comes up short, no matter what team he plays for. Some writers write, but only from a layman's status. May have never played, but, are they ever experts," answered Kirk, who handed C.J. a plate and continued, "enough of that, let's eat!"

"Now you know why he's a co-captain," said Tony in a whisper to C.J., "he leads by setting one hell of an example. I try to keep him calm, you know."

C.J. smiled as he went along the buffet line, "they take care of each other!"

After breakfast, some fellows sat around the lobby talking, some took a walk, and some simply went back to their rooms before taking the bus back to the Carrier Dome for the big show.

In the meantime, the Miles drove from Elk Neck State Park down to BWI airport and took U.S. Air's flight #3852, which left at 8:30 and arrived in Syracuse at 9:50. John had a rental car reserved and it was off for some lunch before going to The Dome.

Sharon was nervous all the way and didn't say much, except short answers when Dora or John spoke to her. Her mind, of course, was on Kirk.

"Sharon, he'll do all right. He's as prepared as he can be. Have faith now, enjoy your lunch," stated John as they waited for the hostess to seat them in the Denny's Restaurant, and he put his arm around Sharon.

She broke into a smile. "I know, I wish I could see him for just a couple of minutes, though," Sharon responded.

"He's got work to do, honey. He needs this time away from us," stated John. Sharon didn't answer because the hostess took them to a booth.

Meanwhile, the players had arrived at the Carrier Dome and were in the locker room. Normal pre-game activities were going on as the players dressed and prepared to take the field for their practice warm up. Butterflies were everywhere as the hour drew close to game time. Finally, they left the locker room and headed for the field. Playing inside on this autumn day would be welcomed from a weather standpoint. It was close to 90 degrees outside, but inside the dome it was a comfortable 72.

There was a loud chorus of 'boo's' as fans spotted the enemy uniforms coming out of the tunnel onto the field. The Maryland team went to one end of the field, using the 50-yard line to the end zone as their warm up area. There were a few cheers here and there. Tony remarked to Kirk that he felt sorry for the poor Maryland fans sitting in the grand stand. Kirk yelled back that they wouldn't feel so bad if Maryland won!

When they arrived at their end of the field, the team broke into several quite organized groups, after doing team exercises. The quarterbacks were taking turns throwing passes to receivers. Punters were trying to get high, long kicks into the air. The offensive and defensive teams were going through various plays. Running backs were taking hand-off's and the kick-off man was placing the ball on the tee and booting the ball into the end zone on the fly.

Then there was one particular player, a linebacker by trade on the Maryland football team wearing number 55, practicing extra points. While Kirk often fooled around kicking when practice was over, this would be the first time 'it was for real' since high school. "Keep your head down, keep your head down," he kept telling himself. Kirk had never felt comfortable with the newer soccer-style method of driving the ball, but used the old straight up Lou Grozza style. He was doing just fine.

Of the dozen attempts, 11 went through the uprights and 1 hit the vertical post on the left and careened off to the side. The coaches then had Kirk back up 10 yards and try some field goals. They placed the ball on the 19, pretending that the ball would be snapped from the 12, with a 7-yard drop for the actual kick. The ball had to travel 29 yards because the goal post was situated 10 yards behind the goal line. Kirk did all right, hitting 4 of 6. Then they dropped 10 more yards and Kirk hit 2 of 4 from that distance. Finally, another 10 yards which would equal a 49-yard attempt. Only 1 out of 4 made the distance and that one just got over the cross bar.

"We'd better get well inside the 30 or get a large fan," remarked Kirk as he left to rejoin the defensive unit.

As the school bands assembled to march on the field for the playing of the National Anthem, the players completed the practice warm up and left for the locker room. They were still waiting for the game to get started, however, there was a more relaxed atmosphere among the players as they assembled to review the game plan and get last minute instructions.

In about 15 minutes, they were on their way back to the playing field ready to play the game. Make no mistake, the butterflies were still there and would only pass once the game started and they got down to the business at hand, however, the waiting was over. This was what all the practices, and drilling were all about. Game time!

As Kirk came running out with the team, he momentarily looked up and around the large, indoor stadium. He had tried to spot Sharon before, when the team was out for the practice. Didn't and figured that with the capacity crowd filling the stadium, that right now it would be impossible. He was correct. He wouldn't be looking around anymore, now, because, as they say, "It's game time!"

The coin toss was about to occur and as a co-captain, Kirk walked out onto the field at the 50-yard line with teammate Billy Williams, a senior running back from Baltimore, accompanied by one of the officials. Kirk was to make the call while the coin was flipped in the air. "Heads," stated Kirk in a loud, clear voice. The coin clearly fell on tails.

"Syracuse has won the toss and elected to receive the kick off," stated the referee to the cheers of the hometown crowd.

At this point, Kirk decided on which goal Maryland would defend during the first quarter, although it really didn't matter, because there was no wind or sun advantage when playing under the dome. The officials maneuvered Kirk and Billy so that their backs were to the goal they would defend and the Syracuse players faced them across from the large emblem painted at the 50-yard line. The referee went through the motions explaining the kick off and which goals would be defended and thus, this ceremony was over.

"I should have told you to call tails," kidded Billy as he and Kirk trotted back to their teammates.

"He screwed up again Coach," continued Billy with a wide grin on his face as he gave Kirk a playful shove.

"Let's huddle up men," said a voice as the players formed a unified circle that spilled onto the playing field itself. The 11 players from the kick off unit trotted out onto the field. Doug Sanford, who would kick off, was the last. He spoke with Coach Wyneski and then ran out, holding the kicking tee, which he would place the ball on for the kick. The players lined up at around the 32-yard line with Doug placing the ball on the 40 for the kick. Doug would start off running, kick the ball to the receiving team and his teammates would likewise start running to tackle the player receiving the kick.

The Maryland players were careful not to cross the 40 before Doug kicked the ball, because the result would be a 5-yard penalty and Doug would have to rekick from the 35. Everything went well. Doug really laid into the ball and it soared over the Syracuse goal line and past the end zone. There would be no runback and the Syracuse offensive game would start at their 20-yard line. Kirk was in his normal position as middle linebacker and was glad that the defensive unit was on the field first. Not that he didn't want his team on offensive, but only because the waiting was over and he'd get a taste of the action, get rid of the butterflies and finally play.

The Syracuse offensive series started with a running play off tackle, but the initial hole was quickly plugged as Maryland had anticipated they'd run in order to let their backs get the feel of the ball. Kirk was one of Maryland players that filled the hole and held Syracuse to just a one-yard gain.

It was now second down and 9 to go for a first down. Syracuse now tried a sweep to the right, but the Maryland defensive end was doing his job as he crossed the Syracuse line of scrimmage and held his position, not taking the fake that would have brought him into the middle of the back field. He slid off the initial block and hit the other back hard enough to juggle the ball loose. The ball bounced around until the Maryland defensive tackle fell on it. Because the ball had been fumbled in the Syracuse backfield, Maryland could have advanced the ball. But the Maryland tackle wanted to be sure of the recovery, so he just pounced on the ball and held it tightly until he heard the referee telling him, "OK son, you can give me the ball. I'm one of the neutral guys!"

The Maryland players were pounding him on the back as he got up and gave the football to the official. As Kirk trotted off toward the sideline, he looked for Billy Williams, just as Billy always looked for Kirk. "See you in the end zone," called Kirk as they touched hands. Billy was all business and just nodded.

As the defensive unit reached the sidelines, the defensive coach got them together to calm them down. They had done extremely well and played as a unit, but only 2 minutes and 15 seconds of the 60-minute game had clicked off the clock. "Let's settle down and keep the rhythm. We've got a long way to go in this one." The business-like atmosphere came back as the players gathered near the sideline to see how well the offensive unit would do on their series of downs. The ball was resting just 18 yards from the Syracuse goal line as their defense tried to wrestle the momentum away from Maryland's early good fortune.

Maryland would try to strike fast. Normally they would do much the same as Syracuse, letting their backs handle the ball, probe the line and corners, but this was an opportunity, and they wanted a quick 7 points, rather than have to settle for a field goal attempt. The Maryland quarterback faked a hand-off to the fullback, into the line and rolled out right. He pumped to throw a pass into the end zone, saw that there was good double coverage and then threw a pass to Billy Williams, the running back who had delayed and then did a crossing pattern between the charging linebackers and the deeper safeties. Bill caught the pass at the 13-yard line and continued to cross the field at an angle, picking up additional yardage as he went. He was hit at the 9 and slid off the attempted tackle, breaking it and then changed direction straight to the goal line. Billy gained 13 yards on the play, more than enough for a first down. It was now first and goal from the 5-yard line!

Maryland, it seemed, would try to go straight up the middle, especially with 4 downs ahead of them. The quarterback again faked to the back, this time to the second man, while the fullback hit the hole and became the blocker for the second back coming through the line. The fake worked as the Syracuse line and linebackers jammed up the hole in the middle.

In the meantime, the tight end made a block, driving his man to the middle and then slid to the inside in the vacant area. The wide receiver had run a route taking the defender away from the middle. A quick pass to the six-foot, five-inch tight end just inside the goal line spelled pay dirt for the Maryland team. Score, Maryland six and Syracuse zero! They had scored a touchdown!

The celebration was going in, both on the field and on the sidelines. Kirk was right in the middle of it when one of the coaches came up to him. "If you're not doing anything in the next few minutes, would you go out there and kick the extra point," stated the coach as he smacked Kirk on the fanny.

"Oh my God, I forgot," returned Kirk with a surprised look on his face. Kirk trotted out onto the field, trying to look calm and collected. Actually, even in the air-conditioned dome, the sweat started pouring down his forehead and back from nervousness. He arrived at the huddle and worked to calm the nerves.

"OK, Kirk, nail it," came the word as the huddle broke and the players took their positions for the point after touchdown attempt. Kirk didn't answer, but tried to concentrate, just as a golfer would on his first tee shot at an important match. "Got to keep the head down," he told himself.

Up in the stands, Sharon turned to her dad, "There's our boy Kirk, kicking the extra point!" but before John could respond, the public address system announced, "Number 55, Daniels for the extra point attempt."

"Good luck," came from the holder as he prepared to take the snap from the center. Kirk again didn't answer, but glanced up at the goal post and made an imaginary kick and flight of the ball.

At the count, the ball was snapped to the holder, Maryland's back-up quarterback, and a good ball handler. It was good that he could handle the ball well, because the hike was high and he had to reach to catch the ball and put it down quickly for the kick, especially with the on-rush of the Syracuse team trying to block the extra point attempt. Kirk waited as the ball was being placed down but almost kicked it before it was set. He hit it a little high on the ball and instead of going end over end as would happen with a straight-up kick, it sailed through the uprights just above the cross bar. Score! Maryland 7, Syracuse 0.

Kirk had scored the 13th point of his career at Maryland, having scored two defensive touchdowns before. He was being patted on the back as he started off toward the sideline. The world had just been taken off his shoulders. What a great feeling! He was all smiles!

"Sorry about the snap, great kick, man," said the Maryland center as he caught up with Kirk just before he reached the awaiting teammates. Kirk just patted him on the shoulder, then turned as the holder came over to shake hands.

"Thanks Terry," said Kirk. "You did a great job getting the ball down."

"It was a great kick under pressure, man, nice going," returned Terry.

By now the team had engulfed Kirk on the sidelines and he felt terrific, he hadn't let them down, at least not yet, and the game was still young. The rest of the first quarter was a defensive battle. Maryland didn't get inside Syracuse's 35 and Syracuse got as far as the Maryland 25. Syracuse attempted a field goal totaling a 41-yard try, but it missed, wide right.

The score remained 7 to 0 until midway through the second quarter when Syracuse connected on a 63-yard pass play. Maryland was playing a zone defense. The wide receiver went past the up man and was picked up by the safety. When the receiver made a cut, the Maryland defender slipped on the artificial surface and fell. The pass was caught and it was off to the races. The other safety tried to run the Syracuse receiver down, but he easily crossed the end zone, dropping the ball after he scored and raised both arms above his head in triumph. Syracuse made the extra point kick to tie the score at 7 each. The Syracuse crowd went wild as their fans watched the touchdown. The defensive battle took over again and the score remained the same throughout the first half.

The players headed for the locker rooms as the Syracuse marching band took the field for the half time entertainment. They put on a great show as usual, and the acoustics of the indoor stadium complimented the music. Sometimes, in the great outdoors, the sounds get lost. The crowd gave a loud ovation at the end of the performance, but one had to wonder if the cheers were for the band or the Syracuse team as they trotted back onto the field. Some of the cheers turned to boos as the Maryland team came running out of the tunnel and went to their side of the field. The second half of the contest was about to start.

Maryland received the second half kick-off and went on offense. They started the drive on their own 37-yard line. The kick-off was short, being received on the 16. It was a low line drive. This didn't give the Syracuse team enough time to effectively cover it and Maryland was able to return the ball 21 yards. Maryland was maintaining a sustained drive using mostly the ground game. They worked their way down to the Syracuse 14-yard line using only two passes. Both were complete for short yardage gains. Maryland, it seemed, would pass on first down as they did before when they were close to Syracuse's goal line. However, they faked the pass and gave the delayed hand-off to the fullback who took it up the middle through the hole made on the trap blocking at the line of scrimmage. The 'draw' play worked well and Maryland had the ball first and goal at the 3 yard line.

At this point, Maryland had Syracuse's defense reeling, expecting the pass and not getting it. Also in Maryland's favor at this time was the time of possession. With more than seven minutes off the third quarter clock, Syracuse had not had their hands on the ball yet. After the huddle, the Maryland quarterback took the snap and faked a hand-off into the middle with two running backs crashing into the piled up line of scrimmage. He then rolled left on a keeper and headed for the far side of the end zone, going wide to evade the linebackers. As he was being tackled, he hit the ground just over the goal line for Maryland's second score.

Again, it was a jubilant time for Maryland. For Syracuse it was another ice water bath. They worked to deal with this rugged dogfight of a game. They had been favored by a touchdown and now found they were behind by one. Plus, the clock was working in Maryland's favor right now. The extra point unit took the field and Kirk felt more confident, not only because of a second score, but also because he was now loose.

The snap, placement and kick were almost a routine. Kirk hit the ball well. It soared high over the crossbars and right through the middle. Maryland added the point to their score. Now the scoreboard read: *Maryland 14* and *Syracuse 7*. The Syracuse fans were unusually quiet at this time.

Maryland held tight for the balance of the third quarter as Syracuse never did get on track with their offense. The Maryland defense, which had been highly touted before the season started, was living up to their early billing as one of the best in the country. Syracuse was held scoreless in the third quarter and going into the fourth and final quarter of the game, Maryland continued to lead by the 14 to 7 score.

Syracuse had an early fourth quarter drive started but it was halted at the Maryland 36-yard line and with fourth down and 6 to go for a first down, Syracuse set up to attempt another field goal. They figured that there was still plenty of time in this last quarter. If they went for the touchdown now or even the first down and didn't make it, it would have an adverse effect on their team for the balance of the game. The field goal attempt would be a long one, almost 53 yards including the drop back for the kick and the extra 10 yards to the back of the end zone where the goal posts were. The Syracuse kicker had, in past years, kicked field goals of over 50 yards, so with the stable conditions of the Carrier Dome, it could be done.

Syracuse set up for the field goal attempt. The ball, though, was snapped directly to the kicker, who was also the backup quarterback, and fired a pass to the end. The end had made an initial block, then slid off to receive the pass, just at the line of scrimmage. He ran inside and headed for the first down. The Maryland defense, weary of the long field goal attempt suspected a fake and alertly covered the play. They rode the end out of bounds at the 31, very close to the 30-yard line. The nearest official dropped a marker at the point the end went out of bounds. It was too close to call and the referee called for a measurement. From across the field the chains were brought to get an exact look. Syracuse was half a football short of the first down.

It was a great try, but Maryland had held and took over on downs. The defensive battle continued. With a little over three minutes to go, Syracuse finally got good field position on a punt return. Maryland was forced to kick from their own 32.

Bill Davis got good hang time, however, his kick was short and the Syracuse punt returner called a fair catch at the Syracuse 47-yard line. Syracuse struck fast with two long passes and had a first down at the Maryland 9-yard line. Two runs later, they were at the 1-yard line. A fake to the middle, a roll out by the Syracuse quarterback and a short, hard pass to the corner of the end zone brought the Syracuse fans to their feet cheering wildly as Syracuse scored with just over two minutes on the game clock. The extra point attempt was perfect and the giant scoreboard showed the game tied at 14 apiece.

Syracuse kicked off and Maryland could not take advantage of having the ball for what seemed to be their last possession. They got as far as the Syracuse 39-yard line before they lost the ball in downs. It was out of range for Kirk to attempt a winning field goal. 56 yards would be difficult for any regular kicker. They attempted a pass, but it was batted away at the last second. Syracuse took over with a minute to go!

The Maryland defense proved just as tough. Syracuse tried a running play and two passes to get down field for a field goal attempt to win the game, but neither pass was caught and the running play was held for no gain. Maryland had used one of their four time-outs, to halt the clock after the run. The clock stopped automatically after an incomplete pass. Syracuse would be forced to punt. Maryland would get the ball one last time.

The snap was high and the Syracuse punter had to reach for the ball. It gave the Maryland defense time to get in and the kick was blocked! The ball bounced off to the left of the punter. An alert Syracuse lineman fell on the ball. The Syracuse fans cheered, thinking that it would be their ball, but that was not the case. Syracuse would have to give up the ball on downs.

The clock was stopped as offensive and defensive teams moved on and off the field. Maryland would take over on the Syracuse 38-yard line with only 27 seconds showing on the clock. It has been a closely fought contest, dominated for the most part by each team's defense. Maryland's defense had forced two Syracuse fumbles that stopped drives and had three quarterback sacks to their credit. They had completed an outstanding afternoon's unit of work and could only stand on the sidelines and hope that the offensive unit could win the game.

A tie would be somewhat of a moral victory, especially since Syracuse was a strong favorite to win. To the young men who had played their hearts out, it would leave them with an empty feeling. The clock showed only 27 seconds remaining in the game. It was obvious to just about everyone in the stadium that Maryland would pass. Maryland did exactly that.

The first pass attempt had to be thrown away as the Syracuse defense blitzed the Maryland quarterback who had no time at all to set himself and look downfield for his receivers. The second pass attempt was a quick out to Ducky Walters, the wide receiver. He made a move on the outside linebacker but picked up only 8 yards as the Syracuse defense closed and forced him out of bounds. The clock showed 16 seconds left.

The next play was to be a pass into the end zone and go for the touchdown or to pass the ball well beyond the end zone so that it could not be intercepted. With whatever time was left on the clock, Maryland would then try a field goal if all else failed.

In thc grand stands, Sharon, John, and Dora were on their feet like everyone else in the stadium as the exciting finish of the game drew near. On the sidelines, C.J. was keeping a low profile, almost out of sight, as he stood nervously waiting for the outcome of the game, and hoping!

The Maryland center came over the ball, snapped it, but there was a bad connection between the center and the quarterback. The quarterback dropped the ball, reached down, picked it up and knew instinctively that he had no time to continue the designed pass play, so he crashed forward toward the goal line. There was no hole and he managed only a yard gain. He quickly got to his feet, called a Maryland time out and slowly trotted to the sidelines to speak with the coaching staff. "A bad connection, my fault, too damn anxious," he said as he reached the coaches. He received a pat on the shoulder as if to say, "Don't worry about it, you had a good game," but it did not help much.

Kirk was called over. "It's a reasonably long shot, but what the hell, Kirk, let's go for the field goal, relax and kick the hell out of it," stated head Coach Wyneski, as the back-up quarterback, went back in to hold for the field goal attempt.

The clock showed only eight seconds left. The ball rested on the 29-yard line. The Maryland team huddled. "Relax Kirk, it's only a game," came a voice in the huddle. It helped break the pressure and everyone laughed. They broke from the huddle and started to take their places for the field goal attempt, but just as the Maryland players got set, Syracuse called a time out!

They'd make Maryland and especially Kirk, think about the situation a little longer. The team went back to the area where they normally huddled. Kirk looked over to the coaching staff to see if they wanted him to come over, but they motioned 'No' and Coach Wyneski clapped his hands and then gave a referee first down sign, pointing to the goal post. It was all a bit exaggerated and, of course, designed to relax Kirk a little.

Kirk further scanned the sidelines, not wanting to look toward the goal post or the Syracuse team at this point and spotted C.J., looking toward the dome roof, fingers crossed and his mouth moving, as if he were offering up a prayer. Kirk had to smile at his friend's concern. It brought a second of relaxation, which was quickly shattered as the referee's whistle blew, signaling that play was back on.

Kirk set himself for the task at hand, "OK, keep your head down," he told himself as he made an imaginary kick toward the goal post. The ball would be kicked from 7 yards behind the line of scrimmage at the 36-yard line and with the goal post resting 10 yards behind the end zone, the total distance Kirk had to kick the ball was 46 yards. A tall order.

The set up was at least straight, no angle, and for that, Kirk was grateful. He took a deep breath and put his eyes on the spot Terry would place the ball. Kirk was concentrating so hard, that he didn't even notice the Syracuse players jumping up and down to distract him, nor did he appear to hear the crowd noise, which was, of course, pro-Syracuse and screaming to also distract him.

Terry caught the ball, quickly placed the ball's laces out of the way and set it for the kick. Kirk did not hurry himself, kept his concentration and kept his head down at the point of placement. He hit it solid and low, the ball shot over the jumping Syracuse players' outstretched hands and continued its flight to the goal post.

The ball was running straight, but the distance...It was coming down now...It looked to be short! As Kirk finished his follow through he now was looking at his kick, trying to wish the distance to the kick. Terry had gotten up from his holder's position and was standing next to Kirk, worrying along with him.

The clock now showed zero. All eyes in the stadium were on the ball as it headed for the uprights. The ball cleared the crossbars, just by inches, but it cleared!

The Syracuse fans were stunned. The noise of the cheering Maryland fans sounded like a whisper in the huge indoor stadium. The stadium scoreboard showed the final score, *Maryland 17* and *Syracuse 14.*

The Maryland players on the sidelines bolted onto the field to join the ones who participated in the last play of the game. Kirk stood for a few seconds almost motionless, trying to realize that he did it. He actually kicked the ball 46 yards and Maryland had won!

Terry gave Kirk a big bear hug and by now all the players were celebrating around Kirk, hugs, slaps on the back. The conversation and congratulations were lost in the noise as everyone seemed to be yelling and talking at the same time. By now, the Syracuse and Maryland coaches had met on the field and congratulations offered all around. It had been a great game, an absolute battle on the football field. The Syracuse players, showing good sportsmanship, were now on the field and talking with the Maryland players and coaches. There was great respect for each other. It was a great victory, and one damn tough loss.

In the grand stands, Sharon had been jumping up and down with excitement. John, while he yelled a bit, was for the most part his conservative self and just stood there watching the scene, as proud as if Kirk was his own son. Dora likewise had cheered the sensational kick, but she was now also watching the scene as it unfolded on the field. When Sharon turned to face her mother and dad, tears were streaming down her cheeks. She was proud, excited and quite drained from cheering not only as a fan, but as a player's fiancée. It was almost too much!

C.J. had stayed behind as the players dashed onto the field, but now he walked over to Kirk as the team headed for the tunnel. Kirk spotted C.J.

and waited for him to catch up. "I don't know what to say. Congratulations man. You were terrific. I think I wet my pants," stated C.J. as he and Kirk shook hands.

"Thanks C.J., this is a game I'll remember," answered Kirk as they reached the tunnel and headed to the locker room. "Did you see Sharon at all?"

"No," answered C.J., "and I forgot what section they were in."

The press was waiting as Kirk, C.J., and quite a few players joined those already in the locker room celebrating the 17-14 victory. Kirk was asked dozens of questions on the way to and in front of his locker. He patiently and thoughtfully answered the questions, praising his fellow teammates for their performance and speaking on behalf of what the game actually was, a team effort.

He also spoke on behalf of the Syracuse players, not because Syracuse newspaper writers were there covering the Maryland locker room, but because he had also been on the losing side of an important close game and knew what was going on in the other locker room. They were a great team, made up of fine, young men, and this afternoon, they just came up short.

After showering and changing, Kirk was preparing to leave the locker room. "Where's C.J.?" Kirk called to Tony, who was already dressed, but still celebrating.

"Went out to find that lady friend of yours," Tony replied. Kirk didn't answer, but continued dressing and spoke to players and coaches as they came over to congratulate him on the winning kick.

Kirk had scored five points today with the two extra points and the field goal. It brought his total score up to 17 points. It's nothing to shout about when you figure what the offensive backs and ends score, but each point was important and can be remembered. He had never really had anyone to share the two defensive touchdowns with, but now that there was Sharon, he couldn't wait to be with her to savor what happened today. It made him feel especially good!

As Kirk left the dressing room, C.J. met him. "I've found them, come on." C.J. stated and he motioned for Kirk to follow. They went outside, not too far from where the buses were parked when Kirk spotted Sharon. She didn't wait, but ran up to Kirk and threw her arms around him. He held her tightly for a minute and kissed her, without saying a word. Then he held her again.

"I'm proud of you," said Sharon as she held onto Kirk.

"I had a lot of help," answered Kirk as he shook hands with John and gave Dora a kiss. "It was along afternoon."

"I've just never seen a more exciting game," said John, "but then, I guess we've never had a reason to be so personally involved. Man, you were cool under fire," John continued.

"Well, I'm glad it looked that way from the stands. I think my knees must be black and blue from knocking against each other," answered Kirk as he put his arm around Sharon again and winked at C.J.

"Don't let him kid you," chimed C.J. "That sideline is one crazy world. Some of those guys could become paid assassins. Some I think are 11-feet-something tall, and the confidence they show, man, I've never seen anything like it, and the sound of the hitting!"

"Enough C.J., you're going to make Sharon think there's danger out on the big playground. It's just organized sandlot ball," kidded Kirk and they all had a laugh.

"Are you hurting?" asked Sharon quietly as they walked toward the main parking lot.

"Not really, a little sore, but that's to be expected," answered Kirk, who stopped, looked back and saw that the other players were getting onto the bus. "I guess this is as far as I can go," he continued.

In the meantime, C.J. made arrangements with John to drop him off at the Marriott to pick up his car and head back to Elk Neck. The Miles would be staying at the Ramada Inn this evening and flying back in the morning. They invited C.J. to have dinner with them and John said that the Marriott's restaurant might be just the right spot. They take plastic!

As Kirk was leaving to join the others on the bus, he gave another quick kiss to Dora, shook hands with John and C.J., thanked them for traveling all this way to see his football game and took Sharon up into his arms and kissed her again. He then started for the bus.

As she watched Kirk walk away, Sharon held up one finger to her dad, as much as saying, "One minute", then she started after Kirk. "Hold on there Star, I can't resist seeing a man in uniform off," called Sharon and then caught up with Kirk and took his hand.

Kirk had to smile as he looked at the girl he loved. "I'm not wearing a uniform now though. Will this outfit pass?" kidded Kirk.

"Close enough," returned Sharon and they walked hand in hand to the bus. There wasn't much time because Kirk was the last one on and, in fact, the other bus was already pulling out for the bus ride back to the Syracuse airport.

"I love you darling. See you back home," said Sharon and they kissed once more before Kirk climbed onto the bus. The bus started out, but Kirk did not take his seat right away, but stood and waved to Sharon.

It wasn't long before the second bus caught up with the first one because of the slow traffic. They followed each other back to the airport and the awaiting U.S. Air charter flight to BWI. While leaving the bus and walking to the plane, it was hard to tell if the Maryland team had won or lost. They were a tired and sore lot of men. Perhaps the celebrations would erupt once again, when they were all together on the plane, rather than separated on the two buses. As they got closer to the plane, you could see that the party was starting. The locker room and field celebrations were from the excitement of the moment. What they had accomplished as a team was now setting in and they were able to relax together as a unit on the plane ride home and savor the hard-fought victory.

The party did take place, as unscheduled parties would do. It was spontaneous, lively fun, but a certain maturity had set in. They came as an untried team, confident of what they thought they could do and now they flew home having proven themselves in a hostile arena against a very tough opponent.

When they landed at BWI and taxied to the gate, one of the players called out that he could see a lot of people waiting for them, as he peered out of his window and looked at the terminal gate waiting area. He was right. Several hundred University of Maryland fans and students had come over to greet the winning team. As the players deplaned, the crowd cheered and welcomed them!

Sunday turned out to be a day of rest for most of the players. Some had to go to the infirmary for additional treatment and others used the training facilities, including the enjoyable whirlpool, but it was a day of catching up with themselves before heading back to class and also getting ready for next week's game against the University of Virginia.

Kirk went to the training center early and had a quick breakfast before taking his jeep and making the drive back to BWI. He didn't know if there would be anything special that would keep him on campus and since there wasn't he wanted to meet Sharon's plane. She didn't know that he was coming. They really didn't have time to discuss it, and, Kirk thought it would be fun to surprise her. He called U.S. Air earlier to verify the flight and left himself plenty of time. It was a pleasant drive and Kirk basked in the feeling that all was really well with the world.

Kirk parked the jeep in the short-term parking lot and strolled into the main terminal building. He walked over to the TV monitors, checked the flight information, saw that the plane was on time and noted the arriving gate. After passing through the security check, Kirk found the gate and sat down to wait. Taking note of the time, he found that the wait would be a long one. He had arrived 45 minutes early. So, up he got and it was off to the snack shop for a couple of donuts and coffee.

While he was sipping the coffee, Kirk noticed a stand that contained about three or four newspaper machines. He checked his change and walked over to buy a Sunday paper. He finished the donuts, tucked the paper under his arm, got a refill of coffee and went back to his seat at the gate, settled in and turned to the sports page to read all about the Maryland victory over Syracuse!

It was interesting reading. There were even several pictures of the game, including one of Kirk kicking the final field goal. "Well, you can see I'm keeping my head down. I think I'll keep this picture," he told himself.

Kirk checked his watch just after hearing the announcement that the U.S. Air flight was arriving from Syracuse. "It's right on time," he noted and got up to watch the plane taxi to the gate. Several passengers came up the ramp before Kirk spotted Sharon and her folks. He waved and they waved back.

"Oh my God, it's Kirk Daniels, the star of yesterday's victory over Syracuse University. Oh, can I have your autograph? What a thrill!" called Sharon in a fairly loud voice as she left the ramp and entered the terminal and ran over to Kirk.

Kirk was turning three shades of red from embarrassment and wished he could find a place to hide. He was also a bit angry with Sharon for doing this, even though he knew she was kidding him.

"I wish...," Kirk started, but Sharon cut him off.

"I know, I'm sorry," she said, "I was only kidding, but I know I embarrassed you."

Before Kirk could respond two men who were on the plane and, obviously, with the Baltimore newspaper came over, having recognized Kirk, after Sharon's kidding outburst. They asked Kirk several questions and wanted an interview.

Kirk was gracious and spoke with them for a few moments. He took emphasis off himself and talked of the total team effort that made the victory possible.

In the meantime, Sharon stood near and listened as Kirk spoke with the men of the press. John said that he'd head on down to the baggage area to claim the suitcases. Dora went with John after telling Sharon quietly that she'd find Kirk a stick, so that he could beat her!

After the men from the newspapers finished taking notes and recording the conversation with Kirk, all four walked toward the baggage claim area. While standing there with Sharon, waiting for the luggage, several U. of M. fans came over to Kirk to ask for an autograph. He asked their name, just as he had back on campus when he signed autographs for the kids hanging around the practice field, but as Kirk was later to tell Sharon, he too, was thrilled. This was the first time that adults had asked him!

After the luggage was delivered, Kirk walked with John and Dora to their station wagon and helped them load the car. Kirk was going to spend the day with Sharon in Towson and drive back to College Park that evening. John and Dora were heading back to Elk Neck, so the good-byes were said at the airport. They'd see him Saturday, after the Virginia game.

Kirk said he'd made some dinner reservations during the week to beat the crowds, but John said no, he'd already called Tag's in Laurel. Everything was already set, for whenever they arrived.

As John and Dora pulled out of their parking space, Kirk picked up Sharon's suitcase and pointed toward the short-term parking lot where he'd parked the jeep. He started off carrying the bag, but Sharon stopped him and had Kirk set the suitcase down and flipped out the wheels and handle, so that it could be towed. "Save your strength for me!" was her comment.

Kirk gave her that look of 'don't tempt me' and Sharon came back with a teasing little girl look.

"You know, one of these times, when we're all alone, you may just push me over the edge and that will be that," stated Kirk as they neared the jeep.

"You promised my mother and father, your future in-laws. Remember over dinner? Eating food my father provided and my mother slaved over? Cooking your favorite things to maintain my virginity until our wedding night? Remember?" stated Sharon in a kidding manner.

"That was a long time ago. Things are changing rapidly!" answered Kirk.

"Long time ago? I've only known you 121 days!" exclaimed Sharon.

"Well you get more delicious-looking by the day and I can't help it one damn bit," returned Kirk.

"I hope you feel that way 40 years from now," answered Sharon in a softer voice as they reached the jeep, then she put her arms around Kirk. "It's tough on me too, and knowing that you've been with other people doesn't help. I just want you for my own."

"Look," started Kirk, but Sharon interrupted.

"I really don't want to know what was. All that's important is after me and I don't mean to tease you too much, just enough," Sharon replied.

Kirk held Sharon for a moment, kissed her and loaded her suitcase into the back of the jeep. They drove out of the airport grounds and onto the Baltimore-Washington Parkway toward Baltimore.

"I was thinking about the Inner Harbor for the day, perhaps lunch at the All-American. They have great hamburgers. And maybe we'll take in the fish tank," stated Kirk as they continued on toward Baltimore. "I've never been inside the place."

"Sounds great," was Sharon's reply, "but I don't think that the National Aquarium should be referred to as the fish tank!"

"Well, that's what the guys called it, I didn't know the official name. I thought it was just part of the city of Baltimore's Crab Festival," kidded Kirk. "In the future, I'll watch it!"

"The city, the country, forgives. Where do we park?" returned Sharon.

"There's a sign: fish tank parking," noted Kirk to the sign that read *Inner Harbor Aquarium Parking* and he drove on right past the turn, continuing straight on the one-way street.

"You did that for a reason, right?" questioned Sharon.

"Yes, I wanted to see if there was a closer parking lot plus, I missed the turn," answered Kirk. "I'll go around the block."

"Oh don't worry about it," returned Sharon. "People pay good money on the town bus driving around Baltimore like this. I understand the city is famous for its White Steps. Does the group pass any of those houses?" laughed Sharon as Kirk gave her that look!

Kirk drove around the block and this time did not miss the parking lot. The lot was located directly across from the National Aquarium. Next to the Aquarium was a World War II submarine, plus an old lighthouse ship. Both had short lines waiting to board for a tour. They crossed the street, but headed to their right toward the nearly 200 year-old ship, the Constellation.

"Let's see the Constellation first," said Sharon as she pulled Kirk along.

"Oh that's fine with me, as if I have a choice," replied Kirk. Kirk bought combination tickets to tour the Constellation lighthouse ship, and submarine. They boarded the Constellation and walked back in history as the tour guide showed them the grand old ship and relayed stories about her exploits throughout her colorful career. There were a couple of places that they peeked into, but could not go, because repair construction was taking place. The tour though was great and both Sharon and Kirk came away with a sense of involvement in American history.

Before walking over to the aquarium area, they went into the mall area and up the steps to the All-American Restaurant for lunch. They told the hostess that they'd wait a few minutes for a table by the window, so that they could enjoy lunch while watching the harbor activity.

Asked if they'd like a drink while waiting, both said 'iced tea' almost at the same time. The hostess was expecting some other answer and instead of leading them to the bar, noted that a table should be vacant shortly. Kirk and Sharon smiled over the hostess' cute way of handling the situation. It wasn't long before they were seated with a tall glass of iced tea in front of them.

The hamburgers were simply great. Maybe they tasted even better because of the outdoor scene and because they were together, but lunch was enjoyable. Then, it was off to the 'fish tank'! Kirk noted that they should go to The Aquarium first, since they didn't know how much time they'd want to spend there. Then they could see the other boat exhibits when they came out. That's what they did!

As expected, the National Aquarium was spectacular and they spent so much time there, that when they came out, it was closing time for the lighthouse ship and submarine. They'd catch it another time.

Kirk wanted to go to the Chesapeake Restaurant, a Baltimore landmark, before dropping Sharon off in Towson and heading back to the University of Maryland. They picked up the jeep and drove to the restaurant. Sharon wondered if they should have called ahead for reservations, but Kirk said that they couldn't be that crowded. Sharon, in disbelief, asked how a popular restaurant, like the Chesapeake, could not be crowded on a Sunday evening.

"We should call ahead," she exclaimed!

"We'll chance it," was Kirk's reply, as he drove on.

As they approached the restaurant, Sharon smugly stated that she was right and "just look at the crowd waiting in the lobby." They parked the jeep and walked toward the restaurant. Sharon said little, but reinforced her viewpoint that they should have phoned ahead for a reservation. Kirk didn't answer. He just let Sharon speak her mind, but smiled to himself.

They entered the Chesapeake Restaurant and Kirk pushed his way and excused himself as he made his way to the reservation desk, holding Sharon's hand as he went, almost dragging her through the waiting crowd.
"Oh Mr. Daniels, and this must be Miss Miles," stated the tuxedo-dressed Maitre d'. "Your table will be ready in just a few moments. Please, enjoy a drink in the lounge and we'll call you."

"Thank you Peter," answered Kirk as he escorted Sharon to the lounge.

"It'll take me just a few moments to catch up," said Sharon as Kirk held her stool and motioned for the bartender to come over.

"Gin and bitter lemon for Sharon and I'll have a Coors," said Kirk.

"Coming right up sir, and hello Sharon, I've heard a lot about you," answered the bartender as he started to make Sharon's drink. "Great game Kirk," he said quietly, so as not to draw attention to Kirk.

"Thanks Jimmy," said Kirk and he caught Sharon's look. "Jim and Pete are classmates of mine," he said in answer to Sharon's look.

"Alright, everything's clear now. In other words, all the time I was worrying about you being embarrassed by not having a reservation, you were putting dear ole Sharon on. Right assessment of the situation?" questioned Sharon as Jimmy put the drink in front of her and had to smile as he saw the dagger expression in Sharon's face.

"That's partly true," answered Kirk with a half smile.

"Well, what part of my assessment was not true?" continued Sharon.

"That's a good question. Oh look, Pete has our table ready. Let's take the drinks and continue the discussion there," said Kirk as he nodded to Peter and reached into his pocket to pay the bar tab.

"I'll have this put on your dinner bill," said Jimmy with a wink.

"Thank you Jim," said Kirk as he and Sharon left to join Peter, who was waiting with menus. Peter showed them to a table located near the back of the restaurant where they could relax. It wasn't long before a young man showed up with glasses of water, rolls, and butter. Then a waitress came, but Kirk told her that they'd need a minute before ordering dinner.

"What do you think?" asked Kirk as he glanced over the menu, but really didn't look because he already knew what he wanted to order.

"What I really want," answered Sharon, who paused for a moment, "is my explanation, but I'm not certain you have one, right?"

"Not one that you'd accept in your frame of mind," kidded Kirk. "Now," he continued, "what would you like for dinner?"

"The old delegation bit. Well, I'm not having any of it. And as far as dinner, since you certainly seem to be on a roll here, please, you order for me. Surprise me!" needled Sharon with a sly grin.

"Would you mind going to the ladies room?" questioned Kirk as the waitress came back over to their table for the order.

"I don't have to!" said a shocked Sharon. "Why would you say that?"

"How can I surprise you then, you'll hear what I say to the waitress," answered Kirk, and he had to laugh to himself.

"It will be my turn some day. Just remember that," returned Sharon.

"Well, time to order," said the waitress cheerfully.

"A couple of grilled cheese sandwiches, tomato grilled inside and two glasses of water, with ice should do it," said a smiling Kirk.

"Ice in the glasses or on the side in a bowl?" questioned the waitress.

Pete, who was seating a party of four at a nearby table overheard Kirk and came over to his table. "Are they giving you a hard time Patricia? We've had trouble with this guy and his lady friend before. Watch what he orders and make certain they don't run out on you," he kidded with a wink to Pat.

"OK fellow, if you don't want this guy to bounce you out of here," Pat stated, but Pete stopped her before she finished her statement.

"Maybe we should reconsider," Pete stated. "This guy plays linebacker at Maryland and if we make him mad, he'll simply beat the hell out of me later." And they all had a good-natured laugh.

"He'll get serious about the order," chimed in Sharon "otherwise I'll order for myself and he'll have to wolf down both grilled cheese sandwiches!"

"Wow, see how fast they turn on you?" answered Kirk. "OK, Pat, I'll be Mr. Serious. We'll have two cups of crab soup, and then garden salads with oil and vinegar on the side. For the main course, crab cakes for me and crab imperial for my fiancée, both with French fries and whatever vegetable of the day you're serving," said Kirk, who paused for a moment, then added. "For dessert, chocolate something for the lady, here, and I'll have fresh strawberries with heavy cream, not whipped cream, but heavy cream." Then Kirk handed Pat the menus.

"You did very well," said Pat, "much better even than grilled cheese. You did, however, forget the beverage. Iced tea now and coffee later?"

"No, we'll finish our drinks now," then looking at Sharon, "do you want some wine with dinner?"

"No, iced tea is fine and maybe decaffeinated coffee with the chocolate something," she answered and reached across the table to touch his hand as the waitress nodded, smiled, and left.

"I love you," Kirk responded as he squeezed her hand.

"I love you, too, darling," answered Sharon.

The dinner and the evening continued to be most pleasant. The food, of course, was delicious and the service outstanding. As they left the restaurant, Kirk stopped to speak with Pete and Jim. He thanked them and told them he'd see them later at school.

Sharon and Kirk walked out into the clear, warm Baltimore night and strolled hand in hand to the jeep. Neither one said anything, although they did exchange glances as they walked along. Glances were followed by the smiling look of two people very much in love.

Kirk drove to Sharon's apartment, but did not go upstairs to say hello to her roommates. He was tired from the game, the travel, and the day in Baltimore.

"I'm not exactly tired," he explained, "just a bit overextended!"

Sharon, of course, understood, then made Kirk promise that he'd call as soon as he got to his dorm. She'd call him if he forgot.

"I'm awake, won't fall asleep at the wheel," he reassured her. "And I will call as soon as I get in, I promise."

They held each other for a moment then Kirk kissed Sharon goodnight and got back into the jeep. With a wave, he was off, heading back to College Park.

It was a normal, enjoyable ride in the jeep. The wind blew all around him. You really know what the word driving in a convertible is all about when you have a Jeep!

There were thoughts of Sharon and their future, his thanks for a friend like C.J., who along with Sharon got him the jeep after the VW was totaled in the crash.

After Kirk parked the Jeep, he put the top and side curtains on. The walk to the dorm was a short one and just after entering his room, he made the phone call.

Sixteen 16

The preparation for Maryland's second football game, and home opener, was just as intense as the Syracuse game. With a hard fought victory under their belt, they had a quiet strength and confidence as they prepared for the University of Virginia. While Maryland would be considered favorites, they would not take the press clippings for granted. They had an attitude of "Let's take it to them and not let up. A winning attitude!"

Sharon and Kirk did not see each other during the week. Classes had started for both and they were equally busy. The nightly phone calls, just before turning in, had to serve as their link this week. Kirk, of course, would also be involved in game preparation Friday evening, as well as spending the time with players and coaches, so the two of them had to be content with after the game on Saturday.

The week went by quickly. Keeping especially busy will often do that. Saturday morning was bright and almost cloudless. It would be a day in the high 70's, with no forecast of rain, a beautiful Fall day.

Even as the players came out for the pre-game warm up, the grandstands were almost full. Many of the tailgate parties had come early and also those faithful fans had entered the stadium early in anticipation of the first home game. The players thoroughly enjoyed the atmosphere and it showed. The Syracuse Victory, coupled with a beautiful day and home fans, gave them that certain confidence and looseness that also showed. The fans cheered the players as they caught practice passes, punted and kicked field goals. They cheered even harder as the players went back to the locker room for the final preparation and to put their game jerseys on. It was a warm, wonderful feeling to be a member of the University of Maryland football team this afternoon.

Sharon, John and Dora had select seats in the stadium and were on hand for the practice. C.J. had an even better seat, or standing spot. He'd be on the sidelines once more. Coach Wyneski saw to it. Kirk and Tony didn't have to ask, "Make sure that good luck equipment manager of yours is here!"

The Maryland team stayed in the locker room until the pageantry for the first home game was completed. The coaches didn't want them coming out too soon and lose their edge. They'd wait until the last minute.

Just as the band had finished the National Anthem, the fans spotted the Maryland players coming through the tunnel and onto the field. The Maryland cheerleaders were lined up to welcome them. An almost deafening roar went up as the players ran through the streamers set up and held by the cheerleaders. They were cheering for this game and an obvious ovation for the big victory over Syracuse, which they could only hear on local radio or read about in last Sunday's newspaper.

Virginia had won the coin toss and would receive the kickoff. The Maryland defensive unit would be on the field first. Kirk always liked that. He'd rather "get on with it," as he would say, not have to "get cold" waiting for the offensive unit to complete their set or sets of downs. Of course, if the offensive unit scored, that's just great, but considering all, he'd like to get his feet wet first, so to speak. Interestingly, the offensive unit always wanted to get on the field first, for the same reasons as the defense.

The kickoff was not too deep and Virginia, with a good runback, brought the ball all the way to their own 48-yard line. Virginia would start their series of downs at almost mid-field. Virginia was always a team with surprises and this game was no different than others. Knowing that they were considered underdogs against Maryland, they went right after them. The opening play was a fake to the middle, a roll out to the left flank by the quarterback and a pass across the grain to a wide receiver crossing. The pass was complete, deep in the secondary in the middle of the field at almost the Maryland 33-yard line. The receiver kept to the crossing pattern and out distanced the Maryland safeties. Less than two minutes of the game had clicked off the game clock and after completing the point after touchdown kick, Virginia was ahead by 7-0. Maryland had been taken by surprise and paid the price. After receiving the Virginia kickoff, Maryland gave the Cavaliers the ball back on downs and during the first quarter, managed only a 27-yard field goal by Johnny Conklin, who was back in action. Virginia's defense held as tough as Maryland's during most of the second quarter. Maryland scored a touchdown in the closing seconds of the first half after a recovered fumble on the Virginia 24 gave the Terps excellent field position for a change. It did take Maryland 6 plays to punch in for the score, but they got into the end zone. Maryland converted the PAT and at the half, led 10-7.

The Maryland locker room, at half time was quiet and businesslike. Virginia had come to play and so far, had made a good showing. It was now time for Maryland to show what they were made of.

Maryland started right off at the second half and through a sustained drive that took over 6 minutes off the clock, scored again. The party atmosphere regained itself in the stands, as the fans felt more secure that Maryland was finally taking control of the game and setting the pace.

Maryland scored one more time in the third quarter and led 24-7 at its conclusion. In the early minutes of the fourth and final period of play, Virginia again scored on a long pass, when the Maryland safety tripped during the coverage and fell down. The pass covered 41 yards and after a blocked point after touchdown attempt, Maryland's lead was cut to 24-13. Maryland came right back though and scored two more touchdowns. As the game clock wound down, with Maryland in possession of the ball, the scoreboard showed what would be the final score, *Maryland 38* and *Virginia 13*. The Cavaliers played tough, but suffered their second loss of the young season, having been beaten the week before by Duke University. Their next opponent would be Virginia Tech.

Kirk stopped before heading out through the tunnel and waited for Sharon, John, and Dora. C.J. had walked off the field with Kirk and waved as the trio got near.

"Don't touch me," Kirk said to Sharon as she came up to kiss him. "I'm sweaty and filthy. I'm not fit to be next to until I shower."

"You didn't look this bad out there," kidded Sharon as she reached up and kissed him anyway. "I love you, I love you, now go clean up!"

"Great game," said John as he shook hands with Kirk.

"Thanks, John. It was a battle out there today," said Kirk, while smiling at Dora continued, "I'll give you a hug later."

"Thanks," kidded Dora. "You do look a mess!"

By now several fans had gathered near. Kirk told the Miles he'd catch up with them later. Then he and C.J. went on through the tunnel toward the locker room. Kirk felt a bit beat up today and the hot shower would feel good. When Kirk and C.J. entered the locker room, the celebration was well under way. With two victories already behind them, the team collectively was enjoying the feeling that triumph brings. They joined in the celebration. The shower could wait a few minutes.

Kirk was glad to fall into the background as just one of the players today. Last week he had been the center of attention and even though he played just as hard this week, he could fade into the background as simply a member of the highly talented Maryland defense. He was polite when members of the press asked how it felt to be just another player. C.J., though, almost got into it with the sports writers, but Kirk interceded and calmed him down. He was almost used to the Press. C.J. was, of course, not ready to handle some of the stupid questions posed by them.

"Suppose you had missed the extra points and the field goal last week?" questioned C.J. to Kirk "They wouldn't be around now" but before C.J. could continue, Kirk stopped him.

"Don't even think about me missing these kicks. You and I should wash your mouth out with week-old beer that's been left outside in a dirty glass," stated Kirk. "I'll handle the press. They've got a job to do. Some just do it poorly, others are very good at their jobs."

"I'm sorry, you know what I mean," answered C.J., "and where did you ever get the idea for the beer tonic, man, that's nasty!"

"It just came to me. Something horrible, you know. Come to think of it, you might just like it," kidded Kirk.

C.J.'s facial expression said "Yuck" as he reached out and gave Kirk a light punch on the arm.

"Let me shower up and I'll meet you outside with the Miles," said Kirk as he held his arm and limped toward the shower!

It wasn't too long, maybe 20 minutes, when Kirk emerged from the locker room door and greeted Sharon, Dora, John and C.J. He by-passed everyone and went directly to Dora. "I'm clean now, it's OK to give me that kiss," said Kirk as he gave Dora a hug and kiss.

"I'm next," said Sharon, as she moved in close to Kirk. He put his arm around her and pulled her close as she reached up and kissed him.

"Com'on you clowns, let's go have some dinner," stated John as he motioned for everyone to follow him and started walking toward the parking lot.

"Where should we go?" chimed in C.J., "Anyone have an idea?"

"Let's try Tags," answered John. "Especially, since we have a reservation!"

Everyone laughed, and it was off to Tags!

Kirk and Sharon would take his jeep. C.J. had his car and John drove Dora in the station wagon. John told Kirk that they'd drop Sharon off on the way home, so he wouldn't have to double back. That would work out fine, because Sharon had planned to come down to College Park on Sunday with a girlfriend. Then, the light came as Sharon spotted Tony, coming out of the locker room. He waved thinking that Sharon was waving 'hello' but then a sharp sweep of her hand and arm as in 'come here', brought Tony over.

"Hi Sharon, Mr.- Mrs. Miles", said Tony in a hospitable manner. "Great games, right? Ole Kirk did OK" as he was stopped by Sharon.

"Tomorrow afternoon, say 1:30 or 2:00 p.m., at your dorm. Be there," said Sharon in a firm voice. "Be there!"

"I've got to be," started Tony "someplace else, but..." he stopped.

"A stable mate, named Peggy, Mama would approve," said Sharon.

"I've got to be at the dorm around then," corrected Tony "Then all of us will come home for pasta and Mama's special gravy, right?!"

"I think we've been invited for dinner," kidded Sharon as she squeezed Tony's cheek!

"I have to work tomorrow," stated C.J. in a low voice, almost to himself.

"I'll eat your share and tell you all about it," answered Kirk.

"Until tomorrow," said a smiling Tony. "I played very well, tell her that."

"I'll lie like the devil for you," answered Sharon kiddingly. "Until tomorrow!" The group finally left College Park for the drive north via route # 1 to Laurel. The table was waiting for them when they arrived and the small celebration at Tag's Restaurant began. No menu was offered, as they say, "We'll cook for you!"

As usual, it was a most enjoyable evening. The food was excellent, although if you asked Kirk what he had, he couldn't tell you, but it would sound good from his description.

C.J. came out with an, "Oh, by the way, my Aunt left for Florida yesterday and you can move in anytime you want. Her girlfriends went early, so she decided to join them."

That was greeted by a punch on the arm by Sharon, along with a "Why didn't you tell me?"

"I *did* tell you," was C.J.'s reply. "I just found out today."

"Today began a long time ago, this is tonight," responded Sharon!

After the 'Thank Yous' for a wonderful evening, Kirk walked Sharon to the Miles' car to say goodnight. C.J. left for the State Park. After saying so long to the Miles, a very tired Kirk pointed the jeep back down Route No. 1.

Kirk awoke the next morning still tired and sore from yesterday's game. He certainly wasn't alone as evidenced by the gathering of players for breakfast. They were, of course, very pleased about the victory, but a price had been paid. Most importantly though, there were no major injuries. The young men would heal rapidly and be ready for the LSU game scheduled for next weekend.

One of the players was heard to remark that "the Virginia players felt worse than we do. They came away with nothing to show, except a second loss" It had been a physical game, so the Virginia players would also be black and blue this morning.

Sharon telephoned to say that she and Peggy would arrive around 3 p.m. maybe 2:30, but in any event, she'd be late. Peggy's car was at the gas station getting a new water pump. It had gone out the day before. Kirk offered to come up and get them, but Sharon, knowing Kirk could use the relaxation said no, just let Tony know of the change and that the wait would be worth it! She also told Kirk that her folks would help her move into the mobile home in a couple of weeks, and that he and his friends should not worry about any of the moving. She anticipated that Kirk would have offered, and that half of the football team would help out but the one thing that was uppermost in her mind now was to let Kirk keep his focus on football. It wasn't just thoughtfulness that guided Sharon during this most important final college football season, but an understanding, of the importance, plus, of course, a very deep love for one of the players.

Tony was standing outside as Sharon and Peggy pulled up to the dorm in Peggy's five-year old Chevy Monte Carlo. He walked over to the car and opened Peggy's door for her. Sharon opened her own door and got out.

"I'm Tony, one of the stars on the Maryland football team," he said with a wide grin as he helped her out of the car and closed the door.

"I've heard so much about you for the last 40 miles," answered a smiling Peggy, as she reached out and shook hands with Tony.

"What am I, chopped liver? You could have just as easily opened my door too," stated Sharon in mock anger.

"Mr. Sharpie is coming down the steps," said Tony referring to Kirk as he left the dorm and strolled over to Peggy's car. "He should have been here to open your door, Miss Prissy. Anyway, what have we here, a clone, or are all your stable mates so called Miss Sharpies," answered Tony in a stage whisper which could be heard across the entire campus.

Peggy had to laugh to herself. "No, not all the Towson girls are as Miss Sharpies as we are Tony," she responded.

"You heard that, you heard what I said?" questioned Tony "You have good ears!"

The entire free world can hear your stage whispers," joined in Kirk as he greeted Sharon with a kiss and winked at Peggy. "Hi Peg" he continued.

"No kidding. I'll have to learn to speak in softer tones," laughed Tony. "Well," he continued, "shall we all head for Mama's?"

Before anyone else could answer, Sharon said that first, she wanted to stop at the mobile home, just to see it again and to see what she needed to bring, or if she should clean it first. In reality, she simply wanted to visit it and, well, the Cherry Hill Mobile Home Park was just down the road, and C.J. had given her the keys.

After a short drive in Kirk's jeep, they arrived at the Mobile Park. They checked the office, but it was closed, then Kirk drove to C.J.'s uncles place, but he wasn't at home either, so they left a note and headed over to the mobile home C.J. had arranged for Sharon to use while she was practice teaching in the Silver Spring area. This would also be Kirk and Sharon's home after they were married at the end of November.

Sharon handed Kirk the mobile home key just before they got out of the jeep. He walked up onto the small porch and opened the door. Sharon wasn't far behind and Kirk held the door as she went in. Tony looked around, as if inspecting the Park and pronounced that the "place looked good... neat, clean." Peggy took it all in, grabbed Tony and headed for the porch. Kirk waited and continued to hold the door for them.

"This is even nicer than I remember," remarked Sharon to no one special.

"It's terrific," stated Peggy, "how many bedrooms does it have?"

"Just enough, one," kidded Kirk. "The sofa folds out though, if we need to take in renters, or C. J. needs a place to stay!"

Tony looked around. He walked to the back first. "This is very nice, I didn't know these trailers were this nice," he finally commented. "There's actually two bedrooms in the back."

"They call it a mobile home," corrected Sharon.

"Sharon, let's face it, you're hitting on the small points. Think for a minute. This home, is not very mobile, in fact, they probably have the wheels off and it sits on blocks. However, some truck trailed it behind, to get it here, a trailer. See what I mean?"

"You've just taken the mobile home industry back to the dinosaur age, but I must admit you've got a point. Glad you like the trailer," stated Sharon.

"Com'on gang, let's head for Mama's house," called Kirk as he opened the door and beckoned everyone to follow.

Once outside, they piled back into Kirk's jeep and it was off to the Italian feast at Mama's house.

The drive took about forty minutes. When they arrived, Kirk had to look for a parking space. He found one, half a block away from the big three-story Baltimore row house.

"Seems as if you're in luck," stated Tony. "You'll get to meet the family."

"There must be twenty cars parked around here." stated Peggy. "Is this for your house, or is there a restaurant near here?"

"No, it's just Sunday," answered Tony as he showed everyone to the side door. "They'll think I've brought company and not just friends if we use the front door" he explained.

"This I understand," commented Sharon "We do the same thing. Right, Star?"

"Right," said a smiling Kirk, remembering the first time he met Sharon. She brought him in by way of the back door, commenting that they only use the front door for company.

Once inside, Tony, who was now a celebrity in the family, because he not only was attending college, but also because he is one of the starting players on the Maryland football team, was mobbed by family. He was all smiles and greeted everyone back with hugs, kisses and handshakes. Peggy, Kirk and Sharon stayed in the background, enjoying the scene. The noise level was very close to the decibel reading of a rock concert. It was happy noise. Tony's father came into the large parlor and put his arms out. Tony was there in a split second hugging his father. Mama came in from the kitchen and Tony had his arms around her, then plastered a big loud kiss on her cheek. Finally, in a loud voice that made everyone listen, Tony introduced Kirk, Sharon and Peggy in that order, telling the family a little about each one. He said that everyone was to introduce themselves, because there wasn't enough time in a day for him to explain everyone to his friends!

Mama beckoned the girls, who followed her into the kitchen. Papa brought Tony and Kirk a large glass of red wine, not in a wineglass, but in a glass that a lot of Italian families drink wine from. It was a generous serving. The wine was excellent. It wasn't long before Kirk was deep in conversation, discussing mostly football, some college, where he was from, and how he could land such a beautiful girl. He felt right at home, talking loud to be heard while other loud conversations went on around him, laughing, enjoying the fantastic family atmosphere which takes place in Italian households. Somehow his wineglass got refilled and he was munching on stuff that he didn't know what it was, but he went back for more, it was delicious!

Then, everyone got called for dinner. The dining room was across the hall, but also had an entrance to the kitchen. The dining room table wouldn't accommodate everyone, but no worries. The kitchen door would be left open and the children would eat in there, while the adults would eat at the dining room table. Tony whispered, in his stage whisper, to Kirk that only a year or two ago he had to eat in the kitchen!

Dinner was exciting to Sharon and Peggy. Kirk had been here for dinner before, but not on a Sunday. He could hardly believe the amount of food, both in variety and volume. There would be enough for everyone to take home for later, and that was the way it was supposed to be.

Conversation at dinner was just as loud as before, several conversations were taking place at the same time. Kirk was involved in two and contributed to a third. It was wonderful! As expected, everyone was taking extra helpings of Mama's gravy. When people asked for her recipe, she always gave the same answer. "You can come over and watch!" Peggy and Sharon started the meal saying, "yes, they'd love more spaghetti sauce," but by meals end with second helpings, they had graduated to, "please pass the gravy!"

As the meal ended, clean up began. The men were sent back into the parlor while the ladies stayed to help out. Dessert would be served in a little while, after everyone rested. Sharon and Peggy tried to stay and help, but Mama insisted they leave the kitchen and relax. They did manage to help clear the table, but that was all they were allowed to do.

Tony was called in to take charge of Sharon and Peggy. His orders were to bring them back for dessert and not before. Tony motioned to Kirk, who was in the parlor to join them. He took the trio to his Father's den. It was a large old and comfortable room, which also served as an office for his father. The room had high ceilings. An old four blade ceiling fan had hung just above a light fixture in the center of the room. A large dark wooden desk, a beautiful, dark, wine colored, leather chair, along with three leather side chairs and a leather sofa gave a certain richness to the den. The walls and ceiling were paneled in rich mahogany. The other focal point of the room was sitting in a large birdcage. Tony went over to the cage and flipped up the door. The bird came off his perch and down to the door, pausing only a second, then came out and walked up the side of the cage to the top. There he went to one foot, taking the other one and opening one wing full feather. Then he did the same with the other leg and wing. Finally, he opened both wings full feather and dipped, showing off his full beauty.

While the bird was going through the ritual of showing himself, Tony was talking to him. "Pretty Bird. Oh, Pretty Bird. Just look at you, Harry!"

"Harry," said Sharon, "the bird's name is Harry?"

"Yes, and to add to all this, Harry is a girl cockatiel," started Tony.

"Why Harry, if it's a girl," questioned Peggy. "Do you have another named Sam?"

"Very funny," returned Tony "When we bought him, her, they said it was a boy. About a year later, there was an egg at the bottom of the cage and Harry was sitting on it. Talk about surprises!"

"She is beautiful," commented Sharon. "Hi, sweetheart," she said to the bird.

"Does she talk," questioned Peggy as Tony put his nose down to the bird's nose.

"No, not yet. I guess with some of the meetings that go on here during the week, it's just as well," answered Tony as the bird stretched to touch noses with Tony. They rubbed, Eskimo style for a few seconds, then Tony straightened up and put his finger out to the bird. Harry hopped on and then flew up to Tony's shoulder. She seemed quite content and started to preen herself. Kirk, in the meantime, was looking at some of the books on the bookshelf behind the desk. "You know, there are some very old books here."

"Yes, well, this was all my Grandfather's, before my Dad's," answered Tony. I guess I still don't appreciate all that is here, maturity needed, I imagine?"

It wasn't long before one of Tony's uncles came into the room to tell them that dessert, coffee and expresso were being served.

"Com'on little boy-bird," said Tony as he bent down and Harry jumped back onto the top of the cage. "Got to put you away." Tony then put his finger back and Harry jumped on. He then lowered his finger to the cage door opening and Harry entered the cage. She went cheerfully over to his seed dish and started munching away on a sunflower seed.

Kirk, Sharon and Peggy watched while this was going on, and it was Peggy who finally said, "I thought it was a girl, why'd you say little boy-bird?"

"Well, he she really doesn't know and we've always said boy-bird, so why confuse him now. You know what I mean?" answered Tony.

"Somehow that does make sense, but you are a bit strange," commented Peggy.

"A bit strange. That's very kind," chimed in Kirk.

"But Peggy, my dear," started Tony as he ignored Kirk's remark completely "also kind, charming and handsome, in a way." Then pointing the way back through the doorway, "Let's have dessert!"

Kirk and Sharon went out the door first, as Peggy stood back for a second, placing her hand across Tony's arm.

"Not quite handsome, cute, very cute though," she kidded!

As they came back into the dining room they came upon a dessert feast. Pastries, cakes, ice cream "Do you want coffee or expresso, help yourself. Com'on take more than one." It was fun!!

They were leaving, for almost twenty minutes. The good-byes were not only long, but even new conversations cropped up.

"You must come again. We'd like to get to know you better," said Mama as Kirk, Sharon, Peggy and Tony finally left. They promised.

"I'll be back very soon, for my laundry," kidded Tony!

"Don't bother unless you bring this lovely Irish lass with you," answered Mama as she gave Peggy another hug.

"I'm only half Irish," stated Peggy. "Mama, my mother is Jewish," she continued in a serious voice.

"Half Irish, half Jewish, a combination that made a beautiful young woman. You teach me chicken soup, I'll teach you gravy," answered Mama as she hugged Peggy again.

Tony gave his mother another big hug as thanks for being so nice to his friends. He then also gave a special hug to his father.

Kirk, Sharon and Peggy went down the steps to the street level. Tony started down, but stopped to hear what his mother was saying.

"Remember, bring this one back. I really like her," his mother said in a loud whisper!

"I will Mama. I love you, you too, Papa," Tony said and he choked a bit, holding back a tear trying to be a man, but loving his parents so much.

Sharon and Peggy decided that they'd like to stop at their apartment house first, get some things and stay at the mobile home, camp out, so to speak, since neither had early morning classes.

The trip to the girls' apartment was fun, as was the drive back to the Maryland campus. They laughed and joked all the way, reliving the hours spent at Tony's house. They picked up Peggy's car then all went to the mobile home. Kirk and Sharon looked around the kitchen before heading back out to the Seven/Eleven store to pick up some snacks, but everyone decided they were still full from dinner and dessert. No one even wanted coffee!

Peg and Tony decided to take a walk. Kirk and Sharon stayed behind to spend some time by themselves. It would be another long week as Kirk balanced classes and practice. He'd have a lot on his mind this week as they prepared for the Saturday night game in Baton Rouge against the LSU Fighting Tigers. The team would fly down on Friday, get in a practice and play football in Tiger Stadium, or Deaf Valley as it was known throughout the Southeast Conference.

The week went fast or so it seemed. The nightly phone conversations Kirk and Sharon had were, as he often put it, "like reaching an oasis." It felt so good, just to hear her voice, to talk about each other's day, discuss their future and to tell each other, "I love you."

"You'd better tell me that forty years from now," she'd say.

"I'll do more than just tell you," he'd reply.

On Friday morning, The Maryland football team left BWI airport on a charter with Continental Airlines 727 for Baton Rouge, Louisiana. The players were excited about the trip and it showed. They were a loose gang of guys, joking and playing all the way to Tiger town. The coaching staff let them alone. There would be plenty of time for being serious. LSU was coming into the game with a win and a loss. They had defeated Texas A & M in Baton Rouge in their first game, but with 3 pass interceptions and 2 fumbles, fell at the hands of Florida in Gainesville in the second game. The LSU defense was one of the toughest in the nation. The 28-0 victory over A & M attested to that. Even in the Florida game, they grudgingly only gave up 13 points, as they lost 13-10 in an important SEC game which was considered a major upset by the press. Maryland, despite two solid performances and two victories, were underdogs by two touchdowns, but the players at Maryland didn't believe the betting lines and were convinced they could win their third straight game! After they landed in Baton Rouge, the buses took the team to the Holiday Inn. Usually the team stayed at Marriott Hotels, but the nearest one was over 80 miles away in New Orleans, a city Maryland would love to play in on New Year's Day at the Sugar Bowl, but, first things first.

The team held the practice session in Tiger Stadium. It was a light workout enabling the players to familiarize themselves with the surroundings and walk through their basic plays. The stadium itself was intimidating. It held around 80,000 people, all but a handful who would be a noisy bunch of LSU fans.

John, Sharon and Dora flew down on Saturday morning. They arranged to stay at the same Holiday Inn where the team was residing. C.J. couldn't make this trip since he was working the weekend. He'd catch the game on television. It was being televised nationally on the ESPN network. Game time would be at 8:30 Saturday night, Eastern Daylight Savings time, 7:30 local time.

Kirk and Sharon managed to spend some time together on Saturday afternoon. Then it was off to Tiger Stadium for the Maryland football team. The players knew there was a task before them and it wouldn't be long before the game time attitude became evident in the locker room. The press would be very limited in their time allowed in the locker room before the game. There really would be no time for discussions with the media as final game preparations took place with the coaching staff.

Finally it was here. Game time and the players headed for the field. Maryland won the toss of the coin and would receive. The kickoff was deep and into the end zone. There would be no run back. Maryland started on their own twenty-yard line. The first two plays were runs that only gained six yards. A third and four yards to a first down pass was overthrown and Maryland was forced to punt the ball. It was a good high and deep punt. The hang-time permitted the Maryland defense to cover the play well and the LSU receiver signaled for a fair catch. LSU started on their 32-yard line. The Maryland defense held tough and forced LSU to also punt the ball away. It was a defensive battle throughout the first quarter. The only break came when Kirk intercepted a pass over the middle. It was thrown short of its mark and Kirk leaped up to pick off the pass. He was hit hard after only a three-yard gain. The ball was on the LSU 28 yard line and after three plays Maryland only managed to move the ball to just the 21 yard line. The LSU defense had stiffened once again. Maryland attempted a field goal, the ball being placed on the 28. The kick was straight and carried well past the additional 10 yards over the end zone placement of the goal posts for a three point score. At the end of the first quarter the scoreboard showed *Maryland 3* and *LSU 0*. Maryland knew that to have a chance to win here in Baton Rouge, they had to hang tight and not let the game get out of hand early. It's extremely difficult to try and play catch-up against LSU at home. Maryland's defense had done their job, now to get the offense on track! The second quarter almost mirrored the first. The defensive battle continued. With two minutes and eighteen seconds on the clock, Maryland hit again on a field goal. The offense had stalled on the LSU 14-yard line and they chose to settle for the sure three points. Maryland now led by the score of 6-0. The ensuing kickoff was short. LSU started the run back at the 17 yard line, bringing the ball all the way to the Maryland 41. They had excellent field position for the first time and after nine plays, punched in for a touch down! They added the point-after-touchdown and with only 26 seconds remaining on the clock until the half, LSU took a 7-6 lead over Maryland. It was a shock, ice water thrown on the Maryland players. The defense had been nearly flawless throughout the first half, now this!

Maryland kicked off the second half, again with a short kick and LSU took advantage once more. They ran the ball back to the Maryland 39 and could have gone all the way, except the kicker made the tackle. LSU struck early with a long pass into the end zone and with less than two minutes off the third quarter clock, LSU took a 13-6 lead. Adding the PAT, brought the score to 14-6. It was exactly what Maryland did not want, to play catch-up in Baton Rouge on a Saturday night. Maryland had a sustained drive mounted late in the third quarter, but it died on the LSU 20 and they had to settle once more for the 3-point field goal. The Third quarter ended with LSU still in the lead, but now it was 14-9. The Maryland defense held tight during the balance of the third quarter. At last the fourth and final 15 minute quarter got underway. The biggest problem the Maryland offense had though, was the LSU defense. They were equally tough, but put to the test, as LSU fumbled the ball on their own 27-yard line. Maryland recovered the miscue. LSU's stubborn defense held once again as 2 running plays and a completed pass only netted 8 yards. With fourth down and two on the LSU 19-yard line, they lined up once more to attempt a field goal. The 3-point conversion would still leave them 2 points behind LSU however, they'd be only a field goal away from capturing the lead. The ball was snapped, but it was a fake field goal attempt. The ball was snapped directly to the kicker, Johnny Conklin. The holder, got up and took on the role as an extra blocker. Conklin, in almost a shotgun position quickly threw a pass to #89, Rick Tosinski the tight end, who in a normal field goal attempt was the right outside blocker. Rick had thrown a glancing block, then cut out wide right and headed for the end zone. He caught the pass at the 11-yard line and raced into the end zone. Touchdown! Score, *Maryland 15* and *LSU 14.* The clock showed that there would be plenty of football left in the game with 11 minutes and 23 seconds to go. The crowd, which had been it's usual noisy self, was now noticeably quiet. The sudden score, a touchdown from what looked like a field goal attempt had stunned the partisan LSU faithful. For the point after touchdown Maryland broke from the huddle and lined up for a 2-point conversion. It would give them a 17-14 lead, if successful and force LSU into thinking touchdown, rather than field goal, since a field goal would only bring them a tie. The ball was snapped. The play was a quarterback draw. The big Maryland line did their job and the quarterback ran, then made a head long drive to the end zone. There was a huge pile of uniforms, LSU purple and Maryland white at the goal line. The officials were busy untangling the bodies, looking for the one holding the ball. They found the ball and the Maryland quarterback at the bottom. He had scored! Maryland now held the 3-point lead. The Maryland kickoff was deep and caught by the receiver 2 yards into the end zone. As he caught it, the other receiver called to him to put a knee down for touch back. He did, knowing he'd have trouble getting very much yardage as the Maryland kickoff specialty team was bearing down on them. LSU would start this series of downs from their own 20-yard line.

The Fighting Tigers were conservative during the series, especially being so close to their own goal. They were in what could be a sustained drive, mostly on the ground, nothing fancy. With the ground game, the clock was ticking off time in what seemed like chunks! LSU had advanced to the Maryland 38-yard line, with the clock showing 6 minutes and 28 seconds left in the game. On the next play, the LSU quarterback looked deep and was ready to unload a long pass into the end zone, when he was blind sided by the defensive end, who had circled around and drove the quarterback to the ground. The ball popped loose and bounced around for what seemed like an eternity, but was really only seconds. An LSU player fell on the ball. It still belonged to them, however, the sack caused a 9 yard loss. LSU would start second down from their 47. Two plays later LSU had only gained 1 yard. They were out of field goal range and would have to punt. It was a great punt. The kicker had aimed for the coffin corner and nearly hit it. The punt went out of bounds at the Maryland 6-yard line. It was a terrible place to start from, but at least they had the ball, and the lead. LSU's defense was up to the task of holding Maryland. After giving up one first down, they brought a halt to the Maryland advance on Maryland's 23-yard line. Maryland would have to punt. LSU could get good field position out of the exchanges. The clock showed less than 3 minutes now as the Maryland punter hit a high, but not long kick. The LSU punt receiver called for a fair catch at the LSU 48-yard line. LSU had good field position. A tired Maryland defense came back onto the field. It would be a tough series of downs, especially with the Fighting Tigers starting just shy of the 50-yard line. They needed only 20 yards to be within reach of tying the game with a field goal. The LSU quarterback took the snap, faked a hand-off to the running back and rolled out right. He hit his tight end 9 yards downfield. The tight end took a solid hit, bounced off and gained another 7 yards before being brought down on the Maryland 36-yard line. At the defensive huddle, the Maryland players looked to regroup. LSU was now in field goal range. With 1st down and 10 yards to go, LSU tried to strike fast. They threw a pass into the end zone, but it was batted away at the last second as the Maryland safety got what looked like just a finger on the ball, just enough to deflect it away from the receiver. It was now second and still 10 yards to go for another 1st down. The second down play was a draw. They tried to make it look like another pass play, but Maryland was having none of it. Kirk, from his middle linebacker position filled the hole that the LSU running back was coming through. He hit the running back with a crushing tackle, driving his helmet deep into the running backs middle. The tackle was so hard that it completely knocked the wind out of the running back, forcing him to drop in his tracks. As he fell from the blow, the ball popped out for a fumble. A Maryland player pounced on the ball, at the Maryland 37-yard line, and the ball was theirs! The LSU player was still down and needed attention from the sideline.

Kirk got up quite dazed from the collision, and started off, staggering a bit, toward the LSU sideline. Tony, who had started toward the Maryland side, spotted Kirk and ran over to him. "You'd be better received on our side," he called and then took Kirk by the arm and led him the other way. "Great hit!" called several players from the offensive unit as they came onto the field and passed Tony and Kirk. Kirk did not respond as he tried to clear his head. Kirk was taken from Tony and over to the bench where the trainer sat him down. The team doctor soon joined them and removed Kirk's helmet. Tony looked over his shoulder to see how Kirk was, then started over, but he was called back by one of the coaches. There was nothing Tony could do and with so little time left in the game, the coaching staff needed all the players to keep the present situation uppermost in their mind. Equally worried, were Sharon, John and Dora. Being in the grandstand was a world away from knowing if Kirk was all right. At home, C.J. was watching the tackle being rerun on the television. He had also been taping the game for Kirk and Sharon. The TV commentators were still talking about the hit Kirk had made, just at a time when Maryland needed to make a big play. Then they broke for a commercial with the clock showing 1:56 to play. It was the 2-minute warning. C.J. hit the pause button so that the commercial did not tape. He didn't sit back down but waited nervously for the commercial segment to end, and he wished that the game was over right now!

Meanwhile, they were still working on Kirk as the officials took the cue from the man on the sidelines, who represented the television network, that the commercials were over and the final 1 minute and 56 seconds could proceed. The Maryland offensive unit needed to pick up a first down, maybe two to run the clock out because LSU still had all their time outs left and could keep stopping the clock with them. LSU probably thought Maryland would run to keep the clock running between downs, or force LSU to expend one of their four time outs. Maryland's first play trying to surprise LSU, was a play option pass. The quarterback rolled left, but instead of passing, he pitched back to the trailing back and threw a block. The play gained seven yards, to the 44-yard line. It was now second and 3 for the Terps. LSU took a time out. The play had removed 28 seconds from the stadium clock, which was also the official clock for the game. On the next play Maryland did pass, but with the receivers covered. The quarterback threw the ball wide and high into the sideline. They had hoped to complete the pass, pick up some meaningful yardage and place additional pressure on LSU, but it didn't work and now it was 3rd down and still three yards for the first down. The clock showed 1 minute and 18 seconds left in the game. On the next play, Maryland tried to run a sweep. LSU, had stacked the center and trying to gain 3 yards of real estate there would be extremely difficult. The play gained almost 9 yards to the LSU 47, when the running back was hit by two LSU players. The ball squirmed loose and bounced toward the foul line, was scooped up by an LSU safety just before it hit the foul line. The safety simply ran on out of bounds. LSU had the ball back with 48 seconds still on the game clock. The ball would be placed on the LSU 45-yard line. The Maryland defense trudged back onto the field. Kirk, was still on the bench. He would not be back in tonight's game. The blow to his head, from the tackle had caused a slight concussion and, of course, they would take no chances by sending Kirk back out, even though he protested their decision and wanted back in!

LSU threw a safe pass into the flat and picked up 8 yards. The receiver went out of bounds at the Maryland 47. The next play was a pass over the middle, which gained 13 yards. LSU, with 29 seconds on the clock, took a time out. The ball was resting on the Maryland 34. The TV networks broke for another commercial. The waiting...!

LSU's fans were almost in a feeding frenzy as they sensed VICTORY! So many times before, their team had snatched a victory from what seemed like certain defeat, in the last seconds. On the other side of the field the Maryland defensive coaches were using the time out to try and stop LSU's quick short pass completions. They had the defensive co-captain with them giving last minute instructions as the officials called time back in. This was it!

As the LSU quarterback received the snap from center, it was obvious that Maryland was blitzing in an attempt to get to the quarterback with a sack, or at the least, to put enough pressure on him and force a quick, hurried pass, even a throw away pass. The quarterback rolled left to get away from the rush. He picked up a couple of good blocks, which also gave him a little extra time and threw across the grain to his wide receiver who was running a post pattern. A Maryland safety dove for the ball, trying to make an interception. He got a finger on the ball, but tipped it upward and into the hands of the receiver.

The ball was caught on the Maryland 13-yard line. The Maryland safety bounced on the ground, diving for the ball. He reached up to try and grab the LSU wide receiver's leg and foot, but the side stepping receiver dodged the defender and even though he stumbled in making the catch, managed to maintain his balance and get into the end zone. Help had been on the way as the other defensive backfield players raced toward the pass reception, but they were too late. The noise level of the crowd and the jubilation of the players told the full story. LSU had taken a 20-17 lead. With the clock now stopped for the PAT, 16 seconds still lit the night sky on the game clock. The exchange on the snap for the extra point was in the dirt. The back-up quarterback, who also acted as the holder, dug the ball out. He quickly placed it down for the kicker, but the exchange took too long and although they managed to get the kick off, it was blocked at the line of scrimmage. It simply had no height and was batted down. The score remained 20-17. Maryland would have a chance, not much of one, but there were 16 seconds on the clock and they would get the ball one more time. The LSU fans, realizing that while it certainly looked good, none-the-less became noticeably quiet. Maryland had played LSU much tougher than anticipated. The 2 touchdown favorites were doing all they could just to hang on.

The kickoff was not the traditional long high shot, but a line drive type kick, which would bounce around and be difficult to field. Of course, it would not take precious time off the clock until the ball was touched by a Maryland player. The ball took a crazy high hop as it hit the ground on the Maryland 34-yard line. Maryland, anticipating this type of kick, had loaded the field with pass receivers and backfield men, ball handlers. The ball was caught after the first hop by a Maryland halfback. He followed instructions and headed toward the LSU side of the field, but at an angle so that he could get out of bounds and stop the clock. He went from his own 30 to the 39-yard line, a long distance from the LSU goal, but, they still had the ball. The game clock showed only 8 seconds left, time for one, maybe two plays. The Maryland quarterback walked over to the referee just before going into the huddle. "If my man is in bounds, look for me, I'll be calling a time out right away."

"You've got it," was the official's answer and he blew his whistle to set the 30 second time to get the play off before calling a delay of game penalty.

LSU lined up in a prevent defense. They'd rush just three men, have five men lined up as deep linebackers and have three safeties. They'd give Maryland the short pass, but nothing long. Maryland took advantage of this in order to get two plays off. The first play was a pass from the shotgun formation. The quarterback lines up about 5 to 7 yards deep, very much like playground football. From this formation he can see all of his receivers and it permits the quick release. The ball was snapped, (hiked was the old term), and the pass was complete in mid-field at the LSU 48-yard line. The receiver, Ducky Walters, picked up an additional 4 yards to the LSU 42, where he was downed. The pick up was meaningful. The LSU defenders had expected the pass to go to the sideline and all the wide receivers were covered very well. The center portion of the field was open and Maryland was actually forced to go there. The clock was stopped with just two ticks left. Maryland, at this point, had 2 options, a long *Hail Mary Pass* into the end zone or a field goal attempt. The field goal attempt would be a long one. With the ball being set at the 49 for the actual kick, and the goal posts at the back of the end zone, the kick needed to travel 59 yards!

Maryland had used the clock wisely and rather than make a quick decision they called a time out in order to have a discussion. The *Hail Mary Pass* would be just that; LSU would, of course, load up for it, and chances for a completion were very slim. On the other hand Johnny Conklin's longest game kick was a 54 yarder last year. This would certainly be a test.

Even if Kirk was not sidelined right now, Johnny would get the call. He is the kicker, and this distance was well over Kirk's range. The coaching staff decided to go for the three points and a tie.

Johnny had a conversation with the coaching staff and walked, rather than ran, out onto the field. He didn't want to hurry himself, this was too important. The snap would have to be a hand motion. The LSU fans had once again joined the game. Tiger stadium wasn't known as *Deaf Valley* for nothing!

The snap was a good in-line snap. The ball was quickly placed down and hit lowly and solidly by Johnny Conklin. It looked great, traveling high and long. The fans had universally become quiet as the ball traveled its course toward the uprights. Johnny was watching, twisting his body as if trying to help the ball. It was on line, but short, hitting the ground just below the goal posts. Johnny had nailed it, but the distance wasn't there. LSU had won 20-17. Time had expired. Kirk was the first player off the sideline to catch up with Johnny, who when he saw the kick was going to be short, just dropped his head and walked toward the side line. "It's OK man, you gave it a great shot. It was our only shot, John" said Kirk as he put his arm around Johnny Conklin. Other players soon joined them, knowing how badly Johnny felt and wanting to console him and share the loss. They were a team!

The LSU fans were jubilant, celebrating a hard fought victory. Down on the field, the LSU players were simply shaking hands with the Maryland players and coaching staff. They had dodged a bullet, so to speak, and knew it. It had been a battle all evening and LSU had tremendous respect for their Maryland opponents.

Sharon, John and Dora made their way toward the locker room area to get a glimpse of Kirk to be certain he was all right. At home, C.J. turned off the tape recorder and slumped in the chair. He had gotten to know a lot of the players during the two previous games and felt the pain of their loss. He, like the Miles, was pleased to see Kirk come off the bench to meet Conklin. Kirk would be OK.

As Kirk came through the tunnel with the other players, he caught a glimpse of Sharon and gave her the high sign. "I'm OK" and joined the Miles for a moment before going into the locker room. "I must look like I've been in a battle," he said as he gave a light kiss to Sharon and shook hands with John."

"I know," he continued, "I'll give you a hug later," he said to Dora, who smiled and squeezed Kirk's hand.

"Are you OK?" she asked with motherly worry.

"I'm fine," answered Kirk "just had my bell rung a bit. Part of the deal sometimes. I'll see you all back at the Holiday Inn," he continued and picked up the rear as his teammates made their way into the locker room.

Kirk first had to see the team doctor again, before he took off his uniform and showered. The Maryland trainer had walked off the field with Kirk. He kept his distance as Kirk talked with the Miles, but pointed him to the team physician, as soon as they entered the locker room. There were three other players also seeing the doctor and several other players that were being worked on by assistant trainers.

"They must be giving something away free," kidded one of the players as he waited in line for the trainer. It was perhaps the only bit of humor spoken in an otherwise quiet locker room. Victory had been so close. Even a tie would have been something. They had suffered their first defeat and it showed. The Syracuse and Virginia wins were special. They had molded this group of young men into a team, a winning team. Now, they'd have to unite as a group and come back next week to challenge a strong North Carolina State team.

The coaching staff gathered the players together for an impromptu team meeting. "Before we all get too down on ourselves," Coach Wyneski started, "I want to tell all you fine young men how proud I am of the effort you put forth this evening. We came in here, according to the press, with no chance to win. We were at least, a two-touchdown underdog. Well, LSU and their fans won't soon forget this Maryland team! To quote Vince Lombardi, the former great coach of those Green Bay Packer teams, 'We just didn't have enough time to win this game.' Again, thank you gentlemen, this game is behind us. Next week we're back home against North Carolina State. Let's look forward!!"

The talk meant quite a lot to the players. The coaching staff knew how hard they tried. It helped, but there were still some wet eyes as different players coped with the fact that Maryland did not win. They were defeated! It hurt! The locker room continued to be quiet as the players went through the motions and left for the bus ride back to the Holiday Inn.

As the players filed off the bus, Sharon stood waiting for Kirk. She came up to him and reached up as she put her arms around his neck and kissed him. Normally the players would kid Kirk and Sharon, but not tonight.

"Are you really OK?" she asked as she took his hand and they started for the hotel lobby.

"For now," he answered, then added, "but don't bring this up to me 30 years from now, with remember that time you banged your head in Baton Rouge!"

"OK Star, I feel better now. You're part way back. Let's go to the pool area and be by ourselves," kidded Sharon as she squeezed Kirk's hand and tugged for him to follow her to the chase lounges by the pool.

"John and Dora?" questioned Kirk.

"Smart parents, knew I wanted you to myself. They'll see you at breakfast. Let's put these two lounges close to each other so that you can hold me in your arms and console me for having worried about you," stated Sharon as she and Kirk settled on the lounges.

"You should be the one consoling me," answered Kirk as Sharon moved closer and put her head on his chest and snuggled close to him.

"But you knew you were all right, that is, after a time. But you weren't all right when you started toward the other bench and Tony had to get you," said Sharon quietly as she felt Kirk hold her near, touch her hair and kiss her head gently. "I love you so much, Kirk."

"I love you too, sweetheart," answered Kirk in a quiet voice.

They laid on the lounges for what seemed like a long time, neither saying anything, but Kirk would kiss Sharon's head and feel her beautiful hair on his face. Sharon reached for Kirk's hand and held it tightly, not letting go. Finally Sharon, still lying on Kirk's chest asked softly. "Does a loss like tonight's hurt as much a I think it does, I mean..." Kirk sensed what Sharon was trying to ask, interrupted her so that she wouldn't stumble over her words not knowing exactly what to say.

"We, as a team, worked extremely hard for a win and came up short. We were in the game to the last. We weren't blown out, embarrassed. It does hurt. At the end of the game, the LSU quarterback came up to me and said, 'This will be a game I'll talk about for years. You guys are incredible. I'm sorry, someone had to lose. We were lucky to get out of here with a win.' That makes it a little easier. We don't have to hold our heads down as losers, we have their respect and that counts for something. Each of us will have to handle this in his own way. I get quiet. Tony had tears in his eyes. This is our last year and we want it to be a banner year. I think we'll all be OK and ready for North Carolina State."

Sharon stayed quiet, but moved even closer to Kirk. It was the first time that Kirk had opened up, shared his feelings with anyone about a game situation like this and he was so glad to have Sharon. It made life! Neither Kirk nor Sharon wanted to leave; but it was late in the evening, even for the Baton Rouge Central Time zone. Nevertheless they lingered awhile longer.

The Miles made their way back home traveling by air through Atlanta and then on to BWI in Baltimore. It seems that everyone in the south travels via Atlanta! Kirk flew on the team charter directly from Baton Rouge to BWI. It was a long quiet flight. The coaching staff, having said their comments back in the locker room did not interfere with the player's individual thoughts. They were not a happy bunch of young men, however, they'd bounce back as the team started preparation for N.C. State.

The North Carolina State game would be Maryland's fourth of the season and the second conference game. They felt that they could both pass and run on State. The basic game plan would be to get on the scoreboard fast and let the defense do their thing. If the University of Maryland could get an early jump, then the plan also called for them to exploit the running game and therefore control the clock throughout game.

This game went according to the plan. Maryland had the ball first and with a series of short passes and running plays, they moved into the North Carolina State end zone on the first possession. A recovered fumble on the State 24-yard line gave Maryland excellent field position and they struck quickly for another score. Maryland led 14-0 at the end of the first quarter. During the second quarter, Maryland scored again on a sustained drive. State managed only a 46-yard field goal. At the half, Maryland was on top 21-3.

The second half was operated in just a business like manner. Maryland controlled the ball as planned and put 10 more points on the scoreboard. The Maryland defense did not permit State to get close enough to even attempt a field goal. The final score was 31-3 in favor of the Terps. Their record was now three wins and one loss. They were two and zero in the Atlantic coast conference, having defeated Virginia two weeks ago.

There was no real celebration by the team. The LSU game had made them grow as a unit, mature, so to speak. They were extremely pleased with their performance, as was the coaching staff. There would be, however, no time to enjoy the victory. Maryland was already deep in preparation to meet last year's number one team on their home field, the University of Miami at the Orange Bowl.

The team met Sunday morning for the first of these meetings. There was no practice this day, but tomorrow it would start in earnest! Kirk went to his room after the meeting, changed and then drove the jeep to the Cherry Hill Mobile Home Park. C.J. had driven to Towson earlier in the day from Elk Neck State Park to help Sharon move into his aunt's mobile home. Sharon had plenty of help from her roommates with the packing, especially one girl in particular, who was taking Sharon's room in the apartment. They'll all be down in two weeks for an open house party after the Duke football game, so there were no tears of departure, just the excitement of a big move. Sharon and Kirk were one step closer to getting married. After loading the station wagon, which Sharon's parents let her use for a while and C.J.'s car, they drove to Cherry Hill, arriving just a few minutes before Kirk.

"You're just in time Star," called Sharon from the doorway. "Whatever you see, bring it in!" She ducked into the door, then came out onto the porch again. "Hello darling, hope your meeting went well," and went back inside! Kirk had to smile as he looked at the loaded wagon, then glanced at C.J.'s car, loaded on the inside and with the trunk lid up, only a small amount had been relieved from that cargo hold.

Just then C.J. came out from the mobile home, "Hey man, glad you're here. Any of the other guys coming over?"

"No, I didn't bother to tell them I was coming here. Let'em relax and do their own thing. Everyone's got a lot on their minds right now," answered Kirk.

"I understand," commented C.J. as he reached into the trunk for some more things. "Here, give me a hand," he said to Kirk.

"Wish I could, but you know how it is, still sore and stiff from yesterdays game. I'm trying to stay healthy for the Miami game," kidded Kirk.

"I'll flatten all four of your tires and drop a frying pan directly on your toe if I wind up unloading the vehicles. Get my drift?" reasoned C.J.

"Here, let me give you a hand with those things," stated Kirk in a jovial voice, and he picked up an armful of stuff and followed C.J. into the home.

It really didn't take too long, with Sharon staying inside and unpacking as well as directing where things were to go. When they were through, the place looked cozy, like home.

Kirk suggested that they eat out at a little Italian restaurant just off campus, but Sharon wanted to relax at home and eat dinner there.

C.J. offered up the compromise and told Kirk and Sharon to relax, he'd drive to the restaurant and bring the meal back. "Spaghetti, meat balls and antipasto all around, OK? I know, I'll get plenty of bread," and C.J. was off.

It was a fun meal. Sharon came up with a bottle of Italian red table wine from her wine cellar. Well it was actually a table top wine rack from the apartment, but no matter, it went well with the meal.

C.J. did not stay long after the meal. It had been a long day for him and he was on duty at the State Park at six the next morning. Besides, he knew that Sharon and Kirk needed their time together. After "Thanks" from Kirk and Sharon, C.J. was off to Elk Neck.

Sharon and Kirk came back inside, turned on the TV and gathered together on the sofa. Sharon curled up in Kirk's arms and tucked her head under his chin, as she often liked to do. "I love you, darling," she said. Usually Kirk responded with the same, or kissed her, but not this time. Sharon lifted her head only to see Kirk sound asleep! She smiled, looking at her man, who put in a hard days work yesterday against North Carolina State and one today, then quietly placed her head back to the same position.

The balance of the week went rapidly as full schedules prevailed. On Friday morning the team flew the charter to Miami. They had the usual practice sessions and then before anyone could catch their breath, it was game time. The press coverage was greater than the Maryland players had seen before, but then, they'd never played a number one team before. The situation was similar to the LSU game, in that, Maryland was a big underdog, according to the Las Vegas oddsmakers. This time it was by three touchdowns. Miami, they reasoned had four wins and no losses and had won a total of 19 straight games. No doubt about it, Maryland had their work cut out for them, so they wouldn't be embarrassed. Game time!!

Maryland did receive the opening kickoff, but could not move the ball and was forced to punt. Miami, with their pro-set, struck quickly with their drive consisting of runs to the outside, short passes and a scoring strike on a crossing pattern. It looked like this might be a long afternoon for the boys from College Park. Even on the next possession, Maryland was halted by the Miami defense. However, the Maryland defense, having received the initial shock, stiffened and played tough as a unit. They held Miami scoreless throughout the balance of the first quarter and even forced Miami into a field goal situation after they received a great field position just before the half. The kick was blocked after a poor snap and the half ended with Maryland trailing just 7-0.

During the second half, the defensive battle continued. The Maryland defense halted drive after drive. They were actually on the field too long. The offense could not maintain a drive until well into the third quarter. However, the Miami defense had their way and finally on fourth and six on the Miami 26, Maryland sent the field goal unit onto the field. Conklin hit it well and Maryland was on the scoreboard, even though they trailed, 7-3.

In the fourth quarter, the battle continued. On a third down and long on their own 29-yard line, Miami attempted a pass. Maryland was blitzing and before the Miami quarterback could release the ball, it was knocked from his hand. The ball bounced on the ground. Kirk, as part of the blitz, was right there, caught the ball as it bounced again and raced for the Miami end zone. No one was in front of him and his teammates had thrown two blocks against the pursuing Miami players. Kirk scored. It was like lightning had struck. Maryland had the lead 9-7 against the nations number one team. Johnny Conklin added the extra point to have the scoreboard read *Maryland 10* and *Miami 7*. The clock showed less than six minutes to go in this nationally televised game. The commentators could not believe the battle Maryland was raging in the Orange Bowl. For them and their audience, the game was a bonanza. They had been talking about a blowout just two hours earlier, when Miami put the first points up on the board. The commentators and the nation were learning about this Maryland team. But Miami was not dead. They were a powerful well-coached and disciplined team and they would not lose their cool. Maryland's defense would be put to the test again. They had been on the field much more than they should have today. They were a tired and beat up bunch of young men.

Miami gained good field position on the kickoff. The kick was not particularly long and did not have much height. It got into Miami hands too soon and Maryland did not have the luxury of covering the kick very well. Miami would start this series of downs on their own 43, two first downs and they were within field goal range. Miami looked to work toward the Maryland goal and use the clock as well. With less than three minutes on the game clock, Miami had picked up the two first downs. The ball rested on the Maryland 28-yard line. Maryland needed a break and almost had one, as a short pass was touched and nearly intercepted by the left safety. The ball fell harmlessly to the ground, however, and Miami still had possession. The clock stopped with the incomplete pass. Maryland players and coaches were clock watching, it showed two minutes and 10 seconds. Miami tried a sweep, but the Maryland line with Kirk, charging behind them caught the play in the Miami backfield for a 6-yard loss. The two-minute warning was called by the officials as the clock read *1 minute and 51 seconds*. The ball was now on the Maryland 34, almost out of field goal range, it would be a 51-yard attempt from here. The television network broke for a series of commercials. Miami had their back to the wall, so to speak. It was now third down and 16 yards to go for a first down and perhaps the game. From a shotgun formation, they passed. Complete to the 21, three yards shy of the first down. Miami could go for the sure tie. They were now well within field goal range. They called time out. The clock showed only 54 seconds remaining in the game.

When time came back in, the officials set the ball, but Miami did not huddle, they came instead, right to the line of scrimmage and once again into the shotgun formation. From the shotgun, the quarterback had the option to pass, hand off or run the ball himself, although rolling out or running the ball himself would be his last choices right now. He needed a quick release to keep the drive alive and before the Maryland defensive line paid him a visit. The ball was snapped. A quick pass to the flat just past the first down marker and Miami had the first down. The receiver picked up 4 more yards and went out of bounds at the Maryland 14-yard line. The play had taken only 11 seconds off the clock. On a quick trap play up the middle, Miami only gained 2 yards to the 12 and called time out again to stop the clock. They thought Maryland wouldn't expect something up the middle. They were wrong! A glance at the clock showed 22 seconds left. During the time out the networks showed more commercials. The commentators loved it, they still had their viewers! Miami came back to a huddle after the time out was concluded. They lined up in a pro-set with the quarterback over the center and not in the shotgun as they did before. The ball was snapped. The quarterback faked a hand-off to his running back, rolled right and hit his tight end at the three-yard line. He tightened the grip on the ball with both hands and headed for the end zone. The Maryland safety came up and hit the tight end, but couldn't bring him down. Other Maryland defensive players swarmed to help out, but it was too late, the big Miami tight end fell just inside the goal line. Inside the goal line! Miami had scored. They now had the lead 13-10. Miami added the PAT, which put the score at 14-10. The Maryland team was devastated. The clock showed 11 seconds were left in the game, not much, but the game wasn't over yet. It had been a battle and Maryland would battle until the time clock showed zero. Miami knew this was a game to be remembered. They were favored by over 20 points and with less than 15 seconds on the game clock, they finally took the lead again. The fans, who had cheered Miami throughout the game, had been pulling for upset during the fourth quarter. Maryland had won them over and had gained a tremendous amount of respect from football fans in the stadium and those watching on national television. They'd all be checking the Sunday papers for the balance of the football season to see how Maryland was doing. They had won the hearts of the fans!

Miami was set to kick off now. The network had shown commercials and replays of the touchdown to the Maryland fans throughout the country. Watching it was almost too much to take. They were so close.

The kickoff was a low line drive, designed to bounce on the ground, be difficult to pick up and eat up the clock as the Maryland players touched the ball. The ball was fielded on the 22-yard line. The ball carrier fielded it cleanly after the ball had hit the ground and taken a high hop. He ran forward to the 30 and just before being hit, went out of bounds to stop the clock, which now showed only 3 seconds left in the game. Maryland used a time out to set the last play. It wasn't just a play, but it was also a time out to calm the offensive unit down, let them mechanically run the last play, rather than have them nervously come to the line. There would be butterflies in their stomachs, but at least they'd pull together and run the play.

The Maryland team lined up in the shotgun formation and sent four receivers out. The ball was snapped and the quarterback let a *Hail Mary Pass* fly toward the end zone and down the middle. He passed as far as he could. The ball was caught by the Maryland wide receiver who had run a post pattern on the fly. He caught the ball on the Miami 24-yard line, but Miami, who had been in a prevent defense, tackled him just after the completion. Maryland had great field position, but the game clock showed no time, Miami had won 14-10.

There was no real jubilation among the Miami players. The Miami defensive unit shook hands with the Maryland offensive unit and talked to them. It had been one of the hardest fought battles the Miami team had experienced and they respected the Maryland team like no other they had played. To the very last second, Maryland would not quit. They had shown that they are a team with character. The balance of the stunned Maryland team, led by Kirk, came onto the playing field to be with their teammates. They talked briefly with the Miami players and then headed for the locker room. It was a long walk. In the grand stand, the fans were cheering the Miami victory. They had the right, after all, their team had won. Some may have wondered why the Miami players weren't as ecstatic as the fans, that is, those who have never played in a game like this. It doesn't matter what sport, those who had, knew what the players had been through and how they felt.

The Maryland locker room was quiet. They had lost a game in the closing seconds and it hurt. Most of the players simply took off their uniforms and showered, not saying anything. Others talked quietly among themselves, comforting each other. The coaching staff had spoken to them just after they entered the locker room. They stated how proud of the players they were. It was a true and sincere talk. The press was kept outside, but still, the absolute agony of this particular loss was too fresh. They knew the Miami players and coaches had their respect, but it was still a loss!

The plane ride home was equally as quiet as the locker room had been the night before. The players were not even up to speaking with the newspaper reporters, even though the press had treated Maryland quite well. Maryland's record had fallen to 3 wins and 2 losses. The 2 losses were by a total of 7 points. The losses, though, dragged Maryland in the national rankings to number 21. It would be a long climb to get back into the top 10.

The upcoming schedule, while not favoring Maryland, did give them an opportunity of playing against more evenly matched teams. Of the final 6 games, Penn State and defending Atlantic Coast Conference Champion, Clemson, would be the toughest games.

The Wake Forest game would be quite festive, with all that goes with Homecoming Weekend. Kirk had a busy schedule between classes and practice. The highlight of each day though, was driving the jeep over to the Cherry Hill Mobile Home Park and having dinner along with an evening of relaxation with Sharon.

Maryland was a heavy favorite to bounce back from the Miami game and defeat Wake Forest. The Homecoming crowd was not disappointed as Maryland received the opening kickoff and scored their first touchdown on just 5 plays. It wasn't that they were trying to make up for the Miami game, you cannot do that. They simply stayed with the game plan as they do each week. Wake Forest is just not Miami and perhaps the early season predictions of a solid Maryland year would come true, after all. Maryland was leading 28-0 at the half and had this game well in hand. During the second half Maryland put 14 more points on the scoreboard very quickly and the fourth quarter started with Maryland ahead by 42-0. In the fourth quarter, Maryland made wholesale changes, taking out all of the starters on both the offensive and defensive units. The changes enabled Wake Forest to move the ball and they scored twice before the game clock ran out. Maryland upped their record to 4 wins and 2 losses on the 42-14 victory.

The following game, number 7, would also be a home game. This, like the Wake Forest game, was a conference battle. The opponents, Duke University from Durham, North Carolina, brought a 4 win-2 loss record into this game. With Maryland's record in the conference at 3 wins and 0 losses, the Duke game had special meaning. After the Duke game, they'd only have 2 conference games to go. It had been years since Maryland had won an Atlantic Coast Conference. but getting by Duke would be no small task! The Duke game had special meaning for Kirk. He had invited all of his co-workers at Elk Neck State Park to this contest. John and Dora Miles had only missed the Miami game, but this would be the first game that the Elk Neck gang would see together. C.J., of course, would be on hand. The coaching staff had kiddingly blamed the Miami and LSU losses on him because he wasn't on the sideline as the good luck charm. He'd be at his regular post for this game and promised not to miss anymore games, under penalty of... you don't want to know! C.J. stated that he had watched both games on TV, but the coaching staff said that TV didn't count. Just be there live, or else!!

In addition to the normal work Sharon was doing as a practice teacher, this week was special for her too. After the Duke game, there would be an open house at the Mobile Home. Since Kirk was busy between school and football practice, Sharon's friends, plus C.J. had helped with the preparation. C.J. had the job of inviting the nearby neighbors, figuring that this was a nice way of meeting them, plus if they were at the party, they couldn't complain about the noise, especially considering that most of the party would be outside.

Saturday morning was overcast, with the threat of rain, however, by the early afternoon, the sun broke through and it would be an above average temperature day for this late in the fall. Game time, was a 1:30 kickoff. The grandstand was packed. Another sell out crowd would be on hand to see Duke play the Maryland Terps. The field was in perfect condition. The sun had dried the early morning dew from the Astroturf, so the field would not be slippery to play on. There was almost no wind.

The game did not start out well, for the Maryland fans. After receiving the kickoff, Maryland fumbled on the second play from scrimmage. Duke took possession on the Maryland 23-yard line and after two quick pass plays, punched into the end zone from the one-yard line. The big Duke fullback seemed to be stopped at the line of scrimmage, but through a strong second effort he slipped off the right tackle and broke the plane of the end zone for a touchdown. Duke added the extra point and the scoreboard read *Duke 7* and *Maryland 0*, with 13 minutes and 11 seconds still left in the first quarter. The balance of the quarter seemed to belong to Duke also. The Bluedevils only allowed 2 first downs to Maryland and as the second quarter started, Duke was once again knocking on the door. The quarter started with Maryland backed up to their own 9-yard line. A quick pass to the flat behind the goal on a timed play brought another score for Duke University. Through a bad snap from center, the PAT was blocked. Duke led 13-0. Maryland's offensive unit showed some life after a Duke pass was intercepted on the Maryland 41-yard line. In a sustained drive, which ended in an 8 yard run, Maryland was finally on the scoreboard. This drive almost brought the half to a close because of the time consumed during the 13-play march to the end zone. Maryland trailed 13-7 after adding the PAT. They went into the locker room to regroup for the second half of this important game.

Duke wasted no time in getting started after receiving the second half kick-off. Through a mix-up in the Maryland return coverage, plus a poor line drive short kick, Duke's receiver broke through Maryland's defense and the speedster was off to the races. Before a stunned Maryland crowd Duke was ahead 19-7, using barely any time from the clock. Duke added the PAT and the score now read 20-7.

It would be an uphill battle and Duke, now feeling in control of the game, was gaining more confidence as the time ticked off the game clock. A stubborn Bluedevil defense permitted only a field goal during the balance of the 3rd quarter. The fourth and final quarter started with Maryland trailing 20-10. A break did come to Maryland as a fumble occurred in the backfield on an exchange between the Duke quarterback and running back. The ball bounced up into Kirk's arms, and being a live ball, which could be advanced because it was in the backfield, he took off to cover the 19 yards toward the Duke goal. He was helped by one of his defensive linemen who had led the way into the Duke backfield. The big lineman blocked the Duke running back as he tried to tackle Kirk. The Duke quarterback was also taken out of the play, which let Kirk score. Maryland added the extra point and now trailed by only 3 points.

The defensive battle continued throughout the rest of the 4th quarter. Maryland attempted and completed a 48-yard field goal with two minutes and ten seconds to go in the game, bringing the score even at 20 points apiece. Duke could no longer move the ball, because Maryland's defense had completely shut the Duke offensive unit down. Maryland was fairing no better as a stubborn Bluedevil Defense stopped each Maryland drive. A break finally came with only 41 seconds showing on the game clock. The ball was on the Duke 26-yard line and the Duke quarterback dropped straight back to throw a pass. The ball was deflected by one of the Maryland linemen, who leaped and got a hand on the ball. Another lineman from Maryland dove and caught the ball before it hit the ground for an interception. He was downed at that spot, the Duke 25-yard line. It was a tremendous break for Maryland. Their offensive unit charged out onto the field, all but the Terp's quarterback, who was on the sideline getting last minute instructions and plays from the coaching staff. After the offensive and defensive units exchanged sides, the linesmen reset the clock and down marker. Maryland would huddle only once and a series of plays would be called, to best use the time remaining.

With Maryland being in field goal range, it appeared, as they lined up on the 25-yard line, that they'd run a couple of consecutive plays up the middle and then go for the field goal and a 3-point victory. This was not the case. The quarterback took the snap, faked a hand-off up the middle, and then threw a quick pass to his big tight end. The pass was complete and the tight end moved forward to the right flat, gaining yardage as he cut a path toward the Duke goal line. He was hit on the 18-yard line, but kept his balance and picked up 4 more yards, holding the ball with both hands as he was brought down. The ball rested on the Duke 14-yard line. The clock showed 29 seconds and was moving. Maryland called a time out. The quarterback eased over to the sideline where the coaching staff was waiting to discuss the situation. Should they run one more play, or should they go for the field goal right now? Go for one play. The last play went to the right and left a poor angle for the field goal attempt. Maryland would run toward the middle, call time out after the next play, then go for the 3 points and the game. The ball was snapped, a quick trap play and the Maryland running back was into the Duke secondary. He was hit once, twice, but kept his feet and moved to his right and into the end zone. A Maryland touchdown! The score came with only 16 seconds remaining in the game. Maryland added the PAT and the big scoreboard showed *Maryland 27* and *Duke 20.*

The game wasn't over yet. Duke had already run a kickoff back for a touchdown. The Maryland team was well aware of this as they lined up for the kick. It was a high and long kick, rather than a line drive bouncing-type kick that is often used in a situation like this. The Maryland players swarmed toward the ball carrier, who fielded the kick on his own 8-yard line. The runner was brought down on the 19-yard line. The clock had started when the runner touched the ball and as he was brought down, it showed 4 seconds remaining. Duke would have one more play to run. They called for a time out just as the officials set the time clock for the play. It would give Duke a little more time for the decision on what play to run and exactly how it was to be executed, however, most everyone in the football stadium knew it could be only one play, a *Hail Mary Pass*! With time back in, the ball was snapped to the quarterback, who was in a shotgun formation. Four receivers went out: two deep on a fly pattern and two deep on a crossing pattern. The pass was thrown deep, as far as the Duke quarterback could pass it. It was headed right down the middle as it came down. Four Maryland defenders and two Duke players were trying to catch the ball. Maryland had to be careful not to have pass interference called, because it would give Duke another play, this time from about the Maryland 30. A Duke receiver caught the ball, but was immediately tackled. The ball was at the Maryland 28-yard line, however, the clock showed no time. The game was over and Maryland had survived to win 27-20!! It was a tough loss for Duke. They had played hard, took advantage of the breaks, but could not quite pull it off.

Maryland's record now went to 5 wins and 2 losses. More importantly their record in the Atlantic Coast Conference was now 4 wins and they were without a loss. They had 2 remaining conference games, one against the University of North Carolina and the other against undefeated Clemson, last years Conference Champion. No easy task lay before them!

Sharon, as usual, waited for Kirk to leave the field. They met just as he came through the tunnel. C.J. had walked off the field with Kirk, and joined Sharon, in addition to the Miles and the men from Elk Neck State Park. Kirk stopped and chatted a few minutes with the men, who, of course, thanked Kirk for the tickets. Sharon had already made them promise that they'd stop at the Mobile Home for the Open House, before heading North toward the State Park. Kirk said he'd catch up with everyone later and started off to the locker room. C.J. said he'd see Kirk later also, figuring that Sharon could use help getting things ready. The locker room was a noisy place as Kirk entered it. The team was not only celebrating the victory over Duke, but perhaps, relief, that they came with a victory at all. This game was a close call. Even though Maryland had been favored to win by 6 points, it was a last minute effort that turned what looked like a loss, into victory number 5. In the ACC, you just can't tell! After showering and seeing the trainer about a bruised shoulder, Kirk left to drive the jeep over to the Mobile Home Park. He had to park quite a distance away from Sharon's new home and his new home in a few weeks, after the wedding. He thought to himself as he walked toward the trailer, that all he had to do was follow the noise and he'd be there. Seems that most of the party had spilled to the out of doors.

C.J. spotted Kirk and went over to the beer tap and poured a large glass for him. As he handed it to Kirk he asked, "How's the shoulder? You really came down on it hard on the one play?"

"I'll be OK," was Kirk's reply, "thanks for the beer," and he took a long drink, swallowing in installments, enjoying the coldness of the beer. "Nice cups," continued Kirk as he looked over the University of Maryland logo large paper cups in Terp colors. "Where'd you buy these?"

"Buy, like in purchase? Please!" answered C.J. "Let's say that they were requisitioned and came along with a party attendee. No more questions, please!"

Just then Sharon came out from the trailer. She walked over to where Kirk and C.J. were standing. She started to reach for Kirk's cup of beer and he simply handed it to her. She took a small sip and gave it back.

"They all threw me out. They said they'd do better with me out of the way and that I should mingle," stated Sharon, who put her arm in Kirk's and continued, "come mingle with me, Darling."

"Hey, cut out the smut talk Sharon, this is an all American boy here," said C.J., as he put his hand on Kirk's good shoulder!

"I know," said Sharon and she took the beer from Kirk again, and took a longer sip this time. "He's going to father our children!"

"How many have you had, or how long have you been at the beer tap?" questioned Kirk.

Before Sharon could answer, C.J. joined in, "That's why they banned you from the trailer, you poor drunken kid!!"

Kirk had to laugh, mostly to himself. "Come on," he stated, "let's mingle."

The party was a success. It was a lot of fun, even though it was basically over by 9:30. Most people had a distance to travel. The clean up was also easy, everyone pitched in and the other players who attended even took the trash bags over to the compactor and made sure the grounds were picked up. It was 10:15 when C.J. shook hands with Kirk, gave Sharon a kiss and took off down the road. He was the last to leave, making certain that all was well in his uncle's Mobile Home Park. "It helped to keep the family together," he stated in a peaceful state, so to speak.

Kirk and Sharon went into the trailer. Kirk sat down on the sofa and Sharon crowded into his arms, snuggling, half asleep. Kirk kissed Sharon on the head and quietly told her that he loved her. She smiled, and moved over closer. It had been a long day for both of them. Having Sunday to themselves would be relaxing, a day for each other, away from their hectic schedules and other people.

It was about six o'clock when Kirk stirred and tried to stretch, only to find that he had fallen asleep also. Sharon was in the same place she was the night before, sound asleep, snuggled on his lap. He felt stiff and gently woke her up, "Good morning," Kirk said softly.

"Good morning," Sharon answered in a sleepy voice. Then it dawned on her where they were. "Oh my God, we've slept together. My reputation for all this time is ruined. Did you take advantage of me? If not, why not? What did you do to me while I was, so to speak, passed out?" Then sitting up, Sharon covered her mouth. "I have dragon breath, don't I? It feels like I do," then pausing for a moment as she sat on the edge of the sofa, "you better still love me!"

"I still love you. I had my way with you, the same as I'm going to do in five weeks and you do have a bit of dragon's breath," answered Kirk, as he got up, then leaned over and kissed Sharon on the top of the head.

"But, are you kidding me?" said a smiling Sharon, as she got up and put her arms around Kirk.

"I never kid about dragon's breath or loving you," stated Kirk, who gave Sharon a squeeze and a kiss on the end of her nose, then continued, "I'm going over to the dorm, to shower and change, then we'll head out and have breakfast."

"Me too. Give me a little extra time to wash my hair," answered Sharon. "And brush your teeth too," she kiddingly called after him as Kirk was getting into the Jeep. "You're a fire-breathing dragon yourself!!"

Kirk waved, laughed and then got into the Jeep, only to pop out again, "Do you want to go over to Silver Springs and pick up the antique mirror for your folks? I forgot to tell you they called to say it's in!"

"Great," answered Sharon and she went back into the trailer. Kirk drove over to the dorm and had the hot shower water pouring on him by 6:30. Since he was stiff from the game and had slept in an awkward position, the hot pulsating water felt terrific. Remembering that Sharon would need a little extra time let Kirk relax even more as he took a much longer than normal shower.

Kirk was back over to pick Sharon up by 8:30. Why go out for breakfast she stated, as she poured him a cup of coffee from freshly ground beans. The bacon was already being slow cooked, the orange juice pitcher was on the table. Kirk liked orange juice and, Kirk would be given the task of cooking the eggs. Sharon said she'd take care of the toast, unless he wanted to scramble the eggs and have pancakes beside the eggs instead of the toast. "Well??!!"

"Hold the toast and get the griddle pan out," was Kirk's reply.

Following breakfast, it was off to the Lion Hearted Antique shop to pick up the mirror they had been waiting for. It was from England, the Victorian period, and exactly what Sharon thought it would look like. It was perfect!

After dropping the mirror off at the trailer, Kirk suggested that they drive to Washington and park near the Jefferson Memorial, take a walk along the river and have an early dinner at Hogates. It sounded like a great idea, after having a man-sized breakfast and taking the walk. Skipping lunch would be perfect. The entire day was perfect!

Monday brought both Sharon and Kirk back to the hectic schedules they kept during the week. For Kirk, it was also preparing for the 8th football game of the season. On Friday morning it would be off to BWI airport and the plane ride to Raleigh, North Carolina. Then the bus would take them to the pretty town of Chapel Hill, where on Saturday they'd play against the University of North Carolina.

Sharon would not make this trip, but would spend the weekend at her parent's house. She wanted to give them the anniversary present, however, there was also the fitting for the wedding dress, invitations and such. There was no need for a photographer, because one of Kirk's friends at the U. of M., who was also the President of the Photography Club, would do the honors. The wedding would take place on the Maryland campus Chapel. C.J., it seemed, had done some scouting and he, along with Sharon's Dad, John, were handling the reception arrangements. Dora decided that it was best to let them go. They were having such a good time with the planning.

Speaking of C.J., he was making the trip to Chapel Hill under orders from the Maryland coaching staff. Even if they could win without him, why take a chance! C.J. had worked out his Elk Neck Park schedule, so that he could make the remaining games.

There was a steady rain as Saturday's game time approached. It was not a particularly cold or heavy rain, as they often had during this time of the year, but the rain would make playing conditions miserable. In a football game on a day like this, it didn't take long to become soaked to the skin. North Carolina won the coin toss and elected to receive the kickoff. They ran their first series of downs and had to punt on 4th and 6.

Disaster almost struck early for N.C., as a bad hand-off was fumbled. Fortunately, for the Tar Heels, the quarterback fell on the ball. Maryland did not fare much better on their first series from scrimmage and they also had to punt on fourth down. The exchange of punts favored Maryland, as North Carolina had to start the next series of downs from their own 9-yard line. The very first play proved to be the break, which started the downward slide for the Tar Heels on this dreary day. The hand-off on a quick trap up the middle netted a four-yard gain, but during the hard tackle, the ball popped loose and Maryland recovered on the North Carolina 14-yard line. The Maryland offensive didn't waste any time. Using the play-option pass, they hit the tight end crossing just behind the line backing corps. The result was a touchdown! The extra point was added and Maryland had an early 7-0 lead. During the rest of the first quarter, both North Carolina and Maryland exchanged punts. North Carolina remained with their backs to the wall, deep in their own territory, however, Maryland, with good field position, just could not punch in another score. The quarter ended, though, with Maryland on the North Carolina 8-yard line and a first down situation, as the teams exchanged goals. It took just two plays to score as the 2nd quarter opened. The touchdown came on a quarterback option in which he kept the ball, rolled right and scampered in from the 3-yard line. The PAT was added and the scoreboard showed the visiting Terps ahead 14-0.

There was no additional scoring during the balance of the first half. The rain was coming down harder as the teams left the field. The locker room would feel good. The players would be able to towel off and get fresh jerseys on. C.J. faired pretty well with all the rain as he stood on the sidelines and offered support to the players going on and coming off the field of play. He had a Terp's rain parka on, which also had a hood that covered his head. His feet though were another problem. They were soaked!

One of the coaches came over to C.J. during the half and told him to get his shoes off. He handed C.J. a pair of football shoes and a clean pair of sanitary socks. They'd serve him better and let his shoes and socks dry out. C.J. immediately made the exchange. As he stood up, he felt a bit awkward, because this was the first time he ever had football cleats on. "Hey, I'm taller," he said to himself, but quietly aloud. Those within earshot had to laugh.

Maryland received the opening kickoff of the second half and through the series of plays discussed by the coaches in the locker room, marched down the field using all but one running play scoring a touchdown. The extra point was added. Early in the second half, Maryland continued to hold North Carolina scoreless, leading the contest by 21-0. There was no additional scoring during the third quarter. Maryland was no longer using the pass. The weather was almost dictating the run. In addition, using running plays took chunks of time off the game clock. The opening play of the fourth and final quarter gave North Carolina their first break of the game and the Tar Heel fans something to cheer about. The exchange between the Maryland quarterback and running back misfired as the wet football fell free on the fumble. North Carolina pounced on the ball! The Tar Heels scored on the first play from scrimmage. A quick pass on a timed play was engineered from the Maryland 11-yard line. The reception and Carolina touchdown was made even easier as the Terp defender fell down in the slippery end zone when he tried to cut and prevent the reception. North Carolina added the point after touchdown, which brought the score to Maryland 21 and North Carolina 7. Maryland still had the game well in hand. All of the statistics favored Maryland and the Tar Heels just could not get lucky enough to pull a game like this out of their loss column. The Maryland defense was ready for the task and would not permit North Carolina to gain another first down for the balance of the game. Maryland's offense was also held in check by the Tar Heel defense and the weather. They continued to run, rather than pass the ball. The final points added by Maryland were insurance, because of a 28-yard field goal. A wet and worn Maryland team took the 24-7 victory into the locker room. The victory was Maryland's sixth of the season against two losses. It was also their third consecutive victory after the heartbreaking loss to Miami. The win would bring Maryland close to the top 10 in the nation, probably number 13 or 14 in the following week's poll. Their place in the national standings would be helped by the fact that the two losses were to top 10 teams, LSU and Miami. Even more important to the Maryland team as a group and to their loyal fans was the fact that they were undefeated in the Atlantic Coast Conference and had 5 wins. It was the best effort a Maryland team had put forth in many years. Only the final game of the year, against Clemson, stood in the way of the ACC championship. Clemson, at 4 and 0 in the Conference, would face North Carolina for their next game. Clemson, with a 7 win and 1 loss record, was rated number 8 in the poll a week ago. Today they defeated Georgia Tech, a team that would join the ACC next year and become its 8th member.

The Maryland team flew home this evening. The chartered U.S. Air flight was greeted at the Baltimore-Washington International Airport by about 2000 students and fans. It was a great welcome home!

With Sharon staying at her parent's home, Kirk convinced C.J. to stay over and not attempt the drive north to the State Park this evening. They'd crash at the Mobile Home so they could sleep in on Sunday morning without being disturbed. They dropped off some things at the dorm, Kirk changed, packed an overnight bag, called Sharon at the Miles', then it was off to join the other players for a couple of beers and to celebrate their victory. They were out a little later than they counted on, actually, they got back to the trailer at close to 3 a.m. and quite literally crashed for the night. Kirk and C.J. were still well asleep when Sharon came through the door at 10:30.

"You lazy bums," called Sharon as she intentionally dropped her pocketbook on C.J.'s head while he lay on the sofa.

"Ouch, Kirk, could you please come in here and kill this women for me NOW," C.J. shouted, then he pulled his cover over his head!!

"I'm busy sleeping," called Kirk from the bedroom, "You're nearest to the front door. That makes you our front line. Take care of it. OK!!??"

"No it's not OK. The front has fallen. Oh damn, I'm awake now," answered C.J. and he pulled the blanket off his head, sat up on the sofa and growled at Sharon.

"Good Morning to you too," said Sharon, in a cheerful voice. "Coffee anyone?" as she went into the kitchen, took the coffee from the freezer, started measuring it for the Mister Coffee Machine and measured the water.

"Whatever you've measured, add more coffee," called C.J., who was still sitting on the sofa. Then he looked back toward the bedroom, "You up yet, Kirk?"

"I told you, I'm busy sleeping. You and Sharon fix breakfast and call me in a half hour," called Kirk as he turned over, then pulled the cover over himself. Sharon held up one finger near her mouth, before C.J. could answer Kirk, then she took a sponge, let the cold water run over it, took a paper towel to catch the dripping of the completely full sponge and tiptoed to the bedroom. She opened the door ever so quietly. C.J. had seen what

Sharon planned and was just a step behind her. Sharon entered the bedroom, eased the cover back off Kirk's head and started to let the sponge water drip onto Kirk's forehead. He opened one eye, looked at her, but before he could do anything, she squeezed the entire sponge on his face.

Kirk had to smile to himself, he figured as much was going to happen. He looked up with both eyes open, wiped away some of the water and said, "Well, I am awake now. Coffee ready?" Then he gave a quick grab for Sharon, but she dashed out of the bedroom and ran to the kitchen.

Breakfast was lively, fun, as they enjoyed the bacon, eggs over easy, hash-brown potatoes, orange juice, toast, and of course, strong coffee! C.J. left shortly after they finished, actually around 12:30 and headed north to Elk Neck State Park.

Sharon and Kirk spent the balance of the day together. Kirk, with three very important football games ahead of him, was a little tense, on edge, as probably all the other players were too. Sharon could see this and suggested that they ride into Washington and take a walk in the Mall, or perhaps around the Jefferson Memorial area. Kirk agreed. It was a favorite area of his, even if there was a crowd of people. They could be by themselves, rather than sticking around the campus.

It only took about 20 minutes to drive into DC. Kirk decided to head for the Jefferson Memorial, rather than the Mall area. He simply wanted to stroll with Sharon around the water of the Tidal Basin and the Potomac River. They spent a couple of hours there and would have stayed until about 4:30, but the sky darkened and they decided to head back. Just as they reached the Jeep, a light rain began to fall. Sharon said, "no" when Kirk suggested they eat out, but said she'd prefer to get take-out Chinese or Italian food. Spaghetti, meat balls, antipasto and extra bread was ordered. Sharon said she had some dry red Italian wine back at the ranch.

They enjoyed a special evening at the Mobile Home, and a special evening with each other.

The next morning brought the basic routine back into focus. Sharon was off practice teaching in Silver Spring and Kirk was in class. He was working especially hard, with Sharon's help, to keep his grades up and keep pace with the other students. This was no small task, especially with so much mental as well as physical time being spent on football. Kirk and Sharon agreed he should take on an even heavier school load during his last semester so the he could graduate with his class in May, rather than have to complete his degree during the summer months. The job at hand right now, though, was class and practice. Penn State University would be in town this weekend and they were one tough group of football players bent on leaving town with a victory.

This would be game 9 for the 6 win-2 loss Maryland Terps. While not a conference game, it was a Big East Contest. Maryland had suffered 2 tough losses to top 10 opponents and Penn State would like nothing better than to knock off Maryland. Penn State has a 5 win - 3 loss record, having won against Northwestern, Missouri, Wisconsin, Minnesota and Rutgers. The 3 losses came at the hands of Michigan, Ohio State and Syracuse. Since Penn State lost to Syracuse with the score of 14 –10 and Maryland defeated Syracuse by only 3 points, the Penn State–Maryland game is being billed as a close match. It would receive television coverage, being the "local" game of the TV double header. UCLA hosting Nebraska would be the second and a nationally televised game.

The week went rapidly as class and practice schedules meshed. Kirk was able to see Sharon each evening. Her moving to the College Park area made this possible. Being with each other, rather than using the telephone to communicate made their hectic lives much more relaxed. It let them share the busy day's activities as well as spend the evenings together, even though Sharon was often marking students papers and doing lesson plans, while Kirk was doing his own homework and playing catch-up on his studies.

The weather forecaster served up a beautiful day for this first Saturday in November. By the 1:30 game time, the temperature was expected to climb to an unusually warm 74 degrees. There was hardly a cloud in the sky, just a few puffs in the distance. The sky was reminiscent of a western New Mexico or Arizona sky. OK, a beautiful western high sky day!!

The Maryland players were quite confident, not over-confident, but they now knew what they were able to accomplish on the football field.

Penn State received the opening kick-off and their first series of plays enabled them to move the ball to the Maryland 23-yard line, before the drive was halted. On 4th down and 8 to go for the first down, the Nittany Lions settled for the 3-point field goal. They had the early lead and demonstrated that they had come to play. Maryland did not do as well during their first possession and had to punt the ball away. Penn State was likewise collared in their second possession and the remainder of the first quarter continued as a seesaw defensive battle. The second quarter started with Maryland trailing 3-0. The defense of each team continued to dominate the game. Scouting reports had been very good. Maryland did not have a sustained drive until the clock showed less than 2 minutes to play in the half. With the ball on the Penn State 14-yard line and only 11 seconds left in the half, the Maryland coaching staff decided to go for the 3-point field goal, rather than try for the touchdown and fail. Putting points on the scoreboard now, before the half came to a close, was important in order to keep the momentum going in the second half of the game. The field goal attempt was good. The ball went right through the center of the uprights and Maryland evened the score at 3 apiece as the half came to a close.

Maryland received the second half kick-off and marched down the field. It looked as though they would take complete control of the game. The drive was stopped though, by a Maryland fumble. The ball popped loose on the Penn State 18-yard line on a bad hand-off in the backfield. The ball bounced around as several players dove for it. When the pile of players were separated, Maryland still had possession, however, the ball was now on the Penn State 24, a loss of 6 yards and it was 4th down and 9 to go for the first down. A field goal attempt was made and as the ball went through the goal posts, Maryland took a 6-3 lead. It wasn't much, but Maryland was ahead! Now, the defensive unit would have to continue holding Penn State at bay.

Penn State also seemed to have tightened their belts, because they shut down the Maryland offensive team for the balance of the 3rd quarter. The quarter came to a close with the scoreboard still reading *Maryland 6* and *Penn State 3*.

The fourth and final quarter started out in the same fashion as when the game began. It had been a hard battle and both defensive teams had been on the field a long time. With the score so close, a break either way could determine the outcome of the game. It was well into the 4th quarter, only 7 minutes and 14 seconds remaining, when Maryland intercepted a Penn State pass on Maryland's 31. They managed to get the ball down to the Penn State 13, when the drive came to a complete halt. Maryland decided to go for 3 points. The field goal was good. Maryland's lead went to 9-3, with a little less than 4 minutes to go in the game. The Maryland kick off was high and deep, coming down on the Penn State 3-yard line. The outstanding kick permitted excellent kick-off coverage and the Maryland specialty kick-off return team was swarming after the receiver, like bees after someone who had just stolen the honey. The receiver picked up the ball on the bounce, at the one-yard line and started upfield. He was barely at the 8-yard line when he was hit hard by at least 4 Maryland defenders and the receiver was hammered and spun around as he went down. The ball popped loose and was recovered by Maryland at the 9-yard line. Maryland had made a break! With 3 minutes and 6 seconds left on the clock, they would try to put the game on ice. There was a delay. The Penn State trainers were on the field assisting their receiver. His "bell had been rung," so to speak and he had to be helped off the field. The television coverage used this time out to catch up on their commercials. As time came back in, Maryland's plan was quite simple, keep the ball on the ground, be sure of the hand-off, score and run out the clock, all at the same time!!

The first play from scrimmage was up the middle and gained 4 yards. A very tired Penn State defensive unit was trying to hold on. The second play was a mirror of the first, simple power against power, will against will. The ball now rested on the one and half yard line. The clock showed a little less than 2 minutes. The 2-minute warning was given to each coach. The TV networks broke for more commercials. As time was coming back in, the TV commentators spoke of the dramatic happenings on the field. Maryland was knocking on the door for their 7th victory. They had 2 remaining games against Navy and Clemson. They'd be expected to win against Navy, but Clemson, the defending Atlantic Coast Conference champions, might be another story. At any rate, a victory today would almost ensure Maryland of a Bowl bid for post season play.

With time back in, Maryland had a quick huddle then it was up to the line of scrimmage. The ball was snapped and the clash of players began. The Maryland quarterback handed the ball to his tailback and he took off and into the air diving for the goal line and the score. He came down in a crash, holding the ball with both hands. The line judge raised both hands over his head, outstretched. A touchdown was signaled! With a minute and a half left, Maryland had the commanding lead that they had worked so hard for. The point after touchdown was added and Maryland held a 16-3 lead. The score held up and Maryland had their 7th victory! It was a hard fought victory to be sure.

An extremely tired, spent football team filled the Maryland locker room. Kirk saw Sharon just after the game ended. She had made her way to the tunnel, where C.J., who had been in residence on the sidelines during the game, first spotted her. He motioned to Kirk, who then made his way over to her. Kirk told Sharon he'd be a while, then he'd meet her and her parents at the Mobile Home, before going out to dinner.

"We could just stay home you know," said a worried Sharon as she looked over her very battered future husband. Then she reached up, gave him a careful kiss.

"I'll be OK. I'd hate to feel like this and lose though," he continued laughingly, then kissed her forehead. "See you later," he said as he headed for the locker room.

After a long hot shower and spending time with the trainer, Kirk met up with C.J. and they drove to the Mobile Home. Sharon had been impatiently waiting and felt a great relief as C.J.'s car pulled up. C.J. and Kirk started walking toward the door, but got almost half way, when Sharon came out to greet them.

"God, do you look good," she said, and carefully put her arms around Kirk.

"I do," said a surprised Kirk, then turning to C.J., "and you said I look like hell. I like Sharon's opinion better," he continued smiling.

"Oh look at that cut on your nose, I didn't see it before," said Sharon as she surveyed Kirk again. "When did you get that?" Then, she looked at C.J.

"Don't look at me, some guy in a white uniform did it, you just thought all that dried blood was dirt," exclaimed C.J.

At that, Sharon punched C.J. on the arm. "Don't talk like that," she said.

"You're right John, a cold beer would taste good," said Kirk as he spotted John Miles coming out onto the porch with two dripping bottles of beer.

"I'd shake hands with you, but maybe even they hurt," stated John as he handed Kirk and C.J. the beer, "They look like you've been in a fight."

"They never hurt too much to shake your hand," answered Kirk as he reached out for John's hand. "Of course, I may not be able to hold a fork," he kidded. Then they all went into the home, where Kirk gave Dora a hug.

"You look like you've been through a war, but you look terrific. We were really proud of you out there," said Dora as she gave Kirk a great big motherly bear hug back. "Don't worry," she said to Sharon, who winked as she hugged Kirk, "I didn't squeeze him too hard."

"Tag's, OK?" said John "Anyone hungry yet?"

"It's almost 6 now," said Sharon "want to call for 7 or 7:30," then she looked over at Kirk to see what he wanted to do.

"Either one is fine," answered Kirk, "we can take 2 cars, that way, your folks can head directly home, unless..."

"No, we're going home and not coming back here," answered John before Kirk could finish his sentence.

"Are you bumming tomorrow too?" John continued as he looked over at C.J., or are you finally coming to work?"

"I'll be there. This good luck charm stuff is way too draining," answered C.J., who put his empty beer bottle in the trash, then continued, "It's pure hell, worrying these guys to victory. I'll be glad to go to work and relax!"

"We're all set," said John, "they'll take us when we get there."

"Drop us off at the campus," said Kirk to C.J., "we'll pick up the Jeep and follow you down, up to Tags. It has been a long day!"

They all met at Tags. John and Dora arrived earlier because they drove straight to the restaurant, while Kirk, Sharon and C.J. picked up the Jeep. At Tags they made only a small quiet fuss when Kirk arrived. The owners were tipped off that he was awfully tired and hurting. "A bit over extended" as Kirk would say! But, as usual, they were made to feel at home in this fine little restaurant in the town of Laurel.

The family and C.J., who was also considered family, really enjoyed the evening. They stayed until almost eleven. The *House* provided the wine and after dinner drinks, with the owners joining later to relax a bit, also after a hard day. After their good-byes, everyone went to their cars. Sharon reached into Kirk's hand and took the keys to the Jeep from him.

"Strap yourself in, I'll drive," she said.

Kirk got into the passenger's side of his Jeep for the first time and fumbled with the seat belt. "It's on the wrong side," he kidded, as Sharon looked over at the trouble he was having.

"Want me to come around and tuck you in?" she kidded.

"I'm just fine lady. Drive on," answered Kirk!!

Sharon started the jeep, backed out of the parking space and made a left onto Route #l South.

Even though it seemed to Kirk that Sharon knew what she was doing, it was hard for him to relax with her driving. He trusted her. It was just one of those *men things,*. no other explanation!

"I can drop you off at the trailer," Kirk said as they neared College Park.

"No, you're staying the night. I'm keeping an eye on you. You need a nurse tonight. No smut, no smut talk, just medicinal nursing. Got it Buster?" exclaimed Sharon and winked at Kirk.

"I love you. I think so darn much I just can't put it all into words," stated Kirk.

"Whether it's the wine or me, I'll take that as a life's commitment," answered Sharon as she turned into the Mobile Home Park and drove to space #399 in front of the trailer.

Kirk made out better, pushing the button on the seat belt to unbuckle himself. Sharon looked over and smiled as Kirk gave the high sign that he accomplished this little feat the first try.

"Com'on, you tired 'ole warrior, let's go inside our little castle and let me tuck you in," said Sharon, as she came around from the drivers side of the Jeep and closed the door behind Kirk.

Kirk pretended to need help as they walked toward the porch, "If you lean on me too hard and make me fall up these steps, you'll think the entire Penn State football team unloaded on you," stated Sharon.

"Man, what bedside manner," said Kirk quietly to himself, but, of course, loud enough for Sharon to hear.

"What did you say. Speak up," said Sharon!

"I said, what wonderful bedside manner you have, taking care of a poor old beaten, trod down person, a meaningful human you are," answered Kirk, who then received a punch on his left arm.

"Ouch. What was that for?" said Kirk as Sharon put the key in the door.

"Your second sentence was much too long to have been fully related to the first. That's why. Do you want more?" questioned Sharon in a tough voice.

"No, I've had enough of a beating for this particular day," answered Kirk as he entered the trailer living room and collapsed onto the sofa, then continued, "Just remember though, you'll never beat any secrets out of me, or even anything from our football play book. I'm tight-lipped!"

"Really," said Sharon as she sat next to Kirk and reached over to kiss him. "Let's see if you continue to be tight-lipped or if you co-operate!"

"Well" said Kirk, as he put his arms around Sharon, there is a point where I'm forced to give in."

Sunday proved to be a relaxing day for Kirk and Sharon. It was, by many standards, a dull, old married person's day. It was also a much needed day of rest for both Sharon and Kirk. They had breakfast at home after Kirk had taken a walk up to the park office area and purchased a Sunday newspaper. Actually, he picked up both the Baltimore Sun and the Washington Post. Sharon was keeping a scrapbook and wanted the articles from the areas' leading newspaper.

During the afternoon, they drove over to the U. of M. campus and went for a swim in the indoor pool. They were basically alone, even though a few people did stop off to see Kirk or wave hello. Those that would have liked to discuss yesterday's football game were put off politely and told, "another time," that he and Sharon wanted to simply relax today.

They stopped at the Giant Supermarket later in the afternoon and decided that since it was a pleasant sunny day outside, they'd get the grill out and barbecue a couple of club steaks. However, once at the meat counter, Sharon spotted filet mignons. They decided to splurge and bought two steaks! The steaks, cooked Pittsburgh rare, along with baked potatoes, green beans, a salad, plus, of course, a loaf of French bread, would make this almost a gourmet cookout. A California 7-year old Cabaret Sauvignon wine from Simi would top off the meal. Sharon, cut her filet in half, and fixed Kirk's plate with one and a half of the steaks, two baked potatoes, the lion's share of the green beans. But he had to fix his own salad plate. It was not that she didn't want to, but just how much salad he'd want on this particular evening, was a mystery. Since both Kirk and Sharon liked Balsamic Wine Vinegar from Italy and extra virgin olive oil, the salad dressing choice was easy.

The balance of the week, like the ones before went by rapidly and at a hectic pace. Sharon was practice teaching and Kirk was attending classes and football practice, as the University of Maryland prepared for Saturday's away contest at Annapolis, against Navy. They spent all of their evenings together and that helped in two ways: one, they were together and two, Sharon helped Kirk with his studies, determined that he graduate in the spring and not have to attend summer school to complete his undergraduate work.

Maryland's football team was on a four-game winning streak. With an overall record of 7 wins and 2 losses, Kirk and the rest of the players had a hard time focusing on anything but football right now. Sharon's keeping Kirk's nose to the grindstone, so to speak, was very important on behalf of his education. He didn't fight her on the studying. Simply put, she was right!

The Saturday morning bus ride to Annapolis was basically a quiet one. It wasn't that the players were still sleepy, because they had been up for a while and had a team breakfast. The mood was simply a businesslike attitude for what had to be done on the playing field this afternoon. The Navy football team was certainly not to be taken lightly.

In their previous 9 games, they had won 5, including a 9-7 upset victory over Notre Dame in Giant's Stadium, in the Meadowland's Sports Complex at East Rutherford, New Jersey. The Navy-Maryland game was also a bragging rights contest for while it was an official away game for Maryland, Annapolis was just not that far from the Washington, DC area.

C.J. was, of course, on hand. He stayed with Kirk on Friday night and attended the team breakfast. He was a fixture now and almost considered a part of the team. C. J. is also the official worrier, especially if the score and clock are working against Maryland. He performs this job very well!

As with any Navy game and especially their home games, there is a lot of pageantry. Maryland stayed in the locker room, after the initial on field practice, as long as possible. The coaching staff did not want any last minute distractions to upset what the team, as a unit, had accomplished during this highly competitive season. A win here today would most certainly propel them into the most important University of Maryland football game in years, as they face their final regular season opponent Clemson next week. With no defeats in the Atlantic Coast Conference,

Maryland, in defeating Clemson would have the coveted ACC title to themselves and a solid bid to play in the Orange Bowl on New Year's night.

Navy won the coin toss and elected to receive the opening kickoff. The kick was short and fielded by Navy at their own 18-yard line. A runback of 16 yards gave them excellent field position as they started the first series of downs from the 34. Navy picked up two first downs on quick opener passes, one to the wide receiver and the other to a receiver coming out of the backfield. The drive was stalled at the Maryland 29 and Navy, on 4th down and 6 to go for another first down, decided to attempt a field goal. They possessed one of the best in the country when it came to field goal kickers. The tough Navy defense, plus three long field goals is what helped them upset Notre Dame and was the key factor in 2 of their other victories this season.

The kick, from the 29, would have to travel about 46 yards in total, with the drop back from the line of scrimmage, plus the 10 yards from the goal line to the end zone. The ball was snapped and the kick, soccer style, was nailed. It reached a quick height over the leaping linesmen and went straight through the goal posts. Navy had drawn first blood and the huge scoreboard read *Navy 3* and *Maryland 0*. C.J., wasn't on duty to worry yet. It was still early in the game, however, he was shuffling his feet a bit and was pacing a little. Kirk walked over to where C.J. was standing and put his hand on C.J.'s shoulder, "We'll be all right, no worries Mate," he said to C.J. in a loud voice in order to be heard over the crowd noise.

"This place is too damn noisy. I don't like it," was C.J.'s reply.

"No place is noisier than LSU's Tiger Stadium," replied Kirk.

"Yea, well, you lost that game," answered C.J. "Now let's get busy and get this thing under control. I'd rather enjoy this game while it's still going on. How much of this can one man stand," he continued!!

Some of the players and two of the coaches overheard C.J.'s loud remarks and had to smile. "What he says. You heard the man," shouted one of the coaches as he pointed to C.J.

"What he says," shouted the players, "Let's go," they yelled to the offensive unit as they went out onto the field for Maryland's first shot at the ball.

Navy's kick off after their field goal was high and deep. There would be no run back as the ball bounced deep in the end zone, then out of the playing field. Maryland would start their first series of downs from the 20-yard line. After three plays and a gain of only seven yards, Maryland was forced to punt from the 27. The punt had both distance and hang time, forcing Navy to call for a fair catch at their own 22-yard line.

"I'm not happy yet," said C.J. to Kirk as the defensive unit bolted onto the field. "Make certain these guys do not gain ground!!"

"We'll hold them," shouted Kirk over his shoulder, "this game is ours!"

The defensive unit did their job. Navy ran three plays. Two of them were passes and had to punt from the 28-yard line. The defense held!

As the defensive unit came back to the side line, C.J. stepped out onto the field and patted the backs and shoulders of the players, "That's the way. All right. Let's go offensive, make the defense proud of you!!"

The punt from Navy was short and with the run back, Maryland's offensive unit would start at their own 42-yard line. They had good field position for starting their second series of downs from scrimmage.

Maryland took advantage of the position and in five plays had first and goal on the Navy 8-yard line. It took two running plays to punch in, but Maryland scored! With the point after touchdown added, Maryland took the lead 7-3. The balance of the first quarter turned into a seesaw defensive battle with no additional scoring. The second quarter continued as a battle of the defensive teams. Neither offensive unit could get untracked, even though each kicked a 3-point field goal. Navy kicked their field goal first bringing the score to 7-6, however, Maryland had a drive underway as the half was coming to a close and had to settle for the field goal. At the half, Maryland went back to the locker room with a 10-6 lead.

Maryland did not waste any time putting additional points on the scoreboard as the second half got underway. They took the opening kick-off and dashed from the seven yard line to their own 44. Three plays later, all crossing passes to three different players, they scored and with the PAT, led Navy 17-6. Navy tightened up, and their defensive unit held for the balance of the third quarter, except for a late 43-yard field goal by Maryland. 20-6 was the score as the third quarter ended. Maryland would kickoff to open the 4th and final quarter. Navy got an excellent run back on the kickoff and nearly went all the way. The Maryland kicker was all that kept Navy from going the distance. A great open field tackle kept the running back from the end zone. The run covered 70 yards. Navy put the ball in play on the Maryland 22. They could not move the ball because of the stubborn Maryland defense, but rammed a field goal through the uprights bringing the score to Maryland 20 and Navy 9.

After the Navy kickoff, Maryland elected to keep the ball on the ground. It was time to work the clock by using the running game to take chunks of minutes off and keep it moving. Even though Navy possessed a fine defense, they had been on the field a long time and it was starting to show. Maryland ran off 9 plays and scored on an 11 yard run. With the point after added, they led Navy 27-9. Maryland's defense, which had not permitted a touchdown today, but just 3 long field goals, remained tough. Maryland, with a number of substitutes now in the game, still chalked up yardage and late in the 4th quarter, added another touchdown and extra point. At games end, Maryland had victory number 8, 34-9. The 8 win-2 loss record was the best effort Maryland had accumulated in quite a few years. The 2 losses were non-conference games and had come at the hands of teams that were currently ranked one and four in the national polls. Maryland had joined the coveted top 10 and looked forward to the final season game, which would be played on Terp's turf, against Clemson, the defending ACC champion. The University of Maryland really celebrated after the win over Navy. Both the team and the school had the feeling that this was their year! The confidence level had peaked at just the right time. The campus atmosphere was one of not only jubilation, but there was also an air of extreme pride. Kirk and Sharon spent as much time as possible together during the week. Sunday, as usual, had been their day and it was spent in Washington's Georgetown area. They drove down after breakfast, parked the jeep and strolled through the area, stopping for lunch at a quaint little restaurant, which had been a brownstone type house. Dinner was spent back at the Mobile Home. Kirk cooked a couple of steaks, one very large, one small, plus three baked potatoes, for two people. During the week they kept as normal a schedule as possible. Sharon and Kirk made time for each other despite the pressures of school, practice teaching, which included grading papers in the evening and preparing for the following day, Kirk's football practice and Sharon's helping Kirk with his schooling. C. J. drove down to College Park on Thursday evening. He bunked in at Kirk's room and was on hand to view the light Friday practice. His role as sort of a cheerleader for the team, plus the official team worrier needed some pre-game preparation also, especially in light of the fact that Maryland would enter the Clemson game as only 3 point favorites. In addition, some of the sports writers thought Clemson had a team that could easily pull an upset and figured that this is what would happen.

At lunch on Friday, Kirk and C.J. drove into the town of College Park and went over to Sizzler's. They made an outstanding hamburger, and then there was that salad bar. It provided a meal in itself!

Between trips to the salad bar, C.J. was talking about what was being written in the papers and asked, "What do the guys think when they're worked so hard all season and mostly read, 'possible upset'?"

"It's no big deal," Kirk answered, "they simply want to bring some extra hype to the game, sell some newspapers and say 'I told you so' if the people from South Carolina would somehow get lucky."

"Well I worry. They've got a good team. They've got a 9 and 1 record, with no ACC losses, and are ranked #10 to our #9. Three is not much margin of error here, you know?" C. J. stammered!

"And they know there's no margin of error, otherwise we'd blow the game wide open on them," answered Kirk, as he took a long sip of iced tea.

"You're like ice water," returned C.J., who had just a sip of iced tea.

"When it comes to football and especially what goes on during the game, you're absolutely correct. I have to be and I can't let up for even one play. It simply has to be that way, too much is at stake," Kirk replied.

"I guess you're right, the winning attitude at work," stated C.J.

"Besides," stated Kirk as they finished up, "I save my love for Sharon, my brother C.J. and monster big friends, like Tony!!"

C.J. smiled, "You really have to be, no, need to be two different people when you're involved in a sport like football, basketball and maybe even baseball in order to excel at the sport."

"Well, at this level of the sport, you need to be a bit more intense and it's down right hard work to bring out the best talent you have to offer. There are some guys with more natural talent, but don't be fooled, they've got to work their butts off if they want to excel. Someone on the other side is certainly trying his best to make you fail," continued Kirk.

"The job of the linebacker, make the offensive fail," kidded C.J.

"Now you're getting too deep for me. I've had just one philosophy course, but you've just reached the advance stage of the subject," answered Kirk as if he were very serious. "You're getting over my head!"

"What?" started a puzzled C.J.

"What you just said. I try to make the offensive fail and the offense team tries to make me fail, by blocking me as well as the other defenders, in order to score points. You should sign up and teach the course," kidded Kirk.

"Whatever you just said, meant let's get out of here, drink up. And I'm driving back," said C.J. and he picked up the Jeep keys.

Saturday morning meant the team breakfast and meeting prior to the players heading out to the stadium for practice as they loosened up before game time. There was a definite air of electricity and excitement as fans gathered early for tailgate parties, or just to be in and around the stadium for this final and most important game, against Clemson. The weather was nearly perfect, 55 degrees and sunny. Pre-game activities were abundant, so much, that it rivaled the pageantry of homecoming weekend. Crowds of people passed the many street vendors as they filed their way toward the stadium, like they were on a pilgrimage. On the field, Maryland, in practice jerseys were at one end and Clemson, in traveling white uniforms, trimmed in their traditional orange and purple were at the other end going through pre-game warm-ups, exercises and plays. Extra points and field goals were being kicked and punted. Footballs were also in the air. After the practice, the teams returned to their respective locker rooms for final preparations, instructions and to put on their game jerseys, as well as their game faces. The latter would bring out individual personalities, as each man prepared himself in his own way for the task that lie ahead for 60 game minutes of tough football.

Meantime, on the field, the pageantry continued, as the marching bands entertained the now nearly full stadium.

The teams remained in the locker rooms during this period. But then the call came and the players filed through the tunnel toward the playing field. Clemson came out first and was introduced. Then came a thunderous roar as fans spotted the first Maryland player at the tunnel entrance. The introductions of the players from Maryland brought applause and screaming as if it were the first game of the World Series. It continued as the team trotted toward their home side of the field. The officials brought the captains from each team to the center of the field at the 50-yard line for the coin toss, which would decide which team would receive the opening kickoff. As a senior and co-captain, Kirk had been designated as the individual who would state the call for Maryland.

"Tails," called Kirk in a loud, clear, affirmative voice!

"Tails it is." stated the official, after the coin he had flipped into the air, landed. Tony, who had accompanied Kirk onto the field, had a surprised look on his face.

"We'll receive," said Kirk, even before the official could explain the options.

"And which goal will you defend," asked the official to the Clemson captain.

"We'll defend this goal," stated the Clemson captain as he pointed to the goal behind him.

The referee went through the motions of showing the crowd what had just taken place, with his arms in the receiving possession for Maryland and using the kicking motion with his leg to show that Clemson would kick. Then he said, "Gentlemen, best of luck, have a good game!"

Kirk reached out and shook hands with the Clemson captain, "I'm not going to wish you good luck," he said smilingly.

"I know," came the reply, " we'll be at each other!"

Then the co-captains headed for their respective sidelines.

"Are you crazy or just nuts," said Tony to Kirk in as soft a voice as Tony could muster. "Calling tails, calling tails??!!"

"Did it work out?" asked Kirk. "Anyway, C.J. said to call tails."

"You were just lucky," answered Tony.

"Of course I'm lucky. I've got you as a friend. Now let's get the damn job done," said Kirk in a strong meaningful voice!

Up in the stands, John, Dora and Sharon were well situated for the game. Kirk had secured tickets on the fifty-yard line. John had borrowed a set of binoculars for the game, in addition to the two he had brought from home. This way, Sharon would have a set to herself, as would Dora.

C.J., in the meantime, was quietly pacing in a small area, shuffling his feet side to side. He also didn't know exactly what to do with his hands. They were in his pockets, on his hips, at his chin. He just wanted the game to start. C.J. was now looking at the ground, deep in thought when Kirk came over to him and put his arm around him.

"It's in the bag, relax man," said Kirk. "By the way I called tails out there like you told me to and it worked!"

"I didn't tell you to call tails. Tails?" said C.J. with a surprised look on his face.

"You didn't? Well someone must have, I'm not crazy enough to do that on my own, besides I told Tony it was you, big guy," stated Kirk as he went over to the area where the defensive unit had gathered.

"Gutsy call. It worked man, it worked!" shouted Tony when he spotted C.J.

C.J., with an exasperated look on his face, just waved a high five back.

Maryland's receiving team was now on the field, as was Clemson's kicking unit. The kicker placed the ball onto the kicking-tee, gave a quick count of his players to make sure there was eleven, checked the official with a nod and moved into position to kick.

The kick was nailed. It carried to the four-yard line where the Maryland receiver fielded it on one hop. The receiver started straight up the field, but then cut to his left as the Clemson players descended on him. The cut toward the left and sideline enabled the receiver to evade two tacklers and pick up almost 9 more yards before he was downed on the 19-yard line.

Maryland's first series from scrimmage was not as successful. After a completed pass for short yardage, a quick hand off in an unsuccessful trap play and a dropped pass, Maryland was forced to punt. The punt was high and deep, great hang time and Clemson called a fair catch at their own 26-yard line.

Clemson faired no better than Maryland and the stage seemed set for a defensive battle. The first quarter was just that, long solidly hit punts started each team off deep in their own territory.

For most of the first quarter, it seemed like a punting contest. Neither team got even close enough for a field goal attempt. Each series ended, just out of reach, which is what caused the punting game to dominate what turned out to be a scoreless first quarter.

The second quarter started as the first ended. The defensive battle continued. Both Clemson and Maryland knew each other's players and plays very well. It was obvious that teams had been scouted, films viewed time and time again, plus this game decided the Atlantic Coast Conference Champions and a solid Bowl invitation. The winner would spend New Year's Day in Miami as a participant in the Orange Bowl. The looser would also be in Florida for post season play, but up in Jacksonville in the Gator Bowl. Prestige, plus Bowl money is on the line.

It was well into the second quarter when Maryland caught the first break of the game. Kirk tipped a pass as he leaped to intercept the ball. Ron LaCost, the free safety, dove for the tipped ball and caught it, just before the ball hit the ground. Ron held on tight as his body bounced on the hard surface to make sure he didn't drop the ball. Maryland fans cheered wildly. It was the first real chance they had. Maryland would start this series at the Clemson 34-yard line. They were just about in range for a field goal.

The first play from scrimmage was a draw. Maryland, figuring that Clemson would expect a pass and try to strike quickly, caught Clemson with the draw and picked up almost 12 yards. The ball was set just inside the 22-yard line. Maryland had a first down and in a game this tight, the coaching staff did not want to open it up yet. Getting on the scoreboard was most important right now. Maryland kept to the ground game, but during first and second down managed only a pick-up of 6 yards, with the ball resting at the 16-yard line. They went to a safe pass in the flat to gain the first down, however, with the primary and the secondary receivers both covered, the pass was intentionally overthrown to the out of bounds area. Maryland would settle for a field goal. The field goal attempt would be 33 yards in total, not quite a chip shot, but well within reach. The ball was snapped, set by the holder and driven by a solid kick through the middle of the uprights. Maryland had drawn the first blood. The scoreboard, much to the delight of the Maryland fans showed them leading 3-0, with only 2 minutes and 47 seconds left in the first half.

The kickoff was not as long as it should have been. An up receiver caught the ball in the air at the Clemson 14-yard line. He handed it to one of the deep men who was coming up and then he came forward himself to throw a block. Clemson had good coverage on the return. Maryland hadn't the time to cover the kick off well and Clemson gained almost 35 yards on the return. With 2 minutes and 32 seconds, Clemson would start what would be their final series of the half from their own 48-yard line. They had extremely good field position. Only the clock and Maryland's defense could stop them. Clemson wanted to get into field goal range, at least. They came out shooting. While Maryland had been for the most part conservative on their field goal drive, Clemson needed to strike fast and fired a completed pass on a post-pattern for 26 yards. The next play was also a pass, this one to the flat. Clemson picked up another 11 yards. Clemson had the ball on the Maryland 15-yard line as time was called for the 2-minute warning. The actual time left on the clock for the first half was 1 minute and 54 seconds. It was a welcomed time out as the Maryland defense tried to regroup. As the Clemson quarterback went to the sidelines for instructions, Kirk trotted over to the Maryland coaching staff during the time-out to review what they thought Clemson would throw at them.

Clemson tried a draw play on first down, trying to catch Maryland in an over zealous charge. It didn't work and cost Clemson a down, plus a 2 yard loss. With the clock showing 1 minute and 3 seconds, Clemson came right up to the line of scrimmage without a huddle. A quick timed pass was executed into the left flat in the end zone. The ball was lofted just after the snap and the Clemson end ran under the ball and caught it for a touchdown. The Maryland fans were stunned! Clemson had grabbed the lead 6-3. They added the extra point and with the clock showing 1 minute and 14 seconds, the scoreboard told the story, *Clemson 7* and *Maryland 3*.

Maryland would have another chance before the half ended to do something. The series of plays to be used was being discussed with Maryland's quarterback and other offensive players as the specialty kick-off receiving team moved into position to receive the kick. Maryland cheerleaders were going through their routines, but for the most part, the seriousness of the moment was uppermost in the minds of Maryland's fans and they were focused on the playing field. C.J. was also focused on what was happening and had almost worn a path in the artificial carpet. He had stayed out of the way during the first half, leaving his worry post only to check on players that came off the field a bit shaken up or injured. Kirk had come over to him a couple of times to see how C.J. was getting along and also to ease a bit of tension built up in himself. C.J. served well as the team's worry stone!!

Clemson's kick-off was deep and sailed out of the end zone. Maryland would start at the 20-yard line. Because no one touched the ball, no time had ticked off the game clock. Maryland had 1 minute and 14 seconds to put some more points on the scoreboard.

This series of downs would be much more wide open as Maryland needed to get down field in a hurry. They also needed to use the clock and their time outs wisely. Three completed short passes brought Maryland to the 43-yard line. Clemson was in, almost, a prevent defense, not wanting to give Maryland the opportunity to burn them with a long completion. The clock now showed 44 seconds remaining in the half. While Maryland was gaining ground, they were still in their own territory. The next play was designed to at least bring them within field goal range. All receivers were out. The formation was the shotgun pass set-up. The ball was snapped. The quarterback could not find an open receiver down field and was again forced to dump the ball off to the short man. The gain was to the Clemson 41-yard line. The clock showed only 31 seconds left. Maryland called time out. The coaching staff and quarterback conferred on the sideline. There was nothing the defense unit of Maryland could do now except cheer and rally their teammates to the task ahead. Maryland went into a quick huddle as the quarterback came back onto the field. They broke huddle and lined up. During the huddle, 2 plays were called. No matter what happened on this play, they'd try to keep the drive alive and even catch Clemson off guard by moving to the next play quickly. The formation was again the shotgun. The ball was snapped, instead of a pass, the ball was handed off to the running back, almost on a delay. Clemson, again in the prevent defense, had gone long with the receivers, two of which were on their horses, doing the fly pattern, off to the races, straight down the field! The play worked. Maryland's back went straight through the middle, picking up yardage by the chunks. The runner cut to the left sideline as Clemson's defense reacted to the play and closed in. The hit was vicious. Two tacklers driving into the Maryland ball carrier. A third hit from the free safety coming at full run, slammed into the Maryland back and the ball bounced free at the Clemson 17-yard line. A mad scramble ensued as the ball bounded free toward the 16 yard line. The Maryland running back was not one of the players going after the ball. He was lying motionless where he had been hit. 3, 4, 6 or 7 players from both teams dove for the ball. Official's whistles were blowing as the pile of players continued scrambling on the ground. The officials quickly went to work undoing the pile, player by player. The officials were on top of the players, talking, yelling to get up, "OK, you don't have the ball, com'on outta there" finally, the player with the ball, tucked in, holding on for dear life in a Clemson uniform! The referee signaled, "Clemson's ball!"

Time had been called. An official time out was in effect, as soon as the pile-up occurred. Clemson would start back up the field from their own 16-yard line. The clock showed 14 seconds remained in the first half. The Maryland fans like the ball players were stunned! The entire stadium was unusually quiet. The Maryland running back was attended to and was helped off the field. The Maryland band was in place, ready to march onto the field for a gala half time show. They'd have to work extra hard to put on a great show. Performing would have been easier if Maryland had scored.

Clemson came to the ball after a brief huddle, actually the play had been called on the sideline. It would be simplified by the situation at hand. Clemson was deep in their territory. The clock showed 14 seconds remaining in the half. Any miscue by Clemson in ball handling would permit Maryland to call time and kick a field goal. Clemson did exactly what everyone thought they'd do. The ball was snapped to the quarterback and he went to one knee. The clock showed 9 seconds and counting. Kirk called time out.

"Let's make them snap it again," said Kirk to his teammates as Clemson went back into a huddle. "They need the practice."

Kirk's move was a good one and was understood by the coaching staff on the sideline. Kirk could have let the time run out and let the Maryland team trudge to the locker room. However, the score was only 7-3. They had another entire half of the football game to play. He didn't expect Clemson to fumble on the next play, but he didn't want his teammates to give in. They've come way too far this season to lose the momentum now. Also, he didn't want Clemson to think they had the upper hand. They had just dodged a bullet and he wanted Clemson to think about that and the fact that Maryland could gain ground on them.

"Man, are you guys lucky," called Kirk from his middle linebacker's position as Clemson came to the line of scrimmage. "You dodged a bullet, but we'll be back. There's a whole half to go you know, and this is one tough defense. Think about that in the locker room. Right guys?"

"Yea!" came a shout from the defensive players on the field, to a surprised Clemson offensive unit and also to the surprised group of Maryland players on the sideline.

"Yea!" came a shout from Maryland's bench.

"All right, pipe down," shouted the umpire as he stood over the ball. "Let's get on with the play before I throw a flag, delay for unsportsman-like conduct."

The umpire moved off the ball and into his position. The referee set the play. The ball was snapped and again the Clemson quarterback dropped to one knee. The play clicked off 7 seconds, but this time Kirk let the last 2 seconds of time run out. He had made his point to his teammates and to Clemson. The players headed for the locker room. Clemson with a 7-3 lead made the dash without much fanfare. They were at Maryland's home field and also, the score was too close to make a point of their lead at the half. The Maryland players likewise headed to their locker room. They were very businesslike. The defensive team had performed well and kept the Clemson scoring down.

The offensive unit was now showing that they could move the ball. Even with the score against them, Maryland was showing that winning confidence. It would be up to the coaching staff to build on that during the half, so that the momentum was not lost in the locker room.

C.J. jogged in with Kirk and Tony. "I think we've turned the corner," he yelled above the Maryland fan noise. "So let's be sure we hold down the Clemson scoring and then put up more points on our side of the ledger!!"

"Good idea," yelled Tony. "Let's tell the rest of the team, this will be the second half game plan!"

Kirk just smiled, Tony was the one player who could keep the team loose. Player after player entered the locker room and the ritual of the half time began. After players had used the restrooms, had something to drink, toweled off, some re-taped, then came team meetings for second half instructions. The Maryland locker room was all business. The players had been through this all season long and knew how much this particular game meant. They would be ready for the second half.

Just as the players were getting ready to leave for the field, the loud booming voice of Tony brought the room to silence. "Just as we were leaving the field, C.J. brought everything into proper perspective for the overall game plan for the second half. He stated that we should hold down Clemson's ability to score, and put up more points on our side of the scoreboard. If we do this we'll make him proud. He's been our inspiration all season long. Let's make C.J. proud. All right?"

"Yea," came a thunderous yell!! There was also a lot of laughing as the players filed out toward the tunnel and the playing field.

C.J. was the inspiration. Tony delivered the message. The air of victory over Clemson was there, now they had to do it on the field within the allotted time for second half.

The bands had finished playing and were marching off the field as the players reached their respective benches. Clemson had came out first and were greeted with boo's, just so they'd remember where they were. The Maryland team was, of course, cheered loudly as they appeared in the tunnel and made the dash for their bench.

Clemson would receive the second half kickoff.

Thc Maryland kickoff was deep and also had good height. The receivers who were waiting at the 5-yard line when the ball was booted, retreated behind the goal line. The ball was caught 4 yards deep in the end zone. The ball was not run out. The other receiver motioned to stay put. The

Maryland kicking team was well in the neighborhood, meaning the run back would be short lived. Clemson would start their series of downs from the 20-yard line. Since there was no run back from the end zone no time had clicked off the clock. It would start at the snap of the ball. Clemson tried a quick pass from the flat, but the ball was batted down at the line of scrimmage. It happened so fast that Maryland did not have an opportunity to intercept the pass. The second play of the half was a draw. It went nowhere. In fact the play lost a yard. With 3rd down and 11 to go for the first down, Clemson was forced to pass. The Maryland pass rush was strong, giving the Clemson quarterback almost no time to set up and complete the pass. The Maryland secondary was also doing a very good job of covering the receivers. The pass was thrown well out of bounds. There was no point in Clemson's trying to complete the pass. With the pass rush and good down field coverage, to throw into a crowd at this early state of the second half would simply not be a smart move. On 4th down and 11 yards to go for a 1st down, Clemson punted. It was a good punt, solidly hit and with good hang time, permitting Clemson to cover the punt well. Maryland called for a fair catch at their own 37-yard line. They would have good field position. Maryland's first series of downs in the second half was much more conservative than their fans wanted. On two runs off tackle they managed 8 yards. Third down was a quick pass to the tight end after a fake to the runner going to the middle. The pass was complete for a gain of 7 yards and 1st down. Maryland had moved into Clemson territory, just over the 50-yard line. Maryland went right back to the ground game. They made two more first downs. With the ball resting on the Clemson 29-yard line, their defense finally stiffened. The Terps continued on the ground for two plays, moving the ball to the 22. On third and 3, they tried a draw play, figuring that Clemson would be looking pass. It didn't work, gaining only two of the needed three yards. On 4th down and a little more than a yard to go for the first down, Maryland decided to go for the field goal and put more points on the scoreboard. The kick, a 37-yard attempt with a slight left angle, was hit solidly and shot straight through the goal post. A huge cheer from the Maryland fans let the kicker know it was good. The kicker, of course, at the time of the snap and kick, is keeping his head down, making certain he sees what he's kicking. "Let the fans tell you it's good" is the usual word from the coaches.

Maryland had now closed the gap to 7-6, still behind Clemson, but the Terps seemed to have the upper hand on the field of play. The drive had consumed more than 6 minutes from the game clock. They'd need to work quickly and use the clock wisely if Clemson's defense continued to hold.

Maryland's kick off again, sailed well into and then bounced out of the end zone. Clemson was not being permitted to run the ball out. Clemson fared no better on offense than they did before. Maryland's defense had dug in and was determined not to be out played by Clemson' offense. A punting contest ensued during most of the third quarter. Maryland could not even get close enough to attempt a field goal. Both teams had outstanding defensive and specialty teams, and it showed. It would take a major break, which could give the offensive unit a decent field position to start from. The almost seemingly punting contest put each offensive team deep into their own territory as the series of downs started and neither team could attain a sustained drive. With only one minute and eighteen seconds remaining in the third quarter, Maryland intercepted a third down pass at the Clemson 44-yard line. It was the break they needed. The left cornerback was dropped almost on the spot as he went high in the air to pick off the pass. Uppermost in his mind was to hold onto the ball before trying to pick up additional yardage toward the Clemson goal line. Just as he came down and started to run he was hit hard and driven out of bounds. The ball would be spotted at the Clemson 43-yard line. The noise level was almost deafening as the Maryland defense left the field and the offense trotted on.

Maryland quickly huddled, broke and lined up. The quarterback came to the line behind his center, looked around and held his hands up, waving for the crowd to quiet down a bit so that his team could hear the signals. The play was a pass to the flat, a safe pass that only gained 4 yards. The following play was a roll out quarterback option. With receivers covered, he ran up the middle, then cut left for a few more yards. The play netted 8 yards and a Maryland first down. The third quarter came to an end with the ball resting on the Clemson 31-yard line. Clemson still had the lead, 7-6, but with Maryland now within reach of a field goal, this could change shortly. Maryland and their fans could hardly wait for the fourth quarter to get underway. It seemed to take forever for the television commercials to end, so that play could begin for the final quarter. The Maryland play calling continued to be conservative. This was a time to keep cool heads and take the lead, much too much was at stake for the Terps.

Maryland stayed on the ground. Jack Macklin picked up another first down before the Clemson team brought the drive to a halt at their 11-yard line. A third down pass was thrown out of the end zone when the quarterback could not find an open receiver. With a little over eleven minutes remaining, Maryland set up for a field goal. If it was successful, Maryland could regain the lead.

The kick would be not much more than a chip shot, 28 yards in total, but sometimes these are more difficult than longer kicks. The snap and set were perfect and the ball quickly gained altitude as it was kicked over the jumping and outstretched hands of the Clemson rush. The officials told the story with their signal of "Good!" Maryland fans were almost in a joyous frenzy as the scoreboard showed *Maryland 9* and *Clemson 7*. Maryland's kick off was not as deep this time, coming down at around the 8-yard line. The receiver returned the ball to the 22. On two quick passes, Clemson moved to mid-field. There the Maryland pass rush kicked into high gear and the drive fizzled. On 4th down, Clemson, at the Maryland 44, was forced to punt. It was a booming punt that sailed into the Maryland end zone for a touch back. Maryland would start from the 20-yard line. A short kick toward the corner would have worked out much better for Clemson, because the net gain on this kick was only 24 yards. Maryland's rush did have something to do with not giving the punter much time, they were coming, trying to block the punt. Maryland's defense, again keeping Clemson out of field goal range was extremely important. Only seven minutes remained in the game.

Maryland continued to play conservatively. They were maintaining a drive through runs, short, quick passes and the draw play. They were also taking chunks of time from the game clock. The drive stalled at the Clemson 27-yard line when on second down Maryland fumbled in the backfield on the hand-off. They recovered, but lost three yards and the down. They fared no better on third down when a pass was knocked down at the goal line. They went for the "whole thing," but it didn't work. A field goal was in order again. Maryland once again kicked the ball through the uprights. The score was now 12-7. The clock showed less than five minutes as Maryland set up for the kickoff. The Maryland defense would be asked to rise to the occasion once again. Clemson could still win this game with a touchdown. They would be throwing, probably long, because the main thing working against them, in addition to the Maryland defense, was the huge scoreboard clock. The kickoff traveled just to the goal line. The receiver looked to see if he was behind the goal line. He wasn't and so off he went to gain as much ground as he could. First he went up the middle, then cut toward the right. It was a good runback. Seeing the Maryland players closing in, he wisely went out of bounds, rather than take a chance of picking up a couple more yards and perhaps losing the ball on a fumble. Going out of bounds also stopped the clock. Clemson would start what could be their last big opportunity from their own 29-yard line. The runback had only taken 13 seconds off the clock. Four minutes and eighteen seconds were left in the game. The Maryland defense came onto the field determined as ever!

No team can be successful in football without a very strong defense and Maryland's defense had brought them a long way this season. Clemson started this series of downs with a completed pass over the middle, just as Maryland was in a blitz. The pass was good for almost twenty yards. Maryland had blitzed and through the quick release of Clemson's quarterback, they were burned. The ball was just shy of mid-field. The clock started to run again, once the chains had been moved for the first down. Clemson ran a draw play, picking up nine yards as they crossed into Maryland's territory. They were now trying to use the clock to their advantage, score a touchdown, and leave no time for Maryland to come back. Another completed pass, this one to the right flat, another first down for Clemson at the Maryland 37-yard line. They were getting within field goal range, but a field goal would do them no good, Clemson needed a touchdown!!

Clemson threw another pass, but it was batted up into the air at the line of scrimmage. Kirk, from his middle linebacker position, dove for the ball and caught it just before it hit the ground. Maryland had made their own break. With only two minutes and fourteen seconds remaining on the clock, Maryland had possession on their 35-yard line. The Maryland fans cheered wildly! They could sit on the ball and win 12-7, however, two minutes and fourteen seconds can be an eternity too, especially with Clemson having all of their time outs remaining. Maryland elected to try a play option pass on first down. Having been conservative throughout the game, they figured Clemson would expect a running play up the middle to use as much time as they could. But, Maryland, knowing that Clemson could call a time out, tried to out smart their opponent. Maryland's quarterback faked the hand-off to his running back and the back carried out the fake perfectly, as he hit the pile up at the line of scrimmage. In the meantime, the quarterback rolled left, carrying the football low behind his hip and leg, bootlegging the ball as his tight end made a block at the line, then went into a vacated area almost eight yards down field. The quarterback continued to roll left and made the play look as if he were going to run the ball. Finally, the Clemson outside linebacker made his move and charged toward the Maryland quarterback, who was still two yards behind the line of scrimmage. The quarterback stopped, brought his right arm up and threw a crisp pass to his tight end. The pass was not the bullet, often used to get the ball to the receiver in a hurry, but one, with no tight coverage on the receiver, designed to be completely catchable, almost as in practice. The tight end came back a yard, caught the pass and started down field. He drew a lot of traffic as they say! As he crossed the forty, heading for midfield, he switched the ball to his left or outside, so that if he fumbled the ball, hopefully it would bounce out of bounds and Maryland would retain possession. Two Clemson defenders caught up to him at midfield. He was hit and pounded to the ground just over the midfield point. The play had caught Clemson off guard. The last thing they wanted Maryland to do here was to gain sixteen yards, have another first down and move into their territory. The play kept Maryland's fans on their feet. They hadn't settled down from Kirk's interception yet and this play brought them almost to a fever pitch.

On the sideline, after Kirk had come off the field and been congratulated by his teammates, C.J. moved from his position to where Kirk was standing with the rest of the defensive team. "Great catch, man," stated C.J., "you sure stopped that drive. I was worried you know. I spotted Sharon, she looked confident as hell!!"

Kirk smiled, gave his friend a light punch on the arm, "Yea, we caught the break we needed and it looks like we're making the most of it!"

Kirk did not look back toward the crowd to see Sharon, or her parents. They had discussed this even before the season started. They'd meet after the game. In the meantime, Sharon knew that Kirk had a job to perform and could not be distracted while the game was showing time on the clock. His focus had to be on the field of play.

The play consumed twenty-one seconds. It was twenty-one seconds that Clemson could not afford. The clock showed one minute and fifty-three seconds left in the game as the officials whistled the two-minute warning and went to the sidelines to personally inform the two coaches. The Maryland quarterback came to the sideline to meet with the coaching staff to discuss the plays to be used on the next series of downs. The Maryland defensive team was yelling to the offensive unit telling them to be tough, execute the play, control the line of scrimmage. It was a total team effort that had brought Maryland to this point where they were less than two minutes from the Atlantic Coast Conference Championship. They didn't want it to slip away. In the meantime, television commercials were being run on TBS, the Atlanta Super Station, which broadcasted throughout the country. They were carrying this all-important game this afternoon. This evening, TBS would telecast the SEC (Southeastern Conference) game of the week, which would put LSU up against Alabama. That game would be played in Baton Rouge, one tough place to play on a Saturday night if your uniform didn't have purple and gold as your colors. Maryland knew that all too well!!

With time back in, Maryland ran a quick trap play off tackle, picking up a hard four yards. The clock was still moving as Maryland went back into their huddle. The next play, from the Clemson 45 was a quarterback draw. The play was executed quickly with the blocking being effective as he gained five more valuable yards to the 40! It would be a third down and a little less than one yard for the first down. Clemson would stack the middle, trying to stop Maryland dead in their tracks and force a 4th down decision if they could. Maryland was just as determined to keep the drive alive. Maryland called a time-out. The quarterback trotted to the sideline once again to talk over the situation and get instructions. This was too important a play to worry about taking a few more seconds off the clock by keeping it running. The 1st down if successful was more important. With this being 3rd down and 1, Maryland's coach would give his quarterback two plays to run, in case the first one didn't make it. Maryland was still out of field goal range. Should they try to just get within range? A fieldgoal would give them 15 points. The best Clemson could do then is a tie. Maryland would have a share of the ACC championship. Whatever they were going to do, the decision was made as the officials set the ball and the Maryland quarterback trotted toward the team huddle. They lined up. The ball was snapped. Again Maryland faked the hand-off to the running back. It was the same play they used before, there was a pile up at the line of scrimmage and the running back dove into it as if he had the ball. The right arm came up again as the quarterback set himself for the quarterback option roll out pass. Instead of hitting his tight end, the pass was thrown to the Maryland wide receiver, who had gotten clear and was twenty yards downfield. The pass was complete at the 21-yard line. The race was on. Clemson's defenders were on the chase, trying to tackle the Maryland receiver turned runner. The pass had been perfect, letting the reception be made at full stride. The 21 yards were covered quickly! Maryland scored! It was now 18-7. The clock showed forty-nine seconds left. Maryland was thinking of two-point attempt, but if it failed and Clemson got extremely lucky, a touchdown, two-point conversion and field goal, they could have a total of 18 points to Maryland's 18 points. The PAT would be a kick!

The ball snapped, set and kicked through the uprights. 19-7 was the score. Maryland had all but put the game out of reach. The Maryland fans had really been in the game and now the Terps cheering crowd erupted as they sensed the game was won and their college was ACC Champions. It had been a long time coming and the celebration was underway!! Maryland's kickoff was a line drive shot, which bounced at the 14-yard line and was picked up by the Clemson deep man at the 9. Maryland did not want the long kick, out of the end zone, because they wanted Clemson to field it and get the clock started. Maryland's coverage of the kickoff was outstanding and they dropped the runner at the 17-yard line.

The officials set the first down chains and started the clock, thirty-nine seconds and counting down. Maryland knowing that Clemson would have to throw the ball, went into a prevent defense. This would enable Clemson the opportunity to complete the short 6 to 8-yard passes, but would prevent them from being successful on the long pass attempt. At least, this was the Maryland plan.

Clemson, now with their backs to the wall came up over the ball, nothing fancy was going to happen. From the shotgun formation Clemson would pass the ball, try to get down field as fast as they could, score, hold Maryland, get the ball again and go back to work. All with thirty-nine seconds on the clock and a tough Maryland defense on the other side of the ball. It was a tall order.

Clemson's first pass from scrimmage was complete at the 24-yard line where the wide receiver was dropped in his tracks. Clemson did not huddle, but came back over the ball right away, again in the shotgun formation. From second down and three, Clemson threw a pass into the prevent coverage, trying to get a quick hit and eat up some yardage. At the 41-yard line the ball was batted away at the last second by Maryland's free safety. The incomplete pass stopped the clock with thirty seconds remaining. Clemson huddled this time, because the clock was not taking time away from them, they could slow the pace a little and organize the next play or two.

Again at the 24-yard line, on third down, Clemson passed from the shotgun formation. The pass was complete at the 32-yard line. Their quarterback had looked long, saw the coverage and went for the short safer pass. It also gave Clemson another first down. Instead of coming quickly over the ball as they had done before, with the game clock running, Clemson used one of their time outs to stop the clock. The Clemson quarterback went to the sidelines to discuss the next series of plays with his coach. The clock was stopped with just twenty-two seconds left in the game.

Kirk, as the defensive captain, did not go to the sideline during the time out. They knew their job, nothing fancy, just pure, hard defense to halt the drive. When time was called back in, Clemson once again went into the shotgun formation. This time they'd send all four receivers long. The situation simply called for this. At the snap, the Clemson receivers were off and running their deep patterns. The players went straight down the field and two crossed, as they tried to divide the Maryland pass coverage and complete the pass.

The ball was thrown to one of the receivers running a crossing pattern. The pass was completed at the 44-yard line of Maryland. The receiver was hit hard almost at once, but he managed to hold onto the ball and gain three more yards before being dropped at the Maryland 41-yard line. The officials stopped the clock as they moved the chains. Clemson immediately went up over the ball, rather than huddle. The clock showed nine seconds left. From the shotgun the same play was run except now, the receivers would go all the way to the end zone and try for a quick six points. The pass thrown was almost a *Hail Mary* because of the 50-yard distance involved from the shotgun position of the quarterback. Just over the goal line the ball came down in a crowd of Clemson and Maryland players. They jumped for the ball. Maryland intercepted for a touchback. The hometown crowd went wild!!! That did it. Maryland would be the ACC Champions!!

The clock showed one second. Maryland would run another play before the regular season ended. The ball was placed at the 20-yard line. It took all that the ushers and security men could do to keep the fans off the field to celebrate. The Maryland quarterback took the snap from center, stepped back two yards and went down to one knee. The Maryland line came up at the snap, as if on a pass play and backed up a step or two themselves to protect their quarterback, but it was not necessary. Clemson did not charge as they would on a normal play. At the snap they stood up and let the *one second* click off the clock. It was a show of sportsmanship for Clemson, who themselves had a great season and were the defending champions. It had been a great game, one especially that Maryland rooters would remember and talk about for a very long time.

The Maryland players dashed from the sideline to join their teammates at the 20-yard line. Several players, Kirk included, sought out particular Clemson players to shake hands with. There is always a lot of respect for the men who had played hard against each other during the game. Many times, the fans in the grandstand do not understand this, but the players, especially the starters on both teams who had gone after each other all during the game in and around the "trenches" sought out their opponents. It was not just a show of sportsmanship, it was sincere. The on field celebration continued as fans joined players on the field. It was something to see. A group had gathered at the goal posts. It used to be a tradition to "tear the goal posts down" after the last game. But then, in those days they were made of wood and easily replaced. These were expensive, made of iron and protected by security guards at each end of the field. No matter, the Maryland rooters, were just plain happy, almost delirious as they celebrated the victory!

C.J. had joined the players in the dash from the sidelines. He did his best to give Kirk a big bear hug. Other players were bear hugging poor 'ole C.J. He'd be lucky if he came away from the celebration without broken ribs! Sharon had made a dash herself. She told her parents to stay, she'd see them later when Kirk went into the locker room. Sharon made her way little by little toward Kirk. She knew about where he was from her viewpoint in the grandstand and hoped that he hadn't moved too far from that spot.

C.J. spotted Sharon at about the same time Kirk did. Kirk was looking up toward the crowd in the grandstand and saw John pointing to the field. He gave John a high sign as he caught the glimpse of Sharon making her way to him.

"Will you hold this," said Kirk to C.J. as he handed him his football helmet. Just then Sharon reached Kirk and he lifted her up in his arms and gave her a high squeeze, then set her down and kissed her.

"I'm so proud of you," stated Sharon. "That was some game you played!"

"Remember to tell our children that," kidded Kirk as he and Sharon kissed again.

Sharon and Kirk walked off the field with C.J. toward the Maryland locker room. As they made their way, fans stopped Kirk to say, "congratulations", "great game," to pat him on the back, to shake hands and feel a part of the victory, the team. As they neared the locker room, John and Dora were waiting. Kirk shook hands with John and gave Dora a hug. They talked for a few moments, but John cut it short, telling Kirk that he and Dora would catch up with them later. John knew that Kirk wanted to get into the locker room and join his teammates. As Kirk and C.J. entered the locker room, with the security guards holding the door for them, Tony came charging across the room. He threw his arms around both guys.

"We were great out there today," he stated in a booming voice!!

"We were great every game this season," returned Kirk as other players came over to shake hands, pound backs and give high fives.

"We just didn't win two of them." Kirk was right, Maryland had been great all year. It was a season to be proud of. Maryland finished the ACC with six conference victories and no losses. They were Atlantic Coast Conference Champions and would represent the conference on New Year's night at the Orange Bowl in Miami, Florida. Maryland had finished the regular season with nine victories and two losses. The two losses, against Miami, ranked number one in the country and number three, LSU were close games. Seven total points accounted for the two losses. Maryland would be ranked perhaps as high as 5th, after this game, because two of the teams ranked ahead of Maryland were upset in their final contest of the year. Maryland's New Year's night opponent would be an interesting one. It would be a re-match with Miami!! The Maryland players were more than excited about that, they felt that they should have held on and defeated

Number One ranked Miami the last time they met. Miami had scored the winning points with just 11 seconds left in the game. They were not at all intimidated by being back at the Orange Bowl. They were looking forward to it! The only problem would be the wait. Maryland had started their season the week after Labor Day and had no open dates. They concluded the eleven game schedule the Saturday before Thanksgiving. New Years in Miami and the big game would be five weeks away. They'd practice, get completely healthy but, oh, the wait!

The locker room celebration continued. C.J. came outside at Kirk's request to tell Sharon he'd meet her and her folks at the Mobile Home. He'd be a bit late getting out of the locker room on this particular afternoon.

John and Dora, knowing that Sharon was planning a party at the Mobile Home told Sharon, that they'd catch up with Kirk on Thanksgiving Day at Elk Neck. John, also being "Dad," gave Sharon some money to help her with the party expenses. C.J., being C.J., had invited his uncle, as owner of the Cherry Hill Mobile Home Park, plus at least half the park.

"If they're all at the party," he reasoned "no one would be left to call the police if the noise level got too loud!!" Well, maybe C.J.'s right!

It was almost two hours after the game when Kirk, C.J. and Tony finally emerged from the Maryland locker room. The three headed for C.J.'s car. Tony was going to drive himself, but C.J. said he'd drop Tony back over at the campus if Peggy wanted nothing more to do with him. Kirk's jeep was already at the Mobile Home with Sharon.

"What kind of food are you having at the party!" asked Tony, as they were closing the doors to the car and he settled in the back seat, but hanging over the front. C.J. had a surprised look on his face as he put the key into the ignition and started the car, but before he could say anything...

"Why, you want to stop at the supermarket?" said Kirk.

"I was only asking, like in what kind of beer! you know," answered Tony.

"I think party food and tap beer, eating and drinking stuff," stated Kirk.

"Your friend here is a wise guy, you know," said Tony to C.J. "You know, I couldda gone to QUITE A FEW parties this evening, invited parties, not crash!!"

"You could not. Peggy and Sharon planned this party," answered Kirk, who winked at C.J. and continued, and you probably have planned to live out this day!"

Tony thought for a moment, then fell back against the back seat of the car with arms stretched out. "When you're right, you're right. Com'on,

C.J., let's go to the party." Then after some further thought. "Really, what are they serving? Not just hot dogs and hamburgers, right?"

"All I know is that Peggy stopped at your Mother's house on her way down here," answered Kirk with a wide grin on his face. "But, we're probably late and the party is well underway. Maybe most of the food is gone!"

"Please do not talk like this. You may not realize this, but as an Italian Prince, I should not be upset. Please drive on," commanded Tony calmly.

"An Italian prince?" questioned C.J. as he made the turn into the Cherry Hill Park.

"Please, C.J., don't get him started," stated Kirk as he pointed to a parking place. "He's the only child, an Italian son, yet. He can do no wrong…he's a Prince!"

"He pretty much covered it. Not bad for an Amerigon," kidded Tony who stepped from the parked car, arms out, mock waving, in a princely manner. "Let the party really begin!" he bellowed.

The party had begun. Several players and girlfriends were already there. It was still fairly warm, but with the party crowd expanding by the carload, it was moved across the street at the Park Recreation Hall instead of just outside the mobile home. Many of the residents were there, pitching in to help set up tables, and to bring in extra food. It had become almost a church like potluck dinner. The crowd was also quite a mixture, many of the park residents wanted to get a glimpse of championship football players, others, who had met Sharon and Kirk were there to enjoy the party and wish them well. It wouldn't be too long before Kirk was also a resident of the park. Wedding plans now called for a December 15th wedding as the official date. It was between the last game of the regular season, Christmas Holidays and the New Years Night game in Miami, also before the Christmas school break itself began. With the wedding scheduled for the Chapel, on the University of Maryland's campus, C.J. was going around the party inviting just about everyone. It was going to be a quiet wedding, so to speak. Someone, with beer in hand, even suggested that the 50-yard line at the stadium might better serve the crowd C.J. was anticipating. He did stop and think for a minute.

"No, it might be too cold for Sharon and Kirk's best man," he answered. "If we only had the Syracuse Carrier Dome!"

The party continued well into the night. Everyone was having a great time. Somehow even dance music started at about 8 o'clock. Seems that the Rec-Hall tapes, plus some tapes from Sharon's collection and C.J.'s car tapes were used. There was a lot of fun going on at the impromptu dance floor, the older folks doing, or rather trying the new dances, the younger people trying out some of the waltz and fox trot steps. It was close to one in the morning when the last of the party goers went home, C.J. was going to drive back to Elk Neck, but Kirk convinced him to stay over and drive back on Sunday. Sharon told them to come over for breakfast, but not too early. She walked them to C.J.'s car, gave C.J. a light kiss on the cheek and thanked him for all his help. "Mr. Peal Mesta", she called him. Then she threw herself into Kirk's arms. "I'm not sure if I'm throwing myself at you or collapsing on you," she stated. "I'm not only overextended, I'm tired!"

"Well, sleep in as long as you want," stated Kirk as he was getting into the car. "If C.J. and I get back here early, we'll put on a pot of coffee and clean up the rec-room." C.J. started the engine, backed out of the parking space and drove over to Kirk's dorm.

"Let's get a few Z's," stated C.J. as he fell into the other bed in Kirk's room, the one he had brought in especially for C.J., back in the early fall. It wasn't long before the room was filled with the sound of snoring, two tired young men, out like a light!

At just about 8 o'clock Kirk's radio alarm went off and on came the country music station playing Johnny Cash singing the Kris Kristofferson song "Sunday Morning Coming Down." C.J. opened both eyes in almost disbelief!

"Am I awake? I am awake!" C.J. sat up in bed and looked over at the still sleeping Kirk, "Oh, I feel like this song," C.J. continued, "I'm awake and he's still asleep," C.J. said aloud, but really to himself. He then got out of bed and walked over to the clock radio, "8:01" it read. The automatic alarm button was in the 'on' position and C.J. started to reach for it to shut it off. "I'm awake and I won't be able to go back to sleep. I think I'll get a shower," then he reached over to the volume control and turned it up twice as loud, grabbed a towel and soap from Kirk's locker, and left for the hall.

"Dum...Dum....Dum...Dum...Dum...." was heard as the shower room door closed. "Hello, I'm Johnny Cash!"

By this time Kirk was up and sitting on the edge of his bed. "I forgot to shut off the automatic" and his voice faded as he realized that C.J. wasn't in the room. Kirk grabbed a towel, looked for the soap and surmised that C.J. had it, so down the hall he walked to the shower room.

"Sorry about the radio alarm. I forgot to turn it off," said Kirk as he caught the soap and walked into the shower stall.

"That's OK," started C.J. as he rinsed off, "you've got to watch the volume though, man you could have awoken the dead if we were near a cemetery!" and he smiled.

"Ya, it was real loud. It must have jumped or something," answered Kirk as he washed.

"Let's stop at Dunkin' Donuts," said C.J. as they left the dorm and walked to the car. "We can pick up some donuts and have them grind some of that coffee for us. They've got a big coffee brewer at the rec-hall. The aroma will get us some help. Guaranteed!"

Over at the rec-hall, the mess from last night wasn't too bad, especially for the amount of people who stayed all evening, plus those who just stopped by. C.J. made the coffee. He also left the door to the rec-hall opened and turned on the ceiling fan. It wasn't too long before some people wandered in.

"Help yourself to the coffee and donuts," said C.J. "We're just here cleaning up a little after last night," as he opened the three donut boxes and offered them.

"Don't you think three dozen's a bit much?" questioned Kirk quietly to C.J.

"No, you'll eat a half dozen yourself. Besides, the birds and squirrels will need a snack too," answered C.J.

By this time several of the people who were at the party last night, stopped to pitch in. The clean up was going well and at a fast pace.

Sharon wandered in just as they were finishing. "I thought you were coming over for breakfast," she said as Kirk handed her a cup of coffee.

"Well C.J. and I got up early and the rec-hall needed cleaning and he had the Huck Finn idea we would get some help to clean up sooner if the aroma of the coffee drew people in," stated Kirk . . .

But C.J. interrupted, pushing the donuts in Sharon and Kirk's face. "Sharon, simply put, it worked. A small army of people were all pitching in for good ole C.J.!"

C.J. was right. The clean up took almost no time at all. It was just past noon when C.J. said so long, "See you on Thanksgiving."

Kirk and Sharon walked back to the mobile home, hand in hand. He held the door for her and they disappeared inside.

"Do you feel like going into DC, or just taking a ride?" asked Kirk.

"No, why don't we just relax at home today. I've got a couple of steaks to cook on the grill. Besides, I know you want to watch and see how the pros play on TV. Your Eagles are playing my Redskins," answered Sharon as she put her arms around Kirk and they kissed.

"I'm not allowed to root for the Redskins?" questioned Kirk. "You know, I've been a resident of the area for almost four years."

"No way," answered Sharon, "the men from Camden, New Jersey, they are fans of the Philadelphia Eagles. Of course, if the Redskins draft you to play for them, then that's another story."

"What if I don't get drafted or I'm a low choice for the Denver Bronco's or some other team far away, will you still love me?" kidded Kirk.

"No one will love you more or make love to you better than me, all throughout your life, Star. You'll forget about all those other girls," stated Sharon, more serious than kidding, and she snuggled in as they sat down on the sofa.

"When compared to you, there haven't been any other girlfriends, certainly no wives, I might add," answered Kirk as he brought her closer and kissed her forehead. Then Kirk hit the remote control for the TV and turned it on.

"That was well put, you know, a little corny, but that's OK too," said Sharon, who continued after some thought. "What do you think of marriage and do you think about the draft, who might pick you?"

"I like the idea of marriage to your parent's daughter and if possible, I'd like to play pro ball," answered Kirk as he looked up at the clock and saw that the game would not be on for another fifteen minutes, at 1 o'clock.

"What about who picks you?" questioned Sharon.

"I really have no control over that. If I get in a couple of post season games, like the North-South, East-West, Senior Bowl for instance, then I could get a higher pick, than no pick at all. If we do well against Miami, that would count too. The higher the pick, the more dollars I'll be offered. The pros could certainly give us a good financial start, 4-5 years of school teachers salary in one, if you know what I mean," answered Kirk on a serious note.

"Well, I hope the Redskins pick you," said Sharon in a bully voice. "That would be the best of all worlds, and with the Ravens in Baltimore, we could have two shots at area teams."

"I know, well, we'll see," answered Kirk, "plenty of things have to happen first, if I don't get drafted, I'll work for a Master's Degree and work on campus, help out coaching the football team. I really don't want to get ahead of myself."

"You're right," remarked Sharon, "I'm just anxious for you!"

"You know, we haven't talked about a honeymoon," beamed Kirk.

"I just thought we'd come back here. Go to Miami for the honeymoon when you play there," answered Sharon. "I promise to make it interesting for you!"

"I know you will but we'll have a couple of days to ourselves, so let's go someplace, like Virginia Beach," remarked Kirk, "Miami can be a 2nd honeymoon!"

"Virginia, Virginia is for lovers. Sounds fine to me," answered Sharon.

"I'll make the reservations. There's a Holiday Inn right on the beach. Every room faces the ocean. It should be cold then, at least during the daytime. There won't be much going on at night in December, so we'll have to think of something to do after dinner," said Kirk with a smile, as Sharon lifted her head and wrinkled her nose at him.

"Oh, I'm sure that after making us wait, we'll think of something to do all night long and for a morning, good morning," answered Sharon as she snuggled back into her place in Kirk's arms.

Kirk had to smile as John Madden and Pat Summerall came on the television with the game.

Seventeen 17

Kirk awoke to the ringing of the phone. He reached over to shut off the alarm clock, then realized that he hadn't set the alarm. He started to reach for the phone, but glanced back at the clock to see it read 7:03. "It's before I was going to wake up," he spoke as he answered the phone.

"Happy Thanksgiving," stated C.J. in a cheerful voice, "and don't start that guilt stuff on me," he continued. "When are you getting here? Let's take the boat out. Come on, it's a great day!"

"I'll be there in a few minutes," answered a still sleepy Kirk. "What boat?"

"Kirk, come on boy, it's me, C.J." stated C.J. in his usual happy, bright manner. "Go get showered, pack, pick up Sharon and get up here. Look, I'll call Sharon and get her started," he continued.

"Right, you call Sharon. Better you than me," answered Kirk, who was now awake.

"OK, don't go back to bed. Sharon said she'll be ready in a few minutes. You're up, right?" continued C.J.

"How could Sharon say she'd be ready. You haven't called her yet. Is this a test?" questioned Kirk, who thought for a minute then said, "Tell Sharon that I'll be there in 5 to 10 minutes." He'll catch a bit of hell from Sharon on that note, serves him right, thought Kirk as he hung up the phone. Kirk pulled himself together and walked down the hall toward the shower thinking little about what he'd pack. "I'll think of that when I'm awake," he thought to himself as he entered the shower room. In the meantime, C.J. placed the call to Sharon.

"Hello," said a sleepy voiced Sharon.

"Oh good, you're awake. Kirk said he'd pick you up in 5 or 10 minutes. It's a great day up here. He even wants to take the boat out," stated C.J.

"Two people are going to die on Turkey Day, you for waking a sleeping Princess, and your friend if he shows up in five minutes," assured a now-awake Sharon. Not waiting for a reply, she quietly placed the phone in the cradle, thought for a minute and picked up the phone again and dialed Kirk's number. There was no answer and after the 5th ring, the answering machine came on.

"Hello, you've reached Kirk Daniels. I'm, of course, monitoring my phone calls and no matter what you say I won't answer, so leave your phone number and your right name and I'll get back to you."

"This is Her. C.J. just called. If you're in the shower, I love you. If you're on you're way here so early, I'm going to kill you, that is unless you put the coffee on," and Sharon hung up the phone.

Kirk came back to his room about 10 minutes later, saw the red light on the answering machine blinking and turned on the machine. Upon hearing Sharon's voice and message, he had to smile!

It was just about 20 minutes later when Kirk left the dorm with his duffel bag in hand. He waved hello to some friends and went to the Jeep. Kirk dumped the throw carpets and straightened up a little, then put the duffel in the back. "Want it looking clean for Sharon," he said to himself. He backed the Jeep out of the parking space and drove over to the Cherry Hill Mobile Home Park. Sharon had already unlocked the door, and as Kirk pulled up, the smell of fresh brewed coffee, plus bacon cooking filled the air as the scent came from the exhaust fan in the kitchen.

"Good morning," was Sharon's greeting as Kirk came through the door and she held out, then pulled back a cup of coffee, waiting for a good morning kiss first. Having received the kiss and a smile, Kirk got the coffee!

"Smells great outside. Surprised there's not a crowd in here," said Kirk, after he took a sip of coffee. "This really hits the spot," he continued.

"Thought you'd rather have breakfast here than waste time in a restaurant this morning," stated Sharon as she got ready to cook the eggs. "Scrambled OK, or do you want them over this morning?"

"Scrambled is fine. Want a fill-up on your coffee?" asked Kirk as he reached for the coffeepot, and filled Sharon's cup, then added cream after she nodded yes. In a couple of minutes they sat down and ate breakfast. Sharon had filled Kirk's plate with a man-sized portion. And said, "no" when he tried to give her some of his. She was fine!

After finishing, Kirk got up and started cleaning off the dishes, put the butter back in the refrigerator and the salt and pepper on the counter top. Sharon smiled to herself as she took the last sip of coffee. She was pleased the Kirk didn't mind pitching in. She got up from the table and washed off the dishes as well as the frying pan, then placed them and the cups in the dishwasher. Kirk in the meantime was cleaning the coffeepot and wrapping a tin-tie around the garbage. He'd take it out so that it wouldn't be in there over the weekend. Sharon finished her kitchen chores by putting the soap detergent into the dishwasher and staring the machine. All in all, everything looked shipshape as Sharon handed Kirk her small suitcase and they headed out the door.

The trip to the Elk Neck State Park took about an hour and twenty minutes. The beauty of the area, with the river in sight a few times, plus the brilliant fall colors of the trees and underbrush brought back to Kirk the sense of belonging that he had all during the summer. Even though he hadn't seen a fall in Elk Neck before, it was just as magnificent as he imagined.

C.J. was already at the Miles house when they pulled up. It was almost as though he had kept an eye out for Kirk and Sharon, because as the Jeep come to a halt, C.J. was standing by Kirk's door. Sharon's dog, wagging his tail was on the other side of the Jeep as she opened the door and got out.

"It's almost 10:30. Where have you been?" questioned C.J. as Kirk stepped from the Jeep.

"Don't start," said Sharon, before Kirk could open his mouth. "I figured we'd get here an hour and a half from now but some how we were both awakened almost before dawn."

"Ya, what she said," stated Kirk as he shook hands with C.J.

"Did you eat. Good. Look, Sharon has to help Mom, you know, lady stuff for the dinner, so we can take the boat out for awhile, right?" stated C.J.

Kirk, trying to catch up. "Yes, we ate breakfast," then he looked over to Sharon.

"Oh, come in, say hello to Mom and Dad and then go play," continued Sharon. They all walked into the house. The all, of course, included the tail wagger!

John came out of the kitchen, gave Sharon a kiss and hug, shook hands with Kirk, then turned to C.J, "You still here?" he kidded. "I thought I saw you leave."

"There's dinner here and the smell of that turkey cooking keeps me on a tether. You're not getting rid of me, not at all." answered C.J.!

"I was afraid of that," commented John.

Kirk and Sharon went into the kitchen and greeted Dora. John and C.J. trailed them with John telling C.J. that the least he could do was take the trash out. C.J. countered that there wasn't any trash yet and that John was simply trying to throw him out of the house on a technicality. As C.J. and Kirk were leaving the house, John handed Kirk an extra wind breaker jacket to take with him. Even though it appeared to be a nice sunny day in the low 60's, it was cool and windy out on the Chesapeake Bay in a boat.

They took the Jeep down the steep dirt road to the beach and T dock area. C.J. had been down earlier to fill the two gas tanks and to put the extra five-gallon Jerry jug in the boat.

"Where the hell do you think we're going," questioned Kirk as he stepped into the boat and saw all the fuel that was aboard.

"I thought we'd just take a little run towards Turkey Point, maybe cross over to Betterton and have a beer. That's all," answered C.J. as he started the engine.

"I'm surprised you don't have a supply of food and booze on board," stated Kirk.

"That's what I meant," answered C.J. who opened the cooler that was stored beneath the passenger's front seat on the left. "That bar we went to over there is probably closed, either for the season or the Holiday. I've got a couple of roast beef sandwiches, too. Also, on board, we prefer grog to the term booze!"

Kirk smiled, loosened the lines, leaving them on the dock, then settled into his seat as C.J. eased the boat from the dock area and headed out into the Elk River, south toward Turkey Point.

"Grog," said Kirk aloud, but really to himself. "Do you want a can of grog?"

"No, I'm fine right now," answered C.J., thinking Kirk was talking to him.

C.J. brought the engine up to about 3/4 throttle, which put the boat onto a plane so that she was no longer pushing water. As they broke out past the first point, the wind hit them and both Kirk and C.J. settled down a little bit in their seats so that the wind hit the windshield and not them. There were a few white caps on the water, but all in all it was fairly smooth. C.J. motioned with his arm in a wave and pointing, that he was going to cross the Elk right now and head to Betterton from the other side, rather than wait until they got to Turkey Point where the white caps might translate to simply rough water. The Elk was almost two miles wide at this point and C.J. pushed the throttle up to full power in order to get across as quickly as possible. Looking around as they crossed, Kirk spotted only one lone sailboat in the distance near the Aberdeen Proving Grounds. Perhaps someone stationed there had the sailboat out. C.J. nodded as Kirk pointed the sailboat out to him. There was no commercial shipping about on this Thanksgiving morning, also a rare sight in a normally busy area on the northern Chesapeake Bay.

In the meantime, back at the Miles' household Sharon was helping her mother set the table as well as helping out in the kitchen. John had brought firewood in and set the fire screen aside as he built a fire in the living room fireplace. Actually it was a unique fireplace, in that it was located between the living room and dining room and therefore visible from both rooms, giving it extra warmth. In no time at all John had a fire blazing away, so much so, that Dora reminded John that it was almost 60 degrees outside and they only needed a small fire for effect, not one that would be beneficial on a snowy day. John got the message and let the fire die down to a comfortable level.

The smoke from the chimney caught Kirk's eye just as they reached the other side of the Elk River. He was looking around, spotted the smoke curling up into the air and tapped C.J. on the shoulder.

"Looks like we'll be in short sleeves during dinner," yelled C.J. over the roar of the engine. Both of them had a good laugh.

It wasn't too long before they were opposite Turkey Point, with its old lighthouse high on the cliff. Betterton was just in front on them as they neared the mouth of the Sassafras River, which also emptied into the Chesapeake Bay. C.J. headed for the docking area. Spotting no lines to tie the boat on to, Kirk reached under the deck and brought up some rope to use to tie the boat up. C.J. slowed the boat to a crawl, and then neutral, then reverse as he brought the boat to a stop neatly in the slip.

"That was very nice," complimented Kirk as C.J. grinned ear to ear about the little accomplishment. Kirk quickly tied the boat and stepped to the dock.

"Practice, my boy. Today 18 feet, tomorrow, a 60-footer," kidded C.J. "OK, you can dream about that. Hand the cooler up, captain," stated Kirk. C.J. handed the cooler to Kirk, checked around the boat for no good reason, it seemed just to be the thing to do. Then he jumped to the dock and followed Kirk to one of the picnic tables that overlooked the bay.

"Everyone must be home cooking the ole turkey. I've never seen this place so deserted," said C.J. as he opened the cooler and handed Kirk an ice-cold beer.

"Want a sandwich now or later," asked Kirk as he flipped the pull-tab on the beer, took a drink from the can, then continued before C.J. could answer, "since when did you start drinking Ballentine Ale?" Kirk asked.

"Make the three ring sign and ask the man for Ballentine Ale," answered C.J. "It's Thanksgiving, tradition and all that stuff, and yes, I only had a Danish and coffee this morning at the diner when they made the sandwiches."

Kirk reached back in the cooler and brought out two neatly packaged roast beef sandwiches. "What does Thanksgiving and Ale have to do with tradition?" Then after a pause, "you drove into North East for the sandwiches?"

"The Ale is a new tradition starting this year and it's your job and that Bride of yours job to keep it going, don't ask so many questions. Also, I knew you wouldn't eat the crap I keep in the cabin's refrigerator, so it was off to the diner!"

"You may have to remind me about the Ale tradition next year and the year after that," kidded Kirk as they both settled sitting on top of the picnic table with their feet resting on the picnic tables seat.

C.J. just nodded, he had a mouth full of roast beef sandwich. The two sat for quite awhile enjoying each other's company and their lunch. Later as they walked back to the boat, C.J. told Kirk to take her back, he'd be the first mate. "OK crew." For the trip back to the State Park, Kirk elected to run straight across toward Turkey Point at about half speed, so that the boat did not pound as she cut through the white caps. After they crossed, the engine was put to full throttle as they sped toward the park's T-dock area. As they rounded the point where the Miles' house sat high up on the hill, the dock area came into view. Sharon had finished her work and accompanied by Duke, walked down the road to greet the returning seamen. All right, it was C.J. and Kirk.

After tying the boat down for the night, Sharon, Duke, C.J. and Kirk piled into the Jeep for the journey up the hill to the Miles' house. With the kitchen exhaust fan on, the aroma of cooking turkey scented the air all around the area. It drew everyone, including Duke, straight into the kitchen door. John was slicing turkey as they entered.

"No, no, tasting of the turkey ahead of time," stated John, as everyone started helping themselves to already carved turkey sitting on the dish.

It was too late, each of the thieves had already taken a piece and was headed for the dining room. C.J. took two pieces and when John started to stab him with the knife, C.J. quickly explained the second piece was for Duke. Well that part was OK, then John however, made C.J. fix Duke's dinner ahead of time, so that he'd be full and not wander into the dining room during dinner.

The gathering at the Miles' house was small this year, just the Miles' family, which really now included Kirk and C.J. too! Last year 19 were at the Thanksgiving dinner which included most of the park employees and families, but this year, everyone had scattered, visiting family in Baltimore or out of state. Even old Mr. Kemper would not be present this year. He had been persuaded to spend the winter in Florida with a nephew and his family. The nephew is a fireman in St. Petersburg. Mr. Kemper and his best buddy, Coco, left 3 weeks ago. He gave John the key to his house at Turkey Point and asked him to check on it. It was quite likely that the Kemper farm would be sold to the State and become part of Elk Neck State Park. Mr. Kemper may well finally retire and remain in Florida.

Kirk and C. J. were told to sit down at the table, actually Sharon told them that they were in the way, so why not go sit at the table. John was just finished with the carving, but would not bring the turkey to the table with those two vultures sitting there, "there'd be none left for the rest of the family!" John also asked C.J. to take the trash out and lock the door behind him. C.J., though was not budging from the table; he'd play garbage man in a little while.

Finally everything was on the table, including turkey. John gave thanks with a very nice talk and prayer, then everyone dug in for the Thanksgiving dinner. In addition to all the normal goodies, Dora had anticipated a run on stuffing and made extra. A very nice Sauvignon Blanc Wine from the Sterling Winery of California Napa Valley was served well chilled. John announced the wine, so to speak, and even though C.J. preferred a beer, he drank wine during dinner. He just knew that John would make him eat out on the porch, looking back with his nose to the window if he asked for a beer.

Dinner was great fun. Dessert was a time for serious thinking, because in addition to pumpkin pie, Dora had baked a mince pie, which John loved, plus there was fresh made carrot cake and special rice pudding, made with cream and included two kinds of raisins. While it was choice time for most, it was easy for C.J, a little of this and a little of that, made dessert!

After the clearing of the table, John told C.J. it was now time to take the garbage out. C.J. made Kirk help, that way he'd be sure of getting back into the house for after dinner drinks. He didn't trust John. The balance of the evening was spent relaxing around the fireplace in the living room. C.J. left first. He was tired and wanted to shower and relax at the cabin. It was back to work for him tomorrow. Kirk, who was going to bunk in at C.J.'s cabin stayed longer and took a walk with Sharon down across the field in front of the house to the point overlooking the Elk River. He'd drive the Jeep over later.

Kirk planned to hang around at Elk Neck during the weekend. He'd see the other park rangers as well as John tomorrow while Sharon and Dora went to North East for a fitting of her wedding dress. An old family friend who was an excellent seamstress was making Sharon's dress and had made several wedding dresses before. Sharon had picked an antique looking gown from a magazine and all the lady had to do was view the photograph, then make the dress in the style according to the picture.

The weekend went all too fast. On Sunday afternoon, Kirk and Sharon drove back to College Park. It would be back to class for Kirk and practice teaching for Sharon during this first week in December. With the wedding only two weeks away, their schedules seemed hectic to people around Kirk and Sharon, but they took things in stride. Kirk already had his tux fitting, as did best man C.J. and ushers, Tony and fellow teammate Jack. Sharon had her final wedding gown fitting. Her Maid of Honor as well as two bridesmaids had already bought their gowns. The wedding would take place in the chapel on the campus of the University of Maryland, with perhaps half the campus population either in the church or outside waiting for the newly married couple to emerge from the church. Some enterprising students from the campus radio station decided to set up a loudspeaker outside, so that those who could not get into the church could, at least hear the ceremony. Some friends from the college TV studio would tape the wedding and give the tape to Kirk. John had arranged for the wedding reception and sit-down dinner for the invited guests to be held back at the Marriott near Baltimore-Washington International Airport. Out of town family and guests would be staying at the Marriott, with BWI being a convenient airport to fly into and out of. Kirk was at the point where almost all he had to do now "was show up," as he liked to say. C.J. had helped with the purchase of the wedding rings, through a friend of his uncles. A deal was made in Washington for the wedding rings, that is.

In addition to classes and football practices, Kirk was keeping busy day and night doing some catch up work on his studies. Sharon was continuing her tutoring with Kirk because both of them were extremely serious about his graduating in the spring with his class and not having to go to summer school, or perhaps having to take fall classes to graduate. It was a lot of work, but Sharon had taken charge on the education, and had a willing student in Kirk. Besides, Sharon stated that she was not going to become the main breadwinner while Kirk lounged on campus as a student, unless he was going for a Masters degree.

Football practices were also part of the daily routine as Maryland prepared for the New Year's Night game against Miami. Maryland, the Atlantic Coast Conference winner was ranked number 5 in both major college polls with their 9 win- 2 loss record. Miami, Notre Dame, LSU were listed 1-2-3, and the 4th ranked team was Nebraska, who would play against once defeated LSU in the Sugar Bowl game on New Year's Day from New Orleans. Nebraska has 10 wins, and 1 loss. Notre Dame, would spend New Years Day in Dallas playing against Southwest Conference Champion, the University of Texas. The Longhorns were ranked number 6.

On his day off, C.J. drove down to College Park to spend some time with the groom to be. Being C.J., he was also checking out the chapel and video set up. The outside loudspeaker system was of no real interest to him, so the college radio station engineers would have to simply get along without C.J.'s so called expertise. C.J. did get things done though and could cut a deal. Through some friends of his uncles, he met with a limousine company and arranged for a limo for the Bride and Groom. And of course C.J. felt that the best man and ushers should also have a limo. One extra car would be fine. They'd share.

Later that day, C.J. caught up with Kirk just after football practice. He got past the guard at the locker room door with a wave and strolled in like he was part of the team, which in a sense he was. Players looked up and either nodded, or gave a "Hi, C.J.," as he passed individual lockers until he got to the corner, where co-captain Kirk Daniels was holding court with some other defensive players as they discussed the upcoming Miami game.

"The basic plan, men," started C.J. as he reached for a stool and sat down, acting and talking coach talk, as he liked to call it, "is not to let Miami score any points. Then our offense scores some points and we win."

"That does sound reasonable," stated Tony, who nodded his head in approval and continued, "does the coaching staff have a better plan?"

"I really don't think so, although they may put in a couple of twists and semi-trick plays to help get the job done," stated Kirk, smiling as he thought of how C.J. had brought the Orange Bowl game down to basic ABC's."

"Com'on, get dressed and let's take Sharon out to dinner," said C.J. as the players all headed for their individual lockers. "Let's go to Sizzlers Steak House!"

C.J. left his car at Kirk's dorm and went with him to meet Sharon. They then took the Jeep to the Sizzlers in College Park. It was a popular spot with the students, especially because of the salad bar. Table talk was equally divided between the two upcoming events, the wedding, now only a week away and the New Years evening game at the Orange Bowl.

C.J. brought the subjects together as he announced to Kirk and Sharon that they'd be checking in at the Diplomat Hotel in Hollywood Beach the day after New Years and staying for three nights, courtesy of several dozen friends. And he presented them with a card filled with signatures as the investors in their future. Actually C.J. had spotted the Diplomats' ad in an airline magazine, and thought it would be a nice sort of extended honeymoon. He passed the card and a large envelope around to their friends, rangers at the park and teammates. Kirk and Sharon couldn't believe it. They had planned a two day stay at the Marriott Inner Harbor in

Baltimore, using the special weekend rate, but this was simply fantastic! "We all love you," was C.J.'s reply to them.

At Kirk's urging, C.J. spent the night, rather than drive back to Elk Neck. After dropping Sharon off, they drove back to Kirk's dorm. Some of the other fellows were still up and around, so they gathered together in Tony's room, called out for Domino's pizza and chatted well into the night. C.J. left early Wednesday morning, stating he'd be back on Friday for the wedding rehearsal and bachelor party, the latter of which he promised Sharon would be tame, as those kind of parties go.

The next few days went in what seemed to be jet speed. Friday was upon them! During the early evening, the wedding rehearsal took place in the chapel at the University of Maryland campus. Both Sharon's minister and the rector of the chapel would perform the wedding ceremony. Sharon's minister had been invited to stay with the rector several weeks before and a new friendship had been formed. The rehearsal went as most do, they got through it. "Don't worry, we'll guide you every step of the way," was the reassurance from the clergy.

Kirk's friends and teammates gathered at a sports bar, just off campus. It was a local hangout during the week and one of the main watering holes during times when a ball game of some sort was being played. The owner had purchased the place about ten years before, when his son was playing football for Maryland, and stayed on to run the business, which had become quite successful. The party outlasted Kirk and C.J., who left just after midnight. Kirk thanked everyone, and explained that C.J. wouldn't live out Saturday if he kept Kirk there much longer, and they headed for Kirk's dorm. After taking a shower, Kirk and C.J. settled down, turned the lights out and went to bed.

"I'm not very sleepy," said C.J. aloud, after they'd been in bed a few minutes. "Are you asleep?" he asked Kirk.

"Not now," stated Kirk, as he startled awake, after just drifting off.

"Me either, I'm tired, but not very sleepy, if you know what I mean," continued C.J., "want to talk?"

"What," said Kirk in a loud voice, "no, go back to sleep!"

"But I wasn't asleep yet," answered C.J.

"Would you like me to put you to sleep?" said Kirk in a low voice as he turned over and adjusted his pillow.

"I get your point," said C.J., "I'm going to sleep right now."

"Good," was Kirk's only reply.

"See you in the morning," answered C.J.

"If you say another word, there's a very good chance you won't," answered Kirk as he pulled his cover over his head.

C.J. didn't answer, but to himself he thought, "the boy does need his rest."

The morning of Saturday, December 15th, was clear and brisk. The high for the day would be in the low 50's. The temperature should still be comfortable for the 2:30 wedding. Outside pictures would be taken in addition to the ones inside the Chapel.

C.J. and Kirk wandered over to the cafeteria for breakfast at about 8:30. After going through the line they found a table and sat down.

"I can't tell if you're nervous or calm," commented C.J. as he took a sip of coffee.

"Why do you say that?" questioned Kirk.

"Look at what you've got on that tray. There's enough for three people," stated C.J.

"Maybe so, but the wedding is at 2:30 and I figure we'd be rushing and getting ready around lunchtime. We'd probably miss lunch altogether and won't eat again until the reception dinner," reasoned Kirk.

C.J. didn't answer, but got up, went back to the cafeteria line and purchased two large Danish, thought for a minute and called to Kirk to see if he also wanted something else. Kirk waved a "no" and C.J. came back to the table.

After they finished the man-sized breakfast, they walked back to Kirk's dorm. One of the fellows shouted to Kirk that Sharon was on the phone. "OK," was the reply, "he'd be there in a minute."

Kirk dashed up the stairs to his room and took the phone. "I thought we weren't supposed to talk or anything until I saw you at church," he said before saying hello, wondering if all was OK.

"We're not supposed to 'anything' but talking is all right," answered Sharon.

"Oh, well, in that case, wanna get married this afternoon? I don't have a job yet. I just have some dollars coming in from my parents insurance money, but I may just have a future," stated Kirk.

"I always thought I deserved to marry a rich handsome man. It looks like I'm settling for potential and cute," answered Sharon who thought for a minute and then said, "see you around 2:30, I love you forever, Kirk Daniels!"

"I love you too, Sharon," was Kirk's answer. "See you this afternoon."

"I thought you weren't supposed to talk to her before the wedding," said C.J., who had walked up to Kirk's room and caught the last of the conversation.

"Talking is OK, anything else is not," answered Kirk.

"Speaking of anything else," stated C.J., "Let's get the Jeep washed this morning, then we'll park it back at the trailer, OK, mobile home. I'll take you to the church on time and after you and the new Mrs. Daniels leave the reception, I'll bring you two back here. While you're taking honeymoon #1, Tony and I will move you from the dorm to the trailer. I'll have plenty of help moving you. It seems like they're fighting over who gets your room. Tony and I will see to it that they don't unload your room from the second story window, OK?"

"OK," said Kirk as he tried to grasp all that C.J. had said.

"Any questions?" asked C.J.

"I don't think so," answered Kirk slowly.

"All right then, to the car wash. I'll follow you," returned C.J. snappily!

They drove the jeep and C.J.'s car to the self-wash. C.J. decided to wash his car also. It took a while and a few quarters to keep the machine working, but the task was done. Then after dropping the car off, they returned to Kirk's dorm where he showered and came back to his room to dress. The scene when he got back to the room was almost that of a Spanish Matador, dressing for the caretta or bullfight. The place was packed with well wishers and, of course, kidding friends with all the normal cliches.

"Can someone help me with this bow tie," asked Kirk as he fumbled with the tie while standing in front of the mirror.

"I thought they'd give me the ones with the clips or something," said C.J., as he also tried to work with the bow tie.

Just then Tony and Jack came into the room, completely dressed, including a perfectly tied bow tie. "Com'on, let's give the kid some breathing room," bellowed Tony as he parted the sea, so to speak and chased everyone into the hallway.

"Who tied your tie?" questioned C.J.

"See you at the church. Good luck. Congratulations, Kirk," stated friends, as they shook hands with Kirk and left the room.

"Who are you kidding?" returned Tony to C.J. as he looked at himself admiringly in the mirror. "God, are you good looking," he said aloud to himself!

"I tied it for him. You having trouble? Here, let me." stated Jack as he motioned to C.J. to lift his chin up while he quickly made a perfect bow tie.

"I'm next," stated Kirk as he slowly shook his head at Tony.

Tony didn't answer, but held his hands out as if to say, "What do you want from me? So, he tied mine too!"

After Jack completed his little job Kirk was given a once over and pronounced fit to be seen by the public.

They all left Kirk's room and headed down the stairway and out of the door. Tony was first out, and in the fashion of a secret service agent in front of The President, he motioned with his hands to part the teammates and friends who had gathered outside.

"Let him pass, part and let us pass," stated Tony, who checked his watch and then said, "OK, we have a few moments for a picture or two. Focus on me," he continued as he saw some people with cameras.

"Do we need you in the picture?" shouted someone in the crowd.

"Very funny," shouted Tony, as he lined the four of them up for the pictures.

"It will, be difficult, but Sharon and I will get along without him on the honeymoon," kidded Kirk to the other two as they posed for the pictures, which were taken on the steps in front of the limo, getting in the limo, and inside the limo. Then it was off on the short ride to The Chapel, which is actually the size of a large church.

Once at The Chapel, the four went through a side door and into the office where they met with both the University of Maryland Chaplain and Sharon's Minister from her church in North East.

Tony seemed the most nervous. Kirk was starting to show some nerves as he paced a little, checked his watch and glanced at the clock on the office wall. C.J. quietly spoke with the clergy, showed them the rings and joked that they'd be in his right tux pocket in case he passed out. Jack found a seat and sat down. He'd been in his sister's and his brother's weddings during the past year and was an old hand by now. Tony's and Jack's jobs as ushers would be relatively simple. All they had to do was escort Sharon's mother and grandmothers down the aisle. Members of the football team, who basically were checking invitations for preferred seating, seated invited guests. Others would be given seats on a first come basis. The rest would hear the ceremony outside. In addition to speakers, two television monitors were set up by the campus station students who would also do the taping for Kirk and Sharon.

Tony and Jack shook hands with Kirk. They said they'd see him later and left the office for the walk to the church doors to greet guests and take care of Sharon's mother and grandmothers. With Kirk being an orphan, of course, there would be no one for him to have escorted down the aisle, but, he considered Sharon's parents as his parents, now. He had thoughts of his own parents. He wished they could be there.

It was just about 2:30 when the limo came into view. It took a few minutes more to wind around the curved streets and come to a halt in front of The Chapel.

John got out first while the driver of Sharon's limo held the door. John then helped Dora and the four grandparents out of the limo. Then John peeked back into the limo, reached his hand in and out came Sharon, looking so beautiful in her wedding gown, with her long dark auburn hair flowing down the gown. Cameras clicked as the grandparents and Dora went inside to be seated. John then escorted his daughter up the church steps. Her Bridesmaids and Maid Of Honor were already there, having been picked up by Kirk's limo, after dropping the group off. They fixed Sharon's veil, checked her over and waited as the singing of, *The First Time Ever I Saw Your Face*, continued.

With the word passed that the Bride had arrived, the clergy motioned to Kirk and C.J. that it was time for them to leave the office and go to the alter. The time for fidgeting was over for Kirk.

"I'll lead, you bring up the rear. That way Kirk won't get away," kidded the chaplain to Sharon's minister.

"Don't worry about me," stated Kirk. "I'm the luckiest guy on earth and I know it!" The words come out, they were sincere, but his voice broke a little as he brought himself together.

C.J. reached out, shook Kirk's hand and gave him a pat on the back as they left the office and took the short walk to the alter where they would wait as Sharon came down the aisle. "Sharon is as lucky as you are," C.J. said quietly. "You're one hell of a guy, Kirk Daniels."

Kirk did not reply, but the smile back to C.J. and the brightened eyes showed a 'Thank you' for many things that have occurred in the warm friendship that began only a few months ago, but yet, seems like a friendship of long standing.

The ministers took their positions, placed Kirk, C.J., Tony and Jack where they should stand and gave the cue to the organist to begin. *Here Comes the Bride*, started playing. Down the aisle came Peggy, Sharon's Maid of Honor. Next came Cynthia Miles, Sharon's cousin and one of her two bridesmaids, Joanne Parker followed her. With this being the Christmas season, the church, in addition to being decorated with flowers for the wedding, had a festive look as it took on the colors and greenery for the Christmas Holidays. The Maid of Honor's dress was a little more burgundy than just red and the bridesmaids were dressed in dark green. John took Sharon's hand, squeezed it and tucked it into his arm as he started down the aisle with her. "I love you, baby," he said softly and forced back a tear.

“I love you, Daddy,” answered Sharon, as she held on tightly to her father.

She was a beautiful Bride, coming down the aisle, the white dress, custom made for her, showed off marvelously with the long train trailing behind as Sharon and John made their way.

Cameras clicked, smiles were all about. You could see Sharon’s beautiful smile, even through the veil.

Kirk was no longer nervous. One look at Sharon took that away. The girls took their places. Sharon and John arrived at the altar. Sharon stopped near Kirk, and John carefully pushed Sharon’s veil back.

Before the clergy started talking, Sharon quietly said “I love you, Star!”

“I love you, too,” said Kirk in a much louder stage whisper.

C.J., also in a stage whisper said, “com’ on you two, let them get on with it,” as he nodded toward the clergy. “I’ve got the rings, you know, when you get to that part,” he continued.

“When we get to that part, I’ll actually ask for the rings. There will be no doubt that we’ve gotten to that part,” said the chapel minister with a smile. “Relax, I’ve done this before.”

“Probably Sharon’s minister has done this before also. That’s a comfort, you know,” answered C.J. quietly and he nodded to Kirk.

“Dearly beloved,” began The Chapel Minister, and the wedding ceremony was under way.

When they reached the part where they say, “Who gives this Bride,” John answered, “Sharon’s mother and I,” then John stepped back and joined Dora.

The ring part also went smoothly, well fairly smoothly. C.J. not wanting to lose the rings had tied them together with a small piece of string in a bow, of course, except the bow came apart and formed a tiny knot. When C.J. took the rings out of his pocket, the problem was discovered. He was nervous, and kept putting his hands in and out of his pocket to make certain the rings were still there, and the bow came loose. This portion of the ceremony was being performed by Sharon’s minister, so Reverend Lang simply took the rings from C.J., who had a look of panic on his face, worked on the knot while they were being blessed by Reverend Miller. In no time at all everything was back in order and Kirk slipped the ring on Sharon’s finger. Since this is a double ring ceremony, The Reverend repeated his words and Sharon placed the ring on Kirk’s finger.

It wasn’t long before, “We now pronounce you Husband and Wife,” was followed by the Reverend’s, “Kirk, you may now kiss Mrs. Daniels!”

Kirk did not hesitate. He and Sharon put their arms around each other and had a long kiss, much to the joy of everyone in the church, who normally saw just a short peck at this time of the ceremony. Cameras near the altar clicked away, taking the picture. The music came up and the group, led by Mr. & Mrs. Daniels, went back down the aisle. Smiles, good wishes and clicking cameras flashed, as they made their way to form a reception line to greet guests at the church entrance.

John and Dora joined the wedding party as congratulations were given to the Bride and Groom. The video camera, from the campus TV station continued filming for Kirk and Sharon.

When the last of the guests had offered their congratulations, it was time to make the dash for the limo. Kirk and Sharon emerged from the church to the guests waiting to see them once more, plus the people who, because of space problems, could not get into the church and saw the proceedings on the TV monitor set up by the campus station.

They paused on the church steps as shouts came from the crowd to "Hold it a moment for a picture," then Sharon took Kirk in her arms and they had several kisses and poses for the camera to the delight of the crowd.

Rice and birdseed were tossed as they finally dashed to the limo. Pictures were also taken during the race to the limo and of the Bride and Groom inside the limo, before the door was closed and they were whisked off to the Marriott for the Wedding Reception.

The auto procession left the campus, drove onto Route 1 and headed for Interstate 495. Headlights had been turned on and cars following the limo continued blowing their horns. The limos stopped blowing their horn once they were on the interstate. After the short trip on Interstate 495, they turned north on the Baltimore-Washington Parkway and drove to the BWI airport exit and to the Marriott Hotel's banquet entrance.

The ballroom had been beautifully decorated for the wedding, as well as the Holiday season. Pictures and videos were taken of the wedding party, parents, and grandparents. Kirk was now an official family member! The wedding dinner was outstanding. John had ordered Filet Mignon for the guests, and Swordfish Steaks for those not wanting meat. There was an open bar and a champagne punch fountain. The band had been instructed by John not to do the cutesy stuff that often occurs at weddings and not to be too loud. They were standing orders! There would be tradition, however, the Bride's dance with her Dad. Kirk took Dora to the dance floor, soon after, and then Kirk got to dance with Mrs. Daniels, after which all joined in the dancing and festivities.

It was about 8:30 when Sharon quietly said to Kirk that she wanted to leave. She said, "Actually, let's start our honeymoon. I want to make love with you!"

Kirk's face got a little red, but he quickly realized that no one else had heard Sharon and he smiled and nodded his head. Then he went over to C.J. and told him they'd be ready in 5 minutes. Sharon went to her parents, told them that she and Kirk were about to leave, then went to where her grandparents were seated. In a moment Kirk joined her to say, "Thank you and good bye."

One of C.J.'s friends had brought his car to the ballroom entrance. It was announced that the Bride and Groom were leaving and as they left the ballroom, a spontaneous clapping took place for Kirk and Sharon. C.J. and Joanne got into the front seat, while Sharon and Kirk slid into the back of C.J.'s car. Then it was off, they thought, to the Cherry Hill Mobile Home Park. But, instead, C.J. turned north on the Baltimore-Washington Parkway and toward Baltimore.

"We need to go to the house and change," said Sharon just before Kirk started to tell C.J. that he was headed in the wrong direction.

"Oh, I forgot to tell you. I had some friends stop at the trailer and put your suitcases in the Jeep and drive it to the Marriott Inner Harbor. The suitcases are in your suite and the Jeep keys will be at the valet car desk. A little service of the house, you know, figured you kids would want to start your honeymoon ASAP," stated C.J., matter of fact, as he continued toward Baltimore.

"Very good thinking," was Kirk's reply, as they neared the city.

It wasn't too long before they pulled up to the front of the Marriott. The doorman opened the car doors and having been already cued said, "Mr. & Mrs. Daniels, welcome to the Marriott. You're already registered, so you can go straight to your room on the concierge level. The bellman just inside has your key and will show you to your suite. Oh, all tips have been given, sir."

Kirk looked at C.J., "What's this suite he's talking about?" he asked.

"Well, an upgrade, so to speak, was arranged," answered C.J., who continued. "Oh, just give the tux to Jack, he'll take care of it for you, when you get back," then C.J. gave a wave as he started to get back in the car. "I love you kids," he said as he got in, started the engine and drove off, not waiting for a reply. Kirk and Sharon looked at each other, and had to smile at C.J.'s remark, they loved him too.

The doorman, in the meantime, held the door open and followed them inside. The bellman quickly realized that Mr. and Mrs. Kirk Daniels had arrived since not too many people came in wearing wedding gowns and tuxedos.

"Come, follow me and I'll take you immediately to your suite. You're on the concierge level. Congratulations, you make a handsome couple," said the bellman, as he held the elevator, showed them the room key card and how to put it into the slot to get to the private floor. Then he told them of the restaurants and facilities. The elevator door opened and as they stepped from it, the bellman pointed out the concierge lounge, the perks it offered and took them down the hall to the end where he unlocked the door and showed them into the corner suite.

"Everything's taken care of," the bellman said as he put the room key on the table and quickly left. Champagne, fresh fruit, and flowers were also on the table.

"Wow, this is some place," said Sharon as she looked around the suite, which consisted of a living room with a wet bar set up, plus a bedroom with a king sized bed. Then she turned and put her arms around Kirk, who had followed her in looking over the place, "What are you looking at?'

"The nice view," said Kirk, as they kissed and he took her bridal veil off.

"The Inner Harbor or me?" asked Sharon as they kissed again.

"We can see the harbor tomorrow. Right now, you're the view I want," said Kirk as he helped Sharon out of her bridal dress.

"It's been a long day," said Sharon as she helped Kirk out of his tux, "I want to take a shower. Want to join me?"

"Glad you asked. That way I won't have to barge in on you," answered Kirk and they disappeared into the bathroom and into the shower.

It was nearly ten thirty when the newly weds emerged from their room and went downstairs to enjoy the Sunday Brunch which was included in the package Kirk reserved on the weekend program. The brunch was exactly that, a huge breakfast and lunch together.

They tried to act like a normal mature couple, but it was pretty easy to see that they were newlyweds, especially in the way they acted at the buffet. In fact, one older lady asked Sharon how long they'd been married.

"Almost one day," Sharon replied and introduced Kirk to she and her husband.

"You make a lovely couple. Don't lose that spark," the lady stated.

After the brunch, Kirk and Sharon went back to the suite for a while, then dressed warmly and took a walk, hand in hand around the Inner Harbor. They stopped at some of the shops, bought some tee shirts and finally made a stop, before going back to the hotel, at a restaurant, where they warmed up with some hot tea and cookies. Check out at the hotel would be Monday morning. They decided not to venture out this evening, but to have dinner brought up to their suite. They might as well enjoy it as much as they can. They might not be spoiled like this too often.

With the Jeep loaded, Kirk and Sharon drove back down the Baltimore-Washington Parkway the next morning to their new home, together, at the Cherry Hill Mobile Home Park. They didn't know what to expect when they got there, especially with the guys moving Kirk out of the dorm. Or did they?

The suspense was short lived once they arrived at the Park. A huge sign hung over the entrance to Cherry Hill: *Welcome Home Kirk and Sharon Daniels N'N'Newlyweds*, the sign read.

"We'll have to save that sign you know…they went to a lot of trouble making it," said Kirk as they drove under it.

"Stop, let's get a picture," said Sharon.

Kirk stopped, backed the Jeep up so that it was directly under the sign, took Sharon's camera, placed her standing on the hood of the Jeep and snapped a couple of pictures. Then it was time to change places. Just as Kirk was getting off the hood, a UPS delivery truck pulled into the park to deliver some packages.

"Stay put," Sharon called to Kirk, then she went up to the UPS driver and asked him to take a picture of them under their sign.

It would be no problem. The entrance was blocked by the Jeep anyway.

The UPS driver took a couple of pictures, handed Kirk the camera and congratulated the newly weds.

Kirk and Sharon then jumped into the Jeep for the short ride to their home.

This Is The Place Where Kirk and Sharon Will Make B*abies,* read a sign draped across their porch, that had also been decorated in a criss-cross fashion with toilet paper, that they had to clear away.

"Your friends, of course," said Sharon as they got out of the Jeep. "I don't think we'll save this sign."

Another sign was taped to the door, *Honeymoon Cottage*, it read.

"Nice touch," commented Kirk "I suppose you feel that your friends should be given credit for this one," he continued, after a pause gathering the bathroom tissue.

"Certainly my friends," stated Sharon as she unlocked the door. "By the way, how many children, do you want?"

"Oh, I don't know, eighteen or twenty," Kirk kidded!

"You'd better file with the State of Maryland as an adoption agency, my body is not producing you more than two or three offspring, my dear husband," answered Sharon in a high pitched voice. Then she hit him on the arm!

"You keep beating me and I'll have the ASPCA down on you," said Kirk as they went inside, expecting the worst from the make shift movers.

"Well, seems like Tony and C.J. were true to their word. All your things are neat and orderly," said Sharon as she looked around.

"I don't think they wanted to be on the answering end of your wrath if it wasn't neat," answered Kirk.

Sharon didn't answer but with Kirk's help they put his clothes in the closet, unpacked the suitcases and went into the living room.

"Do you want to go out for some lunch?" asked Kirk.

"I don't think so," answered Sharon. No one is expecting to hear from us until Tuesday. Let's make the best of it," as she took Kirk's hand and lead him back into the bedroom. "Let's make the best of it."

"I couldn't agree more," was Kirk's reply. The day is young and I'm good looking," he continued with a sheepish look on his face.

Tuesday morning did see a flurry of activity. Sharon was up early and off to practice teach for today and tomorrow. She made the coffee, set out cereal for Kirk, kissed him good-bye and told him she'd see him this afternoon, then it was off in the station wagon to Silver Springs. Kirk got up a little more leisurely. He had classes beginning at 9:00 then football practice at two. He also had classes tomorrow, then for both he and Sharon it was Christmas break time, until the 14th of January.

After breakfast, it was off to the campus. Kirk parked the Jeep in his old spot at the dorm and started off for class. Well wishes, along with some kidding were the order of the day for the 'old married man,' but it was, of course, good natured and taken in that light.

A sign over Kirk's locker read *Light Work for Daniels - the poor man's worn out*, greeted him as he entered the locker room. He laughed, left it where it was instead of taking it down. C.J. would get a kick out of seeing it on Thursday, when he came down on his day off. Kirk wasn't sure who put it there. Jack and Tony probably, at the least, supplied the paper, pen, and perhaps the scotch tape as well.

Football practice went well. The team was loose and looking forward to playing Maryland's first major bowl game in years. The coaching staff talked about the previous game with Miami, where they came up just short of knocking off the Nation's top ranked team. This was not, the players were told, a revenge game or anything like that. It would be simply a game that they prepare for, better than any game in the team's history. And the player's execution during the game would provide them with a win. Enough said. The stage was set and it was off to work.

Kirk almost drove back to the dorm after practice by force of habit. He had to smile at himself as he started to pull into the dorm's parking lot. "Good thing no one's behind me," he thought to himself as he made an erratic move and got back on the road and drove to Cherry Hill. He thought of telling Sharon, but then thought again and simply smiled at himself.

When he arrived at the Mobile Home, Sharon was waiting for him at the door.

"It's almost six thirty. I thought you'd be home a little earlier," said Sharon.

"Me too," answered Kirk "there was a lot to go over, in addition to the actual practice," he continued as Sharon handed him a cold can of Coors beer.

"You look tired," said Sharon and she gave him a quick kiss.

"Don't start," stated Kirk with a half laugh on his face and he told Sharon about the sign on his locker, plus the kidding he took.

"Well, we waited long enough and we've got only one lifetime to make up for it," answered Sharon as she winked at Kirk.

"Should I ask what's for dinner or did you make reservations?" asked Kirk as he settled down beside Sharon on the sofa in the living room.

"To use an old Red Foxx joke, I'm going to cook the two things I make best, meat loaf and blackberry cobbler. You can guess which is the meatloaf," kidded Sharon as she took the beer from Kirk and took a drink.

"I'd better call for reservations," remarked Kirk as he took the beer back.

"You'll love the meatloaf. It's ready for the oven right now," answered Sharon, as she got up and walked toward the kitchen.

"And the blackberry cobbler," questioned Kirk as he flipped the TV on.

"It's out of the frozen food department at the Giant Supermarket. What can go wrong?" answered Sharon. "Trust me!"

Sharon put the meatloaf and cobbler in the oven, checked the temperature, then came back in the living room and settled beside Kirk, who lifted his arm up so that Sharon could nestle close to him. Sharon questioned whether she was too close and hurting his sore ribs.

"No, that's fine," answered Kirk as he brought Sharon closer to him. They relaxed together, watching the news on TV, until the timer bell on the oven went off. It was time to eat dinner. Kirk made the iced tea, while Sharon set the table and fixed a salad.

"Just leave the vegetables in the pan," said Kirk as he cut the meatloaf, "we can dish up things from here," he continued as he took the plates off the table and fixed the portions.

Table talk, was a combination of the day's activities, the upcoming holidays, plus husband and wife stuff, a cute scene if you were a fly on the wall, observing, so to speak.

The next few days were spent rather routinely finishing up school, getting ready for the Holiday season with Christmas shopping and, of course, Kirk's football practices as the Maryland team continued their preparation for the New Year's night game against Miami.

Christmas Eve found the team taking a light workout during the morning. The break would carry through until the day after Christmas when the team flew off to Miami for final preparation practices.

Kirk and Sharon loaded the Jeep at around 4 o'clock on Christmas Eve and drove to Elk Neck to spend the Christmas Holidays with the Miles. Dinner would be around 6. They'll spend the night, plus Christmas Day and return to College Park on Christmas night.

John greeted the newlyweds at the door. "Oh look dear," he called to Dora as he opened the door. "The Daniels have come to join us for supper!"

"Hi, you two," said Dora as she gave a hug and kiss to Sharon and Kirk.

"I have some new beer for you to try," said John to Kirk after they shook hands and John took their coats. "It's from England, an English bitter, I think they call it. Whatney's Red Barrel, from London. I've also got Bass Ale, a six pack of each that the store had as a Holiday special."

John and Kirk settled in the den where John reached into the refrigerator by his wet bar, got out the Whatney's and handed them to Kirk to open. He then reached back in for a bottle of Sutter Home White Zinfandel, opened it and poured Sharon and Dora a glass.

John returned to the den after giving the wine to the girls. Kirk handed John the beer. He took a drink, held it for a second tasting it and nodded approval.

"Ole C.J. will be here tomorrow. I'd stack the refrigerator with cheap beer, but he'd find the imported stuff anyway," said John as he settled into an overstuffed leather chair.

"Like your Christmas tree," said Kirk, as he also settled in a chair, but looked back into the living room where the tree was decorated and lit with all white bulbs.

"Thanks, C.J. and I cut it down the other day. It used to be easy. Sharon and I would find one and that would be that, but with C.J., it's work.

This one's not right, no, that one's not quite right. Lucky there wasn't an axe murder in the woods," answered John.

We sort of have a tree in the trailer," said Kirk smiling. "Sharon and I were about to buy one when Tony showed up with a small tree that Sharon called "cute." It was actually the top, cut out of Tony's tree."

"And...," said John, wanting Kirk's opinion of his and Sharon's first Christmas tree.

"Well, it's about three feet tall and since it came from the top of the tree, it's really perfectly shaped. It took only one set of lights, a dozen balls and one small roll of Garland to decorate the entire tree. Not a bad deal when you figure it," answered Kirk, who then took another sip of Whatney's.

Christmas Eve dinner was enjoyable, quiet, and family-like. Enjoyable. Much of the table talk centered on the upcoming football game. It was interesting, especially for John to hear about it from a player's perspective. Sharon, Dora and John would make the trip to Miami, staying out on Key Biscayne, at the Sonesta Hotel. The team was to be quartered at Miami Springs Villa, which is located not too far from the Miami International Airport. C.J., of course, would make the trip down with the team. They've come too far together to not need their good luck charm for this game.

After dinner, while Dora and Sharon cleaned up, Kirk accompanied John in the park superintendents truck as he made the rounds to be certain that all was well at Elk Neck State Park. They drove slowly through each of the sections, stopping near the cabin that Kirk stayed in during the summer. C.J. was using it now, but he was in town, spending time with his folks this evening. After the park inspection, they drove on over to the picnic area. John simply wanted to check to be certain the huge gate was still closed. After that, they headed back to the Miles' home for an evening toddy before going off to bed and listening for the sound of reindeer bells as Santa made his rounds on Christmas Eve. Santa's sleigh would have to be careful in landing tonight because there would be no White Christmas in Maryland this year.

The Christmas Day festivities started at 8:10 on an unusually warm, clear morning. John noted the time, as he opened the back door and stared at a brightly smiling C.J., his hands and arms packed with gifts.

"Go away," said John as he started to close the door, but couldn't because Duke had put his tail-wagging body into the opening to greet C.J. "Let the dog out and stay with him!"

"I didn't want to be late for breakfast," said C.J. as he pushed his way into the kitchen. "I brought some Philadelphia cinnamon buns for Kirk.

I had a friend bring them down last night, he's visiting relatives in Washington."

"Hi gang," yelled C.J. as he spotted Kirk and Sharon coming down the stairs. Kirk had a warm up suit on but Sharon was still dressed in her p.j.'s and housecoat, looking as if she were still asleep.

"Duke's barking woke me up," said Sharon. "Merry Christmas everyone," she continued, as she walked into the kitchen.

"It was just C.J. trying to break in," explained John. "Kirk, help me throw him out."

C.J. ignored John and gave Sharon a kiss, then Kirk a big bear hug, "Merry Christmas kids," he said then walked over to the kitchen door to let Duke, who was scratching at the door, back in.

"Doesn't anyone listen to me?" mumbled John.

"Daddy, is the coffee ready yet?" asked Sharon

Just then, Dora came down the steps, stopping in the living room to quickly turn on the Christmas tree lights before joining the others in the kitchen. "Merry Christmas," she said as she gave hugs and kissed all around, plus a pat to Duke.

"Let me cook breakfast," asked, but really stated C.J., as he measured the coffee and poured the water into the coffee maker.

"Why don't you two go get dressed," said Dora to John and Sharon. "Kirk and C.J. will help me."

"I'm not kidding," restated C.J., "I'll fix breakfast. Maybe Kirk can help if he wants. Dora, go relax, John, Sharon, get dressed!"

Everyone but Kirk and Duke left the kitchen. Dora went into the living room to lay out all the Christmas gifts in piles for each person.

"Well, now what," said Kirk to the great chef.

"Just relax, better yet, slip out the back door, go around to my car and bring in the bag in the front seat. I forgot it," stated C.J., who noticing Kirk was hesitating. "A surprise breakfast for John."

Kirk didn't bother to answer, he did as he was told, slipped out the door, well not quite because as he started to shut the door, Duke gave out a bark. "Com'on," said Kirk, and Duke happily followed Kirk on the venture to C.J.'s car. The only problem occurred when Kirk opened the car door. Duke pushed past him, jumping into the front seat and directly on the bag. He was all ready to take a ride. "Move over, we're not going for a ride now," said Kirk, as he pushed Duke out of the way and reached for the bag. "Come. Get out of there!" Kirk closed the door as Duke jumped out and went back around to the kitchen door.

C.J. in the meantime had made up some Bisquick biscuits and was spooning the batter into the greased cupcake pan he found in Dora's cupboards. He motioned for Kirk to put the bag down on top of the counter top. Kirk opened the bag and peeked in. "I think the eggs may have a crack or two. Don't look at me, he's the one that jumped in the front seat," explained Kirk when he saw the look on C.J.'s face.

"Well, it is Christmas, and I was going to scramble them anyway," said C.J., as he carefully unpacked the bag, placing the egg carton in the sink, then taking out the packages of country ham, "This is the real stuff, Southern Country Ham. A friend of mine who's a truck driver brought it up from South Carolina."

"They're big slices," said Kirk, as C.J. opened the packages of country ham and placed them in the broiler, where he had carefully made an aluminum foil pan by first doubling it, then making sides to hold in any liquid.

Noticing that Kirk was watching his every move because C.J. was using the care of a surgeon, C.J. said "I make the foil pan this way so that I don't loose the drippings from the ham. It'll be mixed with the black coffee to make a quick red-eye gravy for the ham.

C.J. then went about making a pot of grits, some milk gravy to which he'd also add some drippings for flavor, turned the ham, checked on the biscuits and scrambled eggs.

The smell brought John down from dressing and directly into the kitchen where he opened the broiler door and pronounced, "You can stay," to C.J.

Breakfast was most enjoyable. Country Ham slices have a small bone in the center. John finished his ham by actually picking up the bone and gnawing at the minute pieces of meat still attached. To say the least, he enjoyed the country breakfast!

After breakfast, everyone opened their Christmas presents, then the stocking gifts. It was a fun family time. Duke, of course, had some new toys, raw hide chew sticks, milk bones and a big soup bone.

C.J., he's family! His share of presents was also under the tree. There was no lunch. Dora was cooking a turkey dinner which would be served around two o'clock. They decided on an early dinner so that Kirk could get back home early enough to pack and get ready for the trip to Miami.

Christmas dinner was quite traditional and was thoroughly enjoyed by all. Phone calls had been made and received with friends and relatives throughout the morning. It was a time to catch up with people not seen as often as one would like, plus relatives who couldn't make the trip to Elk Neck this year. Dinner conversation focused on some of the phone calls and remembrances of the individuals, warm thoughts, but also some very funny instances that had happened in past years. It was about 4:30, when Sharon and Kirk packed the Jeep with presents and food. John argued about the FHB, "Family hold backs," but Sharon easily won out and packed for a late snack of turkey sandwiches, stuffing and the like. Even C.J., packed a huge turkey sandwich for later, referring to the great breakfast he cooked as his ticket to some goodies. John was helpless, kidding all the time, of course. As Kirk and Sharon climbed in the Jeep, hasty arrangements were made for Sharon, C.J., John and Dora to meet for the flights to Miami. "I'll phone you," concluded the conversation, however, C.J. would accompany John and Dora to BWI airport, with Sharon meeting them there. Ah, the time. It'll all work out. C.J. would then fly the charter flight that carried the team, with Sharon and her parents taking the commercial U. S. Air Flight.

The drive back for Sharon and Kirk was, as they say, uneventful. It was just a nice drive home for the young couple. As they got out of the Jeep in front of the Mobile Home, Kirk grabbed an armload of presents, while Sharon brought in some smaller packages as she unlocked the door.

"Do you want to make a baby?" called Sharon to Kirk as he came back in with a second armful of presents.

"No, but we can practice," answered Kirk.

"Good. Meet you in the shower," said Sharon laughingly.

"That's as good a place to start as any," was Kirk's reply as he hung up his coat and checked to see that the door was locked, then he disappeared into their bathroom.

A weather front had come in during the night bringing with it some cold December temperatures. Kirk took a peek out the living room picture window as he sipped his morning coffee and noticed that the water on the birdbath had frozen over. He made mention to Sharon to "bundle up," as they prepared to drive him to the college where Kirk would catch the team bus for the ride to BWI airport and Maryland's trip to the Orange Bowl football game in Miami.

The bus pulled out of the parking lot next to the stadium at 8:30. It was just behind the main morning rush hour traffic. Several hundred students, alumni, and well wishers were on hand for the send off. The ball players were, as one surely might expect, as excited as if they had already played the game and won. It was, to say the very least, a noisy trip to the airport.

At BWI, another crowd had gathered to see Maryland's football team off. The team, itself, was more into the festivities. The bus trip had warmed them up, so to speak! Local Baltimore and Washington Television had cameras rolling to record the departure. "Details at Eleven!"

The plane ride started out to be a noisy chartered flight. However, after the meal was served, the players seemed to settle down and a more business like attitude came to light. This was a tremendous opportunity for Maryland and they wanted to be up for the difficult task ahead. If they could pull it off, and defeat the powerful University of Miami team on New Years night, there would be plenty of time to celebrate. The players would carry a victory like that with them for the rest of their lives.

It was approximately a two-hour flight from Baltimore/Washington International to Miami International Airport. Newspaper people from around the country greeted the players as they deplaned. The usual questions were asked of the coaching staff and particular players, Kirk included, were singled out for interviews. As the players left the terminal to board the bus for the short drive to Miami Springs Villas, they were also greeted with near perfect weather. The temperature was 81 degrees, not a cloud was to be seen and there was no humidity to speak of. They drove to the hotel, got keys for the assigned rooms and had the balance of the day to relax. Most of the players chose to settle at the pool to catch a few rays. A team dinner was scheduled for the evening.

Tony, as usual, was Kirk's roommate. The two of them, like in the past, arranged for a rollaway bed to be placed in their room for C.J., who would bunk in their room. Tony, as he had done at the Marriott checked the sofa that was in the room, then he called housekeeping to take the roll away out explaining that only one extra person would be staying and that the sofa-bed would be certainly sufficient for their needs!

C.J. arrived a bit later. He had stayed behind at the airport to help with the equipment, which was taken directly to the Orange Bowl Stadium. When he finally did arrive, the note left on the top of the dresser told him to meet Tony and Kirk at poolside. C.J. quickly changed into his bathing suit and in a couple of minutes he was greeting people by the pool, much as a celebrity would. He spotted Kirk relaxing in a chase lounge, waved a hello and walked over.

"Where's Tony?" asked C.J., as a waiter came up and handed him a bottle of Corona Mexican beer with a wedge of lime on top of the bottle.

"Over there, in the pool checking out the ladies," answered Kirk.

"Thank you," C.J. said to the waiter. "Did I order this?" he questioned.

Kirk smiled as the waiter answered with some fan fair!

"He said to bring it right away, just as soon as the big shot showed up," answered the waiter, with a wink to Kirk!

The balance of the afternoon was spent poolside. It was a time to relax, especially in the light of the next few days worth of preparatory work for the game.

A team dinner concluded the team's so called private together time as a unit until the night before the game. After dinner, the coaching staff gave a talk to the players about the next few days worth of activities. The Orange Bowl committee would be keeping the players occupied, showing them the sights. It was generally a fun time when they were not practicing or viewing films. It was a time to have fun they were told. They'd earned the right to be here!

On New Years Eve, the team rode in the Orange Bowl Parade. The players remarked that they were surprised to hear so many cheers, especially since they were playing against the University of Miami in their own back yard. One of the players was heard to remark that there might be a ton of vacationers down here for the holidays.

The team gathered later at the Miami Springs Villas Hotel to toast in the New Year. Sharon and her parents came over to join in the celebration. They had photographed the parade as if it were a documentary. Both Sharon and John had cameras going. Dora, of course, was the keeper of extra film, camera bags and all around helper. There would be plenty of photos for the other players to have copies, but mostly Sharon wanted a record for her and Kirk. John and Sharon would be back at work tomorrow night with a telephoto lens snapped on. However, back home, Don, would video tape the game as well.

After breakfast on New Years Day, the team went through a light workout, then returned to the hotel for a light lunch and some final meetings. There was not much time for thinking as one might suspect, or worrying about the game, because the press was ever present, seeking out stories that would give them an edge on other members of the press corps. A private light dinner gave the players an opportunity to collect themselves and regroup, so to speak, after the grand whirlwind of the past few days.

It was a quiet bus ride to the Orange Bowl Stadium. Miami had been here before and probably were more loose as a team than Maryland. Also, even though it was a close, hard fought game during the regular season, Miami had defeated Maryland. There was a lot to think about during the short ride.

The players were glad to get into their locker room. It was a familiar scene and they could start to concentrate on the game itself, which would be at hand soon.

A huge cheer went up as Maryland, dressed in their uniforms with practice jerseys on, came out to do their pre-game drills.

"Must be those tourists from the parade," kidded one of the players, who had to shout to be heard. Everyone smiled. A joke or two was just what was needed right now to help relax the ball players.

After the drills it was back to the locker room to get the game jerseys on, pads adjusted, and to review some last minute instructions. The fact that Miami had won the last contest was again brought up, put on the table for discussion. As one of the co-captains, Kirk led the conversation. He pointed out that the loss was during the 5th game. That, in fact, with the 4 point deficit against Miami and the 3 point loss to LSU, Maryland had only 7 lousy points separating them from being even with the number one and number three teams in the nation. He also brought up the fact that the Terps had reeled off 6 consecutive victories to get here. They were the ACC Champions and, he believed in each and everyone of his teammates.

Not much more could be said. "We're ready for this game," stated the coaching staff. "The Miami team is well aware of what Kirk said to you. They know we're good and they know that we are, A TEAM POSSESSED!"

The locker room emptied with players shouting, hooting it up, as they made their way through the tunnel and onto the field. All of the pre-game festivities were over. The bands were off the field and filing into their places in the grandstand. The Maryland cheerleaders had formed an arch and the first of the players through smashed the paper wall held by the cheerleaders. The cheering fans seemed almost equally divided as the two teams came onto the field. The noise level was incredible!

Maryland's bench was on the same side of the field as the press box. Maryland was the host team this year and was wearing their home uniforms.

Kirk, Tony and Jack represented Maryland in the middle of the field for the coin toss. The officials used a special commemorative coin, with each team receiving copies. The coin was tossed in the air. Miami, the so called visiting team, called "Heads!" Heads, it was. Miami had won the toss and elected to receive the kick-off. Maryland stated that they'd defend the south goal. It really didn't matter though, because the wind was not a factor on the cool, clear night. It was cool for Miami, with game time temperature reading 66 degrees. It was near perfect weather for a football game!

The Maryland kicking team came out onto the field to set-up. Between the coin toss and this, the network had broken away for a television commercial, so the players took their time as the officials waited for a signal from the TV network man stationed on the sideline with earphones on, that the commercials had ended and the game could begin. While the breaks for the commercials were often an annoyance, the network had paid millions of dollars in bidding for the exclusive telecast of the

Orange Bowl Game, so they are entitled to try and earn a few bucks by selling commercial time.

OK, we're ready. The Miami team was set up with two deep receivers. The signal by the Maryland kicker was given that he was all set. The whistle was blown and the Maryland kicker started forward. He hit the ball solidly and kicked it off the tee. It traveled deep down the middle of the field. Miami's receiver from the right side moved under the ball as it came down on the 4-yard line. It was caught. The receiver headed up field toward the middle, then veered to his left as he approached the 20-yard line. Some good blocks were made and he almost broke into the clear, however, the Maryland special team forced the ball carrier out of bounds at the 38-yard line. A 34-yard run back, not the best way to get started.

As the officials marked the ball and set the chains, Miami's offensive unit came onto the field and was joined by Maryland's defensive team.

At the snap of the ball, a quick pass to the flat was complete. Miami advanced to mid-field and had gained a first down. It was apparent the jitters had not left Maryland yet. The key was to quiet them and get control before some damage was done.

Miami passed again, this time down the middle for twenty-two yards. Miami had beaten Maryland off the ball at the snap on both plays with their offensive controlling Maryland. The ball was set just shy of the 27-yard line. They were deep in Maryland territory and had another first down. Miami was already in field goal range. Maryland fans were quiet. They were sitting on the edge of their seats, hoping that their team could somehow put a stop to Miami's drive. On only the third play from scrimmage, Miami, on a crossing pattern, threw again. The ball was caught on the 9-yard line and taken in for a touchdown. Miami had used only two minutes and forty-eight seconds of game clock time to put six points on the scoreboard. The extra point was good and Miami led 7-0. This could be a long evening.

Miami kicked off to Maryland. The kick was short, coming down at around the 14-yard line. Maryland advanced it to their own 26. Maryland did manage two first downs, however, their drive stalled at the Miami 48 and they were forced to punt.

The Maryland punt was high and deep, with good hang-time. The Miami punt receiver signaled for a fair catch, waving his right hand high over his head, but then, he got out of the way of the ball, let it bounce on the 6-yard line and then bounce again in the end zone for a touch back. Miami would take possession on their own 20-yard line.

Miami stayed to the air, completing two more passes and moving the ball to the 36. They came to the line once more, got set and the ball was snapped. A bad connection on the snap and the ball bounced free. The Maryland nose guard had penetrated enough to push the Miami quarterback out of the way, then dive for the ball, pulling it in close to his chest with both hands holding it as tight as he could. Other players from both sides piled on, trying to get a piece of the ball. Whistles were sounding as the officials dug through the pile of players, pulling them away, until they finally found the Maryland player who was clutching the ball.

"Maryland Ball. First Down," called the referee as he pointed toward the Miami goal with the umpire standing over the ball at Miami's 34-yard line.

The officials quickly set up the chains as Maryland's offensive team came out onto the field and went into a huddle while the referee set the ball for Maryland's second chance to move the ball.

The Miami defense was up to the task, holding Maryland to a 9-yard gain on two running plays and a dropped pass. The 9-yard run came on the first down, as Maryland surprised Miami with a reverse. They then tried a pass, hoping to surprise Miami again, rather than just go for the 1st down. It was almost complete at the Miami 18, but was in and out of the wide receivers hands. The straight-ahead power play on the 3rd down did not work as Miami bunched up the middle and held Maryland. On 4th down from the 25-yard line, the ball was snapped, placed at the 32 and kicked through goal posts for a field goal. Maryland was on the scoreboard and now trailed Miami by just four points. It had not been pretty, as they say, but Maryland was in this game!

The balance of the 1st quarter was a seesaw defensive battle. The Maryland defensive team had pulled together and was playing their hearts out, not letting Miami get the upper hand. Miami, on the other hand, was just as tough and did not permit the Maryland offensive to gain much ground. The first quarter had turned into a punting contest and so far there was no clear winner as each team started off a possession deep in their own territory.

The first quarter came to a close. The scoreboard read *University of Miami 7* and *University of Maryland 3*.

The second quarter started much as the first quarter had ended. Neither team was able to get the upper hand. Both the Miami and Maryland defensive units were spending a lot of time on the field. This certainly could have an effect on the outcome of the game, depending on which defensive team got tired first. A tired team is just a little slow off the ball. Mistakes are made as players try to do more than their share of the load to compensate for a teammate.

With just one minute and sixteen seconds left in the first half, a break finally occurred. The Miami punter, deep in his own territory, shanked off the kick. It went just twenty-one yards before bouncing out of bounds near the Miami 37-yard line. Maryland though, was still not able to do much with the opportunity. A charging Miami defense gave ground grudgingly, permitting Maryland to reach only the 19-yard line before the short drive came to a halt. Once again Maryland would be forced to try for a field goal. The ball was snapped, placed at the 26 and with the extra ten yards to the back of the end zone, the Maryland place kicker split the uprights with a 36-yard field goal. Maryland had pulled to within one point of Miami as the first half ended.

The teams headed for the locker rooms as the bands marched onto the field for the half time show. The scoreboard now read *Miami 7* and *Maryland 6*. To say the least, the second half should be very interesting.

As the Orange Bowl festivities drew to a close, the teams readied themselves to come back on the field. The Maryland locker room had been one of confidence during the half time break. The defense had played tough and not much more could be asked of them. The offensive coordinator and his coaches went over the plays used during the first half and reviewed the reasons that they thought they didn't work. The staff changed some things and also looked to put in a few special plays drawn up just for this game. There was no great pep talk. Everyone knew his job and they would simply work harder to execute the plays during second half. They could be the Orange Bowl winners. Just 30 minutes of this football game would stand between victory and defeat. "What do you want to do?"

Maryland charged back onto the football field. Miami had already come back on the field and was preparing to kick off. A huge cheer greeted Maryland as the red jerseys come into view from the tunnel. Their fans appreciated the effort they put out during the first half. From the deafening sound, they were behind them all the way.

Maryland's receiving team lined up for the kickoff. It was a line drive kick, which hit around the 12-yard line, bouncing crazily and away from the kick returner. It was finally picked up at the 4-yard line, but by this time the Miami kicking team had penetrated and Maryland's returner was downed on the 8-yard line. It wasn't the best way to start the half.

Just when you think things couldn't be worse, they were. Jack dropped the snap as he pulled away from the center. He wanted to give a quick hand-off to the fullback coming through the middle to open up a little more running room for the team. A Miami lineman scooped up the ball at the 7-yard line. It was Miami's ball, first down and goal to go for a touchdown. This was a huge break for Miami.

The teams exchanged offensive and defensive units. Miami came rushing onto the field, knowing full well that this was the break that they were looking for.

As Jack and Kirk passed each other, Kirk reached out to touch Jack on the shoulder and let him know that it was OK the fumble wasn't the end of the world, or the game, for that matter.

"Don't worry, we'll hold them," yelled Kirk above the roar of the Miami fans.

"I just can't seem to get started," answered a dejected Jack as his eyes met Kirk's.

"You've worked your tail off to get us into this damned game and we've still got the 2nd half to pull it off. You'll be there for us. We all believe in you. We're family, man, we're with you," came Kirk's reply as he headed for the defensive huddle.

"OK, I promised Jack that they would not punch that ball into our end zone," stated Kirk, as he gave the defensive signals, "Let's do it one more time for ourselves!"

On the first down Miami tried to score quickly through the air, but Maryland had great coverage on the play. The Miami quarterback passed the ball over the end zone, rather than risk an interception.

Second down was a run up the middle. Miami managed a one-yard gain. It would now be 3rd and 6 yards to go for a touchdown.

The third down was another pass. This play, a timed pass in which the quarterback threw it right away toward the corner of the end zone, while the receiver was running a pattern to go to the spot where the ball would come down. It nearly worked, but Maryland's corner back got a hand, really a finger, in at just the last second and tipped the ball away.

For 4th down, Miami was forced to bring the field goal unit on the field. It would be basically a chip shot. The holder set up on the 14-yard line, rather than the usual 7-yard drop, perhaps the kicker wanted the extra yard, perhaps he was superstitious. The ball was snapped, quickly placed down and the kick sailed true and through the goal posts. Maryland had allowed 3 points, but not the touchdown. Maryland now trailed by four points, 10-6.

Miami once again kicked off. The ball was caught on the run by the dccp receiver at the 11-yard line. He quickly moved up field, down the middle, then, left his blocking as he cut off right and picked up more yardage, finally being forced out of bounds by the kicker at the 37-yard line. At last, Maryland had good field position.

On the 1st down Maryland used the screen pass to good advantage. They figured that Miami would be coming, and they wanted to maintain the momentum for themselves. The play worked perfectly and Maryland gained nineteen yards, while penetrating Miami territory to the 44 with another 1st down.

Maryland's next play was a draw, gaining eight more yards to Miami's 36-yard line. The following play was a pass to the back, who had delayed a second or two, then quickly crossed between the short and deep coverage. The play gained eleven yards before he was dropped on the 25-yard line.

Maryland had a drive underway and, of course, they wanted to sustain it all the way to the end zone and not have to settle for a field goal.

Maryland faked a hand off on the play option pass, but Jack found no one open, so he tucked the ball in tight and ran left, picking up six more yards before running out of bounds. He could have tried to gain a couple of more yards by staying on the field and lowering his head as he met up with the tacklers, but this was not the time to take a chance and possibly fumble the ball. It was best to play it safe right now.

With the ball now resting on the Miami 19-yard line, Maryland again went through the air. The pass into the right flat was caught by Maryland's wide receiver at the 8-yard line. He was dropped on the Miami 4, a gain of fifteen yards and another first down. Maryland was now knocking on the door for the first time in the game. A touchdown could give them the lead.

Maryland came up to the line. The ball was snapped and a straight-ahead play with the fullback carrying was brought to a halt at the goal line. Maryland had gained almost four yards. The Maryland fans were on their feet. The noise level was incredible. Jack held his hands up to ask for some quiet so that his players could hear the signals being called out. They did quiet down a bit, but they were still standing, expecting something to happen. The ball was snapped. Jack did not hesitate, but dove straight ahead as his blockers moved the Miami line out of the way. He submarined and broke the plane at the goal line for the touchdown. The crowd of Maryland fans went wild as the huge scoreboard showed six points being added for the third quarter. The total point's section on the right of the scoreboard showed *Maryland 12* and *Miami 10*. Maryland had the lead.

The Maryland players were so jubilant that the coaching staff had to settle them down and make certain that they were still focused on the game. There was still a full quarter to go plus three minutes left in this quarter.

Maryland added the extra point. It was drilled through the uprights. The scoreboard read *Maryland 13* and *Miami 10.*

The Maryland kickoff was deep this time and the Miami receiver came only to the 16-yard line. A swarm of tacklers hit the Miami runner, who momentarily lost the ball, but grabbed it and tucked it tight.

While Miami was trying to settle down and go about the business of getting the lead back, it looked pretty clear that the momentum had changed in favor of Maryland. It was also clear that Maryland had to keep the lid on, so that Miami could not reestablish themselves as the driving force in this game.

The Maryland defensive team looked as though they were up to the task, as they have been throughout the game. They did not permit Miami to gain a first down, forcing the punt as the third quarter came to an end.

The Miami punt wasn't particularly good. It was more of a line drive and did not have any hang time at all. This let the Maryland deep receiver catch the ball on the run and advance before the Miami defense could cover the play. Maryland would open the 4th quarter at their own 48-yard line, the best field position they had all evening.

Maryland's first play of the final quarter was a draw. Figuring that Miami might expect them to try and strike early through the air, prompted this decision. The play gained eleven yards and another first down as the fullback charged through the middle, both hands clutching the ball so there would not be a fumble nor would the Miami defenders strip the ball.

Maryland had the first down at Miami's 41. They kept the ball on the ground, grinding out yardage against a very tired Miami defensive team. They were, of course, now keeping the ball out of the air to prevent interception, plus by continuing to run the ball, the clock ticked off precious minutes. A dropped pass would stop the clock.

With the clock showing only eight minutes left, Maryland had a first and goal from the Miami 6-yard line. Two plays later, the Maryland fullback plunged in from the 1-yard line for the score. Maryland fans could not contain the joy in extending the lead over the nations number one team. With the extra point nailed, the huge scoreboard lights showed *Maryland 20* and *Miami 10*, with just seven minutes and forty seconds left in the game.

It would take a touchdown, a 2-point conversion, plus a field goal, for Miami to regain the lead over a team that was playing the game of a lifetime.

Maryland looked like winners as they came up to the ball for the kickoff. They should have been a tired team, but they were not. There will be plenty of time for that later.

The ball was kicked out of the end zone. This was the first time tonight that this feat was accomplished. Miami would start the series of downs from the 20-yard line.

The first two plays were passes. They were short, but they managed a first down at the 32, as Maryland played it loose, not wanting to let Miami complete the long pass. Perhaps they played it a bit too loose, because the clock still showed *5 minutes and 48 seconds* left in the game.

Miami's quarterback was under great pressure from the charging lineman as he tried to dump the ball off to one of his backs, who seeing that the quarterback was in trouble, came back to receive a safety-valve pass. Kirk, from his position as a middle line backer, saw what was happening and rushed to intercept the ball. He cut in front of the Miami receiver, practically took the ball out of his hands on the run, and kept heading toward the sideline to avert the other Miami players. Then he cut down field in a mad dash for the goal line. Touchdown!!

The play brought everyone in the stadium to their feet. Maryland fans were screaming with delight. Miami fans sat in quiet disbelief at what was happening to their team.

Maryland added the extra point, as off the field teammates swarmed around Kirk Daniels. The scoreboard read *27-10*, which also showed only four minutes and forty-nine seconds left in the game.

A tremendous upset was in the making. The national polls would be in further turmoil because in the Cotton Bowl, number six Texas had upset number two Notre Dame 19-13. Number three LSU had convincingly beaten number four Nebraska by 34-14. If this game stood as is at closing, then the final national collegiate rankings would change drastically from the current standings.

C.J., in the meantime had waited outside the circle of players gathered around Kirk. As Kirk started to walk over to the cooler, he was stopped and handed a cup of Gatorade by C.J.

"Not a bad play," said C.J., who reached out with a wide grin and gave Kirk a high five. "I think I can relax a little now."

"Right place, right time," answered Kirk modestly, then after pausing for a moment as he took a drink, "Sure was glad I was there!"

Sharon, like C.J., was also breathing a lot easier. She had been standing, then sitting, then back up the entire game. Even when Maryland did claim the lead, for Sharon and her parents, and pretty much all of the Maryland fans, it was almost like waiting for the other shoe to drop, especially with such a powerful team as Miami who showed all season long that they could strike back quickly. The Maryland defense had made the difference. They managed to hold Miami close, while their own offense worked to get on track. Now, they would be called on again to keep the lid on for the final four and a half minutes.

The Maryland kickoff was not a good one. It sailed low and short. However, Maryland caught a break as the ball hit the ground and bounced away to the right of the receiver. Since he couldn't pick it up on the run, but had to go and pick the ball up on the fourth bounce, it enabled the Maryland defenders to cover the play. Miami returned the ball to just their own 26-yard line. They would have been to, at least the thirty-five, if the break went Miami's way.

Precious seconds clicked off the clock as Miami came up over the ball. They'd have to try to strike quickly, if they were to have any chance at all. Miami was not a team to give up, most especially this Miami team who had come into this game as the team that would most likely be the National Champion.

On first down, Miami threw just under the prevent defense and completed the pass to the 33-yard line. Maryland looked as though they'd give the short pass, but prevent Miami from going long. Second down was a similar pass, but at the last second the Maryland free safety came charging to where the ball was being thrown and nearly picked it off. The ball bounced harmlessly away. It would be 3rd down and 3 for the first down. With the incomplete pass, the clock stopped. It seemed that all the eyes in the stadium looked up at once on the incomplete pass to see how much time was left, three minutes and nine seconds read the highlighted scoreboard. Miami came to the line once more showing pass, however, a draw play was called. Miami wanted to get a first down and maintain possession without having to punt on a 4th down. The draw worked just fine, an 8-yard pick-up to the 41 and first down.

The clock stopped while the officials moved the yard marker and chains. Then after everything was set, Miami came directly to the line without a huddle. The clock started with two minutes and fifty-three seconds showing. The ball was snapped right away and put into the air for a long crossing pattern. Miami, figuring that Maryland would be protecting long, but thinking short, went for a big pass play. It worked and the ball was caught at the Maryland 31-yard line. The receiver was dropped almost immediately. Miami was knocking at the door. Maryland fans were feeling uneasy. This game wasn't over yet. Miami once again came directly over the ball, rather than huddle. The clock was moving 2:36, 2:35, the ball was snapped, "Pass," was shouted by the Maryland defenders, complete at the 18-yard line, 1st down Miami! The officials waved a halt to the game, and announced the two-minute warning. Just 2 minutes left in the game.

Maryland welcomed the break. The defensive unit was simply tired. They'd been on the field of play a long time this evening and it was now showing, two minutes to go!

Kirk as defensive captain, came to the sideline to confer with the coaching staff. He walked with a gate that told the story, he was just plain bushed.

"I think we've got them on the run," he joked.

"Ya and they're using up a lot of clock," answered the defensive coordinator as C.J, came over and handed Kirk a cool cup full of Gatorade. "I do think," continued the coach, "that the 18 is far enough, let's stop them now, they have to punch in, then try and get the ball back. No field goals now, touchdowns are what they need." The worried look told the rest of the story.

"You know," said Kirk matter-of-factly, "the guys, those fellows and I," and he pointed to the rag-tailed and very tired Maryland defensive unit on the field, "were discussing the situation. And we said let Miami have the ball for awhile, use up the clock and get to our 18, then, it should be around the two-minute warning and I'll dash over to the sideline and bring back some words of inspiration which will see us through!" C.J. and the players standing near who overheard started to laugh. They knew Kirk was kidding, but the coach didn't!

"I know, I know," stated the coach. "You've done a great job all night," and he put his hand on Kirk's shoulder.

"Well, don't worry," answered Kirk, "we were just letting Jack catch his wind, we'll give him the ball soon. Miami's just as tired as we are." Kirk then winked at C.J. and trotted back to the field. Time was almost up for the two-minute warning as Kirk called the team together before the officials set the ball and blew the whistle.

"What'd they say," asked one of the players as they gathered near.

"Coach said what the hell's wrong with us, we've come this far, can't we play decent defense for a lousy two minutes. Where's our pride in ourselves, the whole country's watching, and dammit, I agree," answered Kirk as he walked to his position.

Time was now back in and Miami went into their huddle. The play was called and they came to the line and up over the ball. At the snap both teams were in motion. The Miami quarterback faked a hand-off, dropped back for the play action pass, but could find no open receivers. Maryland had covered the play well and the pressure put on Miami's quarterback forced him to throw the ball toward the sideline and out of bounds. There was a receiver in the vicinity, so it was not intentional grounding. The next Miami play was a screen. The Maryland defense was led into the backfield as the quarterback rolled right to throw the screen pass. Instead, he had to bring his arm down, tuck the ball in tightly and make a dash toward the goal. Maryland's defense smelled out the screen and it was well covered.

The play would have lost at least six yards. As it was, the Miami quarterback, cutting back against the grain managed a two-yard pick-up. It would be 3rd down and 8 yards to go in what could be Miami's last effort to keep their season alive. The clock continued as the Miami quarterback was tackled, but was stopped as the quarterback got to his feet and called for a time out. The scoreboard clock showed just one minute and sixteen seconds to go in the season.

While the Miami quarterback went to the sideline for a decision on the next plays, Kirk stayed on the field with the Maryland defensive unit. Team managers started onto the field during the time out with water and towels, but Kirk waved then back. He wanted the team focused for the balance of the game, plus he wanted Miami to see that the Maryland team was ready, right now. The officials whistled time back in. Miami huddled and came to the ball. It was snapped and the Miami quarterback quickly dropped six yards for the pass. It was fired to the wide receiver crossing and caught at the 9-yard line. The receiver was dropped immediately. The ball was momentarily fumbled as he went down, but luckily it bounced right back in his arms. The officials untangled the pile. The fumbled ball had gathered a crowd!

The referee motioned for the chains to determine if the play had made a 1st down, or if it would be 4th down. It was too close and much too important to call without a measurement.

As the linesman brought the chains in for the measurement, it seemed that all the eyes in the Orange Bowl darted to the clock to check the time remaining in the game, fifty-four seconds.

It was a 1st down for Miami. They came right over the ball without a huddle. The ball was snapped. "Pass," was yelled once again by the Maryland defensive team. The ball was fired into the end zone to the Miami big tight end on a crossing pattern. Just as he reached to tuck the ball away for the touchdown, another pair of hands got in the way. Kirk covered the middle from his linebacker position and stole the ball almost right out of the receivers arms, then dropped to one knee for the touchback!! With forty-eight seconds still showing on the game clock, it was over. The victory was Maryland's!!

Kirk was surrounded by his teammates as he made the dash for the sideline still clutching the football. They'd need a new ball to complete the game. Kirk was keeping this one!!

As Jack trotted onto the field and passed Kirk, no words were spoken. Jack simply held thumbs up to Kirk to say "well done" plus Jack could see that Kirk's eyes were wet with tears as the emotion of the game was brought to the zenith. It has been a nerve-racking evening. C.J. was the first to greet Kirk. Actually, C.J. had run a good ten yards onto the playing field. He also saw Kirk's moistened eyes and gave his friend a big bear hug. "What a play," was all C.J. could say.

"Keep this for me," said Kirk as he handed C.J. the football, "it's been through a lot today!"

In the meantime, Maryland had the ball on their own 20-yard line. Jack took the snap and dropped to one knee, protecting the ball as the lineman and backfield players gathered around to protect him and the ball. Miami, of course, called a time out. They had two left and would probably use them. A bad snap, a fumble could occur, you never know. The key however, was that Maryland had three more downs and although the clock would stop for the change over, Miami would be out of time outs.

Kirk looked up toward the stands trying to search out Sharon, but he couldn't find her, then he spotted John, who gave a high sign and pointed to the section closest to the field, where Sharon had made her way to be near Kirk at game's end. Kirk said something to C.J., who was standing next to him and C.J. left to go over to the grand stand. He called to Sharon and some fans that were near. Then Sharon was lifted over the side and down to the playing field. She stood back with C.J., out of the way, because the game was still in progress.

Miami had used one more time out, then on 3rd down, as Jack took the snap once more and dropped again to one knee, Miami let the remaining 14 seconds click off the clock. They showed very good sportsmanship, talking to the Maryland players, shaking hands. It had been a long evening and not only had Miami lost the ballgame 27-10, they also had lost their undefeated season and the National Championship, because LSU had soundly beaten Nebraska 34-14, and no doubt, would be crowned the National Football Collegiate Champion. With the upset of Notre Dame by 6th ranked Texas at the Cotton Bowl 19-13, Maryland could perhaps move up in the rankings, especially on the heels of this convincing victory. Best guess would be up to #3 behind LSU and Miami. As the clock ran out, streams of Maryland fans poured out of the stands and onto the playing field to be a part of the post game celebration. Kirk had gone onto the playing field to join his teammates and to shake hands with the Miami Players. This was a much more pleasant time for him, especially since he had a good game, and, the last time was to congratulate Miami on their 14-10 win over Maryland in game 5.

Kirk turned around to leave the field and find Sharon, but he didn't have to look far, she and C.J. had come on the field to be a part of what had happened here tonight and to be with Kirk. She jumped into his arms and gave him a greeting noteworthy enough, that several press photographers snapped their picture. C.J. of course, got a hold of the photographers and asked that a copy be sent to Kirk at the University for his and his wife's scrap book. It would be done.

Kirk, Sharon, and C.J. walked off the field and through the tunnel toward the locker room. Sharon had told her parents that the locker room would be the meeting place when they were separated, win or lose, she had intended to be at Kirk's side. They'd been through quite a lot during the football season and she wanted to be with Kirk at the end.

Kirk gave Sharon another kiss just before going into the locker room. "Keep this for us," he said, as he took the football from C.J. and gave it to Sharon. John and Dora had not arrived yet, they were still making their way through the crowd so Kirk decided to go in and catch up with the in-laws a little later. Being with his teammates was all-important right now.

The noise level inside the locker room radiated out through the doors and walls. It intensified as C.J. opened the door for Kirk and they disappeared inside. The celebration was officially on!!

Most of the team was already there when C.J. and Kirk entered. Kirk was handed a bottle of champagne. Tony came over with a bottle for C.J., started to hand it to him, then, pulled back, popped the cork which had been loosened, shook the bottle and sprayed C.J. all over! Tony then handed the bottle to C.J. and gave him a big bear hug.

"You're one of us," said Tony as he stepped back and shook C.J.'s hand.

"God I love it, I love all you guys," screamed C.J.!!!

The celebration continued for sometime. Players showed probably all of the emotions there are, some loud, whooping it up, others just sitting in front of their lockers taking it all in and savoring the moment. Kirk was in between but he certainly was enjoying himself and it showed.

Since C.J. hadn't brought a change of clothes and was soaking wet from the Korbel champagne bath, he showered while the trainer put his clothes in the dryer.

Kirk came outside first. He shook hands with John, gave Dora a hug and a kiss, and then, once again took his Bride into his arms. Kirk also explained that C.J. would be out in a little while, he was sort of delayed and he'd let C.J. explain.

While they were talking about the game and waiting for C.J., Kirk signed a few autographs for fellow Maryland students who had come down to Miami for New Years and the big game. He included the students in the conversation and was quite at ease with them. Also other people, as well as some youngsters asked for autographs and Kirk signed for them, asking their names so that he could personalize it. This was something he did with pleasure. Once, after watching the Baltimore Orioles play the Detroit Tigers in a baseball game during his freshman year at Maryland, Cal Ripken (Baltimore's future Hall of Fame shortstop) asked Kirk for his name to personalize the autograph on his game program. It meant a lot to him that Cal would take that little bit of extra time.

Individuals from the press spotted Kirk and came over to both congratulate him and Maryland on the Orange Bowl Victory. They, of course, were also looking for some additional things to include in their newspaper columns. Included in the group of writers were one from the Sporting News and one from Sports Illustrated Magazine.

"Are you planning on a Pro career? Who would you like to play for?" were two of the questions Kirk had to field.

He answered that he'd love a pro career. It certainly doesn't take a rocket scientist to know that the financial rewards of playing professional football would give him and Sharon a great start in life. Kirk, further stated that earning pro-dollars would let him easily go on to earn his Masters degree, rather than trying to do it and teach at the same time. He'd like to eventually teach at the college level and earn his doctorate. He didn't know about coaching college football, hopefully that decision would be years off. "What pro team?" "I don't know, the Washington Redskins would be my first choice. I know the area, having lived here for the last four years, plus some of the fans would know me from playing at Maryland. I'd feel right at home!"

Then before anymore questions could be asked, C.J. came popping out of the locker room. "From what they just said on TV in there, Maryland will be #3 in the National Polls, LSU #1, Miami drops to just #2, Notre Dame, losing to #6 Texas is 4th, Texas is #5. They didn't say the rest of the top 10. Ole #3 isn't bad my friend," stated C.J. as he gave Kirk a high five!

Then it was off the Miami Springs Villas where the celebration would continue, until...!?

By the time Kirk, Sharon, C.J., John, and Dora arrived at the party, the celebration was well underway. Players, coaching staff, Alumni, family and friends plus Baltimore/Washington press members were all in attendance. The party was lively and loud. A band was playing, some people were dancing, others were standing, drink in one hand, hors d'oeuvres in the other, discussing the game, college football in general, pro football and life. It was just normal party talk! Kirk and Sharon spent quite a lot of time on the dance floor. John and Dora danced also, not as much, especially the faster dances were sat out, but they were enjoying themselves. C.J., of course, he was out on the dance floor. He was somewhat of a celebrity himself. Everyone knew C.J. He was dancing with quite a few good-looking young ladies. He whispered to Kirk and Sharon that he didn't know all of their names, however, a certain few that he danced with more often were becoming known! The party lasted into the wee hours of the morning. Kirk was staying at Miami Springs this evening, but would meet Sharon the next day so that they could take the expense paid extended honeymoon at the Diplomat Hotel over in Hollywood Beach which had been provided for by C.J. and a host of friends.

Kirk walked Sharon to the car and said his good night to John, Dora, and his lovely wife. Kirk would take the airport shuttle bus to the Miami International Airport where he'd meet Sharon and her parents. John and Dora would take the flight home. Sharon would keep the rental car for Kirk's and her use over the next few days.

As Kirk came back into the hotel, he passed C.J. and a young lady. Kirk was introduced, said thank you to the offer of a nightcap, but he was going to hit the hay, then disappeared into the elevator. C.J. was still going strong, but Kirk was a bit overextended. He was just plain tired! Sometime during the night Tony and C.J. wandered back into the room, but Kirk didn't stir, even with excitement of being on the Orange Bowl winning team, he was very much off in dreamland.

At just after eight o'clock the next morning, Kirk was up, showered and packed. The shoe was on the other foot, so to speak, because neither Tony nor C.J. came to life as Kirk moved around the room. Just as he was getting ready to leave the room, C.J. came to and stirred.

"Are you leaving? What time is it? Do you need a ride? Let me take you to Hollywood Beach?" questioned C.J.

"Everything is fine, meeting Sharon at the airport, keeping the rental car. Thanks for everything. Tell the body over there good-by, we'll see you both back in Washington. By the way, aren't you on an early flight or did you change it?" answered Kirk as he gathered up his things.

"The later flight, late checkout, very late flight. I'd like to talk, but I need my rest you know," and C.J. was back to sleep before Kirk could say anything more.

Kirk, baggage in hand caught the elevator to the lobby, checked out, and reminded the front desk that Tony and C.J. would be on the late checkout list. He walked through the lobby toward the door where he'd catch the airport shuttle bus to the airport. The driver took his bags and put them in the back luggage section of the bus.

"When do we leave for the airport?" inquired Kirk of the driver.

"About ten minutes. We keep a schedule, especially in the morning," answered the driver. "You have time to get a cup of coffee, there's also Danish pastry on the cart, there, in the lobby, and newspapers too. Tells you all about that big win last night."

Kirk came back into the lobby, fixed a cup of coffee, took a napkin and Danish, reached for the USA Today Newspaper and settled down for a few minutes to read about all of the bowl games played on New Years Day and Night.

The driver came over to Kirk just before heading to the bus to let him know that they were about to leave for the airport. "What airline should I drop you at?" the driver asked.

Kirk thought for a second and said "US Air." He didn't want to go through the long story that he was just meeting Sharon and since John and Dora were flying US Air, that would be good enough.

The trip to the Miami International Airport took just a few minutes. Kirk was dropped off in front of the US Air sign, gave the driver a tip and started to walk into the terminal building, but was stopped by the sound of a horn blowing. He turned and saw Sharon waving out of the passenger's window of a car, which was in traffic, but about four cars away from being at the place where Kirk was standing.

Kirk put his bags down and stepped off the curb, waving two cars past the spot he was standing, but the third car was bent on taking Kirk's spot because it was right in front of the skycap station. The driver blew his horn for Kirk to move out of the way.

"Do you want a ticket?" asked Kirk of the driver in a very stern manner. "Well, move on!" The driver kept going, but gave Kirk a dirty look. He had to think Kirk was an airport policeman.

Kirk then waved John into the spot he was saving, just as an airport policeman came up to Kirk. "You direct traffic very well," said the policeman.

"Am I in trouble?" asked Kirk.

"No, unless you make a habit of it," was the answer.

Just then Sharon, who, of course, hadn't heard the conversation, bounced out of the car and to Kirk's side "Don't drag my husband away, we're still on our honeymoon. Anyway, he was one of the stars of last nights game!"

The policeman had to smile, then said "We sort of had things straightened out until you came along Mrs., I graduated from the University of Miami only three years ago and I'm a big Miami fan. Who is this guy anyway? What's his number?"

"He's Kirk Daniels, #55, middle linebacker," answered Sharon who wasn't quite certain what to say next.

"You're the guy that helped mess things up for us aren't you?" asked the policeman in a stern voice, for Sharon's benefit, that is!

John, in the meantime had opened the trunk and had the skycap take his and Dora's luggage out, leaving Sharon's in the trunk. Then he had the skycap put Kirk's bags in the trunk, all in an orderly fashion. He tipped the skycap, then walked over to Kirk and handed him the car keys.

"Good morning," said John in a cheerful voice, "I'd give him a ticket too, except I think he'll turn out to be a pretty good son-in-law."

"Is this your daughter?" asked the policeman.

"Yes, I know what you're going to say, it is a curse, but hopefully he'll straighten her out the way I had to do with her Mother," answered a smiling John who was glad Dora was out of listening range.

The policeman good-naturedly patted Kirk on the shoulder and shook hands with him. "You did have a good game #55. Good luck to you."

"Thanks," answered Kirk as he ushered Sharon to the car after the quick airport type good-byes.

The policeman stepped from the curb, held up traffic a second, as Kirk pulled away. He gave a high sign in answer to Kirk's wave.

"Well, it's off to Hollywood… Beach, that is," said Kirk to Sharon as he followed the signs for the airport exit.

Sharon reached into the glove compartment and brought out a map the rental car company gave to them. "Looks like we follow the signs for Interstate 95, get off at Hollywood Beach and drive east to the Atlantic Ocean. There should be the Diplomat Hotel."

"OK," answered Kirk, who put his arm around Sharon, after she had put the center armrest up and snuggled close to him.

They found Interstate 95 without a hitch. The signs were clearly marked. They drove onto the Interstate highway and headed north for Hollywood and Hollywood Beach.

It wasn't too long before they were pulling up in front of the Diplomat Hotel, a beautiful Four Star complex situated directly on the Atlantic Ocean.

As Kirk brought the car to a stop under a huge canopy, the doorman came around the car, opened Kirk's door and greeted him, while another doorman opened Sharon's side. They took the car keys from Kirk, opened the trunk and as one of the men placed the luggage onto the cart, the other showed them to the lobby. Kirk tipped the doorman who in turn gave Kirk a claim check for the car, which would be placed in the valet parking lot.

"Good morning," stated the desk clerk in a cheerful voice.

"We'd like to check in. Hope it's not too early," replied Kirk.

"No, we shall be able to accommodate you," was the answer. "Name please," he continued.

"Daniels, Mr. & Mrs. Kirk Daniels," answered Kirk.

"Ah, yes, Mr. & Mrs. Daniels, paid in advance."

" A gift from some friends," said Kirk.

"Nice friends," the desk clerk replied. "Just sign here, it's already filled out."

Kirk signed the registration card and handed it and the pen to the desk clerk, who then motioned for a bellman to take their luggage and escort them to their room.

"Com'on, Star let's go to our room," said Sharon.

"Star?" questioned the deck clerk with raised eyebrows.

"Yes, oh, just a nickname," answered embarrassed Kirk.

"Don't be so modest," kidded Sharon. "He's the linebacker for Maryland who made all those great plays against Miami at the Orange Bowl game last night, ole 55!"

"Sharon!! Now we'll probably get a room overlooking the garbage cans," said Kirk in his 'I really wish you hadn't said that tone.'

"Not exactly," said the desk clerk. "I'm from Bowie, Maryland. I spent a couple of years at Maryland myself. Let me review this. It seems the only room I have available is, well an upgrade to an ocean front suite, cancellation you know, early arrival and all that. OK with you, Star?" Then turning to the bellman, "Front," and as the bellman took the key, "please show Mr. & Mrs. Daniels to their room."

"Like I said, let's start our second honeymoon," Sharon said to Kirk, then with a wink to the desk clerk "There's another reason I call him Star!"

Kirk didn't say anything, he just shook his head, threw his hands up in the air and followed Sharon into the elevator.

Order Form

Ship To *(Please Print):*		
Name:		
Address:		
City:	**St:**	**Zip:**

Number of Books:	USA $19.95 ea.	
	Canada $23.95 ea.	
	Postage & Handling: $3.00 Per Book	
	Total Amount Enclosed	

Order Form

Ship To *(Please Print):*		
Name:		
Address:		
City:	**St:**	**Zip:**

Number of Books:	USA $19.95 ea.	
	Canada $23.95 ea.	
	Postage & Handling: $3.00 Per Book	
	Total Amount Enclosed	

========== ***Make check or money order payable to:*** =========

Wayne G. MacDowell

CasAnanda Publishing

POB 7207

Bayonet Point, FL 34674